Daughter of the Legend

Storm-Mage Chronicles #2,
Sequel to "Apprentice Storm Mage"

A novel set in the world of Dhea Loral by

Douglas Van Dyke Jr.

Daughter of the Legend

Storm-Mage Chronicles Book #2

Copyright 2024 Douglas Van Dyke Jr
Revised 2025

This edition published through Dhea Loral

ISBN: 978-1-949060-13-3
Teen & Young Adult > Fantasy
Teen & Young Adult > Fantasy > Wizards & Witches
Fantasy > General

Written by Douglas Van Dyke Jr
Please Visit:
http://dhealoral.com

Retail Price: $18.00 Paperback

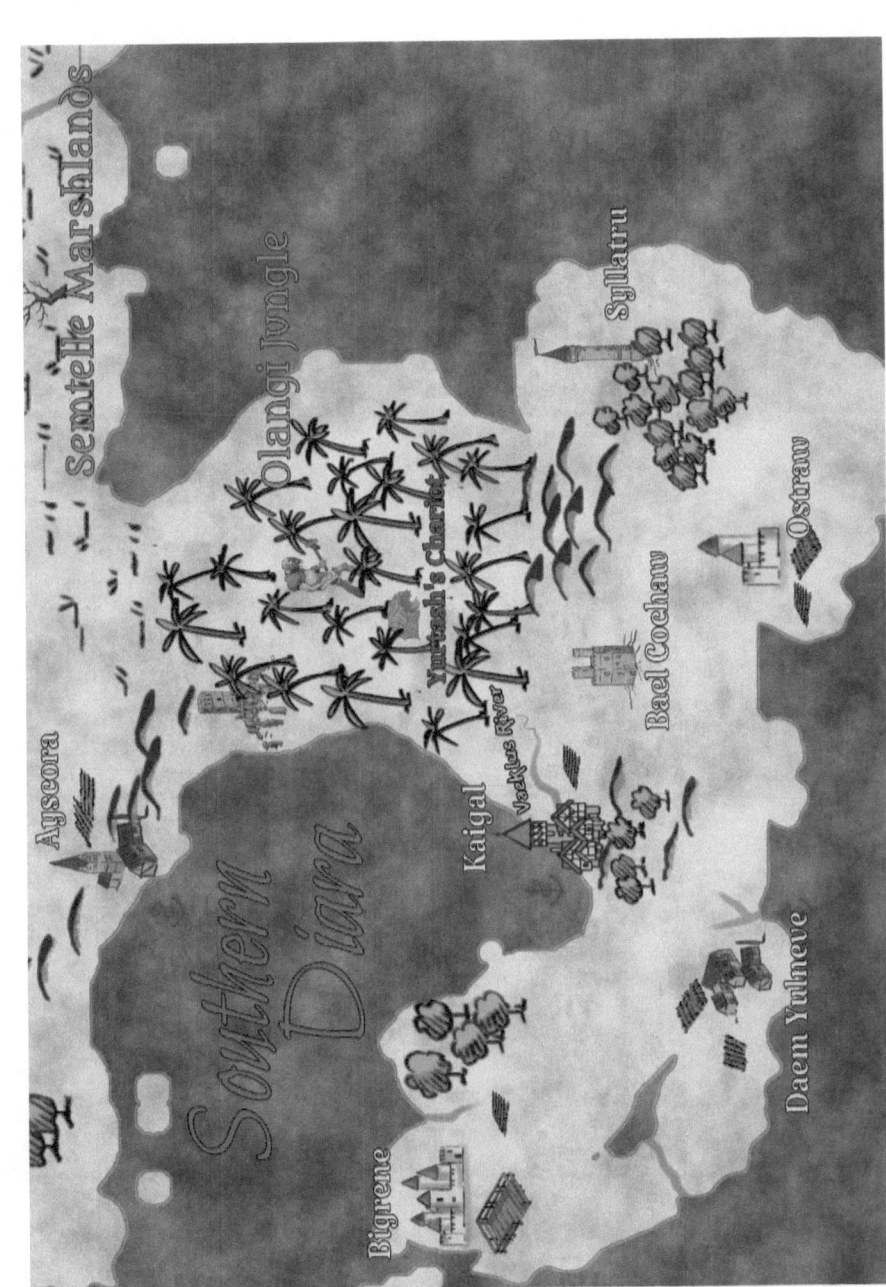

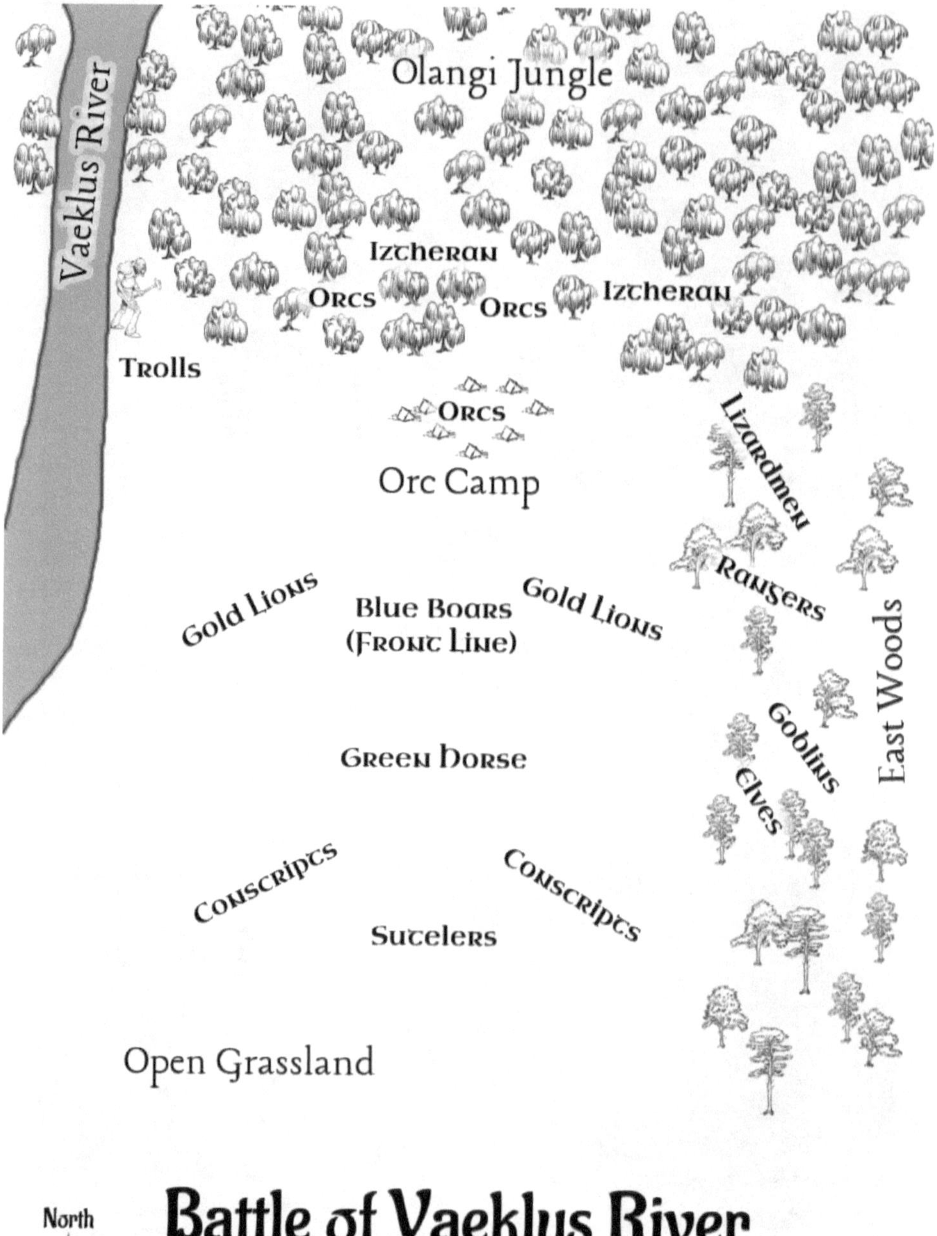

Vaeklus River

Olangi Jungle

Iztheran

ORCS

Iztheran

ORCS

Trolls

ORCS

Orc Camp

Lizardmen

Rangers

Gold Lions

Blue Boars
(Front Line)

Gold Lions

East Woods

Green Dorse

Goblins

Elves

Conscripts

Conscripts

Sutelers

Open Grassland

North

Battle of Vaeklus River

Table of Contents

Acknowledgements

"It takes courage to live through suffering; and it takes honesty to observe it."
C. S. Lewis

I'd like to thank my wife and kids for sparing the time for me to engage in the passion of writing. I remember dedicating a book to my firstborn when he was still in the womb. Now both of my boys are responsible teenagers, and we have some great adventures as a family.

Thank you to my editor, Rebecca Jaycox. I handed her a project that was around three times the length of the original. She took on all this work and is helping my dream come true.

I love the cover work done by Thea Magerand. This is an age in which AI images seek to replace human hands, (and possibly add a finger or two). I'm glad to have some hand-drawn artwork for the fans to enjoy. This one is going up on my wall. You can bet that I'll be seeking out her help to design the cover for book #3.

And I haven't forgotten you, the reader. The reviews and support I've gotten from my fans over the years helps fuel my creativity.

Lastly, I thank the friends and acquaintances that are named on the roster of the Blood-Wolves. I can never forget the many times that we dove into the darkest places of evil and saved the world time and again.

Prologue

Fifteen hundred years ago, the realm of Dhea Loral reached the highest point of its Golden Age. Gods walked alongside mortals, heralding a time of discovery and magic unmatched by anything prior, or since. Starting around this time, small conflicts eventually blossomed into a raging Godswars. As conflicts engulfed both the lands and the heavens, the realm spiraled into destruction.

Twelve hundred and fifty-two years ago, recognizing their failure as caretakers, the gods signed a binding Covenant. They banished themselves from the ruins of the material world, ceding to the mortals more freedom over their own affairs. The agreement ended the Godswars. The inhabitants of Dhea Loral were given only needed comfort to recover from the devastation that ravaged their land, split apart continents, and left entire cities populated with unburied corpses.

Dark Age buried Golden Age. A struggle for survival from First Year After Covenant extended more than a millennium. Whole cultures lost the secrets of metal and many other advancements, reducing themselves to nomadic lifestyles and hunting for food. Extinction claimed several races and creatures. Although the gods provided help, their agreement limited their use of power except through their priests in the world. Slowly, scattered settlements began to thrive and expand once again. Tilled fields began to crawl across cleared valleys, but most of the world remained wild and violent.

In the last two hundred years, as large city-states spread into kingdoms and trade routes expanded across continents and seas, some ambitious gods viewed it as a sign that the races once again prospered. Despite being restricted from physically entering the world, they found ways to manipulate loyal followers as pawns in their newest games. A silent struggle had resumed once more, acting in such a subtle manner that most missed the signs or ignored the danger as inconsequential.

Today, forgotten but perilous fragments of the Godswars remain hidden in regions of wilderness, silently biding their time until discovered once again…

Chapter 1 – Thamin and Thomena

In the oppressing darkness and fetid smell of the slime-encrusted hallway, the mirthful chuckle of his companion seemed out of place.

Hearing the noise, and feeling it violate the silence so profoundly, he glanced at his longtime partner. He whispered in case something was listening. "Marl? We're days into the Olangi jungle, deep in lizardman territory, snooping inside a forbidden temple of theirs…what could be funny?"

"Exactly the point, Thamin." Marl, noticeably gray-haired compared to his companion, walked closer. He kept his sword in his hand in case they were discovered. "We're two humans in the middle of the hostile jungle, lizardmen patrolling all over, a forbidden holy place I ne'er imagined seeing here." The older adventurer gestured at his companion with an open hand. "And you're standing on your head."

Thamin adjusted the balance of weight on his shoulders as he returned his eyes to the vine-covered wall standing opposite of him. His feet helped keep his balance on the wall behind him during the headstand. An elvish clasp tied his hair back, keeping his vision clear to observe his surroundings. Thamin whispered, "I needed to see the symbols from this view, and I discovered something. You're the one who's upside down."

"Say that again?"

"See that staircase down the hall?" The inverted man pointed with his eyes. "The ceiling isn't rough from the wear of time. The steps are hanging upside-down, covered in muck. The current steps were built of mud and rocks sometime later."

Marl followed his gaze. They both heard drops of water echoing from somewhere down the stairs. "Are you sure? How about these?"

His mud-encased boot tapped an old piece of metal, rising out of the floor. Thamin glanced at it. "From this view, it looks like some kind of ornate hook. I think it once held lamps on the ceiling. Now that I have a better look at the support beams on both ends of the hall, I can tell they were once supporting the weight of the ceiling. A ceiling which is now the floor. Now that I look at the wall symbols from this angle, it makes sense."

As Thamin swung his feet down and proceeded to stand upright, his partner took a closer look at the wall. "I thought you couldn't read this strange language?"

Any response was delayed as Thamin readjusted his green cloak. The bow, stringed and ready for use, had drifted over his head, and he had to settle it back in place. He did a quick check of his other weapons to make sure they returned to a comfortable position. His right hand fixed the angle of the axe on his belt; his left hand reached across his body to check the looseness of his swordbreaker. He liked using the swordbreaker in his offhand, because it was a notched blade specializing in catching and trapping enemy blades in its grooves. When Thamin was satisfied with his arrangement, he pointed out a particular symbol on the wall.

"I only know this one: Yurtash."

Marl squinted at the design. "Your god?"

Thamin nodded. "The symbol is upside-down. Once on my head, I recognized other symbols from the Iztheran language, which appear on some of the stone ruins elsewhere in the jungle."

The men spent a moment in silence, each one glancing up and down the hall with renewed perspective, weighing the implications of this discovery. Thamin absently rubbed at his neck, assuaging sore muscles. The soreness reminded him that although he wasn't old, his body wasn't as vigorous as it once was. Feeling his elder's eyes upon him, he met that glance.

Marl ventured, "Does that feel odd? This was a holy place dedicated to your god."

Thamin shrugged. The movement helped ease his shoulders. "Many sentient creatures worship the God of Spirits. Some are good, some have fallen to evil intent. Yurtash isn't a god with an agenda. He favors primal connections, natural lifestyles. He bestowed his powers to me at a young age. It is uncommon to see a structure such as this one in his name. Normally his worship sites are…less grand. This place has multiple levels, statues, precious metals lining murals."

Marl took a step, mud squelching at his boots. "Buried under layers of grime."

As he whispered, Thamin used his innate natura magic to shift his eyes back into a state in which they could pick out better details in the dark. The faded symbols on the wall became clearer. When he looked back towards his partner, the ancient, magical lights that still lined parts of the structure forced his eyes back into human perspective.

He said. "I think I know what this place is…was."

Marl stepped back from the opposite wall, a small, glowing pebble in his hands. He could not adapt his eyes as Thamin could, so he carried his own magically-imbued light source.

Thamin drew out his blade. Marl's light illuminated the popular Diaran offhand weapon. The steel swordbreaker had a cutting edge on one side, but the back was notched with several thick teeth. Thamin pushed the point of the blade into the wall. He twisted it, popping a small sliver of wood loose.

Marl looked puzzled. As Thamin lowered the sword, Marl picked up the sliver of wood. "Not rotted?"

"Magic in the wood itself, not just the glyphs still lighting the passageway." Thamin started to walk down the hall, away from the staircase. "This structure has been sitting upside down in a jungle long enough for the jungle to cover the outside and start to choke the inside, but the wood hasn't rotted, and the metal looks like it merely needs a rag to polish it up."

Marl fell into step behind the younger adventurer. "I knew you were the one to ask about this place. You always seem to figure things out. What's your guess?"

"A divine chariot."

With a snort, Marl answered, "A flying ship from the Godswars? Over a thousand years ago? How'd it end up here, and wouldn't it have fallen apart by now?"

Thamin put up a warning hand as he stopped in his tracks. The hall ended in a larger, magically lit chamber. Only ten feet away from the opening, he thought he'd heard something unusual. Thamin tilted his head in that direction to listen. He only heard trickling drips of water and movement of an air draft rustling some vine leaves. Thamin still had the swordbreaker in one hand, but he allowed his right hand to drift to his axe. He glanced back and noticed Marl holding his long, double-edged blade at the ready. Both men stood as statues, holding the position longer than most could endure. They heard something walking around, somewhere ahead. The footsteps reminded Thamin of the peril of the trip. In time, the sound moved away, and both men began easing forward.

Thamin was still fidgeting with his axe in its belt holder when Marl whispered, "You were saying about the ship?"

"I don't know much, but they weren't all ships. It's better to say they were flying churches." Thamin paused. "They were built with the blessings of gods, so they were highly resistant to fading with time. It would explain the sturdy wood hidden beneath these vines. I believe there is one in Orlaun that still flies."

Marl glanced ahead into the larger chamber they had explored previously. "And as far as being upside down?"

Thamin shrugged. "During the war, some were knocked out of the skies in great aerial battles. Some of the hallways aren't level and look warped, but that could be from an impact. This one could have landed upside down and had centuries for the jungle to grow up around it. By the markings on the wall, it served a god then…"

The two men reentered the large chamber. An amazingly lifelike statue of a lizardman stood sentry, staring at their entry. Nearby tables, decorations, and bloody offerings gave evidence of the room being used as an altar. Sharp tools covered in gobs of flesh and dried blood hung on the wall.

"…and it still serves one now."

Marl took a moment, apparently digesting that news. "A fall would explain the damage to the structure. I guess a divine chariot shouldn't surprise me, not any more than that does."

The elder man pointed with his sword at the lizardman statue standing over the offerings. Both men could not help but admire the craftsmanship facing them. The lizardman figure displayed such detail and realism that it looked like it could come alive at any moment. It appeared as it if was a subject captured in time, mouth partially open in an angry, soundless scream. The scales of the creature were mostly the mottled green and brown colors of the race. A set of bright red and gold stripes on its neck, brow, and short tail gave evidence the subject was male. The presence of clothes and armor on the figure revealed the most shocking aspect.

Marl commented on that as they stared. "I ne'er seen those lizards wear anything more than hides or badly worked leather."

"I've never known them to use writing or symbols. Do you suppose the Iztheran language dotted throughout the jungle ruins may have actually been from the lizardmen?" Thamin added, reaching out to touch the realistic armor. "The dark years after the Godwars must have set their whole race back to a primitive state."

Thamin knew that local scholars considered the Iztheran symbols in the ruins and the lizardmen of the jungle to be separate entities. The hieroglyphs attributed to be from iztheran people came from a lost culture. Little was known about them.

Marl asked, "You think the lizardmen used to write? You're wondering if they are descendants of the legendary iztheran civilization?"

"Now that I've seen this—" Thamin walked partway around the armored statue—"I believe they had to have been something more than they are today. We don't even know who the Iztheran were as a race, but their ruins are located all across the lizardmen's domain." Thamin looked closely at the statue before backing away. "This artwork is simply amazing. I wonder who carved it."

As Thamin cast his eyes about the room, searching for more oddities and listening for danger, he noticed Marl tentatively reach out and touch the statue. His partner tugged on the flap of a leather pouch, even ran his fingers along the scaly arm.

Marl focused on the sculpture with wonder. "What material did they carve it from? The texture feels so right, but it is hard."

Thamin cocked his head to one side at a different entrance to the room. He could hear more footfalls echoing distantly. As intrigued about the structure as he was, Thamin nevertheless began to concede to himself the danger of discovery was too great. The Olangi jungle stretched for days of travel in any direction. He and Marl were accomplished hunters and survivalists, but the jungle teemed with lizardmen and other intelligent monsters. Thamin didn't want angry lizardfolk discovering them here and hunting them all the way back to human lands.

He turned back to express his concerns when he saw Marl jump away from the statue with a shocked exclamation. Both men froze as the sound echoed through the room. Marl held his sword, Longclaw, up to the level of the statue's throat. Thamin kept quiet but raised a questioning eyebrow.

"I was going to try cutting the thin necklace with the magical blade," Marl whispered, "and the necklace moved."

"It must have been added later, maybe an offering?" Thamin half-turned his head to sounds coming from the passage. "We better leave. I think something heard that."

Marl had gotten past his surprise and leaned in to grip the necklace. "It's very fancy. Can you tell if it's magical?"

Thamin shook his head. "Natura doesn't grant me that ability..." He stopped, cocking his head to the side. "The sounds are coming closer. We must leave."

"I'm taking this keepsake for study," Marl proclaimed and pulled the necklace over the statue's head before Thamin could protest.

A guttural sound, full of equal parts loss and fury, erupted from the lizardman statue. Thamin and Marl watched, stunned, as the figure stumbled and fell. Leather creaked, metal armor clanged against the floor, scaled skin stretched as the head turned. The realistic statue had become a living creature, thrashing on the floor at their feet. Both humans stood transfixed by the surprising sight. The lizardman moved erratically, movements clumsy, as if it couldn't fully control its muscles. Despite its struggle, it noticed the sword in Marl's hand and slapped it from his grasp.

Thamin's reflexes came to life. He drew his axe and stepped toward the creature. The lizardman turned its attention on him but seemed unable to control his muscle spasms. Instead, it began speaking strange words.

The plant life inside the room sprang to life, branches flayed about as if alive and searching. Marl sought his sword but was lashed with vines until they dragged him to the ground. Thamin's attack halted as vines whipped around his body and pulled at him. The lizardman managed to gain its feet. It approached Thamin with a stilted gait.

Beyond the creature, from the other passageways, Thamin heard more cries of alarm. His mind conjured an image of a mob of lizardmen dragging Marl and him onto the sacrificial table.

Thamin had no time to contemplate the lizardman's obvious use of natura magic. He called upon his own tricks granted by Yurtash. Just as the lizardman latched firmly onto his axe, the plants released their hold. The creature's eyes widened, clearly surprised that its opponent proved capable of the same sort of magic. Thamin and the lizardman competed to control the plants, causing them to whip about randomly. Both figures withdrew, but only after the stronger lizardman managed to rip the axe free of the human's grip. Thamin rolled into the thrashing vines, but the competition between natura-users kept them confused as to whether to grab or not.

Marl called, "I'm trapped!"

Thamin struggled to his feet. He focused on the plants holding his friend, calling on his own gift to relax their grip. The lizardman stood within reach of Marl's struggles. Even as the vines started to slacken, the lizardman brought the axe down on Marl's neck. He struck a second time while Thamin stumbled through the moving flora. The elder man sagged against the vines holding him. Red blood dripped through the green leaves. Death came quickly. Thamin raised his swordbreaker to attack, but paused at the sight of some new arrivals.

A pair of lizardmen entered the room. They staggered to a stop in disbelief as they witnessed their awakened god. Their forked tongues sampled the air before both dropped into a submissive gesture on the floor. The former statue still staggered in an odd gait when it tried to advance upon Thamin. It pointed at the human and barked commands. The two warriors got to their feet as they turned fanatic eyes upon the intruder.

Thamin did not stop to watch the whole scene play out. It was time to run if he wanted to live. He thrust the swordbreaker into its scabbard. He sprinted for the opposite passage. A gleam amidst the vines on the ground caught his eye. Thamin scooped up the sword, Longclaw, as he ran. He could hear pursuit behind him, even as his boots skidded across muck.

"Fellunus," he whispered.

Natura magic altered Thamin's stride, granting him the sure, agile lope of a hunting cat. The voice of the former statue faded. Perhaps its muscles were still too uncoordinated to pursue? How long had it stood immobile?

Thamin arrived at the stairs several steps ahead of his pursuers and bounded up two at a time. He knew the route to the surface, if only he could stay ahead of the flint spears chasing him. The stairwell lacked light, so he whispered another word of natura, and his eyes penetrated the dark as well as a night animal. A lizardman stepped out from an alcove above, holding a simple club.

Thamin didn't slow. A snake-like stab of Longclaw caught the creature in its unprotected gut. He reached up with his other hand and grabbed its shoulder. He vaulted himself skyward even as he pulled the stunned creature downward. The lizardman rolled down the stairs only to tangle up the other pursuers.

The sword flicked a blood trail among the corridors as Thamin ran. When a larger hallway opened to the left, he turned down that path only to come face-to-face with an alert lizardman hefting a spear. The lizardman's feet were splayed awkwardly amidst vines stretching across the floor, which were trap triggers Marl and Thamin had spotted earlier. Having no time to waste, he dove to his belly alongside the lizard's clawed feet. Thamin's weight set off the trap. The lizardman uttered a brief syllable before dozens of darts, likely poisoned, filled the air only a foot above Thamin's prone form. A moment later, the reptilian body crashed to the floor, setting off the flights of a few more darts. He spared just enough moments to allow the noises to cease. Thamin jumped to his feet. With the feline grace of his spell, he dashed

9

along the length of the lizardman's body, his body putting weight only on vines already tripped by his opponent. Thamin leaped clear of the trap area a moment before an overeager pursuer fell victim. He kept his eyes focused on escape as his ears listened to whistling darts, followed by the fall of another body.

By the time daylight forced his eyes into normal human vision, Longclaw rested in his belt. He exited the structure through a large crack in the wall, likely a result of the divine chariot's crash. Thamin continued to sprint lightly on his feet as he threaded through the overgrowth covering the secret temple. He spotted another lizardman ahead. This one had its back to Thamin, but lifted its head in the air, listening to the shouts of others as the alarm traveled. The human uttered a quick, guttural noise similar to theirs. The lizardman looked over its shoulder. Thamin vaulted the creature, locking his arms onto its head in a practiced grip and throwing his entire body weight against the more muscular opponent. A snap sounded, followed by the fall of the lizardman as its head lolled backwards.

Thamin hit the ground without slowing. He heard lizardmen shouts in every direction except for the deeper jungle ahead of him. Soon they would be tracking him. He would have to dodge them for days before he could get clear of the jungle and into human lands. Thamin had a feeling his primal natura tricks would likely throw them off his tracks. The form of the spirit flowed through him. By the time he hit the next growth of trees, he raced along on all four paws.

***

Across the sea, far from the remains of the Iztheran civilization, the day shone down on the City of Spires, Orlaun. Sunlight filtered through the city's towers and through a window, illuminating the possessions laid out neatly across the bed. The room was small, barely large enough to house two tenants during their lessons at the mages' guild. A teenage girl slowly packed the organized piles of clothing and items into bags. She did so in a slow, careful manner. She kept her clothes folded tight and neat. The youth's possessions went into pockets and pouches with a lot of planning and tidiness. Despite the cleanliness and order of her things, her true emotions resurfaced every time she reexamined a letter on the bed.

Thomena picked it up again, for perhaps the twelfth time that morning. The youth's eyes narrowed, and her brow knit as she sought meanings between the lines. Lips silently mouthed the contents as she read it. Her throat bobbed with a difficult swallow, even as her delicate fingers began to clench the paper tighter. The girl realized her irritability bordered on being of control. With effort, she forced a deep breath and tried to calm her emotions. She wasn't expecting her roommate to return anytime soon, so she didn't realize someone stood at her open door until the visitor spoke.

"So, I'm told that GrayEyes is a master mage now? Are you?"

Thomena, called GrayEyes by her fellow students of arcane arts, discarded the letter so fast that she practically threw it down. She forced a deep breath and smile prior to turning around. "So are my eyes gray today, Tinker? Not silver?"

The visitor, a youth of teenage years no older than the mage packing her belongings, strolled into the room. She chuckled at their exchange of nicknames. "All the boys 'round here seem to think they sparkle, but your eyes are usually a moody gray."

Ignoring her friend's teasing reference of boys, GrayEyes replied, "In any case, Julia, I'm not a master mage by any means. Only my apprenticeship is done." The arcane graduate picked up a pin from her bed. It bore the crest of the Brotherhood of the Circles guild. She turned to display it to her friend as she pinned it on her tunic. "I'm free to stay and continue studying or travel abroad and bring back knowledge."

The young mage caught a glimpse of herself in the mirror by the door. She couldn't help but glance at her own eyes and confirm they didn't sparkle. She also realized she was once again chewing her lip, a bad habit she fell into without thinking about it. The mage lifted a hand to try smoothing out a few stray strands of the deep black hair falling about her shoulders. Like many sixteen-year-old girls, she had long legs, slight curves, and a limber form. Her face was used to smiles, but even she could see that the mirror reflected a forced expression.

Her friend couldn't miss noticing the folded clothes next to the luggage bags. "Looking to travel, I see. Where are you headed?"

Thomena glanced at her letter. "To a home I barely remember."

Julia the Tinker followed her gaze. "To him? That's why your eyes aren't shining. You've been moody ever since you got that letter. He's not worth it."

"Just because your father..." she started to say, but stopped when she happened to glance at Julia's old injury. The top of the left ear was missing, leaving a darkened scar. Worse yet, Julia noticed where GrayEyes's attention had drifted, and she self-consciously tried to cover it with her short, brown hair. The mage sighed as she realized she had soured the whole conversation by pointedly looking at the old

11

wound. "I'm sorry. I shouldn't broach that subject. The truth of the matter is I've had good memories of my father, but I hardly know him. He's only managed to visit me a few times over the years. It's such a long distance to travel. I was very young when Grandfather traveled here, and Father sent me along. I'm grateful for what I've learned in this guild, yet I feel so…" GrayEyes juggled her empty hands in the air. "Disconnected from the person who should have been my closest mentor in life."

Wetness snuck out of Thomena's eyes as she thought about her past. She tried to dab it with a sleeve, disguising the movement by passing her fingers through her hair. Her friend likely noticed, but didn't comment on it.

Julia asked, "And you don't even remember your mother?"

Grayeyes sighed. "Nay. Not one memory. She died while I was still waddling more than walking."

"So, you're going home to the Counties of Diara? Lands of knights, tournaments, bickering nobility, and royal parades? That's a long boat ride."

"Kaigal is not like the rest of those city-states. It borders the jungle and some wild hills. From what I remember, folk out there live on the fringe of civilized lands."

When Julia didn't immediately respond, the mage turned back to her bed. She picked up her wand, a foot-long stick covered in blue arcane symbols, and tucked it into her belt. She proceeded to pack away some of her outfits.

"That sounds even better. Take me with you?" Julia asked.

Thomena turned to her friend in surprise. "I barely remember my homeland. I was so young. Why would you want to go?"

The girl nicknamed Tinker held her hands out to her side. "Look at me! There's nay work in my craft for a girl my age. I don't even have a proper mentor, either. I'm the only one in this mage guild who can be recognized at a distance for my filth-stained, mended-hole clothes. I don't wanna grow old here doing thankless little chores all my life. The people of Orlaun always seem to have their noses in the air every time I'm 'round. I need to go somewhere new, maybe less 'civilized,' where a girl can forge something better than the expectations of the people here."

Thomena paused in her packing to offer her friend a warm hug. "I didn't know you hated this place that much. I'd love some company. I can't make promises on what we'll find."

Julia sat down on the end of her bed, avoiding the piles of clothes. The young mage scooped the discarded letter out of the way yet couldn't help herself from glancing across the writing again.

Julia asked, "Thomena, are you even sure what you're looking for back there?"

Thomena GrayEyes shrugged. "I can't help my curiosity. Now that I'm able to travel, my mind wanders. Out there lies a home I barely remember; a father I don't really know." Silently, she amended: *A father who has rarely seen me.*

She reread the last paragraph of the letter.

I'm very sorry I can't make the trip. I wish duty didn't bind me to this outpost. If your mother was alive today, she'd be so proud to see you follow in her footsteps and become a wizard. I'm happy to know you're safe and living a better life than the course I picked for myself. Stay safe, study hard. I will make every attempt to visit next year when the army here isn't jumping at shadows. With all my heart, Thamin.

Jherad 20th, 1252 AC

Chapter 2 – Memories of Glory

The awakening of his body was a nightmare for Ztakish, but only slightly less so than his fifteen-hundred years of immobility. His senses had quietly observed and listened to everything, confined in the prison of his immovable physique. His mind had been forced to drift into distractions during the long years, but he couldn't truly sleep. He knew an age of the world rolled by while he waited in darkness. The implement of his prison, the elf necklace, currently rested on a rough animal skin stretched across his lap. He glared at it, wishing to set fire to it by his sight alone. Yet, it had become such a part of him for so long he could not distance himself from it. Staring into the facets of its jewels, as he had on that fateful day so many centuries ago, his mind finally roused enough to reform the puzzle of his memories.

One insult came from the words of those humans who had ventured into his chamber. He understood their language, even though the words and accent sounded more foreign than he recalled. "Lizardmen," they had called his people before ignorantly ending his long paralysis. Ztakish glanced at the remains of the human he'd caught. The body was being prepared as a trophy. He would make a new necklace of the bones and set the skull somewhere suitable. The axe won from the second human seemed handy enough, though it was not to his liking.

The greater insult came from the understanding that the humans' words spoke true. The iztheran people once ruled an empire and claimed dominance in their part of the world. They traded goods, waged war, enjoyed their own culture, and appreciated art. Somewhere over the long years, they'd adapted to living as muck-dwelling lizardmen reviled by those human visitors. Being called a "lizard" affronted Ztakish. They were not reptiles other than in resemblance, for their blood stayed warm at night. What had happened to his people to diminish their culture?

There were actual lizardmen in the region who had always been a step below the evolution of the iztheran people, but now, even Ztakish saw little external difference between the two races. His people had descended into a primal existence; their golden age had become a forgotten fairy tale.

Since his release, he made a couple forays into the blinding sunlight. Ztakish viewed what had once been a forest of their empire before the crash of the divine chariot. The land looked completely foreign. The ground that had once been so hallowed to his people and the elves, contested by both, had become a bitter trophy in the hands of the iztheran descendants currently making this their home. He saw some of the ruins covered over by jungle growth. Pillars of stone half-buried in the soil bore faded, weather-smoothed symbols of the Iztheran language. His own people could no longer read them. They didn't read at all. The shamans who carried their stories and histories on their tongues knew only a distorted past. He asked them of the great human kingdom that once flourished upon the plains to the west and was told that had changed, too. From their simple description, he learned the land, as well as the human kingdom, had become fractured. The shamans observed the humans, clad in silver scales and riding four-legged beasts, fighting battles in the open lands. But the reptilian-like people, who had mostly forgotten their iztheran name and heritage, would only observe while cowering in their jungle home.

In the darkness of the Inner Sanctum, the former name of this room of the vessel, he recalled his earliest memories after the fall from the sky. The necklace had kept him in stasis, but he could see and hear everything as seasons passed. The cursed elves who had placed it on his neck likely died during the fall or shortly after, but that was scant comfort. Ztakish hadn't even been standing in the holy center of the vessel when trapped. He'd spent a long time in silent, mental anguish, paralyzed in darkness before the first iztheran rediscovered his body. Back then, they looked starved and poorly equipped. The necklace had turned his body hard as rock. They thought him a statue and set him in their most holy chamber. The necklace had shifted even then, but none would remove it. He became an object, a revered one which they would not rob. Down the centuries, he observed his people remake the temple and worship him. They performed rituals, which became twisted from their original meaning. He saw the fall of his people's language and culture and could do nothing but scream in silent agony. The descendants of Izthera who now proclaimed themselves to Ztakish spoke in a harsh, garbled accent. They seemed to have lost more words than those they remembered. They carried primitive weapons and armor. To them, Ztakish's armor made him a wonder.

Ignorant of the past greatness of their people, these muck-dwellers worshipped him as a god in their image. Ztakish found it unsettling. In his life, he commanded men and led armies. His armor had been common, as had his upbringing. He once brought forth the glory of Yurtash and fought for his people. He couldn't even decipher how many years had passed. The tribe had no concept of calendars or any system of dating time. The condition of his people's descendants brought him despair.

Even as Ztakish silently mused upon their decline, the ones currently serving as his attendants stared at his statue-like demeanor. They submitted themselves to his service, anxiously awaiting his commands. Thinking it must be the aftereffects of the necklace, he often sat or stood very still, even forgetting to breathe until prompted by his body. Now that Ztakish could move, he felt the loss of will for any reason to move. He closed his eyes, a simple act that had been denied him for centuries. He delved into memories, seeking solace. Images of the glories of the iztheran empire marched in grand parade as he dwelled on past pride. Inevitably, Ztakish remembered that fateful day when his fortune, and likely that of his people, turned for the worse...

***

Ztakish felt the wind blow across his reptilian-like scales as he stood at the prow of his ship. "Courage upon you. We will drive the elf influence from our forests this day. This land is ours, and it will be marked as such by the wreckage of their vessels."

With that, the general gestured to the endless canopy of trees, several hundred feet below. Movement in the sky to one side pulled his attention. He focused his vertically slit eyes on the elf vessel emerging from a low cloud.

"Send word to the Inner Sanctum," he bellowed. "Have the priests bring us to port and gain more height."

Nearby, others spoke into tubes running to the interior of the vessel. A few decks below Ztakish, the priests praying in the Inner Sanctum channeled the will of Yurtash to enable the miracle of flight. The divine chariot maneuvered according to his instructions and their prayers.

One of the other iztheran called out, "A second elf chariot!"

Ztakish and the others turned to witness a second elf vessel descending from the harsh sunlight. The newcomer had the advantage

16

of height but would not be upon them before they traded blows with the first elf vessel.

"Stay the course. We must disable them quickly before worrying about the second vessel. I need boarders. Now!"

As iztherans ran around the deck, arming ballistae and readying for enemy fire, a group of tough warriors assembled next to several smaller boats ready for launch. As Ztakish prepared to address them, an aide with a spyglass called out.

"The first ship flies the designs of Laedelious!"

Ztakish received the news without surprise. The elven goddess of forests and wildlands favored ship designs shaped in the form of trees. The branching extensions of the first ship gave away its allegiance. Ztakish turned instead to the pursuing second ship. Its abundance of sails and sea-vessel form made it harder to guess. Even the slightest wind rippled across large sections of canvas. As the aide made known his own uncertainty, Ztakish asked if he could see the figurehead.

The aide nodded. "Seems to be a female elf torso, on the body of a pegasus."

"Westrealei." Ztakish turned to speak to the nearby warriors. "Take the escape launches. Fly up and harass the second ship. It favors the elf faith of wind and air so beware their powers over the sky's elements. Just delay it while we try to strike a blow upon its druid sister." Ztakish waved to indicate the tree-shaped vessel. "Yurtash guide your hunt."

The iztheran warriors, resplendent in thick metal armor and an assortment of weapons, boarded the smaller boats. They launched, a shaman devoted to Yurtash at the helm of every one, guiding its flight. Ztakish gave them no more thought as he turned his attention to the champion vessel of the goddess Laedelious.

The divine chariot of Yurtash, built long, narrow, and several stories high, turned its beak-like prow to just one side of the approaching elf vessel. War machines crowded the upper deck and some ballistae peeked out from large ports in the middle decks. The armaments of the tree-ship dedicated to Laedelious became apparent as it approached. Between the branches of the ship, sling-loaded projectiles could be seen. The spell-fields filling the air, especially from Westrealei's clerics, caused the air currents to lash at all three vessels. Flocks of birds in the skies below the ships took flight from the forest and sought new refuge.

As the first two combatants came within range of their weapons, Ztakish yelled at one of the shamans, "Divine their spiritual center. We must strike their Inner Sanctum fast or we fall once the second elf ship gets in range."

All divine chariots had Inner Sanctums. The clerics, shamans, or druids of the respective gods or goddesses controlled the miracle of flight from those holy centers. The surest way to win such aerial battles involved killing the holy men keeping it aloft. Ztakish had already witnessed his share of such vessels falling from the sky as their holy men died.

Ztakish and the shaman directed fire as both ships exchanged the first volley. Missiles, magical and mundane, raked across opposing decks. Protective magic flared around both ships as enchantments sought to shield crew and ship alike. A few elves from the other ship took to the air using magic. Some of the lizard-blooded combatants invited the call of Yurtash to shape-shift into giant birds and did likewise. The grinding of many gears cranking to reload war machines provided a constant din, punctuated by the sharp cracks of enemy missiles striking their hull. Spellcasters constantly uttered the odd syllables of magic, but those words barely sounded above the chaos of battle.

"More magical fire," Ztakish yelled. "Guide the vessel to their far side; it will delay the second ship."

Bodies rained from the skies as the battle raged. The iztherans fought with the desperation of knowing they were outnumbered over their homeland, using their last vessel. The chariot of Yurtash maneuvered so close it shattered some of the branches of the other ship with its beak-like prow. As the two vessels scraped by along their entire length, the iztheran war machines launched a vicious strike. Fire and magic caused a split in the elf vessel sixty feet wide. Shape-shifted iztherans flew into the open cavity.

Within moments, the great elf vessel began to plunge. Ztakish knew his warriors had dealt a lethal blow to the elf priests in the ship's Inner Sanctum. A great cry went up, mixed with terror from the elves and exultation from the iztherans. Ztakish watched as the opposing ship dropped toward trees far below. Rigging of the ship fell apart as it twisted in the winds. Elves went into freefall along with the deck under their feet. A few lucky shape-shifted iztherans escaped before the crash ripped into the forest canopy. The great weight of the vessel collapsed in upon itself as it settled.

At the edge of his vision, Ztakish witnessed another craft falling. One of the small boarding craft from his vessel plummeted to the ground, bereft of its magic of flight. He turned to look for the second

18

elf ship only to realize his time had run out. Westrealei's vessel drifted on the opposite side of Yurtash's divine chariot—behind where all the war machines currently faced. It opened up a barrage that put large holes in the hull, pitching Ztakish to the deck. Elf archers flew over the iztherans, raking them with volleys of arrows. Small boarding boats from the elf vessel filled the air, dueling with the few remaining iztheran craft.

Ztakish used a few spells of his own. He called upon his natura magic to invoke strength and harden his skin. He attempted to rally his men but found most on the deck lay wounded or struggled against greater numbers. He called out directions to be relayed to the Inner Sanctum. The iztheran troops who would normally relay those directions were engaged in a fight as elves levitated down from above. The war machines on his deck no longer made noise, their actions halted by damage or their crews engaged with boarders. A last volley from the elf ship raked Yurtash's flying temple. The deck heaved as ballistae missiles ripped holes in the wood, its magical protections exhausted. After that, the elves ceased firing out of the risk of hitting their own.

Melee fights danced chaotically across the broken deck. Elves used both magic and force to open access to the lower decks. Some simply used magic to fly into breaches.

Barely a dozen warriors rallied to Ztakish. He encouraged them to fight fiercely. They clung to the hope they could still win with force of arms. Their bodies were naturally larger, stronger, and clawed, unlike the weaker elves. Ztakish led them as they broke through several elf groups.

It wasn't enough.

He watched some of his few remaining men succumb to a charge. Even as Ztakish tried to aid them, he felt an odd sensation creep into his body. His limbs numbed and slowed. Recognizing the magical assault for what it was, he threw all his will into resisting. Elf wizards floated into view. Under their combined force, they overcame his resistance. Ztakish froze in place, his gaze hardened into a hateful glare.

One spoke, but Ztakish didn't know enough of the language to understand. Instead, he listened helplessly as the last of his men screamed their death throes. One of the elves drew forth a necklace and placed it over his head. They spoke to him, using magic to translate the words.

"You are one of their officers. Nay quick death for you."

The second elf in arcane robes sneered. "This necklace will extend your immobility until we are ready to question you."

Ztakish strained to fight the spell but could do nothing. He couldn't even draw breath to voice an insult. His prayers found no answer. The elf magic-users taunted him as they began wrapping rope around his form. His ears and his narrow field of vision found no evidence of iztherans still fighting on the deck. He saw elf warriors still funneling into the hatches leading inside.

The deck lurched, causing everyone to fall prone. Ztakish fell as well, still frozen, while the necklace stubbornly clung to him. Bodies and items slid past his field of view. He caught a glimpse of the clouds, spinning and falling away. Except, the clouds weren't falling, he was. The iztheran in the Inner Sanctum must have fallen to the invaders, dooming many elf boarders in the process. A few on the deck took to flight if their magic allowed. Ztakish's helpless form tumbled into the open hatch of a cargo hold. Inertia flipped his stomach and his eyes became dizzy as artificial light spun around him.

He thought, *So this is what it is like to fall to one's death. Yurtash take your loyal servant.*

Ztakish expected to die. The crash thundered through his ears and he saw great beams split over his head. His senses shook even more as his form bounced along. When the sound settled, he remained alive and aware, unhurt. The magic of the necklace sustained his form in the crash, even as it still imprisoned his body.

All he could do was wait. In the darkness, barely illuminated by magical lights within the divine chariot, he waited an eternity. His vision remained locked on the same shattered wall until he knew every miniscule crack in detail. Sounds came and went as vermin slithered around him. Bugs crawled over his face. Plants and mold formed and died endlessly on the far wall. The rancid stench of wet darkness and the decay of bodies filled his nostrils until he could recall no other smell. Ztakish remained alone with his thoughts until his name became a memory of another time. He created over a thousand curses for his magical stasis.

After an age of tormenting solitude, they found him. His people saw his body and moved him from his resting place. These iztheran had already suffered. They thought he was simply a statue; part of the décor which fit in with the rest of the faded opulence of the vessel. Ztakish's brief spark of hope became another age staring at a different wall.

***

20

Ztakish moved his head slightly as he glanced at his honor guards, his mind returning to the present. The slight motion made both jump. It seemed they still expected him to remain an unmoving god.

They feared him and revered him. He had power in this new life, although the power of his people had greatly diminished. Ztakish could not bear to suffer as witness to the destruction of his people's culture. His mind toiled with ideas of how to move forward. The thought of once again planning around a future had become a foreign concept to him. His people needed to be educated about their past, and only Ztakish could properly unlock a future.

He wrestled with each facet of his old culture, wondering how to begin the process. The means of helping his people rise again needed extensive planning. Their overall goal was the only thing he didn't need to question.

When he fell, he was a warrior fighting a war. In light of his reawakening, the war would be waged anew.

Chapter 3 - Homeland

Thomena and Julia stepped onto the main deck, feeling the gentle roll of the waves and hearing the squawks of seagulls. Both sixteen-year-old girls wore the many-layered clothing typical of Orlaun's style: a gray mantle covered Thomena's shoulders, dark-brown vest for Julia, each worn over dresses with blousy sleeves. Petticoats covered leggings, which disappeared under tall shoes. The thicker, better-tailored wool and lace frills of Thomena's clothes contrasted the more threadbare linen and slightly patched garments worn by her friend. Julia's brown hair was just long enough for her to tie it into a short ponytail using a string. Thomena used a lace strip and some pins to gather her hair into a bun. The breeze of the gulf would have otherwise lashed the girls with their own loose strands.

Thomena whispered to Julia, "How close are we?"

"Less than a mile. I can see the folks moving on the docks. Why are you staring down at the deck?"

The young mage idly chewed at her lip. "I'm trying to remember all the details from long ago so I can compare it to reality. One of my earliest memories was when my ship left Kaigal's harbor. Grandfather stood beside me on the deck, my father waved from the docks, but I tried to memorize every detail of the town so that I'd recognize my way back. Can you see a building by the docks that looks as if it was made out of a giant ship? It should even have a crow's nest and a mast."

Julia, the tinker, held a hand up to shield her eyes. "Aye, I see it. What kind of business is it?"

Thomena grinned. "It's named like a ship, but I recall it's actually an inn. I remember it dominated the harbor skyline. The docks only stretched about a block in each direction."

Julia huffed. "It doesn't stand out all that much. The harbor extends several blocks to each side."

Thomena focused on the image in her memory before raising her eyes to look. Julia spoke truthfully. The inn's mast and crow's nest were noticeable but occupied less of the docks than Thomena remembered. Either her memory exaggerated the inn's size or the harbor had grown. She also noticed a large rock formation jutting out of the water beyond the harbor. She couldn't remember its name, but the sight of it sparked forgotten recognition.

"And Imantz looked upon his childhood home perplexed," Thomena recited a phrase from memory, "for one of them had changed, and he knew not which."

Julia glanced at her. "What was that?"

"A passage from *The Codex*. It sounded fitting."

Julia shook her head, saying, "You recite that book all the time. You won't get me to read it that way."

It was Thomena's turn to huff. "It's not just 'that book.' It has holy scripture and epic tales from many different authors, some of them gods. It wouldn't hurt you to read a bit of it sometime. I find it very enlightening."

Julia joked, "I don't have to read it. By the time we're old maids, I'll have heard you quote every passage ten times."

The young mage laughed, knowing that her friend spoke true.

The tinker waved an accusing finger, though her tone spoke softly. "You keep trying to push your religion on me. What were some of those tenets it extol...extolerated?"

"Extolled."

"That's it!" Julia glanced to the side. Thomena wouldn't be surprised if her friend was rolling her eyes. The tinker continued. "Doesn't it ask you to follow some knightly virtues or something? Some code of honor?"

Thomena held up a hand and began to count them on her fingers. "Truth and Honesty in all things. A Humble soul who demands nay reward and seeks nay fame. Courage to stand firm when others may falter..."

"Okay, just those first three sound hard to follow, especially that whole humble bit. I have a bag of special tools, which may open a profession for me. That day will only come if I boast my head off." A silent moment passed before Julia spoke again. "Wait a minute, how are you supposed to be a successful mage unless you boast to folks about your skills?"

The question pointed at Thomena's own musings during the sea voyage. Part of the sea journey had been paid by the use of Thomena's wind and water spells. She hadn't advertised her skills, merely replied honestly to the captain that her specialty included those elemental schools.

"Honesty about one's abilities is fine; I do have to support myself. Bragging is not allowed." Thomena's thoughts turned inward. "I hadn't really thought of what my future as a mage would bring. I suppose I just wanted to follow in my mother's footsteps."

"Was she a powerful mage?"

Thomena wished she could remember some aspect of her mother's face. "I'm told so. I can't remember her."

She saw Julia staring down at the deck. Hoping to boost her friend's feelings, Thomena offered some optimism. "I know someone will find you indispensable here. You'll find a place to fit in, as I will."

"You're just saying that."

"Honesty is one of the keystones of *The Codex*," Thomena reminded her friend. "I wouldn't say such things if I didn't believe they were true."

Thomena watched Julia's attention return to the shoreline. The tinker frowned as she examined the city. A warm wind blew past, so Julia loosened her collar. Thomena asked, "Not what you hoped? The city?"

"Huh? It looks fine. It's smaller than that over puffed peacock called Orlaun, which suits me well. It has a practical feel to it. Why you ask?"

"You just seemed...like you were frowning."

Julia shrugged and returned her gaze to the docks. "Nay, I'm happy to see land after all this time."

Her answer confirmed something Thomena had begun to observe about her friend. Julia's expressions likely accounted for some of her problems in Orlaun. Her friend didn't realize her face often formed a frown. Thomena resolved she would figure some subtle way to help her friend present a better face to the world.

Julia interrupted her thoughts. "So, your father lives here or somewhere farther inland?"

"Inland. For as long as I remember, he's been at Bael Cochaw. I know 'Bael' refers to a castle or fortification. I don't know how far we have left to travel."

"You mean he set his home in some cold castle away from the markets?"

This time, Thomena could tell the frown was real. She asked, "Are you worried about finding work?"

Julia gave half a shrug. "I can find work anywhere. Cities and towns have a greater need of my real skills. I hate knowing my tools are sitting idle."

"We don't have to rush out of town. I know Bael Cochaw isn't far, but I don't know the exact distance." Thomena reached a comforting arm around her friend. "We can split up while I ask about a carriage coach. You can see what doors may open for your talent."

Julia stared over the rail at the sun-dappled waves. "I didn't cross a large sea in order to park my talents a few days' walk away from you. Your father is down at the end of some road. I won't hold high hopes for a job here until I know where you're going."

Thomena looked across the harbor, chewed her lip. She wasn't sure if her face reflected a frown at that moment. "My future isn't set. I don't think a fort will find better use for my arcane talents than a city. Either way, there's nay sense worrying about it. We'll just have to see what lies ahead."

***

Thomena faced some culture shock when she entered Kaigal. The two girls separated once inside the city, each having her own agenda and splitting up to cover more ground. They planned to rendezvous once again at an open plaza decorated with large statues. Before she left, Julia had pointed out the obvious differences in local clothing styles. The change wasn't as apparent with Julia's humble attire, though the tinker declared she would shed a few layers. Thomena's Orlaun fabrics, blousy extensions, and multiple layers stood out in a crowd. The people of Kaigal walked around with bare arms or shorter skirts, allowing more skin to show. Most of the common folk displayed dull colors: brown or tan hues, subdued greens and blues, as well as shades of gray. Thomena's clothes pulled eyes like garden flowers emerging from a muddy field.

When attempting to buy new garb from a merchant, she was told to exchange her foreign currency at Tinkerhall. The name offered some brief amusement as she thought of her friend's nickname. Thomena went to a guard first, expecting some sort of swindle, only to find that many merchants preferred to do business in Diaran currency. She exchanged a portion of her coins, still feeling as if she was somehow being robbed, and went back to claim her new garb.

Kaigal didn't seem any colder than Orlaun, but by adapting to the local style and reducing the layers of clothing, Thomena suffered from the occasional chill. Dressed in a gray short-sleeve tunic, paired with a long skirt, sporting a subdued-blue cape, she began to blend into the crowds. She wouldn't give up her straps and pouches of arcane accouterments, nor would she hide the pin on her cape representing her membership to the Brotherhood of the Circles mage guild. Thomena owned a second pin announcing her as an honorary vigile of Orlaun, meaningless here, so she tucked it away. A pair of soft leather gaiters covered her boots and protected her skin up past the knee, hiding most of the flesh that wasn't already concealed by the wool skirt. Her old belt kept her lightning wand handy, as well as a dirk intended only to be used as dinnerware.

Wearing less layers made her feel slightly more exposed, but it also allowed more freedom. In the middle of a strange land, she felt like a stranger in her own clothes. She needed time to see if the trade was worth it.

Folks greeted her with phrases like, "Pleasant sunrise," and said farewells with "Grace shine upon you." The latter tugged at her distant memory since she had used the phrase growing up. It wasn't common in Orlaun.

A thought hit her: she might run into her father in the town. Thomena started looking more closely at the faces around her. She felt both eager and nervous for their reunion. She wanted to wrap her arms around him; after all, it had been years since she last hugged him. Maybe four or five...too long. On the other hand, they were living different lives and been separated for most of her life. As a child, she didn't understand it. As a growing woman, she felt a need to ask him about that decision. She didn't want to jump into a heavy conversation subject at the start. Thomena hoped to impress him after having made this trip. She didn't want to disappoint him in any way.

Thomena saw a merchant at a store window hawking kahv, a popular, flavorful drink that seemed to lend vigor to the imbiber. Enticed by the aroma of the crushed beans at his stall, she couldn't resist. She paid double the price she would expect in Orlaun, only to find out Diaran kahv wasn't even a drink. This version consisted of a potent pudding, which disappeared in a few bites. It confused her to have remembered so little of her homeland's culture. Then again, kahv wasn't really a children's drink, and she had been young when she sailed away. Thomena probably never tasted any before leaving for foreign shores.

After much delay from her original plan, she questioned a stableman. "Good man, where might I find the coach headed for Bael Cochaw?"

The rough-whiskered man, her elder by maybe a decade, cocked his head to one side. "A what? Did you say coach?"

Thomena displayed a polite smile and offered a deferential nod as she spoke. "Aye. Is there one that runs the route to Bael Cochaw?"

26

This comment caused the man to suffer a fit of giggles, and he called another, older stablehand over to listen. He cracked a smile as he spoke, "I suppose the next 'coach' that comes along depends on which lord you want. Do you prefer your lords handsome or will filthy rich be enough?"

Thomena's politeness began to wither in the face of their unknown jest. "Are there nay coach services running between towns?"

The old hand asked, "Where are you from?"

"Kingdom of Gheras." When both men looked at each other and shrugged, she added, "City of Orlaun."

The first stablehand clapped his hands once, "That explains it. Well, I suppose the City of Spires has a coach that will take you up to your room on the fourth floor of the inn if you ask it nicely enough." The older stablehand bent over with hooting laughter. The first stablehand resumed after a slight pause. "Around here, the only people who use coaches are rich enough to own them and bring their own armored escort. The rest of us try to get a horse if we can, or we run during the daylight and hide at night."

"Hide?" Thomena, feeling outside of her element, couldn't disguise some trepidation in her voice. "What do you mean? Hide from what?"

"Do you want a list? Some bandits operate between cities, or perhaps some mischievous Gliel might find you. There are a few of them that call the grasslands their home, and they're hard to spot."

As he spoke, Thomena recalled lessons about the small elf-like humanoids. They were no larger than halflings, but very reclusive. Their fey ancestry prompted them to launch tricks upon many unsuspecting travelers.

The first stablehand continued speaking. "Not to mention anything that might sneak out of the jungle and get past our patrols."

The older hand spoke before she could respond. "He hasn't even mentioned the normal dangers you'd find in the grasslands: snakes, poisonous plants, vermin whose bite can give you a pox, maybe even insect swarms."

Knowing that she couldn't afford a horse without spending most of the coins she owned, Thomena asked, "How long is the walk?"

The younger man shook his head, "Two days, but you don't want to walk out there alone. The only safety might be a few isolated farms and," —his eyes roamed her body in a way that caused a shiver to run up her spine, — "some of them farmers might have an unhealthy interest in a lonely young girl."

Thomena felt the color rise to her cheeks. "Well, how would you suggest I travel?"

The old hand shrugged while the younger man responded. "I don't know. I've lived in Kaigal ever since I was born. Never went more than a league from town."

Disappointment burdened her good spirit, but she had the decency to leave them with, "Thank you for your time. Grace shine upon you."

Thomena kept following the street without a clear destination. It dismayed her that she'd already crossed more than a thousand miles at sea only to be deterred by a two-day walk overland. She couldn't even be sure if she'd find her long-separated father at Bael Cochaw, or what their surprise reunion would be like.

After two more inquiries followed similar lines, Thomena wearily ventured into Heroes' Terrace. She remembered the plaza of statues from her childhood, and both girls had passed it coming from the docks, but she didn't pay it much attention. Nothing matched her memories well, and it unsettled her. She walked past the first two statues dedicated to Kaigal's heroes. Children ran among the terraced gardens, running past merchants selling candy. The young mage could not see Julia, which actually felt like a relief. She wasn't in a hurry to inform her friend of her failure to find any safe transport. Thomena picked out a bench and dropped into it with a resigned sigh. At least the sun and the walking had chased away the chill of her new outfit. She reflected on the unexpected comfort of wearing less layers than Orlaun's fashion.

After a time, she gazed at the statues dispersed among the terraces. Thomena never left the comfort of the bench, choosing to appreciate them from afar. She noted the armored figures in grand poses. Each one featured some god of a man in perfect poise. They all bore stern looks and held weapons. Some of their armor was almost comically decorative. Another statue, far different from the rest, drew her attention.

It was the only female statue in the plaza, and she was essentially naked. She had a cloth of some kind, but it was held upon her shoulders, stretching from hand to outstretched hand. The banner draped around her, barely concealing her feminine attributes. It was as if the wind blew it against her front. No grand armor or weapon lent her any amount of modesty. She stood mostly exposed, boldly and unashamedly thrust out to observers. It revealed far too much for Thomena's taste. The cloth swept behind the female form as if it were a grand flag caught by the wind, scarcely covering her backside.

28

Thomena scowled at it and mumbled, "Trust some artisan to carve the men in their fine armor yet leave the female hero practically naked and bared for the whole city to leer."

Between the distasteful statue and her embarrassment at trying to find a means of travel, it left her with a bitter taste for her childhood home.

***

After making several inquiries, Julia began to feel as downcast as her friend. Her worn-out clothes ended many conversations before they began. When folks did stop to talk to her, she could see their attention kept drifting towards her cut ear. Julia kept trying to arrange her hair to cover that disfigurement better. Near the edge of the city, she saw a train of mules and people preparing for a journey. She hoped this would mark a better change in her luck.

As she watched the caravan pack, her focus settled on a huge, muscular man. He likely could be a generation older than her, and his clothing suggested he wasn't native to Kaigal. Hides covered his legs and a thick, leather work apron adorned his chest, but he left his muscled arms bare to the sun. He wore an odd necklace of iron ornaments. He possessed long, blond hair, braided in such a way as to frame a bearded face. The man's footsteps thundered when he walked. When he talked to the other folks of the caravan, his lips barely moved. What most peaked Julia's attention involved the anvil and other smith's equipment the man packed aboard a wagon. Although Julia could only claim a passing knowledge of many aspects of the craft, it was the closest thing to her parents' profession she could expect to find. The bearded man appeared to become frustrated with a chest on the wagon. She watched as he stared at it while patting down his pockets. He grabbed the locked chest and tried to pry it open with his bare hands. Seeing an opportunity, she strode over to the man.

Julia tried to stand tall despite being dwarfed by his stature. "'scuse me, sir?"

The big man looked up in surprise. He made a show of looking around, as if searching for someone else standing next to him, before turning back to Julia. "Sir? Oye tink dat's de first time someone mistook me for a sir."

His strange accent startled Julia, but she tried to recover quickly. The man had stopped and was giving her his full attention. Julia pointed towards the pack animals and men. "I was told a caravan was going out to the small villages. Will you be traveling by Bael Cochaw?"

His mouth barely opened when he spoke. "Who vants to know? You aren't vorking for some bandits, are you?"

She noted the way he glanced down at her patched clothes, the same as twenty others had done that morning. Julia tried to keep her face from betraying her irritation. "I'm Julia. I have a friend that needs to get to Bael Cochaw."

"Yoo-lia?"

"Julia."

"Hoo…hoo-lia? Uffa, nevermind. Ve're not only going by Cochaw, I'm staying once ve get dere. Tanks to de guilds!"

"And who might you be?"

"Gunnard Uunfred, blacksmitt."

Julia found herself adjusting to his strange accent. A smile even crept onto her lips at listening to the odd dialect. "Where do you hail from, Gunnard?"

"Oye come from Norvess. Ever heard of it?" Julia shook her head. Gunnard gave a vague wave in the direction of his homeland as he talked. "It's far nort-east of dis land. Ve are made of several city-states, like Diara. Unlike dem, ve take our sailing and our smitting to heart."

Julia had to admit there was something interesting about the man. He couldn't pronounce her name and his face stayed impassive the whole time, yet he was the most talkative man she'd met that morning without throwing a storm of insults her way.

Julia glanced between the wagon and the city behind her. "Why are you traveling to a keep for your craft? Cities offer more business."

Gunnard narrowed his eyes, the first facial expression she'd seen. "De guilds say who sets up in deir city, dey run everyting. Now I vork for dem. But, since I'm foreigner, I start vere dey send me, so Bael Cochaw gets me first."

His words sparked a concern in the young tinker. Merchant guilds could enforce a hard limitation on starting her craft. Julia asked, "Do the guilds wield that much control? Can one start a business without them?"

Gunnard huffed. "Uffa, nay. De guilds run dis free city. Nay independent crafters here. You vant to vork, you sign vit dem."

His words deflated her hopes further, yet Julia felt like she'd gotten her foot in the door just by talking this long to the smith. At least now, she had found a means of traveling to the fort with a group. That only left one other need. She began to blurt it out fast enough so Gunnard wouldn't have much chance interrupt her.

"Could you use an apprentice? I work hard. I've got more muscles than you think. Done plenty of labor. I can be precise and careful with tools..."

Gunnard folded his arms across his chest and leaned back against his wagon. He looked her up and down more keenly as she continued to rattle on about her usefulness. When he did interrupt her, he didn't even speak. One big, open hand came up, indicating she should stop. Julia's words came to a halt.

"Make muscle," he commanded.

At her confusion, he flexed one large arm. Julia did the same. He reached out and gave her arm a squeeze.

"Not bad for a voman. Ever vield a smit hammer before, hoo...Lia?"

"Nay, but I've worked around smithies and helped with some labor." Julia found it hard to read his emotions, so she pointed to the chest that seemed to frustrate him. "My family used to work with small, complex devices, like locks and gear work. I might be able to help with your lock problem."

It took a moment before she realized his stomach shook slightly. Looking up at his eyes, she thought he might be laughing silently.

"You vant to impress me by picking my lock? Uffa!"

Julia began to panic, wondering if he might call for guards. Instead, Gunnard stepped aside and swept a hand to indicate the lock. Julia stepped forward. Now that she had her chance, her fingers began trembling. Julia unslung a sack tightened across her back. She took out a smaller bag inside it. Gunnard stood where he could look over her shoulders. Inside the bag, she began to unfold some oil-stained cloths, revealing several spotless tools. She set a few on the wagon close to the chest.

Julia saw Gunnard's shadow nod as he spoke. "You take good care of your tools. Vere did you get dese?"

"They belonged to my parents." Julia tried to shut those memories out of her mind. She concentrated on the lock as she started to pick at it with some of her tools.

Gunnard seemed to understand. "Parents died before dey teach you?"

Julia found her palms getting sweaty as she worked at the lock. She felt she knew the right method to get it open, but she had to stop

31

and wipe her palms on her raggedy tunic. "They taught me. Problem is that folks have a hard time giving a young woman a chance."

"And dey knew locks?"

"Actually, they built clocks. It was my father's wealthiest pursuit. They sell for a lot of money back in Gheras. Only lords and state officials showed an interest, so he began to work on locks for the merchant class."

With a click, the chest lid popped open. Julia stood back and glanced at the big smith. Gunnard's eyes reflected his surprise. He turned from Julia and reached over to the chest. The first thing he plucked from the inside was a set of keys. She rewrapped her tools but noted Gunnard kept looking away from her. Heartbeats ticked away nervously as she waited for him to speak.

"You know," he turned back to her, his hand rubbing his chin, "I don't tink dere is a clockmaker in Kaigal. I tink anyone who shows a talent for clockwork can do vell among the guildmasters. Can you make clocks?"

Julia couldn't rein in the eagerness of her body language or restrain the smile on her face as she answered, "Aye! Aye, I can do all the hard work. I have all the tools; a smith can help me make the parts I need. I'm good at woodwork, too."

"I tink maybe you and me can make good business togetter, if you can deliver on your promises, Lia."

"Julia."

"Yoo-lia...Uffa! If you don't mind, I'll yust call you Lia."

***

Thomena and Julia sought the best comfort they could while sitting atop the wagonload of anvils, tools, coal buckets, dry goods, and metal bars, each chewing an apple as the road rolled along. Kaigal disappeared into the distance as the wagons navigated a rut-marked path past sparse farms. Thomena swallowed a mouthful and spoke the first words since leaving the town gates. "I really owe it to you for finding this caravan. I couldn't find anything, and everyone seemed set on scaring me about the countryside."

Julia huffed and hurried to finish her mouthful. "You didn't seem to need me for passage. What did the caravan master offer when he saw you?"

Thomena felt ashamed about it, but she couldn't lie to her friend. "He offered me some gold for me to be vigilant, as well as help protect the caravan if we're attacked."

The young mage noticed Julia casting a side-glance at her new attire. Even though Thomena had bought new clothes, her wand and magic bags were readily accessible and visible to anyone. The tinker looked away but spoke out of the side of her mouth. "I'm glad you made out well."

Thomena glanced at her friend. Julia's words weighed sincere, but Thomena sensed something hurtful behind it. As the mage thought about their journey, she had an epiphany. In the back of her mind, it had preoccupied her that, aside from her magic, she could boast no appreciable craft. Aside from the great unknown that would result from meeting her father, she had been perplexed about how to create a lifestyle and make her living. Julia had spoken her own similar concerns back in Orlaun. Thomena began to realize the difference in how easily they could reach their goals. The ship voyage from Orlaun to Kaigal allowed Thomena on board in trade for casting a few spells. Julia had to work for her passage, learning and performing the skills of a sailor. To join the caravan, Julia had to convince someone to take her on as an apprentice. By comparison, the caravan master offered to pay Thomena for accompanying them. Doors practically opened for Thomena and her magic, but her friend had to work her way through life.

Julia interrupted her thoughts. "Thanks for the apples."

The apples were the only thing along their journey that Thomena bought which Julia accepted. The mage realized their differences might form a rift in their friendship if she didn't work to prevent it.

She leaned closer to whisper so that Gunnard might not overhear. "Julia. I'm glad you found something, but are you sure it's what you want?"

The sparkle in Julia's eyes looked genuine. "He'll teach me to smith, and I'll teach him about clocks. If things work out, I can get back into the craft that raised me. It sounds like clock makers are very rare throughout Diara. There's hope there."

"I can't thank you enough for joining me on this journey. You helped me more than you know." Thomena realized that a slight change in her words and perspective would help bind their friendship closer. "I mean, it's not just my journey anymore—it's *our* journey. We're in this together."

Julia smiled. "Two young girls seeking their fortunes in Dhea Loral."

Thomena grinned. "Look out, realm."

Contented, Thomena leaned back to finish her apple. She relaxed, listening to the world around her. She felt the rocking motions of the wagon wheels in time with the creaking axles. Her eyes went to the clouds, daydreaming about their shapes. Her nose sampled the scents of the grasslands.

Before long, Julia interrupted her thoughts again. "Thomena, do you remember the coaches and caravans in Gheras? Out in the country?"

She nodded. "We didn't go out of the city much, but I recall them."

"More to the point, do you recall the guards?" Julia tilted her head. "Or any of the praetorians, for that matter?"

Thomena smiled. "Well, I did have an adventure with them before I met you."

Julia's eyes went wide. She spun her head to face her friend. "Wait, I forgot…but you never said much about it. You helped Orlaun's guards? Or was it just the vigiles?"

Thomena recalled a phrase from memory. "All of the vigiles are praetorians, but not all praetorians are vigiles." The ends of her lips curled up from the recollection. The praetorians who joined the vigiles became the firefighters of the city. "So, aye, that was part of my mission: to protect them from hazards as they fought fires—"

Thomena was about to say more, but Julia's voice raised in agitation as she interrupted. "How old were you back then? You had to be a child!"

The dark-haired mage pulled her honorary vigile pin from her pocket. She held it out for her friend to take. "I was thirteen and rather bold for my age. I ended up closer to danger than anyone planned. I got burned for it, too. You've seen the small, pale spots on my leg."

Julia resituated herself on the uncomfortable wagon load. The girl looked at the pin from different angles. She turned her focus on her friend. "So, tell me about it. Spare nay detail."

Thomena started to shake her head. "There's not much to tell…"

The tinker rolled her eyes. "It's not pride to admit you did something good. You can give me an honest answer and retain your humility."

After taking a deep breath, Thomena tried to give a brief rendition. "I wanted to learn how to wield fire, but I was too young according to the guild rules. They gave me a daunting assignment: I was to accompany the vigiles to fires and cast protective spells on them. I guess they thought that exposure to fire's dangers would help teach me a proper respect for it. I felt overwhelmed on the first day."

The mage paused, rolling the apple core in her hand while she envisioned how to translate old events. Julia waited patiently.

"Two important things happened during that time. First, I started discovering evidence that suggested another mage was starting the fires." Julia gasped but didn't interrupt. Thomena continued, although her throat tightened a bit as she tried to speak about the next event. "Then I encountered a large fire. Old Market."

This time, the tinker couldn't keep silent. "That's where you got your nickname? The Old Market Mage?"

Thomena closed her eyes and nodded, snorting out a bit of air at the title. "Aye. The Old Market Mage. Makes me sound older than I am."

"I'm sorry to interrupt. What happened?"

Thomena took another deep breath. She needed to steady her nerves to retell this portion. "A lot of vigiles were trapped in the fire. I used a borrowed scroll and a lot of my own spells to breach an escape path. I saved most of them." She tried to keep her tone even, but likely Julia didn't miss the tightness in her friend's voice. Thomena also realized that she was vigorously fidgeting with the apple core in her hands. Thomena admitted, "I didn't save my friend."

It had been three years, yet she was ready to leak tears again over Pommery's sacrifice. Without a word, Julia reached over and plucked the remaining fruit. She tossed it out for the animals to find. The young tinker took Thomena's hands, cradling them in her own and offering a firm, reassuring squeeze.

Thomena nodded at the gesture but continued retelling the past. "There was pressure to quit, inside me as well as from others. I stuck it out and helped find a way to predict the mage's next fire. I tried to use a summoned elemental to battle him, but I still got swept into the fire. I even got trapped under a burning timber."

Thomena looked skyward and sighed. "It turns out, one of my own friends was the mage causing the fires. I managed to talk him into freeing me. Then I grabbed him using a strength spell and didn't let go. We'd caught our criminal, but that also ended the assignment." She cast a sidelong glance at Julia and offered a smirk. "They couldn't allow a child to go running through fires after all that."

The young mage held out her hand, and Julia returned the vigile pin. Thomena concluded, "And that sums it up as much as I'll admit."

"That's…" Julia hesitated. "A big adventure for a young kid."

Thomena just nodded, so Julia offered her friend a reassuring hug. The tinker tried to reposition herself for comfort on the wagon, while the mage tucked her pin away. They rolled over a few bumps in silence.

After a short span, Thomena asked, "Why were you asking me about the guards?"

"Huh?" Julia took a moment to respond. "Oh, I'd almost forgotten. Anyways, what was your opinion of the praetorians?"

Thomena closed her eyes and pictured them. "Orderly. Organized. Always wearing some uniform or another. Despite some seriousness, they had their playful moments." She reflected upon the fun they'd had with her conjured snowballs. "They were a good team."

Julia nodded in agreement. "And note your 'fellow' caravan guards here."

Thomena glanced at them, assuming her friend had spotted some brash, young man and taken a fancy. Julia's continuing observations dispelled that thought immediately.

"No uniforms. All mismatched armor and weapons. Half of them bear scars like me. None of them wastes idle talk, all of them continually watching out for trouble. Sometimes, they seem to be scrutinizing their fellow guards."

The young mage watched how seriously the hired swords and bowmen followed their task.

Julia finished. "Seems a lot different here. These folks really are expecting trouble."

Now that her friend had pointed it out, Thomena noticed these guards seemed rougher than the ones back in Orlaun. In fact, despite lesser armor in almost every case, these men looked tough enough that they wouldn't think twice about picking a fight with the guards back home. She also thought Julia was perceptive in noticing a bit of paranoia toward their fellow guards. Not all had signed up at once. There was no banter, no idle talk.

Thomena whispered to her friend, "Everything here feels different."

"And more dangerous?"

She agreed.

Chapter 4 – Scales in the Jungle

"There, a proper home for you," Thamin spoke, barely a whisper, while sliding Longclaw into the new scabbard.

He loosened and inserted the blade a few times, testing the feel. He mused over the crafting of the scabbard. He thought it was as good as his skill could provide. His fingers passed over the texture of elf beads woven into parts of the leather. With this project finished, he paused to reflect on Longclaw's prior owner.

"Rest peacefully, Marl. See you in the great unknown."

Thamin's words disappeared in the darkness of the barracks, having no one to witness their passage other than the empty bunks of other lost friends. He rose with a slight groan, stretching joints punished by years of abuse. He buckled the single-edged sword onto his belt. Turning to blow out the one small candle illuminating his bed, he paused. Against a wall, in some old, broken mirror, he caught his reflection.

Despite a recent shave, whiskers had already reclaimed their territory. No trimmed beard or mustache interrupted his ever-present rough growth. The worry lines on his brow and eyes defined his facial expression, as well as the smirk that formed whenever he tried to force a grin. Despite a solid shoulder girth and strong legs, he knew he looked lean for his six-foot frame. An elvish clasp, unseen behind his head, kept a lot of his shoulder-length, brown hair away from his eyes.

Thamin blew out the candle. Rows of shutters that were never left open did their best to block the sun's light. Nevertheless, thin strips of bright light still lit portions of the barracks. The irregular stripes of sunlight, blinding if you stood exposed to one, only served to make the majority of the barracks cloaked in a deeper darkness by comparison. The dimness never bothered him. If he looked at the barracks in the light, it would only dig up painful memories.

He heard footsteps outside. They approached with a rhythm and urgency that caught Thamin's attention. Although he expected no trouble, old habits compelled him to check the looseness of his blades once again. Both Longclaw and his swordbreaker could be drawn for action in a heartbeat.

"Accipet," he whispered, and his eyes slipped into a spectrum of light that penetrated the darkness easily, though it lacked color. A quick glance at his side reassured him that his bow hung on the same peg that had housed it for years when not in use.

The boots stopped at the door briefly before a soft knock could be heard. A nervous voice called, "Trollsbane?"

"Come in."

Thamin heard the outer door swing open, followed by a helmeted head peeking around the corner of wall inside the barracks. The head swung about nervously, sun-blind, and unable to make out details in the overall shadow of the building. Thamin could easily see every detail about the footman. He took a step, allowing the newcomer to make out his location through the intermittent stripes of sunlight. The footman jumped at the movement then took a moment to gather his wits.

Thamin broke the silence. "Am I needed?"

The newcomer stuttered his reply, "A-aye. T-the commander wants to see you right away."

Thamin nodded, belatedly realizing the other man likely couldn't see the motion. "Very well. Did he say why?"

"Nay, sir."

He assumed the other man couldn't even see the smirk on his face at that moment. "You don't have to use 'sir' with me. Thanks for the message."

The man hastily departed. "You're welcome...Trollsbane."

Thamin opened his footlocker. In the process of throwing in some leftover leather scraps and elf beads from the scabbard crafting, he came across something that caught his enhanced eyesight. He reached in and withdrew an old doll. The doll was barely more than old rags sewn together, with stitches forming the eyes and mouth. His night vision didn't allow him to see the bright mix of colors on the toy. Thamin stared at it, his mind wandering a thousand miles away.

"You're a grown woman now, making your way somewhere in the world. How I wish I could see you soon." With great care, he placed the old doll back in the footlocker. "Maybe it's just as well that you're living your own life. You could do better than follow a worn bowman like me."

***

"At your summons, sir."

Commander Bedran looked toward the door in surprise, unaware of when Thamin arrived. The armored giant of a commander waved for him to enter then resumed his lecture to a couple sergeants. Thamin strode over and waited patiently for his turn.

He remembered when the fort commander was once a company captain, one who showed an interest in Thamin's talents as a scout and guide. Now, the aging warrior showed considerably more wear than Thamin. Scars crisscrossed Bedran's face and head, cutting through graying hair growth in several places. The commander had difficulty pronouncing some words due to several missing teeth, one clinging on crookedly to the left side of his face. Eyebrows dipped at the center, almost meeting over the nose. The effect gave him a perpetually angry appearance. The commander maintained impressive muscles for his age, his arms thicker than the legs of some warriors.

After lecturing the sergeants, he gave them no chance to reply before turning on Thamin. "I think you and Marl stirred up something when you went into Olangi."

Thamin nodded but waited for the commander to continue. It had been more than a forty-day month since returning from the temple with news of Marl's death. Bedran knew everything about what they'd found in the upside-down temple.

The commander waved vaguely over a map. "We got scales scurrying all over, acting unnatural." He often used the term "scales" to refer to the lizardfolk. "They've become bolder, moving about in larger packs."

Thamin glanced at the map. His attention paused over a silver-tipped pin marking the position of Yurtash's temple in the Olangi Jungle. Parts of the map were blank in that area since no one had explored too deeply until Marl attempted it.

"Are the lizardfolk carrying out more raids?" Thamin asked. It wasn't uncommon for him to track down raid parties.

Commander Bedran fixed him with an incredulous stare. "That's exactly the odd thing about this. Normally, I'd see some raids on some of the early harvests." He turned to the map and stabbed an accusatory finger at places near the jungle border. "I've had scouts and light horses patrolling all over. The reports I'm getting...it's just the opposite."

Thamin waited as the commander gathered his thoughts. Bedran threw his arms up. "The raids started but just as quickly stopped. We've found the tracks of several groups, even caught a couple of scales. They were all going back into the jungle. The ones we caught were all empty handed."

Thamin glanced over the map. "Something in the jungle has them more interested than looting us? That's a first."

"Exactly my thoughts. They love their raiding too much to give it up over a few extra patrols." The fort commander took a swig of a nearby mug. "I think we need to get some eyes inside the jungle."

"My eyes."

The commander confirmed, "Your eyes. Everything we've found suggests they're heading in one direction." He pointed firmly at the silver-tipped pin. "Towards that temple. I can't be sure. An armed force would only get itself trapped and ambushed in that dense growth. I'm sending other scouts in but, well, you're the best. You've seen the temple."

Thamin glanced between the fort commander and the map. The riskiest jobs always seemed to fall on his shoulders. Then again, he always survived when others didn't. For the average soldier, a short trip alone into Olangi equaled a death sentence. Thamin noticed the looks on the sergeants, reflecting similar sentiments that Bedran was asking him to go on a suicide mission.

Thamin simply replied, "I'll find out what I can."

***

They saw the birds circling from a mile away. The scavengers passed over a sizeable cottage just off the road. The caravan master ordered the train to skirt away from the building. Thomena and Julia were jostled in the back of Gunnard's wagon as he tried to navigate uneven ground hidden under five-foot tall grass.

One of the caravan guards rode back and called to Thomena. "Get on the back of my horse, jumble-mumbler."

"What?"

He guided his horse alongside the wagon. "Whatever that is you speak when you cast spells, wizard. Time to earn your passage. Jump on!"

Gunnard slowed as the guard continued to point in back of his saddle. Thomena stood, unsteady, on the edge of the wagon board. The guard, with his impatient huff and dirty face, rode as close as he dared to the wagon wheels. Thomena couldn't believe he wanted her to jump from the wagon to the top of the horse's hindquarters. She had a fleeting vision of landing on a venomous snake moments before a wheel crushed her. She hoped the skirt she bought in Kaigal—

previously thought to be a little too short and open—would allow her the flexibility to make the jump.

She thought, *Is he serious?* The Codex *may want me to be brave, but this is more like stupidity!*

Almost biting her lip, she jumped. She landed hard on the horse and immediately wrapped the other rider in a web of limbs. He cursed and fought to keep his balance. Somehow, Thomena managed to keep upright and get comfortable.

The man yelled, "I didn't think you'd be dumb enough to actually jump. Are you a fanatic of Kelor?"

Thomena ignored his reference to the God of Luck as he kicked the horse faster. She glanced back and glimpsed Julia throwing a worried look in her direction. Thomena turned back to regard the carrion birds over the cottage. She assumed they were going to investigate the cottage and help the folks within, but it was reasonable to be on guard for any hidden threats. The mage checked her wand to make sure it hadn't fallen from her belt. Her hand patted the pouch of gems she could tap into to replenish her magic will if needed. Thomena cycled through her choice of spells, thinking ahead to what might be needed. Fire-based spells wouldn't be an option; the blaze would catch the endless fields of tall grass and go wild. Thomena also had never cared for offensive spells that burst over an area, thus threatening nearby friendlies. She didn't want to cause injuries to any innocents out of her view. In this instance, she would need precise spells to aim around her fellow guard anyway. The trade-off of such attack spells was that they placed her in view of her enemy. As the cottage loomed ahead, and other caravan riders rode near, she put her mind on defensive spells. Her favorites wouldn't work well with her clinging to the rider. Instead, she chose a spell from the earth element, hardening her skin and toughening her resistance to damage.

Her whispered magic, coupled with a nearly unnatural flexing of the fingers of one of her hands, caused the horseman to flinch. "What are you doing back there?"

"Just something to protect me. Who lives here?"

The guard shrugged. "Just some fools that should have stuck closer to a city."

Hanging onto the horseman, Thomena could feel the tension in his muscles. Her own heart beat faster as she began to see animals lying in the grass, feasted upon by scavenger birds. Although they weren't within good bow range of the cottage, the smell of decay drifted to them on the wind. Thomena wished she could block her nose.

She began to wonder about something, so she voiced her question. "Is there a healer coming with us?"

The horseman gave a mirthless laugh. "He's staying next to the caravan leader. If we're wounded, we must get to him, not the other way around."

Thomena wondered why the healer wouldn't come to help with any wounded. A moment later, she got her answer. All the guards turned their mounts parallel to the caravan, veering slightly away from the cottage. Her eyes darted between the damaged structure and the caravan's altered course. Thomena asked, "We aren't going to check out the cottage?"

"Why walk into a devil's embrace?"

His tone and answer shocked Thomena. "What do you mean? Aren't we going to help them?"

The guard threw her an astonished look. "Help them? I thought wizards were smart. All we plan to do is watch for trouble and keep the caravan protected as we pass by. If you see someone stick their head out of a window, especially if they have a weapon, just drop a fire blast on the whole place."

Thomena's jaw dropped. A fire blast? Recalling her time spent with the vigile fire-fighters of Orlaun, the last thing she wanted to cause would be an explosion of flames that could grow wild. This guard's attitude ran contrary to Thomena's virtues. The girl didn't know what scared her more: trading destructive spells with an armed enemy or leaving injured people behind. She stared, disbelieving, at the young man's back. "But someone may be alive. They may need our help. Shouldn't that be part of our duty?"

"Or someone may be waiting in ambush." The guard snorted. "We either came too late or it may be a trap. The caravan is our only concern." He threw a look over his shoulder and lectured her. "I don't know where you grew up, but it sounds rather sheltered. You don't live to be my age out here without learning to take care of yourself."

As with the other guards, he looked ahead to scan the grass for any dangers. Thomena began to realize these guards were more mercenary in nature than she'd hoped. They only performed the specific duties they were paid to do and wouldn't veer from the path of convenience even if other lives were at stake.

Thomena couldn't resist asking. "How old are you?"

She expected him to say thirty. Some scars marred his face. Deep lines formed in his cheeks. Dirt stained the corners of his mouth and eyes. Therefore, it shocked her when he said, "Twenty-three." Only seven years older than her!

The caravan maintained a good distance from the cottage. Thomena watched helplessly as the lone building receded. She absently chewed her lip. She hadn't discounted an ambush, but her heart worried that some resident may have needed their help. She allowed herself to be led away but kept watching for any movement. More scavenger birds joined the feast on the ground, until the remaining ones circling in the sky dwindled to specks.

The guard finally delivered Thomena back to the wagon. This time, she jumped down to the grass, and Gunnard slowed so she could climb up. As the guard rode off, Thomena settled back into an uneasy seat between chunks of metal and threadbare blankets.

Julia perked up. "Well, that was a bit of excitement. I felt rather helpless sitting here and worrying for you."

Thomena didn't immediately answer. She couldn't believe that they might be leaving some wounded person to their own fate instead of lending a hand. The entire situation left her with an uneasy lump in her gut. She tried to remind herself that this journey would be an adventure, not simply a mistake.

Chapter 5 – Rise of Iztherans

Even before Commander Bedran sent him to Olangi, Thamin had been watching the lizardmen with concern. After a lifetime of studying and scouting one of the biggest threats to his homeland, it wasn't hard to miss a number of changing habits. He'd already noted a lot of foot traffic leading back and forth from the direction of the temple. As warlike as the lizardmen acted in the best of times, the signs of increased coordination between tribes shouted at his senses like a bad omen. Thamin could feel the threat emanating from the jungle, but he felt blind trying to discern its nature.

Each time he pondered it, Thamin's thoughts would inevitably focus back on the memory of the god statue coming to life. How did this creature fit into the lizardmen's lives? How much did its reawakening affect the tribes? Thamin felt this creature must be central to the changes in these people. Somehow, he had to determine the level of this threat. He couldn't help but feel responsible for whatever future developed from awakening the ancient lizardman.

He refocused his attention to his surroundings as the voices of more lizardmen drifted on the stifling jungle air. Thamin glanced up. The reddened rays of the setting sun could be seen playing across the upper canopy. On the jungle floor, shadows already held dominion. The darkness wouldn't hinder his abilities, but the lizardmen were better adapted to the low light. More voices drifted from ahead. It wouldn't be the first group he'd come across that day. Thamin hoped he would find an answer soon, dreading the potential discovery at the same time.

Thamin paused numerous times as he listened to the voices. His tendency to remain cautious and alert had allowed him to survive in the jungle territory as long as he had. Thamin continually watched for other dangers rather than just concentrate on the target ahead. He tried memorizing all the terrain around him in case he'd need a quick escape. One never knew when survival might depend on knowing where game cut a trail or spotting a natural hazard. If he had to run, he wanted every advantage.

Their language mostly compromised sounds and phrases best imitated by a slurring drunk. A small part of their communication included human words butchered by mispronunciations. He began to sort one voice above the others, speaking with a tone of authority to the rest. The other voices would fall silent in deference to this one, influential speaker.

The ground cover made it difficult for Thamin to approach. He turned to one of the unasked-for-gifts bestowed upon him by Yurtash during his youth. Although he wasn't sure why he'd been granted natura talents by the god, he appreciated having those magical gifts. Thamin envisioned a hunting cat, moving gracefully. He willed the vision to fill his spirit.

"Fellunus."

A moment later, Thamin's hands and legs started scaling a tree with more grace and silence than any other human. He took his time following an overhanging branch. It offered an unobstructed view of the meeting below. Thamin saw something that gave him pause.

The lizardmen, normally good at seeing even in dark conditions, were using a light source. No torch was visible. The light came from a seemingly magical ball of light floating over one of the lizardmen. This came as a complete surprise to Thamin, who had never known these creatures to use anything magical unless it was stolen. Even then, they used things that were passively enchanted. The floating ball of light indicated that someone or something present had used a spell.

Thamin perched in silence amongst the jungle canopy and watched. The lizardmen gathered in a circle inside a small clearing. Their scattered belongings leaning against rocks and trees. It didn't look like a camp as much as it seemed more of an impromptu roadside meeting. Now he could match the voice to the face, watching the speaker deliver a message with passion and confidence. As the lizardman gestured at…something…in his hands, he sometimes directed the light to float to different spots to better illuminate whatever he held. The way the light followed the speaker, it had to be a spell or triggered arcane item. Since lizardmen were illiterate, neither method seemed possible. Try as Thamin might, he could only recognize that the held items looked like some collection of wooden tiles.

In the mix of foreign and human words, Thamin heard the other lizards refer to the speaker as a "priest." He had never encountered the title used on any lizardmen before. While his mind wrestled with the implications of religion in their society, he continued to observe. Most of what they said couldn't be understood. Insects bit Thamin, muscles complained, but the ranger maintained his silent perch for more than an hour.

45

At one point, another quiet visitor slithered into Thamin's tree. He took note of its color pattern and shape of its head. Venomous. The snake, native only to the Olangi Jungle, paid little attention to Thamin. It curled up around a branch as if ready for slumber. He knew the snake's venom induced sleep in small mammals prior to eating them. It could put a man to sleep, although it wouldn't actually feed on one. Some alchemists prized the venom for medicinal qualities. The snake didn't threaten him, so Thamin returned his attention to his enemies.

The gathering came to an end. Thamin could understand goodbyes being exchanged between the group and their speaker. All of them except the speaker exited the clearing venturing north, toward the temple. The speaker started packing the strange tiles in his bag. Thamin knew he had to examine those tiles. He glanced between the "priest" and the sounds of the departing lizardmen.

His mind sorted through several options. Although he bore no love of these creatures, he didn't plan to kill this interesting lizardmen needlessly. He couldn't take a prisoner. This deep into the jungle, he didn't want one loose to warn others of his presence. On the other hand, he needed to see those tiles and examine this creature at a closer angle. The departing group of lizardmen would quickly be dispersing out of earshot, which would certainly allow Thamin an opportunity without alerting those nearby.

Calling on the powers of the God of Spirits, Thamin turned his attention to the serpentine visitor sleeping nearby. He let his senses fall into the domain of animal spirits. He calmed the snake, comforting it, without consciously knowing what he said. The natura connection with spirits conveyed emotions and feelings without the distraction of words. Thamin slid down the branch and managed to slide one arm under the half-asleep reptile. Whispered words poured from Thamin's lips, lulling the snake in a hypnotic embrace. The snake curled around the human's arm just as it had on the branch moments earlier.

Thamin's task would have been challenging in the best of times. Lulling an animal assumed you acted as its friend. Thamin's plans involved some threat to the animal; therefore, the attempt to hide such insincerity made their telepathic connection more difficult.

Time ran out for him. The lizardman priest got to his feet with his collected belongings all bagged up. Thamin had to act or lose his chance. He allowed the gates of his mind to open, revealing the threat to the snake's safety. "Harm" flashed across their connection, bringing the snake fully awake as Thamin flung his arm forward. The snake fell.

As soon as the snake found itself hitting and entangling a moving body, it reacted aggressively. The lizardman priest flailed in surprise as the snake around his neck plunged its fangs into him. The lizardman did attempt to call out in fright, though the words were lost in the sharp intake of breath following the pain. A second bite…a third. Although the victim was in little danger from the weak venom, he panicked as much as any creature would. The lizardman fell backwards. Thamin heard the crack as its head struck a rock. As the snake wiggled loose, the lizardman struggled to regain his feet. One hand gingerly probed at its pained head as the snake flailed. Thamin, worried the priest would make a sound to call back the others, saw an opportunity. With his head already hurting from a hard hit, the lizardman likely wouldn't piece together what came next. Thamin dropped from the tree, the pommel of the swordbreaker blade connecting with the back of the lizardman's head.

Thamin paused in a crouch on the jungle floor. The reptilian humanoid lay unconscious, venom assisting it into a deep sleep. The snake sought safety in the tall grass. With luck, since he wasn't seen, the lizardman would awaken and only recall hitting its head after a snake dropped on it.

The bag of tiles had spilled on the ground nearby. Thamin didn't rush for it. His senses sampled the evening noises for any sign the others had been alerted. His own presence melted into the background of the coming night. No one came running to check on the lizardman. After night sounds returned, Thamin stalked over to the bag. Like the scaled humanoids, he found his enhanced night vision insufficient to read the marks on the tiles. He flattened low in the tall grass. One hand pulled out a magically-lit coin, attached around his neck on a string. He cupped his hand over it to reduce the chance of other intelligent beings spotting the light.

A symbol marked the surface of the tile. Thamin sorted through several of them. In each case, another symbol would be revealed. He began to scrutinize his earlier assessment of the priest's magical light being a passive item due to lizardmen's illiteracy. These symbols were an alphabet. The beginning of writing. A realization dawned on Thamin that the symbols on the tiles matched the unknown language in the Olangi temple. Could this be a rebirth of a forgotten language?

His attention turned from the tiles to the lizardman. Like many others, it wore clothes stitched together from the hides of other creatures in the jungle. Thamin dipped his hands into its pockets and pouches, looking for anything. His fingers brushed a carved, wooden

47

object tucked under the creature's vest. Thamin pulled it out and examined it under the light.

A holy symbol of Yurtash.

Thamin felt no kinship to this creature who shared his faith. Yurtash's religious beliefs were generally neutral but shared one similar trait among all: the presence of primal, chaotic urges among his followers. The god didn't tend to interfere in politics of civilized lands, organizations, or culture clashes, though sometimes his worship could cause tension among such people. In Thamin, Yurtash's touch helped him understand and adapt to the vast wilderness. In others, it tended to produce aspects that did not blend well with neighboring civilizations.

The implications did not bode well for the nearby human settlements. The sporadically warring lizard clans of the jungle, embracing the gift of the written word, might now be uniting under a common pursuit. Was this some kind of enlightenment? What danger might it present to human lands? By itself, it might not be a direct threat. Nevertheless, it heralded a change in the native society.

***

Ztakish waved his clawed hands over the assembled group of followers bowing before him. They had even begun to view themselves as iztheran. Previously, they had no other identity except the differences between tribes. They hadn't even considered their differences from the more primitive lizardmen subspecies. Now they were becoming united as a race. Iztheran. He made it a mantra, repeatedly pushing it into their consciousness and fusing them with a sense of unity.

The priests received his blessing as they would from their own god. He did not protest their impression that he was part of Yurtash and that his words formed a sacred doctrine. Ztakish took every advantage given to him to elevate his people to a new awareness.

It even surprised Ztakish that, in the holy depths of Yurtash's fallen chariot, the priests spontaneously began to find spells through their faith. Whether the magic originated from divine means, or part of their native natura in the wild, Ztakish couldn't say and didn't care. The small miracles existed and fostered dedication. Ztakish directed the priests, and their religious fervor spread to the neighboring tribes. A dozen iztheran tribes camped in the shadow of the jungle temple, converting themselves into a singular people. A city, primal and maze-like, carved itself out of the vegetation.

Ztakish began appointing the most intelligent and devout minds he found as leaders and gave them tasks. The written word spread. The reptilian race began production of materials they hadn't crafted since their fall during the Godswars. Most importantly, iztherans began to think in new directions.

Before departing from him, one of the priests asked, "What do you see of our future, Holy One?"

Ztakish eyed them all. The rest listened closely, ready to hang on every word as gospel. He stood tall and flexed the arm holding his staff. "I envision a time of greatness for our people. I see us carving out a country and building an army. I see us retaking the lands that were lost in this war."

The other priests didn't question his context of war. They knew Ztakish served in a war and that to him the war never ended. They accepted this fact and impressed upon their own minds the desire to win the ancient, never-ending struggle.

Ztakish continued, "I want us to look beyond this jungle and the nearby swamp. Iztherans should set their goals on the rich fields and bountiful woods beyond. Humans and elves don't even see us as equals. We must change how the world views us."

He reveled in the eagerly nodding heads hinging on his words. "We will be a country. We will arm our warriors. We will retake the lands which belonged to us long ago!"

The priests enthusiastically cheered the idea. They were only interrupted as a scout begged an audience with Ztakish.

Ztakish didn't want to spoil the mood, but he sensed urgency in the scout's tones. "Speak! Tell us what brings you to interrupt our discussion."

The scout prostrated before his living god. "Elves, Most Holy. Elves have been sighted exploring in the south."

Ztakish felt old hatreds flare within him. Visions from the last great aerial battle against the elves flooded his memories. He couldn't deny himself a chance at retribution. He thumped his staff on the floor. "I will assemble a war party. Elves hold the blood of many of my kin in their hands. Let's see if they have softened in the years since they've enjoyed their conquest."

Chapter 6 – Memories of Lelkaya

Two elves conversed in the late hours of the evening while the curtain of night descended quickly in the shadow of the great jungle canopy. Their attention remained fixed on a stone structure covered with partially-hewn vines. Other elves were cleaning and packing away tools for the night. Only a small portion of the structure had been uncovered, but the sight of it filled the elves with awe.

"The matron was right to send us here," one stated, conversing in their native language. "Treemother bless us in our search for ancient knowledge."

The other, a senior member of the archeological group, nodded. "One can only guess what secrets we may bring back to Sellatru. With so many vine-covered structures stretching beyond this, we've confirmed that a large Talo'Seelie population once settled here. The style and motifs of the structures leave me surprised. I suspect this was forest when the city was built."

At the mention of their surroundings, the younger one, one of the warriors honored with protecting the expedition, glanced at the surrounding trees. He did not expect much trouble, even among the jungle-dwelling hunters. A number of trained warriors protected the camp.

He returned his attention to his companion and spoke. "It will take months, years I guess, to unveil most of it."

The senior member nodded again. "Tomorrow we should be able to clear the growth around the door over there. I'm eager to get a look at something not seen in countless centuries. The morning should prove to be very exciting."

The elves could not foresee the twisted truth of those last words, spoken while eyes watched them from the jungle growth.

***

Ztakish listened calmly as his scouts described the elf camp. The scouts, still illiterate, watched in awe as Ztakish translated their visual descriptions into a map drawn in the mud. Slowly, the map filled in with the positions of the elf tents and vine-covered structures. Ztakish pushed them further, asking about areas of hills, low ground, and mud beds surrounding the camp. It fascinated the iztheran party that someone could create a bird's eye representation of an area.

Ztakish pushed them for more information than he needed. He wanted his scouts to learn to spot any little detail of significance. He had been dismayed when their earlier attempts to scout anything had resulted in very basic reports.

"*How* close is the tree line here? Would it take four or ten strides to reach the closest tent?" The replies from the scouts caused him to brush out part of the map. "If you threw spears from this gully, could you reliably hit someone tending the fire?" Ztakish noted two iztheran with spears were the only ones who boasted they could. "How tall is this brush? Could someone crawl on the far side and be out of sight of the camp?"

The questions went on and on. The details began to confirm what he had already secretly observed from afar. The Iztheran warriors accompanying him often derailed their stories with words attempting to placate their god, but Ztakish worked to limit those interactions. It may be beneficial for them to hold him in such high esteem, but he wanted them to get used to speaking openly and honestly when it came to warfare.

As it turned out, Ztakish was an imposing enough speaker, even without their worship. Scars around his mouth from old wounds gave him a permanent angry look. He recalled how it had helped him intimidate lesser soldiers in the past, and it worked even more effectively here.

As evening shadows darkened and the ground map became more difficult to see, Ztakish tried to find out more about his people by asking their strategy. Most were agreeable along the same lines, planning simple and straightforward attacks without thought of coordinating past the initial rush.

Ztakish interrupted their conversation with an abrupt gesture. "You will go into battle with a partner." At their stunned looks, he continued, "You will pick your partner. Hopefully, it is someone you have fought alongside before or someone you trust with your life. When you fight the elves, you and your partner need to work as a team. Try to get on opposite sides of a single opponent. Speak as you fight, so that you fight as if one entity with four arms."

The others traded uncertain glances. Ztakish said. "The elves and humans fight this way. You have to be able to speak and plan when the fighting starts. If you do not, they will adjust and team up on you. We once fought this way, before your time. We were successful because we worked as a combined will."

As Ztakish continued to ask about their strategy, he realized he had to change more than just their individual tactics. "You would attack at night? Why? Elves see better at night."

After some prompting, he persuaded one to answer, "But not at a distance. It limits the range of their bows."

Ztakish nodded. "If you allow them the use of their bows, you give them a great advantage. I intend for us to attack during the daylight, from positions so close they will not have time for bows."

***

When morning's light broke upon the tree canopy, Ztakish lay covered with mud in a bed of tall reeds. The mud covered the bright red and gold markings on his body. The few iztheran warriors lying nearby were likewise camouflaged so that only their moving eyes gave them away.

By that time, the elves were already awake and enjoying their morning drink. Ztakish didn't know its name, but the familiar scent riding the wind evoked dormant memories. Even the nearby ruins generated images from another time.

What did they call this place? He thought, trying to remember, *Lelkaya, or such? I remember when we drove them out. The forest burned, mixed with the same scent from the cookfires of their morning tea.* A rare twitch of a smile graced his features. *An age of the world passed by and they are only just returning.*

Such thoughts brought scant relief from the discomfort he and the others felt. After spending the nighttime hours crawling into positions that came within a short throw from the elf camp, and then holding still in the mud and the bugs, they were all nervous, anxious, and miserable. They all ached to move, yet any movement could alert the watchful elves. His ambush could easily go the wrong way if any of his people were discovered.

Ztakish, watching the elves, made his people extend their wait even longer. Most of the elves stood near the cookfire, but if the attack started now, they might have the luxury of forming a protective circle. Ztakish wanted them to separate. Another hour crawled interminably before the elves set to work. They started off alone and in pairs toward different spots in the ruins. Only a couple remained by the fire when Ztakish decided it was time.

He quietly whispered words of natura magic. His muscles found new strength. His skin hardened. Once prepared, he called his signal. He knew from experience that elves couldn't be easily fooled by imitation bird whistles. Instead, he grunted like a wild pig. Some elves looked his way. The moment they did, they left themselves blind to the iztherans rising from the brush and mud at their backs.

Spears flew. The elves at the campfire dropped with barely a cry. The fragrant pot of tea spilled across the fire. Another elf, perched on a ledge three meters high in the ruins, arched and dropped as a spear took him in the back. He hadn't even managed a scream before his impact on the stones beneath him. More iztherans scrambled out of the mud. In a rush, they descended upon the elf workers. Screams and cries began in earnest. To their credit, most of the elves did prepare at least one weapon or tool as the melee started. The elves tried to move closer to each other but found it difficult due to the iztheran surprise. The sound of clashing metal and wood echoed in the ruins.

Ztakish made sure his warriors could witness him make an early kill. He jumped on one elf, who moved more like a warrior than some of the rest. The elf reacted with quick reflexes, but Ztakish's battle experience proved more knowledgeable. Within three moves, his staff bashed the blade from the enemy hand. Before the elf could recover, Ztakish bowled him to the ground. Pushing the advantage as quickly as possible, the iztheran stomped his weight onto the frail neck. Unsatisfied, he followed up with two more stomps, reveling in the crunching sounds he caused. His warriors cheered as they sought more targets.

Ztakish stood back as they charged, allowing himself a wider view of the battlefield. The jungle contours hid some of the action, though what he observed looked promising. His people followed his command from the previous evening, shouting and coordinating their movements. Each elf faced one or two pairs of iztherans at a time. Many of those slender humanoids displayed skill, but they hadn't been properly equipped or ready for battle. The slaughter went on in earnest, and Ztakish couldn't help but feel a rush of glory and vengeance. He cheered his people onward and they reacted with zeal upon hearing the encouragement from their god-made-flesh.

Blood splashed the leaves and desecrated the ancient elf structures. Ztakish relished the repetition of the slaughter delivered here during the Godswars. Even the elves who fell wounded were denied mercy.

Reptilian warriors, blinded by their fervor, continued to hack their victims. A few iztheran warriors also fell. The survivors would rally against the elf responsible until the seelie warrior was overwhelmed by numbers.

Except, Ztakish noted, in one area by the tents. Two elves, better armed than the rest, withstood the ring of iztherans attacking them. Their swords downed more than a few reptilian warriors. They struck with patience and skill.

Ztakish moved to join the fight. Their training and abilities marked them as more than simple diggers. He realized these elves must be the leaders. Ztakish's hand went to the captured human axe at his side. The old axe that once belonged to Thamin was excellent for melee combat but well-balanced for throwing attacks as well. For all their lightning movements, the elves did not wander from their position. They stayed, linked back-to-back, only rotating to meet their challengers. Ztakish waited for a particularly frantic point of the exchange to launch his attack. Both elves concentrated on their immediate attackers and missed seeing the spinning axe thrown from the edge of the fight.

The throw buried the axe blade in the chest of one elf. It hit with enough force to knock the elf back into his companion. As he fell dead, the remaining elf turned to see the source of the attack. The iztherans, also amazed, stepped back and paused.

Ztakish roared a challenge. Iztherans scrambled out of the way, opening a path between opponents. The elf stood bravely, holding his sword in a guarded pose as he turned his focus on the newcomer. Despite his stance, Ztakish noted the observant elf eyes studying his muddied armor. No doubt, this elf hadn't been alive to remember a time when iztherans went armored into battle. Ztakish walked a few paces closer, holding his staff almost casually by his side.

His body boiled for revenge. He felt his heart pounding at the prospect of spilling the blood of this defiant elf. Iztherans lined up and cheered him. Their worship added to his zeal. The elf remained in a defiant stance, but Ztakish preferred it that way. It made the moment all the sweeter that his enemy didn't cower or try to run. Ztakish's natural instincts took over. After so long at suffering immobility, he returned to being the hunter. If his people wanted a god, he would show them one.

Ztakish spoke something in a growl, but even his own people didn't understand the words. Ztakish underwent a physical change as he set free the natura magic he possessed. Yurtash's favor upon the iztheran marked him as a greenman, known to some as a feral warrior. It allowed a shape-changing ability.

Ztakish's form added mass. His body elongated and fell forward, growing to double its length and even stretching further. Hands and feet became large claws. The mouth became the most defining feature, elongating into a long U-shape and opening to reveal a deep row of dagger-sized teeth. An impossibly large alligator form dwarfed the lithe elf warrior.

The surrounding iztherans stood motionless in awe. One humbled himself by bowing, and suddenly the whole party of iztherans prostrated before their god. The elf stood transfixed. He had only enough sense left to bring his sword into line as Ztakish lunged. A slash of the weapon left another of many scars on Ztakish's mouth, though the attack proved futile. Massive jaws clamped around the elf and crushed his midsection. The monstrous body log-rolled and twisted, rending the muscular elf warrior into a rag doll with all the stuffing torn from it. The twisting monster even injured a couple iztherans as it rolled across them, not caring that some allied bones broke.

For a few dozen heartbeats, Ztakish stood triumphant. He let the elf's remains drop to the ground as he released another primal roar. His people chanted in worship. They called his name in fervor. He listened to their adulations, and it confirmed his future plans for his people. In his new form, his animal urges raged strong, but a good part of his sentient mind retained control. He sensed that all the other elves were dead. His people once again ruled alone over the fallen and almost forgotten city once known as Lelkaya.

A city that would never rise again unless by iztheran hands.

When enough time passed, Ztakish the greenman shrank back to his normal form. He knew his warriors would spread word about what they'd witnessed. His legend would grow and attract more to his side. Ztakish retrieved the axe and led his people away from the slaughter. He paused only long enough to leave one message. Despite his limited grasp of Elvish, he nevertheless knew the key words he wanted known to anyone who found the slaughter. He scrawled the words in elf blood on one of the tents.

***

Thamin crouched by the remains of the pot, observing the tea leaves scattered about the dead fire. His fingers traced wounds on the closest elf, though his eyes scanned the general positions of those slain. The ranger scout pieced together the battle in his mind, finding many confusing elements about the whole event. He got back to his feet and walked over to the blood-tainted tent. Symbols from the lizardmen's temple, from their formerly dead language, marked the tent. Other words seemed to originate from a strange dialect of the Elvish language, but he could understand the message scrawled into the fabric. It delivered a simple and straightforward threat.

"Elves come here; elves die here."

Chapter 7 – Soldier Guide

The caravan arrived in Bael Cochaw with plenty of sunlight left in the day. Thomena commented when she saw the castle, "Do all these outer forts appear like that?"

"Uffa! Vat do you mean?" Gunnard replied.

"It looks larger than I imagined. It has more than four towers and four walls, but it isn't large enough for a city." Thomena counted about eight outer towers, plus a few tall ones from somewhere inside the walls. "There don't seem to be any buildings outside of the walls, like in Kaigal or Orlaun."

Gunnard shrugged. "Don't know. Oye haven't visited much of de countryside. If dere are nay buildings outside, dere is good reason for it."

Julia pointed to the fields on one side. "There are some buildings over there, outside the walls. One looks like it has fire damage."

The smith noticed them, too. "Nay, Lia. Dose aren't buildings, dey're siege to'ers. Someone tried to go over de valls."

Thomena and Julia took a moment studying the distant structures. They finally noticed the large wheels at the base of each, partially covered by overgrowth. From the looks of it, one of the towers had heavy fire damage, the other two sat on broken wheels. Neither girl had ever before seen siege engines, despite seeing many castles around Orlaun. Each of these war towers stood more than three stories tall. Thomena started to feel less safe about the fortress.

Julia whispered, "I wonder who tried to take this place?"

A dry chuckle escaped Gunnard's beard. "Most likely it vas anodder county of Diara. Dey like to bite at deir neighbors."

They rode in silence for many breaths. Thomena happened to be chewing her lip when Julia asked, "What are you thinking?"

Thomena looked up. Of course, Julia had known her long enough to know her nervous habits. "I reread my father's old letters during the ship voyage. About four years ago, he mentioned a big fight near the fort. I had to read between the lines a bit; he wasn't very straightforward. Since then..." Thomena trailed off a bit, looking for the right words. "I think something changed."

"What?"

Thomena shook her head slightly, a grimace on her expression. "I don't know if I can describe it. He talked less of specific things and people out here, but he would talk more of how much I meant to him and how he hoped I was safe. I feel like the tone of his messages changed."

Julia looked like she expected more, but Thomena shrugged her shoulders. "I'll just have to ask him about it."

The tinker turned and stared at the siege towers again. "Do you think he fought out here during the battle?"

Thomena nodded. Her mind wandered back to the wording of his letters. "I'm sure he did, but I believe he kept some secrets. He didn't say much about it."

Thomena and Julia looked up in awe as Gunnard's wagon navigated through a towering gatehouse. They passed under a large, iron-reinforced gate that could be dropped at a moment's notice. Looking to both sides, they judged the width of the fort's wall to be around twenty feet thick at the base. On the other side loomed a second, equally thick gate that could be dropped as well. Ahead, they could see tall buildings competing for space down the main avenue. Some of the buildings even leaned over the road slightly, blocking the light. To the sides, long buildings ran along the wall under the inner ramparts. By the presence of the relaxed soldiers milling around them, Thomena knew they must be barracks. She glanced around, looking to catch sight of her father. She knew that he commanded troops, and every loud voice among the soldiers caused her to crane her neck and see who was giving the orders. The movement did not go unnoticed by her companion.

The tinker gestured her hand out toward the streets. "Why don't you hop out and look for him? This place isn't very big. You could easily find us later."

"Nay, Julia. I'm not going to leap out just because we're here. You found us the ride and I am determined to help you unload."

The caravan broke into different paths as each wagon went about its business. The leader stopped by Gunnard's wagon to finish paying Thomena for her guard role. He even offered a place on the return caravan in a couple of days, at which Thomena refused.

Despite Julia pressuring her, Thomena's dutiful nature made her stay with them. Gunnard reported to a steward, who then had a servant show them the old smithy. When Thomena asked what happened to the old smith, the servant simply replied, "Died, of natural causes." That addendum left Thomena wondering how many folks did *not* die of natural causes.

Thomena helped them unload, further pestered the whole time by Julia. They were interrupted when an official asked to discuss business with Gunnard. The smith excused Julia to seek and grab a list of supplies. Thomena found herself free to start the search for her father. Since Julia didn't have a set time to be back, she accompanied Thomena back to the gates.

As they walked down the line of barracks, Julia whispered to Thomena. Her sharp tone hinted at irritation. "They're all staring at you."

Thomena attempted a casual glance at the soldiers lounging around the garrison. Some were caring for equipment; others engaged in dice, games, or relaxation. She saw several looking their way. "They're looking at *us*."

Julia snorted. Thomena saw the movement out of the corner of her eye as Julia swept her hands to indicate her smith's apron, men's trousers, and patched clothes. "I'm nay flower to look at. You, on the other hand...what are those things covering your lower legs?"

"Gaiters." Seeing Julia raise an eyebrow, Thomena explained. "You saw the tall grass we traveled through to get here. They protect the boots and legs from getting scratched."

"Aye, I saw some folks in Kaigal wearing some...covering leggings. I didn't see anyone wearing them paired with a skirt. Every step you take, your skirt bounces high enough to give those boys a flash of skin."

Her cheeks flushing red, Thomena detoured around the far side of a wagon to covertly try tugging the hem of her skirt down.

"Not that it matters." Julia chuckled. "Take a look around. How many other young women do you see?"

Thomena looked up and down the streets. Julia had a point. There were few women in sight, especially of young age. Most of the soldiers were young men. The two friends did see women in the garrison: generally older, closely-trimmed hairstyles, tough-looking as rocks, hiding any curves under padded layers of armor. In fact, a lot of these women looked more manly than the male apprentices at the guild in Orlaun.

Thomena tried to put a lighthearted spin on the revelation. "There's better chances for you to find a man out here. It seems we may be in demand."

"Until I turn and they see this ugly thing on the side of my head."

Thomena had to resist the sudden urge to glance at Julia's half-ear. She decided to move on from that conversation. "I better start inquiring as to my father's whereabouts. He could be anywhere."

The first young soldier they approached looked eager that two young ladies wanted to talk. A smile took over his features, he stood straighter, and his eyes roamed them without subtlety.

Thomena asked, "I'm looking for a man named Thamin. He is my father."

A quick change came over him. His mouth dropped its smile and his eyebrows rose. "I'm not sure where he is. Excuse me."

While mumbling those last words, the youth walked with new purpose in a course opposite the direction the girls were headed.

Julia cocked her head. "What was that look about?"

Thomena shrugged. "He acted like he found something frightening in the bottom of his mug."

They stopped another young soldier. When Thomena repeated her question, he also appeared to lose any eagerness in talking to her. A few nearby soldiers, hearing the same question, became distracted enough that their drill went awry. An officer saw the confusion and shouted a few choice insults at them. The scene attracted attention from others in the barracks and on the wall.

Upon seeing the two girls for the first time, the officer stopped and offered a bow. He looked quite mature; his polished silver shoulder guards reflected the light. "Pardon my language. How can I help you ladies?"

Thomena answered, "I seek my father, a soldier named Thamin. I think he's in the wolf quarters."

Neither girl missed the sudden hush that descended across the wall and barracks at the mention of the name. Several soldiers stopped what they were doing and looked at her. A couple folks repeated some phrase...or perhaps a nickname? Thomena couldn't hear it. The words sounded like "roll-brain," but that didn't sound right. Even the officer gave a slight pause, his eyes scrutinizing her for some reason. Before she could waste too much time puzzling over it, the officer pointed down the wall in the direction they faced.

"You'll find his barracks over by the east gate."

"My thanks, sir." Thomena quickly turned to hurry onward, unsure why she'd attracted so much interest.

Behind them, the officer had returned his attention to his men. "Enough gawking, you all have assignments. Ingel, I want you making tracks to the supply shop, don't delay. Hammon, march those men a few laps around the wall!"

Julia hurried to keep pace with her friend's long strides. "With all these strange reactions, maybe you shouldn't mention his name."

Thomena's eyebrows scrunched at the suggestion. Feeling a bit flustered, she muttered, "It will be harder to find him without asking folks the name of whom I seek. At least everyone here seems to know him."

"And is that a good thing or a bad thing?"

Julia's question went unanswered as a young soldier caught up to them. The two women stepped to the side to get out of his way, but he circled in front of them and swept into a bow. "Mabry Ingel, at your service."

Thomena and Julia stood stunned. Julia recovered first, catching Thomena's eyes and indicating the man in front of them with a slight smile. Thomena had to admit, he was handsome and looked about their age. Like some of the soldiers who'd been doing manual labor near the barracks, his bare arms glistened with sweat. No helm covered his head, revealing dark hair shaved close to the skin. As he smiled, they could tell he kept his teeth cleaner than most folks. His only imperfection came in the form of a nose blunted from being broken in the past. Thomena remained too preoccupied by other thoughts to admire him for long, even though Julia seemed to be staring.

She remembered overhearing the officer shouting his name. "Ingel?"

"Aye, milady, Gold Lion regiment."

"I recall that officer yelling at you to run to a supply shop. Won't you be late?" Thomena began walking around him.

Not to be put aside, he fell in step alongside Julia. "The shop happens to lie along the same path. I'd be happy to show you to the right place."

Thomena appreciated his offer, though she felt he might be complicating the situation. Her "thank you" to him felt stiff even to her ears.

Julia eagerly jumped into the silent space. "We appreciate your help! I'm Julia, and this is my friend, Thomena."

"A pleasure. I wasn't aware Thamin had a daughter. Have you traveled far?"

Thomena didn't rush to respond, so Julia intervened again. "From Orlaun. It's been a long journey; I've never seen Diara before."

Thomena glanced sideways at Mabry, who stayed in step with the ladies. "How well do you know my father?"

"Oh, I don't know him personally. But he's a local legend. Folks watch when he goes by. There's been plenty of tall tales told about him and his regiment."

Both Julia and Thomena traded raised eyebrows as their pace slowed, though Julia spoke first. "In what way?"

"When we were invaded a few years ago, a lot of villages were plundered. Even Bael Cochaw itself was attacked. The Blood-Wolves got into a tight spot…"

"Blood-Wolves?" Thomena stopped. The name left a bad taste on her tongue.

Mabry explained, "The different arms of Bael Cochaw are represented by different beasts, and a color associated with each one. It makes it easier to identify banners across a battlefield by their color, except the wolves never really carried their banner much."

Thomena assumed he could see the growing confusion on her face.

Mabry explained. "My regiment, the Gold Lions, we're light infantry. We carry a few extra weapons but don't overburden ourselves with heavy armor. The Blue Boars wear heavy armor and use polearms. Green Horse belongs to the mounted knights. Anyway, the wolves were red, but everyone called them Blood-Wolves, and their reputation lived up to it."

She asked, "What was the wolves' specialty?"

"You don't know? I would've hoped you could have told me."

Thomena's hands helplessly extended out from her sides. "I've lived in Orlaun since I was young."

As one, they resumed walking again, though Mabry shrugged. "The Blood-Wolves were special. Part of what made them special was that nothing defined them. Some were heavily armored warriors, some wielded magic, and others had bows or went lightly armed with daggers. They were some of the best-trained men from a variety of backgrounds. I believe Thamin hailed from the local ranger groups? Although, the wolves rarely gathered in full strength. Folks would see small parties of their group come and go from the gates. Anyway, the regiment sprouted legends before the war, tackling monsters from the jungle and elsewhere. When the war started, their reputation made them idols. They were everywhere."

"You keep saying 'were' and other past-reference words whenever you talk about them." Thomena stared, awaiting a response.

Mabry paused a bit before responding. "Not many survived the war. There isn't really a wolf regiment anymore. How is it that Thamin is your father and you don't know?"

She was sure the shock showed on her face. Mabry's question cut deeply into her most secluded emotions. "But they still have a barracks? My father has lived there as long as I've known."

Mabry faltered. "You'll understand more when you see the barracks. We're almost there."

The young man looked over Thomena again. She pretended she didn't notice, though she did perceive Julia edging more into Mabry's view. The soldier ignored Julia and asked, "Did you study to be a wizard?"

"Did the wand give me away?" She realized her attempt at a grin probably looked more like a smirk.

Thomena reached down to pat her wand. As she did, she accidentally jostled a sack next to the wand. A green gem bounced out and landed in the street. Thomena quickly scooped it up. Mabry missed a step when he saw it. Worried, he swiveled to look if anyone else had noticed.

He whispered, "Might want to hide that better. Some folks here would be desperate to get sly hands on something like that."

"It's not there for currency. I need it close at hand to use its magic."

His eyes still glancing around the street for threats, the soldier asked, "What does it do?"

Thomena thought for a moment, trying to find words to describe it so he could understand. "It doesn't do anything; it just holds energy. Using magic wears at a person just like physical strains, such as swinging a sword time and again. I can store some of that energy ahead of time in certain gems like that and then draw from it when I need later."

"Fascinating." Mabry smiled at Julia, who didn't share his enthusiasm. "Where is your wizard's staff?"

Thomena let out a slight laugh despite her reserved feelings. "Every mage needs a staff, right? You can't just *make* a staff; it must *be* made." At his confused expression, she explained. "Something a master said to me. You either find a staff that already holds energy, or it must somehow become linked to you with some personal bond. The mage has little control. You simply find one when you find one. The staff and the mage become linked by some event."

"What's the difference between a mage and a wizard?"

Thomena sighed. The soldier proved to be full of questions, while her mind only wanted to focus on her upcoming reunion. "It's just a different dialect of the human tongue. Region-based word choice. In Orlaun they seem to feel 'mage' is a more respectful title. Out here, I find I'm suddenly a wizard."

She caught sight of a frown on Julia's expression. It occurred to Thomena that her friend showed more interest in the young soldier than she felt, yet Julia seemed to be getting frustrated at her inability to get much of Mabry's attention. Thomena would have preferred more quiet time, so she lapsed into silence, hoping her friend could take advantage of it.

Julia made an attempt. She was used to seeing Thomena shy away from boys, so she understood her friend's silent cue. "Mabry, have you lived here all your life?"

Mabry turned to face her better. "Mostly, though I was born in Kaigal...wow. How'd your ear get messed up like that?"

Julia came to a dead stop, followed a moment later by the other two. Glaring at both, fists clenched at her side, she made a visible effort to talk calmly. "I'll leave you two alone. I really should get back where I'm needed. Good luck, Thomena. I'll see you later." She spun on her heels and hurried away without waiting for a response.

Thomena sighed. As Mabry turned a confused face toward her, she said, "That doesn't win you over to her good side. Just point the way for me."

Ingel's eyes were partly lowered to the ground as he sheepishly stated, "Just through that city gate there. Look for the red wolf on an aged sign."

Thomena glanced at the exit and then looked back in surprise. "Outside the city gates?"

It occurred to her she hadn't seen any buildings outside the walls, but she now stood on the opposite side of the fortress.

He nodded. "They built these newer walls, gates, and barracks after that invasion...after the old barracks became damaged in the assault."

Thomena started to walk away when Mabry pushed his luck. "What happened to her?"

She turned and stared at him. "She'll only tell a friend, and only when they *don't* ask about it. The proper way to find out would be to apologize to her. Try to see past the ear."

Mabry nodded. "I will as soon as I can. Where can I find her?"

Thomena tried to recall a passage. "'Thus Prince Bersage resolved to walk the ends of Diara barefoot until he could amend the hurt inflicted unto his beloved.' That's a quote from *The Codex*."

"What does that mean?"

"It's a small fortress," she spoke as she spun away. "Finding her yourself will go a long way towards proving the value of your apology."

Chapter 8 – Red Wolf Barracks

Thamin entered the war room but melted into the background and watched. The ranger shook his head as he tried to interpret all the competing voices in the room. Commander Shan Bedran of Bael Cochaw found himself besieged on all sides. Couriers and emissaries swarmed his war room and assaulted his senses. The commander didn't even have space to swing his large mace, as he often did just to keep his muscles toned. Every so often, he advanced to the map ingrained on the war table, would move pieces, only to move them back again a moment later. The frustration could be felt across the room, and Thamin had no desire to dance into the chaos just yet.

"Trollsbane!" The commander's voice boomed and echoed off the walls. "I see you slouching over there. Get over here and give me my report."

Not that Thamin actually slouched, but when his demeanor shifted from hiding against the wall to striding into the crowd, he somehow seemed to gain a few more inches in height. He glanced at the folks surrounding the commander. The crowd included village elders and young pages from the other frontier castles.

Commander Bedran tapped impatiently on the war table. His face reflected anger at the best of times, due to eyebrows meeting right over the nose and damaged muscles on one side of his jaw. "Well, what did you find?"

Thamin switched his gaze from the commander to the gathered throng and back again. His meaning spoke clearly to the man who'd known him over the length of his extended military career, though he still spoke for the benefit of others. "This is best for as few ears as possible."

The older man nodded. "If you're not one of my officers, clear out! Get some rest and I'll attend to you once I ponder the whole situation."

A few folks took a considerable amount of intimidation before they retreated from the room. Once his sergeants closed and barred the entry door, the commander blew a sigh of relief as he ran tense fingers through the remnants of his hair. "Did you say that truthfully, or were you just giving me the excuse I needed to put the boot to their hindsides?"

Thamin shrugged. "I don't speak well in crowds, and this is best handled privately."

"Your men followed you. They could hear you shout directions across a battlefield."

The ranger averted his eyes. "That was different. We bled together and they respected me. Those strangers you just dismissed never fought at my side."

The commander huffed. "Oh you'd be surprised at the respect you'd get from any of the people living around here." As if suddenly remembering something else about those who just left, he waved in exasperation at the doorway. "Can you believe it's been the same year after year? They come out here to build a home in the frontiers of human culture and panic that I can't have a hundred men patrolling every little hamlet and farm all the time. They see scales moving in numbers…even if there isn't a raid, they panic. If smoke comes from campfires in the hills, they wet their pants and run. If a few crows circle some dead animal a mile away, they may interpret it as a soldier slain by orcs and figure they'll be next. If they can't stand on a stronger spine, they shouldn't have come out here."

Thamin watched as the older veteran ran a hand over his sweat-filled brow. The absence of all the other bodies alleviated the room of its former humid atmosphere. The commander sat on the edge of his war table, reclaiming a stale drink as he spoke. "I'll have my report now."

"The lizardmen made a new discovery: writing." Thamin continued despite Bedran nearly choking on his drink. "They've been passing around tablets bearing the runes inscribed inside the Olangi temple. I observed one teaching others."

The commander waved his goblet dismissively. "This isn't just random curiosity?"

Thamin knew Bedran trusted his word, but the commander always made the habit of pushing for extra information on every subject. "Several groups…numbers I've never seen before…were converging towards that temple. They called their teacher a priest. He even had a holy symbol on him. Yurtash."

The commander raised an eyebrow. "Your god?"

Thamin nodded. "Same as inside the temple. Yurtash appeals to many who prefer the challenges of nature over the comfort of cities."

67

Bedran smirked, though not in an unfriendly way. "Spoken from one with firsthand experience."

Thamin shrugged. "I also saw this priest wield magic." As the remaining men in the room began to speak up and rebuff the idea, he continued, "Whether he actually cast a spell or triggered an item, I can't say. He wielded arcane spells, not just divine, and is spreading knowledge of writing to the tribes."

As the arguing continued, Commander Bedran wielded his influence to force the others to calm down. Some of the younger advisors, who didn't know Thamin's history and weren't swayed by the tales surrounding him, took the longest to settle.

Thamin said, "Whether you believe me or not, this is what I swear I saw. I have nay doubt the lizardmen are becoming organized and will soon offer us a new threat. They are moving past the primitive race we once knew."

"Those folks who we just booted out the door," Bedran said, returning to his drink, though he winced at it and set it back down. "Many reported lizard sightings. Nay raids nor any attacks at all. The scales just sat back, watched them, and moved on. I have a feeling we may find an attack in our future; one planned like we've never known."

Thamin stepped farther into the room, getting a closer look at the war table map. "There's already been an attack."

As muttered discussions began anew, Thamin pointed at the edge of the Olangi jungle. "Here. An expedition of elves. I assume from Syllatru."

One of the others blurted, "What are elves doing in Olangi?"

The ranger scowled at the young officer. "The elves of Syllatru are our neighbors, and they also border the jungle. This group had occupied some ruins, elven in origin. In fact, there are lots of elf ruins scattered through the jungle, most buried under a thick cover of vines."

Bedran stood by Thamin's shoulder, surveying the map. "What happened?"

"I arrived on the scene days late. Scavengers had already set upon the camp. What strikes me as odd is that the attack happened in the first few hours of daylight."

"Scales only attack at night, wait a moment..."

Thamin looked up as the commander stared at him in an odd way, head cocked to one side. Despite all the news handed to him, Bedran's puzzled look changed to a slight grin, lopsided due to the missing teeth and damaged muscles on the one side.

The commander glanced at the others as if there was a private joke. "How many of you arrived here after the invasion?" Some young warriors spoke out. "You only know of the Trollsbane by tales. Tall tales, maybe?"

Those same men nodded. Thamin could see doubt in their eyes. The ranger accepted that disbelief, because the tales coming back to his own ears were starting to stretch beyond recognition.

The commander continued, "I've known Thamin to be my best scout. He hailed from the rangers when recruited."

Everyone knew the rangers were a secretive group, informal and loosely organized, who constantly patrolled the borders of the jungle and safeguarded the civilized areas. Their number included skilled hunters and trackers.

"Sometimes, I feel he can glance at spoor in the woods and tell me how many points the buck had. I want you to know you can trust his instincts if you're in the field and I'm not nearby." Bedran's eyes shifted back to Thamin. "Enlighten me on this: how is it you arrived on a battle scene days later, scavengers spoiling the site, and know what time of day the attack occurred?"

Thamin took a moment to steady his breath. As he had told the commander, he didn't speak well in crowds, nor in smaller groups when all the attention was riveted on his words.

"The lizardfolk came in from the northwest. The signs were still there, including their camp. Their tracks swung all the way around to the far side of the elf camp, so they could attack from the east. As we said, lizardmen generally attack at night, but if this was any other race, I can understand sneaking around east to attack with the rising sun blinding their opponent.

"The elves were dressed for their excavation: tools free of dirt, packs for artifacts empty, fingernails clean. So, they had dressed and spread out but hadn't finished their work. Finally, there were tavi leaves sitting in the pots and used mugs by the fire."

Bedran cocked his head to the side. "Tavi leaves?"

The ranger nodded. "A morning drink. Elves only make it for morning tea."

Commander Bedran whistled or attempted one, which didn't quite form due to the old wound to his jaw. "You convinced me. Daylight attacks by scales? This is more troublesome by the candlenotch."

"One more thing." Thamin found this most worrisome of all. "They left a warning in blood. A *written* warning in Elvish—an old dialect of it. I suspect it's from the lizard we 'woke.' He must be the intelligence at the center of this."

Commander Bedran asked Thamin a few general questions but spent several minutes conversing with the rest of his staff over the map. Thamin began to wonder if he was dismissed until Bedran turned to him. "I need you to go with all speed to Bael Altlun. They need to be warned, and I need to muster some volunteers from the rangers there to keep eyes surrounding the jungle border. I'll write up the message."

As the commander took up a quill and paper, he added, "And you're going by horse."

Thamin opened his mouth to protest but Bedran smoothly continued, "And I don't care that you don't like horses. You're taking one. It doesn't matter how many have been killed out from under you."

"Eight. I don't need a horse." As Bedran continued to scribble away and ignore him, he added, "I love horses, too much to put them in danger."

"You can't run all the way to Altlun by yourself and get back in time to be of use to me. I imagine you're tired from sneaking around Olangi. You'll ride." That last statement slammed with the weight of the final word on the subject.

***

The moment Thomena strode outside Bael Cochaw's eastern gate, her boots stepped across a trail of cobblestones fighting a losing battle with weeds. Parts of the old barracks included a large, overgrown grass field, where marching feet once kept it tramped into dust. Several long, dilapidated buildings of the old barracks stood on either side of the cobbled walk. Most were in bad shape—all of them looked deserted. She could make out signs of an encircling wall on the other side of the old quarters. Compared to the prosperity and life within Bael Cochaw, the old barracks clung to the fort like an ugly, unhealthy growth. Thomena gawked in shock. No one had cared for this place and these structures in years. Had Mabry lied to her?

Thomena saw part of the reason why some buildings fared worse than others. Even as she walked through, some poor folks were scavenging the stones off the outer walls and planks off the buildings. She imagined the guards must turn a blind eye to those poor enough to loot stone from abandoned structures. Thomena walked slowly, her sweeping eyes taking in every detail. Several flagpoles stood prominently upon the walls and in the open area that she assumed was a parade ground. Not a single banner adorned them. Broken shutters hung from windows, some swinging loosely and clattering when a breeze blew. She passed two horse troughs. One suffered a sizeable hole, the other still held a pocket of fetid water from the last rain. Vines scaled some of the buildings. Thomena could see beyond to where the old walls stood. They were less than half the height of the current fortress. She viewed a portion of the outer wall that showed damage from more than what scavengers could accomplish. A deep tear existed in the wall, with a scattering of stones spreading inward from the area. Thomena imagined that's what damage to a wall would look like if it was hit by an enemy catapult. Another double set of gatehouses faced east, but the portcullis that once stood between them was warped and dragged to the side.

Her eye caught the sun-faded image of a gold lion gracing a door of one of the long buildings. Thomena recalled Mabry was a member of the Gold Lions, which were now housed inside the walls. A lot of the paint had peeled away. Across the trail stood a barracks with a blue boar painted on the door. Thomena got the feeling no one would be returning to touch up the paint. Passing by an open window, Thomena overcame her revulsion and managed to peek inside. The skeletal frames of a hundred beds lined rows within the building. In one corner, she caught sight of a pile of blankets surrounded by several empty bottles. The scene gave her an involuntary shudder. Certainly, her father wasn't living like that?

The young girl forced her legs to walk away from the building. The chipped paint on the next barracks grabbed her attention. The red wolf design, not as faded as the others, beckoned to her. She took a few more steps before trepidation arrested her movement. She remained motionless and stared at the design. In her mind, Thomena surrendered to the admission that she was afraid. She couldn't pin down the exact reason for her anxiety. Perhaps it was fear of the unknown that paralyzed her. Thomena closed her eyes and recited a few of *The Codex*'s proverbs of courage.

When she reopened her eyes, she noticed a few things about the building that promised hope. The shutters were all closed, but none were broken. A couple floorboards in the building's porch steps had been replaced with newer boards. Neither the walls nor the foundation stones were missing any pieces due to looters. The walls remained free of vines. She could tell that someone still cared for this place, and that meant something good.

Thomena walked up to the partially open door and knocked. Despite her resurgence of courage, her voice still croaked when she called out a hello. Several dry breaths went by with no response. Only unbroken silence answered her. The fixed and closed shutters of the building blocked most of the light as well as any sounds.

"Father? It's Thomena."

Her voice sounded meek to her own ears. Her faint words felt insufficient to cross the inviolable threshold. Steeling her voice, she practically shouted, "Thamin! Anyone?"

Her words felt feeble against the prevailing silence. Thomena took her first step inside, though the tightened shutters permitted only uselessly thin streams of light stripes across the floor. She drew her wand, not expecting to need it for protection, but feeling too nervous without its comfort in her hand. Her other hand motioned a spell pattern, calling forth arcane energies to provide illumination. The violated sanctuary became unveiled to her magic as she placed a glow upon her wand.

At first glance, it looked like the building remained occupied. Unlike the abandoned lion barracks, the bed frames of the wolf barracks supported mattresses and blankets. Cloaks and swordbelts hung from bed posts. Shoes sat side-by-side beside bunks. Crafts and paintings adorned some of the walls. On a pillow, a ribbon marked a spot between the pages of a bound tome. A clutter of personal items occupied bedside tables. A deck of cards was fanned out across one bedsheet. Footlockers lined the rows at the bottom of the beds. A few lockers bulged open due to tools, lengthy items, and clothing stuck between lid and base. A desk near the entry held a quill, inkwell, and a sheaf of papers. A baggy hat hung by the doorway. A wizard's bandolier of spell pouches rested on an alchemy table.

A prolonged look at everything revealed the truth behind the illusion of life.

Dust coated nearly every surface in the barracks. An accidental touch of a bed sent a cloud into the air. The mixture on the alchemy table was so old some fungi had overgrown its container. Some of the footlockers suffered holes the size of rats, and corresponding droppings could be seen along the walls. The deck of cards and various papers showed signs of deterioration: fuzzy filaments growing on the surface, brown rings, brittle cracks across the surfaces. One of the beds showed signs of long-term water stains, as did the ceiling above it, mixed with the smell of mold. Her nose wrinkled further at the smell of rot. She idly wondered if it was from decayed food or a dead animal.

Salvageable arms and armor still sat in displays. It felt so abandoned; Thomena wondered why it hadn't been robbed.

The youth would have gladly walked back into the fresh air, but she couldn't deny some signs of recent habitation. A clean trail stamped with boot prints parted the dust, indicating someone's frequent passage between the entry and one row of bunks leading to a far door. She followed it to the back and found a pantry and kitchen. A breadbox held cut portions of a loaf—slightly stale but not moldy. She found more food in edible condition: apples and salted or dry strips of meat. The food occupied bins, which helped seal them away from vermin. Rats left teeth marks in some of the wood, but some cupboard doors had recently been repaired. Apparently, someone utilized this place and even tried to stop the rats from getting to their goods.

A pleasant surprise lay beyond the storeroom. Thomena found an indoor privy more modern than she expected. She could hear the flow of water runoff flowing beneath the seat and a vented chimney airing out the room from above. A metal bathtub sat next to it. No pipes existed to bring in water. From the pair of buckets sitting on the floor, Thomena assumed one had to make trips to a pair of intact rainwater barrels she'd seen outside. A pot and a fireplace against one wall served as a means to warm water for a bath. Dry wood laid stacked to one side. Some shaving implements and soap, recently used, sat beneath a mirror. Thomena knelt before the fireplace and extended a hand. She could feel warmth radiating from the ash.

She retraced her steps back to the bunkroom. Passing by a shutter, the mage attempted to wrestle it open. It didn't wish to be disturbed, but she forced it to give, little by little. Her thoughts tempted her to cast a strength spell, but she disliked using magic on small chores. Thomena forced the shutter to obey with a little effort. At least the window added more illumination than her wand.

As she reexamined the barrack beds closest to the storeroom, one that was free of dust grabbed her attention. The chest at the end of the bed overflowed with contents. Several pieces of wood stuck out or leaned against the bed frame. Among the lengths of wood, she found a longbow staff. It sat unstrung and didn't quite look finished. She ran her fingers along it. It sparked a memory of a figure...maybe her father...whittling away at a long stick. Thomena recalled fleeting images of him crafting bows.

One memory added to the next. They walked in the woods, collecting feathers. It was a fanciful memory Thomena remembered during her days in Orlaun. Now, she could recall it more clearly; they were collecting feathers for arrow shafts. Some sticks of wood, stored in a small barrel behind the chest, would be the right size to make arrows. She eased the lid open. Inside the chest, she saw a few stray feathers.

Bright colors grabbed her attention. A doll? Thomena tenderly picked it up. The colors and fabric looked faded and worn. She remembered holding this doll during her childhood. Thomena stood, turning the doll over in her hands, always returning it right side up to stare at the mismatched eyes. Memories formed and fit together like puzzle pieces. A bedtime companion she could hug. A missing bead. Slim hands attaching another bead in place, even though it didn't match. Thomena tried to focus on the fleeting memory of those slim hands. Her mother's hands. Despite her struggle to remember, the memory melted away as quickly as it came. She couldn't picture a face to go with the hands.

The sound of a boot scuffing wood only a few feet from her jerked her attention back to her surroundings.

An intimidating mountain of a man stood there, but it was not her father. He wore armor and carried weapons, but his face looked the most frightening of all. Scarred, damaged, with thick eyebrows that almost met in the center, he looked as mean as a hungry bear.

Thomena reflexively stepped back and raised her wand. The big man casually held a hand up and gave a slight shake of the head. "You're looking for Thamin."

"Aye," Thomena croaked. Inwardly, she cursed her voice for betraying her nerves.

The big man's pose did not seem threatening, and to Thomena, he looked overwhelmingly confident, considering he stared down the tip of a wand. His deep voice matched his bear-like appearance. "When I heard someone was asking around, claiming to be the daughter of Trollsbane, I took personal interest in meeting her."

Trollsbane. That must have been the title uttered by the soldiers back on the wall.

The big man continued, "Didn't mean to startle you. I'm in charge of the garrison here. Shan Bedran, at your service. Thamin takes his orders from me, but we also have a friendship that goes back several fights."

The man's tone and stance reflected a more lenient character than the way the scars disfigured his face. Thomena felt she could trust him. She lowered the wand. "Trollsbane? How did he come by that name?"

"He earned it, of course, but I wasn't there to tell the story. He doesn't use that title, but most everyone else calls him by that name."

Thomena tilted her head towards the man. "And your title? You are lord of Bael Cochaw?"

Shan Bedran chuckled, helping Thomena realize he was in a better mood than his features reflected. "This is Kaigal's territory. We did away with nobility and the entitlements such men claim. We're run by citizens and the elected council. I'm here because I'm a military man who spent most of his soldier years garrisoned here. I am this fort's commander, that is my only title, and I guard this region in Kaigal's interests."

Thomena realized she hadn't introduced herself. She grabbed the edges of her skirt and curtsied. "My name is Thomena. I am Thamin's only child. This is my birthland but I've been away as far back as my memory stretches."

The big man nodded. "Orlaun? If I recall correctly?"

Thomena noted his eyes roamed over her from head to foot and back, though not in any lewd fashion. He looked to be a practical man judging her against, (she assumed), her father's reputation. "Aye, sir. Brotherhood of the Circles mage guild in Orlaun." She brought up a hand to indicate the guild's pin on her mantel.

"Forgive me for any perceived slight my next question might bring. You look rather young to have finished your apprenticeship as a mage." His tone felt genuinely inquisitive, rather than distrustful.

Thomena's humble nature precluded her from trying to boast, yet his direct question deserved an honest answer. "I worked hard and graduated to journeyman at sixteen. I can go back anytime and study more years to be a master, but I wanted to visit home."

The last words sounded odd even to Thomena's own ears. She felt more at home in Orlaun than in this strange land.

Commander Bedran said, "You must be wondering about your father."

Thomena couldn't mask her eagerness. "Oh, aye! I've been impatient to meet him." Her eyes swept off to the side, at the rows of unused bunks, deteriorated footlockers, and discarded equipment. "And a little confused about his…accommodations."

Commander Bedran pointedly looked around the room, a scowl turning his mouth. "His choice," the man grumbled. "If he'd taken up my offer, he'd be lounging in the comforts of the keep. Instead…"

The man exhaled a small sigh, gesturing across the empty barracks. "He seems to think someone should remain. I think he has a hard time letting go of memories." Shan Bedran's tone lightened as he changed topics. "Oh, you did just miss him. I sent him on an errand not two hours ago, riding hard and fast. It may be a few days before he gets back."

Thomena felt like time was moving against her. "Oh, where to? If I could arrange to get a horse…"

The man brought both hands up and waved her off. "He's got his orders and I need them carried out in a hurry. You'll have to wait until he returns." At seeing her disappointment, he added, "Do you need proper lodging? For Thamin's daughter, I could arrange something."

Thomena's eyes passed over the rows of abandoned bunks. Her nose still crinkled at the musty smell, but she figured she could adapt. "I guess I'd rather pick out a bunk since this place doesn't really appear to be used. Sleeping here, I'm bound to run into him."

The big man looked noticeably surprised, yet he did not try to talk her out of it. "Well, if you should need anything, don't be a stranger up at the keep. I'll make sure the guards admit you if you knock, though I may not always be able to address you directly." He turned halfway and glanced at the door. "I have a wagonload of business to attend and must return to it. Try to find an unoccupied bunk."

Thomena cocked her head to the side. She gestured to the closest ones. The bunks in question had numerous dusty items either laid out on them or hanging on their corner posts amidst cobwebs. None of them looked as if they expected their owners to ever return. She said, "They all look unoccupied."

"Unoccupied by *ghosts*," the commander stressed, taking his leave.

Thomena looked at the bunks and wondered how literally to interpret his words.

Chapter 9 – Unpredictable Allies

"You honor us by joining our cause and our faith. We will speak more of our future plans soon." Ztakish raised a mug of swamp-water brew. The drink had a horrible aftertaste, but it was the toast of choice for his goblin guests. "May a glorious feast await us if willed by Yurtash."

The raggedy group of goblins cheered his words and joined in his toast. The race of creatures, so easily swayed by feasting and reasons for violence, raised their weapons and howled their eagerness. The deal concluded; they were ushered out of the antechamber lying within the wreckage of the ancient, divine chariot. As they did, Ztakish held back the iztheran priest who planned to accompany them.

The chosen warrior of Yurtash instructed, "They are receptive of our god's word, and that is good. Try to restrain their eagerness to do anything rash until the proper time."

The priest bowed in reverence. He slipped the last of his tiles of letters into a pack and then followed the goblins out of the chamber.

Once gone, there was a quiet moment in which only Ztakish and his top rank of iztheran followers occupied the room. He noted the dour expressions on their faces. Many were repulsed by the idea of allying with goblins.

Ztakish felt the need to instruct them. "Some of you disagree with dealing with these creatures. I understand. I find it distasteful to recruit such wretches, but it is necessary. Having fought humans and elves many times, I have always been mindful of their resourcefulness. Even now, our enemies hold many advantages over us. They have quality weapons and armor, and they can sit safely behind thick walls waiting for reinforcements who will come."

The chosen of Yurtash strode around the room, meeting the eyes of his followers. Some were warriors, ranked among the best of their clans. Others wore the robes and symbols of Yurtash. These acolytes were the first priests converted and trained by Ztakish. He'd already won their admiration, but he needed to reinforce the tactics they would need to survive.

"We will only win by building our numbers. Yurtash has ever been an ally of those who dwell within simple comforts, living close to nature and away from stone walls. It is our duty to elevate new followers in his name." As he passed each officer, he spoke directly to them. "Just as importantly, we will need numbers. Our own race has fallen over the centuries. We are a shadow of our past greatness. Iztheran armies alone will not be enough for our task."

As Ztakish returned to his throne, one of his generals asked a question. "You find value in goblins, weak and single-minded? And value in the orcs awaiting your attention?"

Ztakish nodded. "Aye. Goblins take to war with little effort. Their flesh can serve as armor to our own troops, wearing down the enemy numbers. And as for the orcs…"

He motioned to the door, referring to the creatures awaiting their audience. "…they also present large numbers of potential faithful, further spreading the influence of our god. As a bonus, some of them regularly trade in the human lands. They can serve as eyes inside the enemy strongholds."

Some of the lizard-like warriors nodded. One felt the need to comment. "We fought these tribes in the past. They were not friends before you woke."

Ztakish nodded, accepting the observation. He replied, "A common purpose, a common following, can make friends of enemies. We will need many friends. This will be a long journey for our people. Others will resist us. We will need to prepare for an extended struggle to reclaim what was taken."

"Will our enemies-made-allies make problems?" one voice asked.

Their leader waved away the concern. "Some problems will always arise. We must keep their hearts bound by Yurtash and their thoughts focused on our enemies living outside the jungle. My only worry for the near future is if groups like those goblins grow too hungry, too fast. We don't want to alarm the humans and elves."

Ztakish motioned for one of the door guards to admit the orcs next.

***

Geylu, The Long Shoot couldn't believe his luck when he saw a lone rider racing down the trail toward their ambush. The trail crossed through tall grasses and swells of ground, but it led toward the small woods in which the goblin party hid. The goblin became so excited he almost lost his balance on the branch. He'd picked the perfect position for a shot. He hissed to his fellow tribe members. "Rider! A tall-legs on a stretchy-speedy-legs. Be ready."

The other goblins rushed into position, rustling leaves and branches as they got into their ambush places. Their boss, Kranks Many Scalps, whipped a branch at one who was slow to run forward.

Geylu listened to their voices as the rider galloped closer.

"Get to ya spot. Hide!"

"Just one? Don't kill too fast, save for fun."

"First war glory goes to us."

"Quiet! Stay hiding."

Geylu braced his crossbow against the branch. The human rode fast, and he began to doubt his shot. He wanted to claim the entire kill for himself, but he had trouble matching the human's movements. As the rider approached the edge of the woods, Geylu turned his focus towards the horse. As long as he could drop the stretchy-speedy-legs, he could drop the long-legs.

He fired the crossbow when the horse entered the woods. The bolt flew true, striking the stretchy-legged beast just below its neck. As the horse let out a high-pitched neigh, the rhythm of its run became a stumble. Horse and rider passed underneath the goblin's branch, even as the mount tumbled to the ground. The tall-legs had only a moment to throw himself free of the saddle, rolling down the trail beyond Geylu. A small cloud of dirt and leaves puffed into the air.

Geylu The Long Shoot laughed in glee. He didn't bother to reload the crossbow. The goblin shouldered it so that he could climb down the tree and help loot before the others got carried away.

As his horse collapsed, instinct drove Thamin's reactions. He flung his body out of the saddle to avoid getting pinned. The landing did not go smoothly, but he tried to roll with the impact. He tumbled head-over-heels through matted dirt, small roots, and young ferns. The roots and rocks jarred his body. More worrisome, he could hear the unmistakable chorus of goblin cheers.

Thamin knew his time would be short before a goblin weapon jabbed him. He forced his muscles to work together. He utilized the slowing roll to his favor, springing to his feet with the last of his momentum. Despite some dizziness, his eyes glimpsed the head of a spear coming toward him. Thamin used one arm bracer to sweep the spear to the side. His other hand formed a fist and cracked the tooth of the goblin holding it.

The rest closed in fast, hooting and hollering.

Geylu The Long Shoot heard his boss urging his warriors to target the legs. The crossbowman appreciated that they would have some sport before their victim died. He slid his way down the branch toward the trunk.

Thamin grabbed the spear and yanked it from the stunned goblin. The ranger barely managed to get his balance before having to dodge to the side. An old, rusty short sword went through the space his legs had occupied. Thamin promptly speared the goblin wielding the short sword. His reflexes were so sharp that he managed to grab the weapon's handle as its previous owner released his grip. As the stricken goblin fell backward, taking the embedded spear with it, Thamin side-stepped again to avoid another lunge from a third goblin. The third goblin's axe bit into the soil. The ranger stabbed the goblin with its friend's short sword, toppling him to the ground next to his axe.

Thamin finally had a moment to curl his fingers into a natura sign. He felt the connection to the plants of the forest. "Movreal," he whispered.

Plants and bushes became sentient and moved of their own accord. Their appendages lashed out at the goblins. Ferns wrapped around legs and hard branches thunked against arms and heads.

Geylu hummed to himself as he started down the tree trunk. It was an old song his mother had taught him about the many ways to cook rats. He licked his lips in anticipation of their next meal. He wasn't really paying attention to the sounds the woods made as they snapped at the goblins surrounding the human.

Another spear thrust aimed at the human, but he rolled underneath it. Thamin spun low to the ground, sweeping the feet from his latest attacker. His hands moved quickly enough to grab the axe in the soil, roll between two more goblins, then strike at the tripped goblin. He left the axe embedded in his victim.

Some goblins managed to scramble free of the animated flora quicker than others. As grouped goblins readjusted their attacks and tried not to hit their friends, Thamin grabbed one by its threadbare cloak and shoved the creature into its ally. Thamin slid the goblin's dagger free of its scabbard as it stumbled into another tribemate. A moment later, the same dagger spun through the air to take the life of one of its cohorts.

Thamin, still holding one of their poor-quality short swords in one hand, stabbed a new attacker just as he managed to stumble free of the bushes.

Geylu still sang his little cooking song as he descended the trunk. He heard several goblin war cries and screams filling the air on the other side. Maybe he wouldn't be too late to join in some more fun?

Kranks Many Scalps yelled his name from closer to the fighting. "Long Shoot! Reload. Shoot it!"

Geylu's feet touched the ground, and he was only too happy to play his part again. Without really looking up, he fumbled for another bolt.

Thamin discarded the chipped short sword and glanced around. Three goblins still struggled to attack through the clutching branches. One goblin, decorated with more ribbons, colored rocks, and feathered pieces than the others, shouted orders from outside the angry vegetation. The last and farthest goblin was reloading a crossbow near the trail. The ranger crossed his arms only long enough to draw his weapons. He raised Longclaw in his right hand and the swordbreaker blade in his left.

He released the foliage from his natura spell. Grass, plants, and bushes lost their strength as they became docile again. It took the goblins a moment to realize they were no longer being held. By then, it was too late. Thamin's two swords descended on them with all his fury. The longsword swung while the swordbreaker stabbed. His attacks proved to be rapid and precise. As each goblin attempted its attack, he had already danced back out of range, leaving behind a mortal wound.

Only the chieftain managed to block an attack, only to fall victim to the second and third strikes. He didn't survive long enough to retaliate.

Geylu raised his crossbow to his shoulder and sought his target. He realized the forest had gone still and quiet, even as his eyes spotted the bodies of his tribemates. On the far side of them, the human and the chieftain engaged blows with each other. The moment did not last long before Kranks Many Scalps staggered backward and fell dead from his wounds.

The long-legs wore an elvish clasp holding a small tail of hair neatly back. His pose looked tall and firm. The human looked only slightly dirty from his tumble but no less imposing. Both his brown armor and deep-green clothing were well-kept, finely woven, and thick. His two swords bore the blood of Geylu's tribe, and each blade looked sturdier than any weapon they'd ever wielded. Perhaps this had been the wrong person to ambush.

Geylu nervously aimed his weapon. The long-legs grabbed his cloak and swept it into a spin. The goblin's bolt launched at the rotating figure. The point bit through the cloak, sailed past, and embedded itself into a tree.

But then the figure stopped spinning. The human showed no signs of being hurt. Geylu cried in fear as he began to pull the drawstring back for another shot.

The long-legs said something in a foreign language. Geylu did not understand the human speech. It seemed clear enough to be a warning. The human stood twenty meters away, repeating the same words with renewed warning in its tone. It even stuck one sword in the ground, raising a pointed finger at the Geylu. The goblin's nervous fingers fumbled a bolt into place. It raised the weapon for another shot.

The human called out a word of magic, "Mitsarum!"

An energy bolt flew from the long-leg's fingertip and struck the goblin. A shock burned through his body and jolted him backward. Geylu The Long Shoot fell dead.

Thamin cleaned the blood from his blades before searching the goblin bodies. He hadn't heard of goblins attacking this far out from the jungle or the hills in many years. Their belongings offered no clue as to any grand intentions. He found more holy symbols of Yurtash, but the goblins also carried symbols for Dalios as well as those of various goblin deities. Many goblin cultures worshipped local legends, and such legends were recognized by an array of simple forest ingredients mucked together into tiny dolls.

There weren't enough details to paint a firm picture, only enough to reinforce his growing unease. Nevertheless, the commander wanted him to scout out the lands, and Thamin was glad that he happened to thwart this ambush instead of finding someone else's corpse after the fact. He completed his search, though weariness could be felt in his body. The two natura spells he cast had left him feeling slightly drained. Thamin was more of a fighter than a magic-user.

The warrior turned around and looked at the horse he'd been given. Death from the bolt had come mercifully quick. "Nine," he muttered.

Thamin lamented that the God of Luck seemed to be enjoying mirth over his misfortune with mounts. He knelt over the stricken animal and placed a hand on the mane.

"I'm sorry. I was forced to take you, even though I didn't need you. Rest and dream."

Thamin stood and turned his eyes up the road, toward his original destination. He still had a mission to carry out, and he felt that speed was vital. He closed his eyes and focused his other senses on his surroundings. The area had become quieter due to the sudden violence, yet Thamin could still hear the wind, creaking branches, rustling leaves, and a distant chirp. He let the call of nature flow into him, and it created an animal form in his mind. Thamin possessed enough natura for a transformation. He actively willed himself toward the form imaged in his mind's eye. His breathing accelerated, fingers curled, legs shook as muscles spasmed, and the corners of his lips pulled upward into a snarl. He threw his body forward, arching over onto the ground. Muscles and joints shifted as his skeleton reformed. Thamin's senses heightened, receiving more sounds and smells than his human form could distinguish.

When he re-opened his eyes, he viewed the world from a perspective closer to the ground. His animal form paused only to sniff at the air before he sprinted down the trail to his destination. Four legs carried him onward.

Chapter 10 – Working up a glow

Julia had enough chores to keep busy the moment Gunnard set up his blacksmith shop. Lucky for her, Gunnard preferred to sleep in the indoor portion of the shop. This left a second story bedroom for her use. Both of them were eager to partner on making complex gadgets like clocks and locks, but they also had to deal with a logjam of work orders from the garrison. Julia had been thinking about another project they could try to tackle.

During a brief pause in her work, she asked, "Gunnard, you lived up north? Did you ever see the Republic of Lar?"

Gunnard snorted as he sorted through some metal bars. "Uffa! Vhy ask? Lar vas near us. Ve raid dem often, so Oye sailed a long route to avoid dem."

"I've heard they have crossbows that can fire up to ten bolts before reloading."

Gunnard nodded. "Aye. Dose bows sent many Norvess lads to Krakus's embrace. Terrible veapon."

"If the enemy has one, I guess so," Julia answered while brushing some sweat away from her eyebrows. "But if you had one and your enemies didn't, how would that change your feelings?"

Gunnard reached for his mug and downed a sip. She could see a grin on his face. "Oye'd love it if Oye could fire von at my enemies." His eyebrows raised. "Vait! Lia, do you have an idea?"

Julia shrugged. "I've never seen one, but I've tried to envision how I could get some gears set up to replicate the same action. I need to draw it out and see if it works."

Gunnard gave her a friendly slap on the back, but he hit her so hard that it nearly knocked the sixteen-year-old girl to the ground. "Clocks, locks, crossbow gears…Lia, you have talent."

"Maybe, but I won't know until I can plan it."

"Vell, push dose muscles. Ve have mundane vork to finish then ve can craft some dreams!"

Julia pushed herself even harder. The day was unmercifully hot, sweat made her tunic stick to her body, but there was nothing she could do about it.

At one point, she looked up and saw a familiar face. The young soldier, Mabry Ingel, was staring at her from down the street. As soon as she met his stare, he broke eye contact and abruptly walked away. She assumed that he was still repulsed by her ugly ear. It bothered her that he gawked at it in such a manner. Her anger spurred her to put extra force into her work.

***

Thomena lost her patience. At first, she thought sleeping in the same accommodations that her father endured would build her character and maybe help her understand him better. A sleepless night in the old barracks convinced her that it wasn't a Humility-versus-pride Codex argument. The building looked so run-down and creepy that she wouldn't have been surprised to be bothered by a real ghost.

That morning, she sought out all the cleaning gear, an old wheelbarrow, and whatever supplies and tools she thought she could use. "The fort doesn't care about this barracks, so it really belongs to Father now, right?" she rationalized. "And sometimes, even fathers need someone to take care of them."

The first thing she did involved stripping all the old linen from the bunks. Some of the cloth ripped when she tried to move it. All the bad ones, moldy or vermin-chewed, went into a large pile on the marching grounds in preparation for a bonfire. Only a few decent ones remained; she hung those on a line and batted them furiously to knock off years of dust. They needed a good wash. Thomena found a dry horse trough that didn't leak, threw the sheets and blankets in, added soap, then conjured a storm of water to fill the basin and get everything soaking.

Returning inside, she tried to decide on the next chore. "It's time to get this dust out of here."

Thomena spent ten minutes with a broom, trying in vain to sweep everything out, when she stopped and realized she had an easier means. Within a minute, a dust-devil whirlwind maneuvered through the barracks. It sucked up all the spare particles in its path. It also whisked around some of the loose clothing, but the girl reasoned that she could wash or burn those items afterward. Thomena perspired from the exertion, but she guided the windstorm up and down lanes in the building. The effort proved more taxing than she anticipated, but it managed to do an expert job. Without much strength to spare, she walked toward the door while pushing the whirlwind of dust ahead of her. She gave it a final shove to send it outside, only realizing a moment too late that someone's shadow could be seen through the cloud.

The poor visitor got caught in the doorway as a funnel of dust and particles blasted out of the building.

Thomena's eyes went wide and her hands steepled in front of her mouth. "Oh, I'm sorry! I didn't see you. Are you okay?"

Mabry Ingel bent over in a coughing fit. A wool sock fell off his shoulder. He backed out of the doorway while he slapped at his uniform and tried to knock off the filth. "I...will be. Soon."

The young man twisted about and patted down his uniform. A layer of dust, cobwebs, and small threads plastered his front. He sniffled a little and cleared his throat. Thomena's embarrassment and shock overrode her temptation to giggle at the sight.

Mabry eventually managed to speak. "What was that about?"

Thomena stood aside, gesturing at the doorway to the building. "I'm cleaning out this haunted house. That's what it feels like."

The soldier's eyes went wide and scared as he looked into the darkness of the building. He took a step back. "Is Trollsbane in there?"

Thomena realized she was getting irked at so many people using a fear-laced title in regard to her father, yet she knew so little about his lifestyle. She gave a curt response. "Nay. I haven't seen him since my arrival."

The mage watched the young man exhale and relax at the news. She added, "If you're so scared of my father, why did you come here?"

Mabry gave a slight bow as he replied. "I followed your advice. I didn't mean to hurt Julia's feelings, so I went looking for her. She's working up a glow at the forge."

Thomena's brow knitted. "She's what? Aglow?"

Mabry seemed taken back by the question. "When one works up a glow, they are using so much of their energy that they sweat. But we say that only men sweat, while women glow."

Thomena chuckled. "Oh." Still feeling the weariness of her whirlwind, she glanced down at the small drops glistening on her arms. Her underclothes were stuck to her body. She added, "I must be glowing right now. That spell was a lot of work."

Mabry nodded. "But if you're simply glowing like a candle now, she's burning like a torch. It looks like a hot, wearisome job at the forge. Since I wanted to offer the proper effort into my apology, I thought I'd see if I could help her."

"You want a spell to help cool her down?"

Mabry responded with a hopeful nod.

Thomena looked off to the side for a few breaths, trying to think of a solution. She didn't want to leave her chores, but she agreed with Mabry's efforts. A solution took form in her mind.

"Mabry…it's Mabry, isn't it? I have an idea, but you'll have to put more energy into this. I have chores keeping me here, but I want to help her, too. What I need you to do is go collect a pitcher full of fresh fruit. You'll need to chop up the fruit inside the pitcher, tiny as you can, without losing the juice. I'll need one or two spoons as well. Bring it back here, and I'll work my magic."

Mabry snickered. Thomena tilted her head slightly, unsure why he reacted that way. He explained, "It just sounds like the odd start of a quest."

Thomena found a slight smile as she answered, "You'll see the results. It will be worth it."

He started to turn away.

Thomena added, "You'll need to pay for the spell!"

Mabry turned back in shock. "How much?"

"Information," she answered. "I want to know more about this 'Trollsbane' title."

Mabry showed a slight hesitation but he nodded. He rushed off to carry out Thomena's task.

Once the soldier was gone, Thomena's full attention shifted back to the barracks. Mentally tired from her dust devil, she returned to the broom to sweep out the last stubborn dust piles. She had to pick up discarded clothing, inside and outside. Now that the dust had cleared, she finished rinsing the soaking linens. The previous occupants had left plenty of rope. Thomena stretched a few lengths between buildings and hung out the linen for the fresh air to dry.

The windows and shutters became her next targets. She scrubbed the intact windows clean. A couple of them had broken panes, so she knocked out a pail full of glass pieces. As she had noticed when first entering, the shutters had been cared for and were in good condition. None were stuck. Having no real need to fix anything else around the windows, she turned to the next item on her agenda.

It was a chore she'd been dreading because it felt most likely to offend any such ghosts that might still haunt the structure. Several footlockers still had weapons, supplies, and personal items stored. Thomena assumed that all these bunks belonged to people who would never be coming back. She approached the first one but paused, pulling in a deep breath. None of the lockers were locked. She could perceive that these people had trusted each other with their belongings, and none of the townspeople had even come by to loot, whether influenced by respect or fear.

The fact that people left this building alone was one of the reasons why she decided on staying in an area that was technically outside the fort's walls. But that didn't make anything feel right about this abandoned place. In fact, she felt a bit of resentment surface as she worked so hard to put this place in order. Who could she blame this resentment on? The people who were once here left a mess of good things to rot, but some must have died. She couldn't lay blame on the dead. What about her father? If he saw enough value in this place to remain here, certainly he should have taken care of these belongings as he did the building. After all, she could tell he had invested some care into this structure in the past few years. Yet that same amount of work and dedication helped absolve him in her mind. Or maybe, she just didn't want to find fault in him? This left the blame to any survivors that willingly abandoned the place, without giving a final rest for those who had passed on. But who, if anyone, did survive? Thomena knew so little, and so the resentment just boiled deep inside. She still had work to do and ghosts to appease.

Thomena knelt and prayed before opening the first footlocker. "As *The Codex* is my guide and the good gods are my witness, allow me to pass on these items to the living. Let new faces use them. Do not let material possessions disturb your rest in the next existence."

She cracked the first footlocker open, half expecting something to jump out and scare her. When nothing happened, she began sorting the contents. Thomena looked for magical auras as she explored. Most of what she found were clothes, and much of those were in the same condition and smell as the worst of the linen. Whenever she managed to find something salvageable, she thought, *I believe there was a poor shelter in Kaigal. Maybe they could use these.*

A pile of neatly folded clothes began growing on one of the stripped bed frames. Its growth paled in comparison to the stack of dirty and moldy linen out in the marching square.

As Thomena delved into the trunks, she also found spare weapons of every variety. Some beds even had polearms leaning against them. She made several trips out to the wheelbarrow. Her arms strained under the weight of axes, hammers, sharp blades, small shields, and quivers full of ammunition. All of the weapons looked to be good quality to Thomena's untrained eyes, though some had become tarnished in storage. A few radiated magic, so she left those inside the barracks for her father to help sort. Enough clutter filled the wheelbarrow that

Thomena didn't even attempt to add the polearms or spears to the mess. She leaned the long, staff-like weapons against the barracks and made a mental note to have the garrison come collect them.

Thomena also sorted piles of personal belongings. Letters, portraits, jewelry, lumped together by owner. Thomena hoped that if her father could contact the deceased's family members, these valuables could still be returned. Her heart sensed that it might be a lost cause if it hadn't been done by now.

As Thomena perused the containers, it became obvious that a number of the Blood-Wolves had been practitioners of magic. Up until this point, she hadn't touched the alchemy table. As she started finding arcane objects, she began stashing them over by that table. A few scrolls seemed to endure the elements well in protective tubes. The first excitement of the day hit her as she found spellbooks and arcane notes left behind by their authors. Not all the notes were in the common language, but Thomena had been gifted a Language Glass by another student at her mage guild. It appeared similar to a magnifying glass, but the person looking through it revealed their preferred language written neatly over the faded, original, translated foreign language. Her exhilaration warred with her sadness over knowing these items were the unclaimed belongings of dead people. Her father had personally known these individuals to some degree. Thomena wanted to know the backstory yet dreaded the apparent outcome.

***

"Thomena? Thomena!"

She had been so caught up in sorting through a footlocker that she realized Mabry had been shouting her name several times. He still feared entering the barracks. Thomena scrambled to her feet as she recalled the quest she'd dropped on his shoulders. She grabbed the edge of her gray mantle and dabbed at the sweat on her brow. Thomena realized she'd already worked up as much of a "glow" than she'd accomplished since her days helping Orlaun's vigiles.

She called out, "I'll be there in a fairy's wink."

When she saw him, Mabry had set up a pitcher full of different berries, finely chopped, on one of the tables outside. He'd also brought two spoons and two wooden tankards. The soldier looked up sheepishly and asked, "Is this sufficient?"

Thomena smiled, feeling pleased with what he gathered. "Aye. This will be perfect." She remembered the price she'd asked of him. Her smile faded only to be replaced by a serious, business-like visage.

"Once I cast this spell, this pitcher is going to be really cold. You'll have to run it over to Julia because it will start to melt." Thomena crossed her arms. "So, I want someone to explain to me this 'Trollsbane' nickname. Why does everyone seem afraid of my father?"

Mabry's face screwed up awkwardly upon her choice of words. He responded, "First of all, fear and respect sometimes share the same profile in a mirror."

Thomena's eyebrows rose. "I'm not sure I understand."

The soldier occasionally glanced around as he spoke, as if someone else might be trying to listen. "I think the best source of information might be Commander Bedran. He's probably known your father's whole career. The other soldiers swap stories to new recruits, but I have nay idea how exaggerated those tales may be."

Thomena considered mentioning to Mabry that she'd met Shan Bedran. She changed her mind when she considered that if the soldier knew that his commander was withholding stories, then he might do the same.

Mabry paused for a moment. "Bael Cochaw is Kaigal's farthest outpost. We stand guard against any threats coming out of the Olangi jungle, as well as the hills just east of us. There are dungeons in those hills that run very deep, likely down to the Deeprealm." Thomena nodded her recognition, having studied about the vast subterranean world under the surface of Dhea Loral. Mabry continued. "There are some traders using the river Vaeklus to the north, and we have ferry stations along that river. Some people live their lives on either side of Vaeklus, though the ones on the north side of it sometimes rebel against Kaigal's authority. There are settlers in small hamlets sprinkled between the river and the hills, but anything out of sight of the fort is considered wildlands. Aside from the fort, there is an independent group that tries to keep the peace, called rangers. That's an informal term. They don't have any structured organization. A lot of them are trackers and hunters. Some are hermits living off the land. I'm sorry if this bores you with anything you already knew."

Thomena shook her head. "I was a child when I left Kaigal. During the times in my life that my father visited me, we didn't discuss these things. So, what part does Thamin-the-Trollsbane play in this story?"

"He was once, or still is, a ranger. He's been our best scout as long as I've been out here. If anyone else gets a patrol assignment, they mount up on horses, pack their camp, and go as a group. When he goes on a mission, he walks out the gate alone with the small pack on his back. Nay soldiers in this fort would go exploring alone. Neither the jungle, the hills, nor the hidden bandit gangs seem to intimidate him in the slightest." Mabry spread his arms wide. "There's so many stories of him and the Blood-Wolves clearing out dungeons and monster dens, I wouldn't know where to begin. Some members of that group sang or told their tales at the pubs here. Those stories are still repeated by others. You should visit the pubs here, or even in Kaigal, and you'll often hear a tale or two. The Trollsbane has a reputation of winning impossible battles and surviving when others didn't."

Thomena couldn't wrap her head around the brazenness of her father. She nodded toward the Red Wolf barracks. "Is that why there are so many empty beds in there?"

He nodded. "Partially, aye. But although many of them died over years of adventures, a few survived and moved on. They suffered the most casualties around four years ago. Diara is full of would-be kings. One laid siege to Bael Cochaw and Kaigal at the same time. He set an ambush for the Red Wolves. Half the company died, including their old commander, but Thamin led the other half out of the trap. During the action, he killed many trolls who were helping the enemy force. He was a legend before then but...have you ever seen a troll?"

She shook her head. "I only know what I studied in creature compendiums. Aren't they around three to four meters tall?"

Mabry cocked his head. "We use feet and yards out here. I don't know how to measure a meter."

Thomena scrunched up her face as she tried to remember the ratio. It had been a lot of years. "Around nine to twelve feet tall? Very strong, hard to kill?"

"Exactly." Mabry drew his sword and stretched it into the air. "Their face is way up there, not that I've seen one up close." He re-sheathed his sword. "Do you know Bael Cochaw's tactic for bringing down a troll or other large creature? We send out an 'arrow' of five or six riders. The first three are the front of the arrow, all with lances to spear it, but spread out enough that only one or two at most will get in a shot. The line helps confuse it. The following tail of three riders each carries large, two-handed weapons. They train so they can guide their mounts with only their legs. They deliver heavy blows as they gallop past it. The first one targets the threatening arm on that side, the other two go for the body organs."

91

Thomena realized she was staring wide-eyed at the description. Five or six well-armed riders to take down one monster? She forced herself to relax and asked, "Did my father ride in an 'arrow?'"

"Nay, that's just it." Mabry's arms were very animated as he talked, mimicking the next action. "There were trolls bombarding the Wolves during the ambush...trolls can throw huge boulders like mobile catapults...and Thamin charged them alone, on foot! I know he was supported by other Wolves in some way, but the story goes that he still managed to kill several single-handedly. That's how he became the Trollsbane. The Red Wolves became the Blood-Wolves that day. They broke free of the ambush and routed the enemy."

Thomena had to remind herself to breathe as Mabry pointed around the old barracks and continued his story. "An army arrived here to keep the fort from reinforcing Kaigal. You've likely seen the frames of the destroyed siege engines out in the field. Thamin led the remaining Blood-Wolves back here and broke their siege. The keep's men hardly had time to lick their wounds before the garrison marched west. I was still a boy in Kaigal when Bael Cochaw's soldiers hit the false king's army from behind and put an end to the threat."

He finally fell silent, leaving a lot for her to take in. After a bit of thought, she prompted him for more. "And what happened to the Blood-Wolves after that?"

Mabry held his hands wide. "Maybe a dozen survived? They continued to watch the frontier and raid dungeons, but they didn't accept any new replacements. Over the course of the last few years, they all dispersed. One at a time, they moved on to different posts, or left wherever the wind took them, I suppose." Mabry sighed. "Only Trollsbane is left. He still takes on jobs and patrols the wilderness, but you'd have to ask him what holds him here."

A resentful thought went through Thomena's mind. *Or why he stayed here when all his family was a sea away?*

Thomena spent years building up noble reasons why her father hadn't raised her. It felt harder and harder to justify his absence. Was she clouding herself from a truth? She told herself she would know more once she saw him. Surely an answer would come.

Thomena blew out a breath she hadn't realized she'd been holding. She cleared her mind of any other sour thoughts and turned a grateful smile toward the young man. "Thanks Mabry. I will craft that treat now. I don't know how to take in all that news. However, I believe we have kept Gunnard and Julia waiting long enough."

Mabry's expression fell into disappointment. "The second tankard was for the smith?"

"Unless you can plead a sip from Julia's." Thomena shrugged with a playful look. "But you haven't worked up a glow, they have. Gunnard will feel better about Julia taking a break and chatting with a soldier if you supply a cold drink to his hand also. Allow me to concentrate."

Thomena held her hands open with the pitcher of fresh fruit pieces and juice directly before her. Mabry felt a cold breeze encircling them, blowing some of the sand on the ground. The pitcher's contents slowly began to swirl. Thomena's breath misted when she exhaled. Tiny crystals of ice formed just above the pitcher's mouth and dropped into the mix. As the fruit assortment began to swirl around, condensed water droplets formed and circled the inside. Cold crystals and water added to the mixture. Mabry watched in amazement as the concoction began filling the pitcher. Berries and cold crystals mixed into a bubbly material.

Wasting no time, Thomena tipped the pitcher and started spooning the mixture into the two tankards. It ran thick as a pudding. She glimpsed Mabry's rapt attention.

"What was it Master Jonah said that summer?" Thomena mused out loud. "He said that this is the best magic, right here. One can laud over an impressive spell blast, but he favored a soothing treat on a hot day."

A small amount remained in the pitcher when Thomena added both spoons to the tankards and lifted them to the soldier.

Mabry couldn't help looking at it. "There's a little extra left in there."

Thomena stared unflinchingly. "And you have my thanks for it. I've been working rather hard today." As his mouth started to move, she quickly added to the message. "Normally, I'm more generous than this. Remember, your task today was to make an apology to Julia. Do that, be compassionate, and talk my overheated friend out of a mouthful on her terms. Get on *her* good side and you will be on *my* good side. Lots of other refreshing mixes will follow. You better move quick, before it starts melting."

Mabry responded like a true soldier. He took both tankards firmly in his hands, tipped his head respectfully, (and curtly as if he was making some kind of salute), then he turned to deliver the drinks without further delay or complaint.

Thomena gripped the cold pitcher and found a shabby chair. She timidly put her weight onto the worn seat, half expecting it to crack or

93

jab her with a splinter. She glanced back for Mabry, but he was already out of sight.

She thought, *He does seem to be genuinely nice and hard-working. Hopefully he'll make things right with Julia. I feel like I dragged her into…*

Leaving the thought unfinished, Thomena eyed the hanging linens and broken-down barracks. She shrugged. "I don't know. Orlaun had a lot to offer. Bael Cochaw is rough as an oak's bark."

Fatigued from her own work, she started sampling her frozen fruit drink. It seemed to be the first time she had truly relaxed since the ship voyage. Her body melted into the chair as fast as the sun liquified her treat. When the pitcher dropped from her drooping hand and rolled across the ground, the girl lacked the willpower to retrieve it. Without meaning to, she drifted off into a nap.

Chapter 11 – Trollsbane's Daughter

The next day dawned, and yet there was still no return of her father. Thomena wondered just how long these excursions usually lasted. She didn't want to entertain thoughts of how dangerous it could be, especially given Mabry's revelation that most everyone else in the fort went out in groups. She wondered how anyone could sleep in the wilderness alone and not risk danger.

The Red Wolf barrack's transition continued into the new day. Since Thomena felt the strong need to wash up, she made some changes to the indoor washroom tucked into the back of the building. She added some scavenged drapes to add to the privacy already offered by the doors. Warped wood and negligence had allowed a few potential peepholes to form in the doorway and walls, so Thomena sealed everything up as best she could. Some holes got caked over with mud and magic, others had a board hammered over them. She tossed out some old towels and soap, making a shopping list as she cleaned. Thomena found a sink and mirror that was stocked with some nice items, including a shaving kit with carved designs decorating the box and handles. It had to be her father's. Thomena claimed the next best sink and mirror she could find. Up until that point, she'd been living out of her bags…bags that could hold more than they appeared. That changed as she began placing her things around the sink. She either salvaged or tossed out everything else that looked personal in the room. Finally, it was time to reward herself with a soak.

The bath felt invigorating, partly because she used magic to warm the water. The large, metal tub was the most rustic accommodations she'd ever used. Nevertheless, it was the first good soak in which Thomena had indulged since leaving Orlaun. It also didn't feel like the bath lasted long enough before she dressed and embarked on more barracks cleaning.

The young mage required guidance from her father to handle some of the useable items properly, including some magical weapons. That still left a full wheelbarrow of nonmagical hand weapons and a leaning forest of polearms to disperse.

Thomena glanced down the line of staff weapons propped against the barracks, planning to bring over what she could and have the fort's garrison collect the rest. The teenage girl gripped the handles of the wheelbarrow. Almost immediately, she found a flaw in her plan. The combined weight of arms proved to be much more than her own arms could handle. The wheelbarrow was built sturdy enough, but her limbs weren't. The rear posts had sunk an inch into the ground from the weight.

Thomena wasn't the type to curse; she was the type to seek out an answer to her problem. Thomena had the perfect spell to assist her. Pulling on the element of earth, she absorbed some of the strength from the ground and molded it into her muscles. Physically, her arms and legs seemed unchanged. Internally, power flowed throughout her body. The incantation would only stick to her for an hour, but that would be more than enough time.

Thomena squeezed her grip on the handles a second time. Her teeth gnashed together, eyebrows pinched, stomach tightened, feet ground into the dirt. When she tugged, her burden shot up so fast that she nearly overcompensated and fell. A smile managed to sneak past the grit in her teeth as she understood how amazingly her spell elevated her muscles. The mage guild had given her lots of practice, but she doubted that she had tried her strength on anything this heavy. Putting one step before the next, her breathing resumed a normal rhythm as she guided the load back toward the fort's inner gate. The wheelbarrow squeaked and complained, so she forced herself not to rush. Compared to all the efforts she'd put in yesterday, this task didn't feel as bad.

She maneuvered the load through the gate, which was barely manned due to other guards placed around the former gate, on the eastern edge of the old barracks. A few soldiers looked her way, including one female guard, but they said nothing as she shuffled past them. Their eyes drifted between the load of weapons and her relatively small frame.

Thomena answered their unasked question. "Unclaimed weapons from the old barracks. I'm taking them to the new."

The woman waved her past, a slight grin on her face. The rest of them just stared. Other bastion occupants, citizens and guards alike, had the same reaction. They couldn't believe that a teenage girl her size could cart such a heavy load of weapons down the street.

As she approached the training yard, she heard an occasional heavy pounding noise. Each loud hit was accompanied by cheers or jeers from the soldiers in the yard. Rounding the corner, she saw a capable-looking warrior holding aloft a spiked cudgel. She viewed him from the back as he faced a training dummy. A battered, wooden shield stood before a torso composed of a bag of dirt. A sturdy pole ran behind the shield, supporting it through its straps, and was tied to a pair of tall stakes. The dummy sat on a small table, propped up by some thin poles spiked into the ground. A number of soldiers stood in a line to be next, while others watched from balconies and positions on the outer wall.

The soldiers didn't notice Thomena at first. They were busy making wagers and calling encouragement to the armed warrior.

A long-bearded, gray-haired officer stepped out of the barracks, motioning to the men making bets. "Let's not make a spectacle here, keep your eyes on the target. If this was an enemy, this would be nay laughing matter." He gestured to the man by the dummy. "Impress me. Knock down your target."

The soldier raised his spiked cudgel. It was mostly a thick stick capped with a solid-looking steel casing. He roared as he wound up and swung. Thomena watched, hearing the earlier sound of the impact reverberate across the training grounds. Dust and splinters ejected outward as the shield bounced on the pole, but it still held strong. The soldier dropped his weapon by the dummy, waving it off as nothing as some of the young men voiced their amusement.

The sound died out as everyone began to notice the girl hauling an overburdened wheelbarrow into the yard. Silence blanketed the barracks except for the squeaky complaints from the wheel. Thomena pushed it directly over to the officer before letting it set. More creaks came from the container as the rear posts crushed the surface dirt. She stood and rolled her shoulders to relax the stress of the trip.

The officer asked, "What have we here? Normally, if you're not part of the garrison, you're supposed to halt at the low wall over there."

Thomena glanced back to note the spot. She saw a low foundation but no sign. A young soldier on the taller, exterior wall called out to his commander, "That's the Trollsbane's daughter!"

Another defended her by adding, "She's been camping out at the Blood-Wolves' barracks."

She looked to find the voices, but it was hard to tell who spoke since every eye was focused on her. The officer looked over the girl, his eyebrows raised with renewed interest. "I'm Lieutenant Kreshaw, and I command the Blue Boars. Forgive me for reciting the rules of the castle. Let none say I barred the Trollsbane's daughter from going anywhere, even the wall if she so chose."

Thomena glanced at the men in the yard and recalled Mabry's descriptions. The Blue Boar company focused on heavy armor and weapons. The men who had been taking turns at the practice dummy had arms at least twice as thick as any of the boys back at the mage guild.

Lieutenant Kreshaw brought up one hand to smooth his beard. The other hand slowly raised and pointed to the wheelbarrow. "What have you brought us?"

She curtseyed, offering her name as she did. She was getting tired of being referred to as the Trollsbane's daughter. "I am Thomena GrayEyes, daughter of Thamin. These are weapons left behind by the previous residents of the outer barracks. This is all I could carry for now. There is a score of polearms, bowstaves, and other heavier weapons still at the barracks, awaiting ownership of someone who will put them to use again. Could these men use them?"

The officer nodded. "We're fortunate for the collection." His eyes roamed over the stack. "I even wondered how many magical ones may have been abandoned back there. No one wanted to disrespect your father by removing them."

The comment stunned Thomena for a moment. It had her questioning if she had overstepped her bounds in cleaning out the barracks. Did she really consider all the implications? Thomena wanted the place clean, but maybe she had also fooled herself. Maybe a part of her wanted to get rid of the ghosts that had kept her father from her for all those years.

Thomena had kept the officer waiting for an answer. She said, "I left the magical ones in safekeeping. I'd rather wait and consult with Thamin in regard to their disposition."

"Fair enough," he replied. "We appreciate the donation." Kreshaw motioned to one of the men. "Wheel this behind the armory and submit them for inspection by the quartermaster."

Thomena stepped aside as a burly soldier approached. The man got a grip on the handles and lifted. Immediately, a groan left his mouth and his lips tightened into a grimace. The rear posts shook as they rose. A few other soldiers let loose in laughter as the burly man struggled with the load. He didn't get far before letting it come to a rest. He made a show of rewrapping some straps on his hands to get a better grip, as if that was all that as needed. Some young men openly stared in wonder at the girl who made it look easy.

Kreshaw harrumphed. "I should let you take a shot at our practice dummy."

Thomena glanced at it. "Were they trying to break the shield?"

"Or the arm holding it." The officer pointed at the horizontal pole upon which the shield was mounted. "A lot of humanoids in the wild have a natural advantage in strength over us. I try my best to build up these men's arms to crush what they hit."

A few voices shouted out. "Let her try it."

"I want to see what the Trollsbane's daughter can do!"

"She's got arms on her, use them."

The officer barked at his men, "Quiet down, men. Show some decent courtesy." He looked to the side and flashed an apologetic smile to her. "I'm sorry, Thomena. I didn't mean to cause a fuss on your behalf."

Thomena's initial reaction at the men's shouting caused her to blush. She didn't want to be the focus of so much attention, even though she couldn't avoid it the moment she walked such a heavy load into the training yard. *The Codex* warned against prideful thinking; one of its tenets included Humility. Thomena could, and likely should, take a humble exit and leave the stage on which they'd placed her. She knew she shouldn't show off her strength. It wasn't even her true strength; it was the benefit of arcane study.

But the call of the challenge brought other tenets into conflict with Humility. Bravery and Honor both encouraged rising to challenges. She felt a call to test herself. Even her prime tenet, Honesty, wanted to know the truth of her capabilities. Thomena wanted to test her limits.

Humility never was one of her strong points.

She tilted her head to the commander. "It never hurts to test one's capabilities, right? I would like to take a swing."

The officer's eyes widened, and a smile turned the corners of his lips. The men around the yard began cheering louder. He stepped back from the dummy but raised a hand to it, indicating it was her turn. Even the man who was supposed to be moving the wheelbarrow stopped to watch.

Thomena walked to the wheelbarrow, inspecting the weapons she'd stored there. Although some felt lighter than they looked, she knew from some past conversations with her grandfather that any weapon would weigh heavily when wielded for a few minutes of fighting. She also recalled her father saying that bladed weapons could be tricky to master. Since her strength gave her a natural advantage with a straightforward, blunt weapon, she looked for that type.

Thomena pulled forth a small mace from the wheelbarrow. The metal hadn't suffered from any lack of care, and it fit her hand well.

Right now, it felt light as a feather, but when she'd originally put it away without the benefit of her spell, she didn't feel overburdened by it. She decided it wouldn't weigh her down too much without her spell, and therefore might be something to keep for herself. But how well could she use it?

When she approached the target, the officer made her pause. He said, "They're still declaring wagers."

Her Humility balked at that, but she wasn't going to turn down the challenge. Instead, she focused her thoughts inward. Her arm gently swung the mace at her side, getting used to its feel and weight. When the soldiers called on her to go ahead, she narrowed her thoughts to the dummy before her.

Thomena once chased after an opponent when she helped the vigiles. She tried recapturing that single-minded focus. *This* was her challenge. *This* was a potential enemy. Every day in life presented new challenges to her growth, and *this* was her moment. Both of her hands gripped the handle. She first raised it directly at the shield, pointing it at her target and feeling the angle of her arms. The yard went quiet as the soldiers watched, but her awareness narrowed to her task. Slowly at first, she moved the mace back and forth for practice swings. After three lazy swings, her tempo increased. Thomena felt ready.

Someone on the wall shouted, "Swing hard." Seconded quickly by another shout. Thomena let loose like a coiled spring. She roared the first battle cry of her life…which to other ears could sound the same as someone realizing they were stepping on a snake. She hit the shield as hard as she could and heard a snap. At the same time, the mace sent a shock into her fingers as it reverberated from the contact.

Thomena's eyes darted to her hands. She still had a grip on the weapon despite the stings in her skin. Both her arms and the mace looked undamaged.

"And that's how you do it," Kreshaw announced.

The shield dangled from one of the support stakes since the pole supporting it had cracked apart.

The officer continued speaking as soldiers settled their wagers. "Good enough to break a human's arm."

A part of Thomena found that comment disturbing, but her thoughts only revolved around her victory. She had known that learning the earth-based spell would come in handy for many chores over the course of her life; its usefulness in her defense had never entered her thoughts. Thomena decided to keep the weapon. There were plenty of belts and harnesses still at the barracks. She would find one suitable to house the mace. Success buoyed her soul and would put a spring in her step for the rest of the day.

***

Julia walked under the eastern gate to enter the old barracks section. She hoped to find Thomena there and wondered about her friend's reunion with her father. Setting up the blacksmith shop with Gunnard and catching up on urgent requests had taken every moment of daylight for the last few days. Her only times outside the shop had been to eat. Even sleeping involved a simple cot in a small cubby, partitioned by a hanging cloth, upstairs from the work area. She didn't complain: she earned decent wages and had a roof.

The first surprising thing she saw involved a group of young soldiers each carrying an armload of polearms. Most of their feet were pointed in her direction, but their heads were cranked around to stare back into the barracks. Rounding a corner, Julia could see the distraction. Thomena stood in an open area of the old parade grounds, surrounded by a field of weeds, but she posed still as a statue with her arms slightly apart from her body. Since she faced away from them, they barely put one foot in front of the other. The soldiers openly stared at Thomena and whispered amongst themselves.

Julia's muscles tightened, eyes narrowed, and teeth clenched, though whether it was more from their disrespect or due to jealousy of her friend, she couldn't be sure. The tinker wished she could get boys to stare at her like that. On the other hand, she didn't mind shaming their actions. After all, they were sizing up her dearest friend like she was a market display.

"Do all soldiers here get paid to stare at young girls?" she snapped at them.

Five strong, young men nearly broke their necks whipping their heads around. Two of them dropped some polearms. They helped each other recollect the weapons while Julia stared daggers and walked by.

Her face softened when she entered the parade field and approached her friend. A sudden feeling of caution caused her to stop short. She didn't know what Thomena was up to, but it was likely tied to magic, and magic could be very dangerous. The tinker simply watched and waited as her friend poised motionless but not quite silent. Julia could detect faint sounds from Thomena's throat. Grunting? Humming? The tinker looked down at the wild grass and weeds at

Thomena's feet. Some of the reeds stretched to the top of Thomena's dull leather gaiters.

Julia's eyes widened as she noticed that the tops of the reeds were blackening. Thomena's fingers flexed a bit, and the tips of the plants wilted. Julia thought it was impressive, even though it may have been unnoticeable if she stood ten paces farther back. Thomena apparently didn't share that sentiment. The mage suddenly moved, shaking out her hands and uttering a grunt of frustration.

"Oh, folly." Thomena sighed to herself. "You can do better than that."

"Looked like you did something," Julia offered in comfort.

Thomena let loose a startled gasp and spun around. The moment she recognized her friend, her face beset with worry. She stepped close to take Julia's hands in hers as she stuttered. "Oh! I-I'm sorry. I d-didn't realize you were so close. I didn't hurt you, did I?"

Julia's face softened, "What do you mean? I am well."

"But, I could have..." Thomena paused to take a deep breath. "I was practicing a spell. I could have hurt you if you stood too closely. I guess my concentration had me blind and deaf to the world."

Thomena seemed genuinely shocked, so Julia pulled her in for a reassuring hug. Thomena's return hug nearly squeezed the life from her. The tinker squawked, "Do you have that strength spell on you?"

Thomena broke contact and stepped back. She flexed her fingers and looked down at herself. "Nay. I had to think about that for a moment. The spell expired a couple hours ago." She shrugged repentantly. "My apologies again. I could have seriously injured you, and now that has me spooked. I felt like I was riding on top of the world this morning—that I could accomplish anything. Now, I feel like I'm just sliding back down the other side."

"Riding the world?" Julia's tone sounded playful. "What happened? Did you see your father?"

Thomena and her friend found a couple chairs and sat down. She explained her challenge at the barracks. When the tale came to a close, Julia pointed at the slightly-blackened grass. She asked, "And was this another challenge?"

Thomena nodded, rubbing a hand across the sweat on her brow. "It's one I couldn't complete at the mage guild. I thought I might give it another try."

The tinker nodded at the spot. "You're doing something. Burning grass."

The observation made Thomena giggle. "Well, aye, it's something. But it isn't the full effect I hoped for. It's really hard to accomplish."

Julia didn't say a word. She stared back, awaiting more of an explanation.

Thomena said, "It's a defensive spell. You see, I'm already very attuned to wind and water elements due to my focus. It's only because of my connection that I can even dare try this spell. People have me worried every time they talk about how dangerous it is out here. And I thought, what if I'm grabbed by someone? Or immobilized? How can I defend myself? And this spell may make it possible. If I succeed, I can draw a charge from the air around me and let loose a short-range electrical pulse."

Julia's face scrunched up. "A what? And you can do it without moving? Wouldn't that be a great thing for all mages?"

Thomena nodded. "I could draw in and release an electrical jolt out to a range of maybe two or three meters around me. Trying to do it without moving or speaking is the nearly impossible trick. It's not an easy task for any mage, and it doesn't work for any ordinary spell. This one comes strictly from my attunement to the air. It's like a door in my mind that needs the right mental key to open." She pointed at the unruly weeds. "This overgrown eyesore was the perfect target on which to practice."

Julia asked, "What now?"

"For now, we move on to something else. I'm weary from all of today's efforts. How have you been?"

The tinker narrowed her eyes at the mage. Julia said, "Well, it's been really busy at the forge, but Gunnard and I are already putting together plans for new ideas. It was hot yesterday, then Mabry ran up to us with a frozen fruit concoction. We were forced to stop and enjoy it."

Julia forced a harsh tone, but she knew Thomena sensed the playful inflection hiding behind it.

"So Gunnard and I were absolutely *forced* to take a break. I had to make a pig of myself in front of this strange boy or risk the sweetest-tasting treat this side of the Sea of Krakus melting into slush. And you seem to find this funny."

Thomena raised a hand to cover her smile, but her composure quickly broke into titters at Julia's mock indignation. Thomena managed a few words between giggles. "I'm sure you enjoyed it."

"I feel like I was ambushed." She said, throwing up her hands.

Thomena doubled over and laughed louder. She managed to ask, "I thought you wanted more attention from the boys?"

Julia felt cornered. "I am trying to build upon my craft out here. I'm working with the only smith that will take me and we're busy. We've got plans for clocks, locks, and even a repeating crossbow. I'm not here to be the target of some meat-headed, soldier boy! What would you do if some lovestruck young peacock strutted toward you, with all the worries you have right now?"

"You just saw what I'd do." Thomena gasped between giggles. "I redirect them toward you. Ha, ha."

Julia put hands to hips, even as they sat facing each other. "Well, that's just…what a traveling partner you turned out to be."

She turned a salty look toward the weeds, but it didn't last long. Soon, Julia's own composure broke down into giggles. She tried hiding her face from Thomena, but the mage could see her shoulders shaking and hear the muffled laughter.

It took a moment for Julia to compose herself enough to add more. "Furthermore, you made it too cold. As I'm rushing to drink it, I get this splitting headache. I put my hand out, a futile chance to stop it, and he misunderstands and he *takes my hand in his*. I'm sitting there feeling scandalized, but no boy has ever held my hand like that, and I couldn't just pull it away."

Thomena chuckled. "So, did he get a taste of the fruit mix?"

Julia adopted a queenly tone as she replied, "I graciously bestowed upon him the undeserved honor of a few bites."

Thomena's smiled widened. "Is he forgiven?"

"I don't know, it depends."

"Depends on what?"

"Well…" Julia turned toward Thomena, her face quite red and her expression made it seem like the next comment would drop her through thin ice. "We'll find out how well he treats me tomorrow when he's agreed to buy me dinner at the inn."

Thomena's jaw dropped moments before she exploded in laughter. Julia offered a playful slap on the shoulder in response before falling helplessly into her own mirth. Both girls spent a couple minutes erupting in sniggering fits. Every time one gained her composure, they'd catch the look on the other one's face and break out in amusement again. A few unladylike snorts snuck in to the embarrassment and further amusement of both. They took several minutes to calm down, at which time Julia changed the subject.

"Thomena, have you met your father yet? I'm guessing not, or you'd have mentioned it."

Thomena sighed. She gestured vaguely at their surroundings. "Nay, he hasn't returned from whatever mission he's on. I have been busy cleaning out and sorting the possessions of dead people. Tidying up the place and cleaning out this whole mess has occupied every waking moment. All this time, I keep thinking of what we'll say or how he'll react. I don't even know how I'll greet him. I've envisioned our reunion in my head a dozen times, each different. It's hard to predict. I feel like I don't really know him anymore—it's been so long."

"Sometimes, that's better than knowing your father," Julia lamented, running fingers across her injured ear. She thought better of her words a moment later. "I'm sorry, that wasn't really helpful. You must have a list of questions on your mind."

Thomena nodded, chewing her lip. "I should write them down, so I don't forget any. I'll just have to see where the conversation wanders. He'll likely be as surprised and full of questions as me."

"Do you think you'll get all your answers?"

Thomena started shaking her head without the need for much consideration. "Nay. Hopefully, the most important ones will be revealed. We've been apart for so long, I just want to get to know him again."

Julia knew her friend valued honesty, yet she questioned how honest Thomena's reasoning could be with her own self. She prodded with a tough question. "What if you don't like the answers?"

Thomena shrugged. She started chewing her lip before visibly forcing herself to stop. "I'll have to quell my doubts. This is a different world than the one I've lived in. He's a hero to these people, standing as a larger-than-life figure. Among other things, he *must* be wiser than most. I'll have to extend my trust to him. I would like to believe he's a man of honor."

"I hope…what's the dwarven term?" Julia's face screwed up for a moment, but then she snapped her fingers and said, "I hope he's not an empty keg."

"Agreed."

Both women quieted as they heard the approach of a galloping horse. The noise approached from the east, through the undermanned gates on the far side of the barracks. Moments later, the rider entered their sight as he rounded the Red Wolf building and raced for the older East Gate. His lack of both composure and proper dress alarmed the girls. The man rode with wide, panicked eyes. Sweat gleamed from his forehead. He wore a nightshirt, underclothes, and wool socks, but nothing else. Similarly, the horse had reins but no saddle. The man seemed too hard-pressed to care. He didn't even spare a glance at the two friends before galloping within shouting range of the gate.

"What news, rider?" a guard yelled from the wall.

"Dire indeed!" he shouted, slowing only slightly and huffing for breath despite the fact that he was mounted. "Hedger's Hearth has been laid to waste. Our buildings burned, people scattered. I still hear the echoes of their screams behind me."

The man said no more as he rode into Bael Cochaw, toward whatever help would come too late. In the yard, Thomena and Julia traded shocked stares.

Julia reached out to hold her friend. "And your father is somewhere out there?"

Chapter 12 – Face to Face

Commander Shan Bedran walked laps around his office. The large man's frame stepped heavily, as if a mountain rumbled along. He swung a heavy mace with one hand, switching it to the other hand every few laps to build his muscles evenly. Normally, his choice weapon involved a two-handed sword, but even the sizeable sword seemed light after sessions of swinging the mace one-handed. Of all the young men serving in the fort, few could match the thick arms of their commander. More reports of seemingly random attacks had begun reaching his ears, so he passed the time keeping his body strong and ready.

An insistent knock thundered his door. His two squires jumped up in surprise, one of them heading to help open the door even as the commander barked out, "Come in!"

The door opened and his prize scout entered. Thamin strode through the doorway, light of step compared to the commander's rumbling walk. He didn't appear to have washed up from the road. His boots and cloak tail were discolored by dirt and the green stains of the prairie grass, housing a few burrs that had hitched a ride. Several days' worth of whiskers shaded his face. Thamin's water bag appeared thin from a lack of contents. A glance at his hands revealed more dirt, but Bedran also noted some bruising and skin tears from a fight.

"I wish I could say my trip was uneventful, but that would be a lie." Thamin paused halfway across the office. "Ready for my report?"

Commander Shan gestured to a map on the wall with one hand, even as he set his mace aside with his other hand. The old soldier suspected that Thamin hadn't yet ran into his daughter, since he seemed to have skipped visiting the barracks to clean up. He decided to open with a different inquiry. "Did the horse return with you?"

Thamin's posture stiffened. "It was a casualty during an ambush."

Bedran couldn't help but laugh despite the tension that had been on his mind all day and the mention of an ambush. Thamin had survived many ambushes during his service. "So, that was number nine, was it not?"

Thamin's eyebrows lowered, and his jaw grew firm. The commander's mood sobered in order to get down to business. Bedran waved a hand for Thamin to continue.

"I took a wide route, circling north to the edges of the jungle, to Bael Altlun. Along the way, I hit a goblin ambush. It was just a small patrol. I left nay survivors. By itself, I wouldn't think anything past a rogue bandit group. Once I got to Bael Altlun, the fort was barricaded. They've seen tracks and heard things skulking in the night. The countryside is getting restless, and now so is the fort."

Thamin approached the big map and pointed to his route. "Then I swung east, scouting the farthest hamlets. There's been more signs of humanoids coming and going from the eastern hills."

Commander Shan scratched at his beard. "What are the scales doing?"

"Nay more signs than usual." The scout shrugged. "I had suspected them of being behind the excitement, but other than tracks, I haven't seen any. Once I get cleaned up and restocked, maybe I should explore the river valley."

Shan Bedran put up a stalling hand. "I have enough scouts hitting several areas. You don't need to go far from the fort. You might even consider just relaxing here a bit for once." As Thamin started to say something, the commander added, "You have a visitor in the barracks."

Thamin paused in his step. The commander remained silent as he realized Thamin's thoughts were sifting through the possibilities. "I wasn't expecting a visitor. One of the Wolves?"

Bedran grinned, even though the damage to his teeth made for a hideous appearance. "Maybe someday, at the rate she is gaining reputation around here. I have a lot of distracted young guards looking inside the walls as much as outside." The commander crossed his arms and adopted an accusatory expression, as if Thamin was guilty of something.

"You're not going to tell me who it is?"

Bedran laughed. "I think you better scout this one out yourself."

The edge of Thamin's lips curled into a slight grin. "Very well. I've given you enough surprises over the years, I can allow you one of your own."

As the scout turned to leave, Bedran said, "And don't worry about rushing out into the wild again. One more or less scout, even you, won't be a big influence to whatever happens."

***

108

Thomena happened to be reading some Red Wolf mage's spellbook when she thought she heard footsteps on the boards outside the building. She quickly marked her spot with the spine ribbon and set it aside even as the door opened. Thomena jumped up from her bed and patted her skirt to brush out any wrinkles. It amazed her that someone would dare to walk right in unannounced. She opened her mouth to inquire about her visitor, but her voice caught as she saw the figure framed in the doorway.

There was no mistaking him. She may have gained some height in the past few years, but he still stood a head taller than her. His firm jaw displayed untamed growth from his days on the road, but he still wore the green and brown colors he favored for blending into the woods. His leather armor and clothes bore the scratches and patched evidence of hard use. More worry lines than she remembered framed his brown-eyed, piercing gaze. He looked as tough as this wild land, but the sight of her brought a smile to his face.

Thomena froze in place, arms by her sides. Her lungs swelled with unspoken words, but she decided to let him speak first. She wanted to see his honest reaction.

She could tell that he recognized her. Despite the years of separation and growth, her gray eyes, calm expression, black hair, even the way she was chewing her lip—all of it belonged to the baby girl who once struggled to hug around his muscular calves. What Thomena could not realize, from her father's perspective, was the way her noble bearing had changed even more than her height.

Thamin broke the silence. "Thomena, is that really you? You're nearly a full-grown woman now, and I've missed too much. Where's my hug?"

Thomena found some relief in that he acknowledged missing her. She stepped forward and met him halfway across the floor. His big arms wrapped around her, offering a firm, fatherly hug. She didn't even mind that he wore several days' travel worth of odors. His embrace offered her a priceless refuge. Thomena's heart beat to a rhythm of "It's him, I'm really home!" She closed her eyes and enjoyed his warmth. She felt one of his hands pat her head and cradle it close to him.

"So tall," he admired, disbelief choking his voice. "I could almost rest my chin on your head. Oh! We need to make a new mark for this occasion."

He pulled away, and she looked up through a puzzled gaze. "What do you mean, a new mark?"

109

"Come here, to the doorway."

They walked to the outer door through which he'd just entered. He pointed to the topmost of a series of scratches on the door frame. Even so, the top mark was down around the level of his thighs. "This was how tall you were when you left for Orlaun. I used to measure your height here. Your mother wouldn't let me damage the walls at our house." Thamin glanced down at her gaiters and boots. "How thick are those soles?"

Thomena smiled as she looked down. "I knew I'd likely need good padding, so there is a thick set of layers between me and the ground. Allow me to remove them for a true measurement."

Always honest, she took the time to loosen the gaiters and remove the boots. She allowed herself to be positioned against the doorway. Her father took out a knife and sawed a new mark into the frame.

Thamin nodded to it, saying, "There. Take a look. You're more than twice as tall as back then."

Thomena stepped forward, joining her father and turning back to examine the old scratches on the door. A number of marks measured her early years, but the new scratch jumped much higher than the rest.

A question entered her mind that she hesitated in broaching. Thomena appreciated that their reunion started tender, but many of the questions burning through her thoughts could upend any of that. Nevertheless, he presented an opening, so she felt the need to ask her first question.

"Father, I thought I remembered us having a house in Kaigal. Why are you out here at this fort?"

Thamin nodded. "We did, but that home was damaged in the same attack that resulted in your mother's death. Once your grandfather and I came to the decision to get you into a good college in Orlaun, I saw nay need to rebuild. I sold the property. The memories tied to that place...were too harsh. With my service to Kaigal's defense, this fort provided all I needed."

While she realized his answer contained logic, it didn't satisfy the myriad of other questions in her heart. Before she could ask more, he spoke again.

"If only Jaena could see how you've grown." He reached out and slid some fingers through her hair. She saw how his visage softened even more as he thought of his departed wife. "And if she could see your magic. Not like I've seen it, either, but you must have used it to clear out all those weeds? Your masters in Orlaun commended you in their letters."

She nodded. She watched his eyes as he talked. Thamin seemed to be honestly admiring her, but she also saw his frequent glances at the barracks and beds. His eyes appraised her even as he soaked in the changes she had made to his environment.

Thamin's visage turned to challenge her as he asked, "I know you had a graduation, but surely you aren't a master of wizards yet?"

Thomena grinned as she shook her head. "Nay, not a master. I haven't even read a quarter of that vast library of theirs. I'm a journeyman in the ranks. I can literally journey for a time to perfect and research the arcane arts, or I could have stayed at the guild. Some journeymen disappear for a year or two before returning to the guild, hopefully with new books and knowledge to share."

Thamin motioned to some chairs and tables, and they both took a seat. Thomena slipped her boots back on, unsure if they might go outside. She realized his face had lost none of that challenging interrogation. She could tell from his visage that he sought as many answers as she did to quell his curiosity.

She decided to dampen the coals of any potential argument while playing the proper hostess at the same time. "If we're going to sit down and chat appropriately, let me set the table proper."

 Thomena kept some treats and desserts handy, planning ahead for their reunion. She had a vague remembrance of her mother hosting guests and her father reflecting on her manners years ago. She was gone only a few breaths before returning from the kitchen with a plate of fresh-baked sweets and two tankards of cider. She arranged the table neatly, serving her father first, and then she sat across from him.

Despite some seriousness lurking in his eyes, Thamin nodded at her conduct. "So much like your mother. And treating me as a guest under my own roof?" He paused only briefly to take a sip of the cider. When he dove into his next statement, she was reminded how direct he could be when pursuing a subject. "This is a long, difficult journey for a young woman who is untested by the world. It's nay day trip to skip from Orlaun to Kaigal. Do you possess so much confidence in your abilities?"

Thomena sensed that he must be testing her. "'Pride undermines all diligence,' or so *The Codex* says. I didn't make the journey alone. I felt capable of protecting myself from most dangers I'd expect to find."

Thamin broke into a smile when she mentioned her holy text. "That's my girl. Still persistent in your virtues? I honor your devotion. Your mother would be pleased." After a slight pause, he added, "Who came with you?"

"A tinker named Julia—you've never met her. She did odd jobs at the mage guild but wanted to find a new future. She's working and staying with the blacksmith here at the fort."

He nodded, and she wondered if he had suspected a boyfriend or such. Thamin's next words chided her, though in a smiling, gentle way. "Still, that was a dangerous trip. I told you I would visit you when I could."

She didn't return the smile. His line of questioning tugged at one of her fears. "Do you wish that I stayed in Orlaun? Could you so easily part with me for more years?"

It was as if he saw the hurt lingering in her eyes more plainly than she realized she had revealed. He took her closest hand in both of his, hugging it firmly. "My precious child, I only worry for your safety. This is a land which one must continuously be vigilant against the threats surrounding it. The monsters of the jungle and bandits of the grasslands pose significant threats. Despite the danger, the 'civilized' city-states and counties of Diara constantly shift power and bicker over every scrap of farmland."

Thomena didn't pull back her hand, but her eyes narrowed, and her jaw jutted higher. "You don't appreciate me being here," she accused. "You would prefer that I stay miles away?"

He shook his head. "If you would have asked, I would have discouraged you from coming. There is peril out here just beyond the reach of your senses. However, even if I had told you nay, I can see you would have come anyway. I am grateful for that. I guess I grew more world-wise than you when I was your age, and I worried Father on several occasions. Perhaps I just needed to see you old enough to take action on your own behalf. Only you can answer whether you're ready to face the world, but you never know what challenges it holds for you."

She glanced down at her hand as he softly released it. He redirected his own to sample the baked treats she'd provided. He'd left her an opening, but it took her a moment to decide what to say next.

When next she spoke, even Thomena realized her words sounded tentative and slow. She needed to get some thoughts in the open. "If home was destroyed, and this land so dangerous, why didn't you also go to Orlaun?"

Thamin sat back as he answered. "I was still young then, but my whole livelihood revolved around scouting the wilderness. I possessed many friends who assisted me, guided innocent folk around safely, advised leaders about threats and solutions. To this day, it's hard to

112

imagine uprooting to another home. I've crossed the breadth of Diara but found no place that welcomes me more. Kaigal needed me, more than a big city like Orlaun could."

Thomena deemed it an honest answer, even if it was an unfulfilling one for her part. She was about to say something when he continued.

"I've worked hard over the years to try taming the rough character of this land. Not just for the toughened folk that live here, but also to provide you a place of peace and opportunity when you came back. My number one wish has always been to earn a good home here for your return. I've made a difference many times." He paused to gesture vaguely beyond the walls. "But I know it doesn't appear that way."

Unsure that she could find true satisfaction in his answers, she deflected towards humor. "As long as you left me a place to build a tower and fill it with a wizard's labyrinth of books."

"Well, you got your start."

His finger pointed at the spellbook she'd set on her bed. The veteran scout looked over the barracks. "I have to thank you for doing what I could not. I've faced dungeons and monsters that could shake a man's confidence. Buried companions. Yet, it was hard to imagine trying to dispense of their belongings. I tried once. The ghosts of their possessions were more than I could face."

"You blame yourself?"

"I was responsible for their well-being," he clarified. "For a number of years, they followed me as their leader. All such decisions have consequences, and so, not all of them came back."

As father and daughter shared their dessert, he questioned her about the changes she'd made around the barracks. Thomena recounted the sorting of all the equipment, the disposal of the non-magical weapons, and the inventory of magic weapons and armor that she'd been unsure how to handle. For a long time, she did most of the talking while he threw out occasional questions. He nodded his head slightly, helping her feel like she'd been useful and productive while awaiting his return.

He reinforced those feelings when he commended her. "You did a good job sorting these things and keeping the right ones. Some of these magic weapons I'd like to keep around. Even magic weapons aren't immune to destruction, and I've lost several over the years. The ones that wouldn't accommodate my style can go to the quartermaster. He'll find a good home for them. As for the spell books...wizards are scarce here. Keep what's useful, and I'll show you who can properly disperse the rest."

Thomena gathered up the finished plates and delivered them to the small kitchen. When she returned, her father had his full attention on her again. Thomena felt a judgmental stare focused on her.

"What is it?"

Thamin sighed. "I don't know how to feel about your business with the vigiles. When I first received word, it scared me. I thought it was foolish of you and poor responsibility on behalf of your guild."

She felt the urge to defend herself but fought against having an outburst as she realized her father was leading up to some new conclusions.

His eyes slid away from her, staring off into a distant corner of the room. "But that wouldn't have been fair of me. Nay matter how much I worry about you, you've grown enough to make your own path."

Thomena swallowed her first response, recognizing the dangers of prideful speech. Instead, she decided to turn the discussion around. She resumed her seat, and her gray eyes faced him as she asked, "What were you doing at my age?"

A mirthful "Hmmpf" escaped his lips. His gaze turned to her. "I was falling in love with Jaena, in between her studies and my wilderness skirmishes. Don't let that embolden you. I was really too young for considering marriage while at the same time fighting bandits and monsters. It's a tough land out here, however, and people living in these wilds grow old early."

He sat back, pausing before his next words. "I'd seen my share of fighting and running scared—by my own choice—before the age you are now. My father, Gregros, lectured me about it. Yet, I had my talents and my determination to help people, and they needed me."

Thamin took a deep breath and stood up. "I've been fighting back the wilds with nay progress to measure my work. I've spent nearly a score of years trying to plant the seeds of a home in this soil, but homes don't take to root here so easily, or safely. These days, I have been reminded that even when the evils of the wilds have waned, it's just a matter of time before they flourish again."

She stood up with him. He reached out and put her gentle hand between his calloused ones. Thamin said, "About your earlier question. I'm glad that you accepted the adventure to come visit your home. You've reminded me of what's most important in my life. I don't want to seem like a charlatan. It would be improper for me to lecture on your adventures when my own started so young."

Thomena found something in that statement that her heart had been seeking more of during their conversation: genuine love, concern, and acknowledgement. She was glad to know that she was a priority in his life, despite the absence. It was easy to find her smile again. "I'm glad to hear it. I'm looking forward to spending some time together, as much as we can. I don't have any scheduled time at which I must return to the guild. I can journey for years."

***

After spending the afternoon reminiscing and addressing the various objects and weapons Thomena had set aside, she opened up a new line of inquiry that had been nagging her.

"Father, how long will you be resting in Bael Cochaw? Your duties have kept you away for days, and I prefer to enjoy your presence for as long as I can."

Thamin now wore a different set of clothes, made for comfort instead of the road. A bath and a shave had done much to make him more presentable. Her father relaxed his back in a woven chair, padded with blankets. His feet stretched out across the only thick rug in the building.

"Commander Bedran offered me to take a short leave to spend my time with you. I'm grateful for his offer, but I find myself uncomfortable with abandoning my scouting duties. There is some strange influence spreading from the jungle, and trouble usually follows."

He couldn't have missed the frown that washed through Thomena's expression. In her mind, she struggled to understand his conviction to duty over his family. If their roles had been reversed and he had visited when she had been helping the vigiles, she would have dropped all responsibilities to be with him. Could he not do the same?

"Are you really so vital?" she asked. "Must you journey again so soon?"

She could sense it was no idle boast when he said, "I'm the most dependable man he has for sniffing out danger."

Thomena was almost resigned to accept his departure when a defiant thought entered her head. "You can take me with you."

She tried to muster a determined will as she stared him in the eyes. "We both want more time together. You said I was important to you. Therefore, take me with you and show me around the land."

His face lacked expression as he met her stare. Thomena couldn't match him and averted her gaze. She eyed the far wall, aware that his eyes focused straight on her.

"Hmm," he muttered, letting the sound hang in their air awhile.

She almost jumped when he spoke again.

"If it came to a fight," he asked, "can you handle yourself? I was ambushed only days ago, lost the horse I rode."

Thomena's gaze jerked back to his, concern in her eyes. She spoke before considering her words. "Why do you risk yourself like that? You disapprove of my adventures, yet you seek out danger."

"Life *is* danger." Thamin's words, though spoken quietly, nevertheless carried the weight of conviction. "It has danger whether you seek it or not. While the rich man sits content in his robe sipping tea, a poor man outside is freezing to death. The rich man may have nay knowledge or appreciation for the struggle. Any random alley may host a desperate man with a knife.

"Nature's animals, in their home environment, risk death every hour that they sleep, hunt food, or look for a mate. The wild is full of predators hunting for prey. A beautiful garden can still play host to a deadly game of cat and mouse.

"Even in a bountiful civilization like the city of Orlaun, there are those who set fires. It's better to be vigilant and watch for danger before it draws near."

Thamin paused to let his words sink in, awaiting Thomena's reaction. She chewed her lip. Her father recognized her habit, knew she was deep in thought, and allowed her time to respond.

After a few breaths, she asked, "But why does it have to be you who always goes? You who patrols out of sight of your family?"

"Why did you join the vigiles and stand face-to-face against mage-crafted fires?"

Thomena felt that his words would lead him into a trap. She declared her answer with a hint of elation that she would be turning the question back at him. "I did it because I was selfish. I lacked patience to wait for the appropriate time to learn fire spells. In my rush to push my skills, I watched a friend die."

Her answer didn't seem to break his composure. He coldly faced into her hot stare with ease. The room itself seemed chill and dark when Thamin found his response.

"And how many people would have died at Old Market that day if you hadn't displayed your best qualities in the fright of the moment? How many others might have died if you hadn't eventually caught the wizard responsible? How many innocents did you protect, 'Old Market Mage?'"

In her mind, she groaned. She thought, *They told him.* Despite Thomena originally being honored that she'd earned a title that day, *The Codex* scripture warned against pride. Many titles could lead one astray from duty. She lamented the fact that the title had followed her across the sea.

"I'm not a fan of titles." Thomena couldn't think of any other answers. *She* had fallen into the trap instead of him.

Watching him nod, wearing a solemn visage as he did so, she realized there might be a similarity between how she felt about titles and how he perceived his own. Trollsbane.

"Anyway, I'd hoped you would volunteer to come with me. As you said, we'll be able to spend time together and discuss our adventures."

She tilted her head, and her forehead scrunched up. "You just got done arguing with me of how dangerous the land can be."

He nodded. "True, and it was nay lie. We're only taking a short walk to some nearby hamlets. I assume you haven't camped under the stars before?" She shook her head. "This will be a first time then. A father and daughter adventure." His stern visage cracked with a bit of remorse. "Also, when I was young, and left sweet Jaena and you behind, I didn't return in time. Kaigal stood besieged, and I was unable to save her from death. Maybe you'll be safer beside me." He grinned. "At least safer than the fort will be if all its young guards are looking inside the walls instead of outward."

Thomena's cheeks bloomed red.

Chapter 13 – Village of Veldale

Father and daughter hiked down a trail matted with horseshoe prints, sometimes hopping the wagon-wheel ruts to avoid mud spots. Grasslands stretched across the horizon, interrupted by low swells of the land and ridges of trees. They passed by ponds too small to deserve a proper name. Thomena saw larger hills on the eastern horizon.

When asked about them, Thamin replied, "The hills mark the eastern edge of Kaigal's influence. The elves of Syllatru claimed the lands beyond them. The elves sometimes try to push westward to border Kaigal, but the hills bend to nay flag nor central ruler. Even the city-state of Ostraw to the south, has extended into the grasslands but won't dare reach into those hills."

The way he talked, Thomena pounced on a hunch. "I'm guessing that you've explored them, haven't you?"

He nodded. "But even I won't go into those hills alone. That land is pockmarked with dungeons and savage humanoids. They were quite a source of adventure in my youth. Even Jaena faced down caverns full of monsters, with friends at our side. We uncovered treasures and artifacts buried from the eyes of cultured man since the Godswars."

For a moment, Thamin's eyes and smile seemed aglow with memories. As she watched, his expression fell back into a solemn enclosure. He lamented, "I'm sure we've already found anything worth finding. Nay reason to go stomping in those lands anymore. Nay cause to continue chancing death and angering its natives."

Thomena had told Julia about meeting her father and her first impressions. Her tinker friend was hard at work, so she kept the conversation short and uplifting. Julia had been shocked to hear that Thomena would be walking out into the wild again. Julia gave her a verbal list of things to watch out for and prepare. By the time Thomena left, she could tell that her friend was even more anxious than when they'd started talking. Hopefully, she'd be returning soon with good news.

Thomena and Thamin's conversation lapsed for a time as they hiked farther north. Thomena had been told that they were heading in the direction of the great Olangi jungle, but they'd be nowhere near seeing it. That didn't stop her from straining her eyes to the north after cresting every hill, hoping for a glimpse. The hopefulness put a bounce in her stride during every ascent.

Nevertheless, she wasn't used to the walking distance or the pace. She called a temporary halt to readjust her pack and fidget with the heavy weight hanging from one hip. The mace hadn't bothered her at the start of the trip, but now it had bounced against her hip more than a thousand times. Once she readjusted her belt and straps, she nodded her readiness and walked onward.

As they moved, Thamin's eyes focused on her choice weapon. "Why a mace? Wouldn't a lighter weapon suit you better? Or even a wizard's staff?"

"I'll use a strength spell, should the need arise. They last an hour, but I wouldn't want to use the spell unnecessarily and drain my mental strength."

Thamin nodded. "I've seen such strength spells used by wizards before. Good choice." After a pause, he added, "Even in this open land, danger may be upon you without time to incant a spell. Do you have a reserve weapon? That eating dirk may do in a pinch, but a longer dagger with a guard would be preferrable."

She shrugged. "I thought the dirk would do if I get surprised."

"Without a guard," he pantomimed a stabbing motion with his hands, "your blade might hit something hard to penetrate, like leather. Your hands could slip down the handle, cutting yourself on the blade."

Thomena's fingers absently rubbed the handle of her dirk. She hadn't thought about the dirk being a danger to herself. Her mind drifted to thoughts on the other topic he'd mentioned. "I would like to have a wizard's staff, but one is not necessarily bought, nor crafted. A proper staff holds some kind of connection to the wielder."

She glanced at Thamin, but he watched her in silence, awaiting more. "The words and runes of staff creation bind better when the wood is obtained from something or somewhere personal and emotional to the wielder. Some wizards walk around with a mundane staff just hoping to force a link. A good staff starts off imbued with energy just by some connection. It doesn't even have to originate as a staff. It's possible that I could summon one out from the very timbers that make up the Red Wolf barracks, due to sharing a relative connection through you…"

Thamin started chuckling. Thomena broke her stride at the unexpected reaction. "What amused you so? Something I said?"

119

He continued walking but pointed a finger at her. "You. You sound so much like your arcane teachers."

"Well, I spent my whole life around them." A moment after her blunt, honest answer, she recognized how closely it pointed to the questions in her heart. Rather than give away her thoughts, she turned the conversation slightly to a similar subject had nagged her. "What about that weird sword-like thing on your right hip? Why is the middle outline so wide?"

Her father slipped loose a leather knot near the guard. He drew it forth for her to see. Her confusion was understandable. The sword's handle and tip were normal, but the guard and close half of the blade were broad and jagged. Holes and grooves interrupted its profile.

Thamin said, "That's a swordbreaker. All those holes and edges are designed to trap an opponent's blade when used by someone skilled in such ways. It's my left-hand weapon, so that it might be easier to trap a right-handed enemy blade. I would then be free to finish them with a blow from my right-hand weapon."

Her eyes widened. "You can break swords with it?"

He winked before returning the sword to its scabbard. "Not really. I wouldn't normally bet arm muscle against steel."

"But since it still has a point, you can choose to stab with it?"

"Aye."

She looked at his other scabbard. "You also have a sword as your right-hand weapon?"

He nodded, drawing that blade. "This is Longclaw. It has a magically keen edge. It also belonged to a friend of mine who passed away recently." He returned it to the scabbard.

The conversation almost lapsed, but Thomena wouldn't allow it. Her father stayed silent during too much of their time together. "We've been apart for so long I feel like I know so little about you. I'd like to ask some questions."

When Thamin acquiesced, she fired off question after question and didn't relent. Even if she already knew a specific answer, she asked anyways just to keep the conversation going. In her own honesty, she couldn't hide herself from the fact that she only did so to load his conscience with guilt. Maybe she could indirectly get him to realize that there remained a chasm between them, and she needed him to put the effort into rebuilding the bridge he'd let collapse due to his negligence.

According to his answers, he liked strategy boardgames. His hobbies included just enough leatherwork and bowyer knowledge to care for his equipment. Thamin rarely touched alcohol. He didn't like the taste of it and refused to risk losing his edge. He favored goat's milk or fruit cider. Thomena had tasted ale but likewise didn't care for its flavor or smell. She preferred tea or broth. Their conversation turned to food, so Thamin offered her a loaf of leskam.

Thomena ripped off a chunk and studied it before taking a bite. "Thank you. This is leskam, correct? From the elves?"

He nodded. "It's an elven recipe. It holds lots of nourishment for traveling."

She took a second look at his gear. "You have a lot of elvish influence about you. Elvish trail rations, elf-designed bow, and an elvish-knotted hair clasp."

Thamin unconsciously reached up and touched the clasp. Due to the length of his hair, he favored tying some of it into a tail behind his head. "A friend decorated the bow after we looted it from enemies. This bow is enchanted to shoot faster and farther than a normal bow, so I'd have been a fool to leave it go. Other than that, I scout out past Syllatru and have made myself known to their culture. There's also a number of elves amongst the rangers. I've become fond of their crafts."

"I wanted to ask you about the rangers." Thomena paused to finish swallowing a bite. "Tell me more about them. The memories of my youth are still mired in fog, and there was little written about the subject in the guildhall."

Thamin nodded. "We are a loose-knit organization that protects people out in Diara's frontiers—not that there are many frontiers left in Diara. The Olangi Jungle and the Semtelle Marshlands in the far northeast are the last 'uncivilized' territories on this continent. There are other places as dangerous as the eastern hills, including some ruins, and so there are ranger lodges in many places across this land. We aren't political, and we don't take sides in the fights between counties…other than defending our own homes."

When Thomena attempted to push the questions towards the Blood-Wolves, she hit a wall. Thamin would hint at his friendships but never offered out names or answered openly about their history. She sensed a well of sadness hidden behind his stoic visage. The loss of many of them must weigh heavily upon him. Apparently, a few had survived and eventually left Bael Cochaw to pursue other interests. She couldn't find a reason why he hadn't left and joined her in Orlaun, other than his efforts to make this home a safer place.

Thomena paused for too long in thought. She felt like she was overdue in asking another question and keeping the conversation rolling along. Thamin's gaze focused off to one side. Thomena didn't see anything, so she started to ask another question. He shushed her with a quick downward slash of his hand. His pace had nearly come to a stop.

Realizing that he sensed some danger, she whispered a spell. Her skin hardened as the earth-based spell lent her flesh the resilience of rock. One hand dropped to the wand at her belt.

In a flash, Thamin's bow was at the end of his arm and an arrow nocked into place. The ranger let it fly, whizzing away in a blur. Thomena barely tracked some motion in the grass. The girl heard a high-pitched squeal as some grayish mass, perhaps only two feet long, rolled to a stop in the brush. The squeal faded.

After a few moments, he turned back to the trail and resumed his pace.

Thomena asked, "What was that?"

Thamin whispered, "In the wilds here, if you want to stay safe, you have to know everything that's going on around you."

"I didn't get a good look at it."

"Coyotes are predators here, usually roaming at night." Thamin walked as he spoke. "I saw one running scared from something, coming our direction. I had to wait and see if what chased it was a threat to us. It killed the coyote but then got our scent. Ravenous little buggers that don't have much fear. I took care of it."

Thomena's brow knitted. "What killed the coyote?"

"Gusster." When she didn't reply, he glanced over his shoulder and saw her head tilted. "Large vermin from the jungle. Normally you don't see them on the plains, unless they were following potential food sources. I wouldn't worry about it anymore."

If anything, she worried more. She'd studied illustrations of various monsters of the world during her time at the school. Although she didn't recall a gusster by name, she'd seen pictures of rat-like creatures that grew larger than normal and carried all sorts of diseases in their jagged teeth. Thomena had a feeling that she might endure some nightmares tonight.

***

"Is that our destination?" Thomena could see plumes of chimney smoke rising from thatched rooftops to meet the late afternoon sun. They'd already passed a few outlying farms.

Thamin nodded. "That's the village of Veldale. There's maybe a score of families living in this area, just over a hundred people form this community."

Her walk slowed as she started to fuss with her wind-tortured hair. "Tell me a bit about it."

The ranger explained more about Veldale as they drew near. A dozen buildings sat on a cart-rutted path, overlooking a pond. Tilled fields surrounded the community. A trading post served as the hub of the village. It offered cider, ale, and warm food, as well as tools and feed for the locals and their animals. A couple barns and gated corrals sat at one end, allowing for the trading of livestock. A postmill-style windmill sat on the only hill. Thomena had heard about the structures but never seen one. It pivoted on one post in order to best catch the wind. Along with the windmill, a watchtower standing above a walled barracks represented the only tall structures in the area. A militia of only eight men manned the small garrison at any given time. Thamin also pointed out a modest, three-room schoolhouse that served the area. He commented that the locals had built it only four years ago and scratched their initials around the foundation. Aside from a few houses, the only other sizeable building belonged to an elderman who was elected to oversee the area. Since it was a public house, it could shelter a few travelers for the night.

"But I don't want to inconvenience them," Thamin said in reference to the idea of shelter. "We'll stay long enough to get a warm meal and see if anything is amiss, then we have one more village to visit before circling back. We have our own blankets and I have a tarp we can tie off as a rain shelter if we need. I hope you don't have anything against camping in the wilds?"

Thomena's stomach knotted. "It will be my first time."

Any worrisome thoughts about camping were soon swept away at their village reception. People saw their approach and hustled to greet them. Children of different ages ran out first, heedless of their parents' calls. They laughed and chased each other around Thamin, asking about his travels and life at the fort. Thomena smiled in greeting but barely got in a word as eager conversations jabbered around them.

"Thanks fer showin' me the deer tracks! I's seen several 'round our farm."

"Have you been to the big city? What's Kaigal like?"

"Who's this girl? She's pretty."

"…and tell Josh to stop throwing dirt on my rag doll, Lila. He listens to you…"

123

"I found this flower. You have it."

Thamin didn't stop walking even as he responded to the children's questions and stories. Thomena barely got a dozen steps before she had to lean over to receive a flower in her hair. She wasn't allowed to stand again without picking up a girl of perhaps four years and carrying her. The child rambled on about different colored birds and whether or not they were getting along at the pond. Thomena, weary from the walk, wished she had put a strength spell on her. Thamin noted her predicament with a sly smile but kept walking. She kept the pace, carrying the girl in her arms as they reached the village buildings.

Thamin suddenly stopped, his eyes on some older men on the trading post's porch. They stood solemnly, offering him a salute. He respectfully returned the gesture. Thomena also paused while some unspoken formality took place. Once it was done, everyone relaxed and became informal again. They called to him to join them for a game just as other adults on the street resumed their greetings.

Thomena appreciated when a woman approached and reclaimed her child. She followed Thamin up to the trading post, eager for a chance to sit and rest. The children began to disperse as the village wise men congregated around a few tables on the porch of the trading post. The young wizard paused, unsure if her presence was disruptive of some assembly. Thamin eased the moment by introducing her to the elders. In return, they promised food would be prompt and motioned for her to have a seat.

The weary road left her too spent to focus on the conversations. Just the act of sitting down and relaxing made her feel like she could nod off and miss the afternoon. The simple wooden chair served her backside as well as a pillowed lounger. Only the enticing scents from the building's kitchen and the rumble in her belly kept her awake.

She watched as Thamin took turns with the elders playing a game of "Twelve Men Mill." Thomena hadn't played the game, though she knew a bit about it. They were moving different colored stones around a web-like design. Whenever someone lined up three pieces in a row, they were allowed to remove one of their opponent's stones from the board. As she watched, Thamin eventually beat one elder at the game. As the food arrived, he split his time between eating and playing, getting a commanding lead on the second game as well.

Thomena dabbed at her mouth with a washcloth before voicing her support. "You are doing well, Father. You must play this game a lot."

Every villager on the porch burst out in chuckles at her observation. Intrigued, she asked, "What did I say?"

"He always wins," one answered. "I wouldn't ever bet against him."

Another wise man took a seat across from her and elaborated more. "I was the one who taught him this game. Maybe twenty years ago?"

"Not that long ago," Thamin answered, "and I don't always win."

The man waved off the comment. "Close enough, I'd say. He won the first game he played, then he won almost every game since then. Once in a year, he might lose, and every time he does, I think he did so on purpose. His skills are legendary. People here practice all the time to see if they can be victorious someday."

Another man added, "He's a masterful strategist, whether it's 'Twelve Men Mill' or actual warfare. Since none of us wish to challenge his feats on a battlefield, our hopes are reduced to beating him at the game."

"Enough about me," Thamin politely asked to deflect the conversation, "let's resume your earlier subject. You were giving an opinion on bannermen?"

They had hooked Thomena's interest with her father's gaming skills, but one of the village elders apparently loved the earlier conversation enough to not give it up so easily.

The aging villager spoke passionately. "Being a bannerman is considered an honor. Every young lad feels flattered to have the post, but it's the most dangerous place to be on the battlefield. I understand why so many die. Nay weapon except the banner pole, and the enemy focuses on them. That is like asking for suicide."

One townsman interrupted. "Blame the color guard, not the bannermen. It's their job to protect the flag and its bearer."

Thomena didn't want to feel lost in the conversation. She assumed that if she participated, she might even be able to turn the focus back toward her father somehow. Additionally, they were speaking of Honor, one of the tenets of her religion, and she desired to learn more. Her higher-pitched voice cut through the older men's debate.

"What is a bannerman, and why is their position so dangerous yet considered an honor?"

Even as Thomena joined the conversation to find a way to turn it toward her father, Thamin butted into the discussion at that moment to help steer it away from him.

Her father explained. "Bannermen are flag bearers on a battlefield. In the confusing clash of swords and polearms, men try to rally their line with their flag's position. The armies of Diara try to fight in organized lines, arrows, or circles; but whatever the formation, the flag marks the center of each unit. This makes the banner and its bearer a target for the enemy." Once Thamin finished his statement, he focused on the game as the other men took turns debating.

One of the men jumped in. "That's why it's so dangerous. The banner helps control the flow of battle and the placement of your allies. As such, enemy troops try to capture it if they can, bringing honor to themselves and confusion to their foes. The position carries high honor, but many bannermen don't survive long."

A farmer added, "My cousin got a letter when her son was picked to be a bannerman for a sword group. You could tell he wrote about the promotion with pride, but she treated it like an invitation to his funeral."

The elders' voices continued tossing comments back and forth. "It takes a brave lad to keep his head during the battle, following the commander's orders, and leading his friends into formation. Many brave boys die that way."

"It wasn't much better when they used bannermaidens."

"Poor girls…"

"Why did some noble think that was ever a good idea?"

Curiosity grabbed Thomena's attention once again. Her voice cut through the deeper baritones as she asked, "Bannermaiden? Did a woman carry the flag on a battlefield?"

"Not even a full-grown woman. Girls of marrying age, pretty ones at that!"

The town's Elderman explained. "At some point, a noble got the notion to put a girl as guardian of the banner. Sometimes, they even rode on horseback so that all the armies can see them better. You see, chivalry still has a strong grip all over Diara. Nay army wanted to target a girl or hit her by accident. On the other hand, many young lads from her army would risk anything to protect her and catch her notice."

Another voice picked up the description. "The company flags still marked the most dangerous area of the field. The fighting around each was fierce, and enemies wanted to capture the banner and the girl. However, nay knight would risk unnecessary harm to the bannermaiden."

"Few lords were willing to order an archery barrage with a girl sitting high and pretty in the middle of it."

"Some kingdoms even used such girls to seal agreements after the battle. Some of the post-battle negotiations included their hand in marriage."

Thomena had studied and admired women adventurers. Yet, her eyes widened in horror at the idea of a girl her age riding at the center of a battle. "Did you say they stopped this custom?"

A few of the men began to answer at once, but the Elderman loudly cleared his throat and slashed his hand downward. The others went quiet. It seemed like there might be a right way and a wrong way to answer her question, and the wise man intended to craft a statement to his liking. He spoke in a somber tone. His head tilted downward, eyes to the table. It was as if the burden of a tragic memory weighed on his thoughts. "The custom ended here in Kaigal's lands. After many years and countless events in which beautiful, young maidens met violent fates, the last bannermaiden fell. She didn't die...thank the gods...but her sad fate traveled the breadth of Diara and prompted change. Lords and commoners alike protested the convention and it was abolished. I will not repeat her story for young ears. Know this: never again will our armies put a defenseless young girl in the midst of such violence. A woman soldier is a different thing, if she so chooses, but we won't force young, innocent girls near such slaughter. In Kaigal, it was one of the events that eventually triggered our revolution against nobility, stirring the changes that formed our current council."

A solidly built, middle-aged woman, who had been lingering at the edges of the conversation, forced her way past some of the men with a "Tsk, tsk" as the only announcement to her presence. Arriving at the game table, she planted her feet and raised her voice.

"That's quite enough of such subjects around young ears! This innocent maiden and nay less than a dozen youths are standing slack-jawed and knees quivering from all this scary talk."

She turned to face the young kids who stood within earshot of the trading post. "Now, back to the school with you all. Finish your counting assignment and be done with it by the time I check on you again."

Thomena watched the kids bolt for the schoolhouse, kicking up dust as they ran. When she turned back, she met the woman's gaze. The older lady had transformed from sour to sweet, offering her a broad smile.

In a motherly voice, she asked, "Come now, girl. You and our favorite scout will need some decent food for the road. Knowing the Trollsbane, you'll be spending the night under the stars, won't you?" Confused at the sudden shift in tone, but sensing a good heart in this woman, Thomena nodded. "Well then, let's get you some! I'm Maridel, and I cook in the trading post. Let's find you some decent food for travel and leave these old codgers alone to play their games."

Thomena tried not to be irked at being treated like a youngster. After all, taking pride in her maturity and risky travel went against her tenet of Humility. Plus, the woman had a sound idea.

Maridel ushered Thomena into the trading post and began to pack some rations. Most of their polite discussion centered on the food and the surrounding lands. Some of Maridel's questions turned towards Thomena's travels and where she was staying. The young mage got the notion that maybe the woman inquired in order to set her up with a local boy. Thomena redirected that conversation by trying to pay for the meal. The woman insisted that Thamin's protection earned everything, but Thomena's Codex ethics forced her to put on a strong fight. She ended up having to admit defeat to the other woman and could only offer a thanks in return. At least, Thomena thought, the underlying subject of the earlier chat had been forgotten.

Thomena listened to Maridel's parting advice as they left the trading post and headed towards the school. Maridel said, "I have to check the children's schoolwork. If I miss you leaving, then I hope you'll stop by and visit again soon. Next time, stay the night and join the women here for a proper conversation."

"Thank you," she said, hefting the bag of food higher, "for everything. Oh, my father said the schoolhouse was built only four years ago. It looks large compared to some of the other buildings in town. That must have taken a lot of work."

"Oh, indeed it did. We had to cart extra wood from neighboring villages and the stone foundation blocks from Kaigal. Men from nearby communities sweat over building it for weeks. They all carved their initials along the base."

Thomena shifted the straps of the food bag to one arm. She looked down at the letters as they walked along the side of the building. Most were carved into the wooden frame, just above the hard stone forming the foundation. *The Codex* often lectured against pride, but sometimes it seemed like a good thing. She imagined the pride and joy the team of workers must have felt when carving their marks after bringing a hall of learning to this frontier land. As she smiled, she ran across a solitary letter. Unlike the others carved into the wood, this lone emblem had been boldly carved into the stone itself.

"T"

Thomena's brow lowered and she stumbled a step. Maridel noticed the pause and asked, "Are you well?"

Her mouth suddenly went dry. It took a quick lick of the lips before she could utter, "Did my father help build this school?"

"Aye, he did. Oh, that's his mark. He's the only worker whose weapon could cut his initial into the stone."

Thomena stood still, staring at the lone letter. "I see," she barely mumbled.

She could hear the children's laughter inside the building…the building of learning that *he* helped build. Out here. Out near home. A sudden hot feeling welled up inside her. Thomena felt like she needed more air, and her hands twitched in nervousness.

"Are you well?" Maridel asked, concern in her voice.

Thomena gave a slight jump, having forgotten about the woman. The young mage needed to keep her hands busy, so she loosened her collar a bit. Hopefully, that would help with getting air and warding off the sudden warm feeling.

"Just thinking." Thomena's words were rushed, clipped. "I will be okay. Thank you."

The older woman didn't look convinced, but she offered a nod as she departed. "Well. If you need anything, I'll be right in here." Maridel disappeared around the corner.

Once the villager was out of sight, Thomena gasped in a deep breath. She folded her arms firmly across her chest, keeping them occupied and giving herself some needed support. She stared at the T and seemed to feel it staring back at her. It wasn't just the letter but the whole legacy her father had accumulated. The scout. The ranger. The school builder. The Trollsbane. Everyone out here seemed to know him better than she did, and those who didn't know him personally reacted out of fear or respect.

An added thorn dug into her thoughts as she stood rigidly facing the school. When Maridel had just asked her if she was okay, she nearly lied outright that she was. Thomena barely deflected her words into the hope that she would be fine. She valued *The Codex* tenet of Honesty above all else, but she had nearly lied. How could the conviction of her values be so feeble in that moment?

Thomena realized she had been biting rather painfully on her lip as her thoughts ran circles. She felt the need to move elsewhere. Thamin still sat with the elders at the trading post. She dared not enter that crowd with her feelings in such a state of fluctuation. Nor did she need any more supplies. Instead, Thomena walked down the path to the east edge of the village. She tied the straps of the ration bag around her belt. Her father would likely be wanting to leave soon to continue their route. Maybe she could hurry the process. At the very least, she could be alone with her thoughts.

She didn't really mark the time it took before hearing his steps approach.

"So eager to leave?" Thamin asked, but she didn't turn to face him. He might end up seeing the redness in her eyes.

He spoke again. "I had hoped that we might play a game before leaving. I thought it might be fun."

Earlier, she would have enjoyed spending some time playing a game with him. How long had it been since they'd played a game together? Five years? She'd already spent the last several days, even years, waiting to play a game with him. However, in this moment, she felt raw, hurtful emotions swirling and boiling just under her skin.

She snapped, "Not today. Sounds like I will need a lot of practice." Thomena left her last thought unspoken. *Besides, it sounds like you always win.*

Thomena put one foot in front of the other without further words.

Chapter 14 - Outburst

The last two hours of their day's hike went considerably different than their initial journey to Veldale. Thamin began to open to her more and ask questions. In contrast, Thomena's conversation dropped to mumblings and clipped answers—when she bothered to speak at all.

Thomena didn't think he would notice. His attention remained everywhere at once; sometimes, he slowed down as he scanned spots on the horizon. He even sidestepped open parts of the road while studying tracks. Thamin tried to convey his considerable knowledge of trails and danger signs to her, but she couldn't focus on his words. It was easier to just nod, shrug, or utter two-syllable hums.

The girl's tones and postures were practically shouting her reluctance. He must know that something was up. Though Thamin continued chatting as they had before, she couldn't reciprocate the conversation. Surely, he noticed her change. When would he ask her about it?

"We'll find a spot off the road. It will be reasonably close to a water source yet offer us enough cover to shelter from unkind eyes." Thamin waved his hand around the horizon. "There are enough groupings of trees around…we should be able to find a spot with a decent supply of wood."

Her father's words were lost in the background. Thomena's thoughts swirled down uncertain trails and shaky foundations. Her imagination became like a demon that led her on a narrow path past pits of bad assumptions.

She barely listened to her father as he found a bush of edible berries and helped her recognize its leaves and colors. She added the berries to a pouch for a nighttime snack, but in doing so, her arms moved as mechanically as a controlled golem. Thomena even tasted one at her father's prompting, offering a non-committal grunt when asked her opinion on the flavor. In truth, after only a few minutes had gone by, she'd already forgotten the taste.

She heard Thamin speak of reading the clouds and temperature changes to determine if it might rain overnight. His arm motions drew her gaze to the sky. Instead of seeing the clouds, her mind conjured images of her forgotten mother. Thomena's memory offered only a vague picture of what her mother looked like. She wondered how things might have been different if Jaena had survived to raise her only child. Would she have been raised in Kaigal? Attended a school there? Grown up without any magic at all or taught personally by her mother? Her daydreams distracted her from reality for a time.

When her father picked out a campsite for the evening, he tried to use the occasion to teach her more lessons. He asked what was good about the site? What was bad? How did it rate in terms of possible food, water, or defensibility? Thomena mumbled answers, too distracted by thoughts of a children's school with a **T** carved into the foundation.

The campsite Thamin chose involved a ring of trees on a small rise. There was evidence of the place being used as a camp in the past. A dip in one end had been carved out by humanoids. Some logs and branches formed a small shelter that stretched over the dip—a wide enough cover that a few people could huddle without exposing themselves to any rain. Blackened wood and ash marked a fire ring.

They'd no sooner set their packs down when Thamin finally asked her, "You've been so quiet since the village. Is something wrong?"

Thomena chewed at her lip, staring down at her equipment pile. "I...need to relieve myself."

Thamin pointed to the opposite end of the tree ring, at a spot where a large tree had fallen. Thomena headed that way, inwardly berating herself for her feelings. She found some privacy within the fallen branches, as well as forks in the limbs, which provided good places to sit or squat. Once done, she paused to have a heart-to-heart with herself before going back. Her words formed bare whispers as they drifted up from her core.

"I need to gather up my Courage and face him. I need some kind of answers to help me understand the distance set between us as I grew up. What was that passage?" She closed her eyes for a moment, searching for the words from *The Codex*. "'It can take more courage to face down one's greatest ally, than it takes for one's greatest enemy.' That's how I feel right now. Though I don't know why I value Honesty so highly, I can feel the effects. Even the act of leaving something unspoken is akin to an open wound that begs for attention."

She stood, taking extra time for her trembling hands to fidget with her attire. Thomena continued to whisper her words. "You know he's a good man. He didn't lie about his wanting to protect people, I can tell. He exhibits Bravery, Compassion, Honor, and maybe too strong a sense of Sacrifice. Maybe that's why it's hard to reprimand him or relay my concerns. He stands behind everyone else—everyone but me." She delayed for the length of one deep breath before returning to her father's side.

He'd already managed to add to the shelter. His first tarp stretched across part of the shelter's roof, offering added rain protection. A second tarp stretched out on the ground. Thamin began clearing some wind-blown debris out of the firepit.

"We can risk a small fire before it gets too late. I have some meat strips we can seer over some skewers," he said before glancing up at her. "Interrupt me anytime. I know you have something restless in your thoughts."

He could see right through her, yet Thomena still regarded him as a mystery. His expressions on the road had remained muted. Did he fear something was watching him all the time? Did the man ever really let his guard down? Thomena's thoughts invoked images of the building full of ownerless cots. Could Thomena open up if that had been her past?

She sat on a convenient stump on the opposite side of his preparations. Thomena couldn't directly say what she wanted, so she decided to approach their separation from a subtle angle.

"You don't seem to mind living on your own or facing the wilderness by yourself. Have you ever spent much time in the big cities? Kaigal? Orlaun?"

He probably knew she was dancing around the subject. "I've spent some time in Orlaun visiting you, and I would have been willing to settle in Kaigal with Jaena. I've also traveled to other cities across Diara for one reason or another. Those great cities hold nay attraction to me. Aside from the pressing crowds, people in those cities have...lost something about themselves. I guess that, maybe due to Yurtash's gifts, I've always favored a more primal lifestyle. The call of nature challenges and welcomes me more than civilization. I thrive in the wilderness."

Thomena's eyebrows crinkled. "So, why did you send me to a big city to learn? Was that Jaena's influence?"

"You could say that," he answered, his hands moving with long-practiced ease to build the pyramid of the campfire. "As much as I thrived in the wild, it's not for everyone. Jaena was hoping to give you a similar education like what she had, and maybe you'd show an affinity for learned magic."

"There wasn't any place closer to home?"

Thamin mulled it over for a moment. "I suppose there was but not very renowned, nor very safe for that matter. Also, if I'd sent you to any of the other city-states in Diara, there's always shifting politics and wars that put them at odds. It was possible that one day you might be in an enemy's city. I settled on Orlaun because those guilds were the most reputable, and the city is tougher than just about anyone else. Jaena had made more than one comment about traveling to explore their libraries."

"And grandfather was willing to come? I'm thankful for his guidance and presence, but how much of it was his choice?" Thomena asked.

He nodded. "Gregros spent his career as a soldier out here; he desired some 'softer' living. It sounds like he's done well for himself there. He said he'd be happy to watch over you."

She caught herself chewing her lip again. She ceased as she asked one of her deepest questions. "Why didn't you follow us out there? You could have watched over me yourself."

Thamin whispered a word, creating a spark of flames at his fingertips. The tinder at the base of the stick pile caught fire. Thomena recognized it as natura magic. It couldn't be learned or taught; people were born with the primal ability to draw it forth. Others had to learn arcane sciences just as she had done. In Thamin's case, the god Yurtash had granted him the ability in his youth, whether he wanted it or not, and it set his destiny as a man of nature.

"I did watch over you. I visited as often as I could during the years. Your masters exchanged letters with me and kept me updated on your progress. My father kept in touch."

It wasn't the answer she wanted. Thomena didn't think Thamin had intentionally neglected her, but he didn't realize how much she needed him for those years. "A sea separated us. What kept you over here?"

Thamin looked at her over the rising flames. His inquisitive gaze landed more intently than she saw in most people. "This is home. It's a home plagued with restless armies, ambitious nobles, savage monsters, and dungeons filled with evil secrets. Yet, it's still home. I was part of a company of brave souls that defended Kaigal's independence against threat after threat. I became good at it, and eventually I was the one in charge. I've been fighting to..."

"To make this a better home, so you said!" Thomena's retort hit more sharply than she'd intended, partially pressured by emotions she felt boiling inside of her. "Why couldn't Orlaun become home?"

He shook his head. "A big city like that has nay use for me."

"What about my needs?" Thomena closed her eyes and put a hand to her head. She didn't want to come across as selfish, but she didn't know any other way to get her point across. "You built a school. Here. In Diara. How many schools have you built?"

Thamin held up two fingers.

"Two? Two! I suppose neither of the schools you built were good enough to teach me?"

"Neither would have taught magic..."

"That's beside the point!" She paced and huffed a couple times, trying to get better control over her feelings. Her fingers fidgeted. "Those kids in Veldale probably know you better than I do. You built them a school and it sounded like they looked at you as a kind of father figure."

Thamin didn't give a response. He couldn't even meet her eyes.

Thomena's eyes began turning red and she angrily wiped away tears. "I guess galivanting across the countryside with your friends and risking your life against monsters had more appeal than raising your only child? How often did you miss me?"

She began to throw words hot and fast at him, barely taking a breath. "You weren't there when I first started lacing my shoes. The first day I was supposed to learn at the wizard guild, I ran home to Gregros in tears because I was scared to be alone. Where were you when someone made me daily meals? Where were you when I first got up on a horse?"

She saw that every question stabbed him like a dagger. He winced and brooded over the fire. When she took the briefest of pauses to breathe, he started to reply. "Grandfather was there to..."

"He isn't you! Bless him for helping me through life, but that should have been you. Other kids had a parent greeting them and asking about their day. I did not. I watched families stroll in Orlaun's parks, while I studied alone. Where was your guidance? Your interest in me? Your encouraging words?"

She continued ranting, tears coursing down her cheeks. She'd worked so hard to contain the flood gates of emotions, but now they broke forth and ran unchecked. "Where were you whenever I had nightmares and needed comfort? Where were you when I was teased and didn't have anyone to talk to? Why weren't you ever there to dry my eyes when I cried? Where were you whenever I was sick? Where were you to teach me about camping when I was younger? When would you have taught me about the wilderness if I hadn't tracked you down in Diara? Where were you when I became a woman and Grandfather went red in the face trying to calm me down and explain it? Where were you when I passed my mage tests and I wanted you to attend and congratulate me? Why weren't you there to comfort me when Pommery died?"

Thomena hyperventilated. A part of her felt guilty about lashing into her father like this. But a bigger part felt he deserved it. These questions had been a thorn under her skin over the course of her life. Thomena didn't realize how much pain she'd buried and ignored. She had to let it all out. Exhaustion settled over her after she'd unleashed the floodgates of hurt and resentment. Her voice raised in pitch and lost strength as she continued.

"I have nay memories of my mother and few enough memories of you. What did I do to deserve that? Did you even want me? Was I anything to you?"

Thomena bit off any more comments. She knew her last questions had gone too far. She felt a pang of guilt at everything she'd said...but all the pain of her argument felt true, and she couldn't take it back. Thomena tried to calm her breathing. He deserved a chance to answer her anger. She cleared her eyes long enough to focus on Thamin and judge his reaction. This strong warrior of a man, the local legend, hung his head in defeat. He seemed to age during her words, or maybe it was the light of the fire. His shoulders drooped, his hands wrung uselessly, and some tears escaped his eyes. The stoic man she'd known had been crushed. It hadn't been trolls that crushed him. Nor had it been the loss of his friends. Words, *her* words, had knocked him down.

Thamin took a long moment before a few heavy words were offered.

"I'm sorry. For everything I failed at. I guess I wasn't a good father, and you deserved better."

Thomena stood silently, hands clenching and unclenching at her side. She wanted more. She *needed* more. One exasperated breath followed another, and nothing else was said. He couldn't meet her gaze, nor did he offer anymore words. Thomena would find no answers or explanations tonight.

She turned to her bedroll and threw herself into it, restlessly tossing, stopping occasionally to wipe at her eyes. Thomena faced away from him and hugged herself, trying to minimize her shaking body. Subdued sobbing eventually gave way to a fitful sleep.

***

Thomena opened her eyes and saw orange shades of light in the clouds. A new day dawned. Memories of the previous evening rushed back to her mind. She questioned what to do next. She quickly decided that she'd said her part and would try to be patient for an answer. She hadn't meant to unload so much of her past on him in one torrent of words. Once she had started, she just couldn't stop.

She took a deep breath.

You've said everything there is to say, she told herself, *it's up to him to find an answer.*

Thomena rolled over and glanced at Thamin. He sat near the dying fire. She knew he could see her rise in the corner of his vision, but he didn't look her way. He didn't say anything as she packed her blankets and gear.

"Stop. Don't move."

The abruptness of Thamin breaking the silence, as well as the urgent message, left her frozen in place. Her eyes glanced over at him as he stood up. Thamin's gaze darted back and forth, sniffing the air.

He suddenly bolted out of the camp's enclosure of branches. Thomena watched as he made haste to get to the top lip of the hill. Belatedly, she drew out her lightning wand.

A moment later, he came running back. Thamin spoke in a rush. "I'm sorry I don't have time to answer last night's questions. We have to move, now."

Thomena rushed to pack the remainder of her gear and sling it across her shoulder. All sorts of worries danced in her head, but she forced herself to breathe calm and easy. Once ready, she followed Thamin back up the hill. Atop the highest point, he pointed westward, and she followed his finger.

A plume of smoke rose on the horizon. It was difficult for Thomena to judge the distance. An old fear settled in her gut, reminiscent of her time helping Orlaun's firefighters. It wasn't until Thamin spoke that the full realization hit her.

He said, "Veldale is burning."

Chapter 15 – Tracking Prey

Thomena did her best to match Thamin's strides as they ran back along the trail. His pace went by evenly, seemingly relaxed despite the distance they were covering. She faltered often at first. She'd never run so far and so hard in her life. Her lack of endurance delayed him, but he slowed his strides so that she could keep up. Thomena hadn't thought that the smoke was so far away, but every time she could see it, it never appeared to be getting close enough, fast enough. She had been so distracted during their evening walk that she hadn't paid much attention to the distance. It took more than an hour of jogging to reach the edge of the hamlet's fields.

Some of the surrounding farmhouses were burning; some were untouched. The main source of the smoke belched from the center of the hamlet. The remains of the trading post, elderman's house, and the watchtower barely extended more than a few feet off the ground. Fires still devoured the collapsed walls and roofs. The postmill had lost two of its four fan blades, and the inside mill mechanism was exposed through the burning gaps in the sides. Thomena's heart skipped a beat when she saw the school. There was little left above the stone foundation.

Neither of them could see any movement in the village, nor could they hear anything except the sounds of the fires. No one still fought; no survivors walked around; no one worked to extinguish the fires.

Father and daughter entered the outskirts. Some of the acrid smoke began to get into their lungs. Thomena reached out and grabbed his arm. "Wait, Father. Let me use a spell to help us search."

Thomena began shielding them with Rylak's Bubble. A mix of water and air elements formed a soft "bubble" of air around their heads. "It won't provide breathable air, but it will keep out toxins and ash."

She began casting another spell on herself. Thomena's ice shield made it look like she was covered in frost, but it would keep her cool near the flames. When working with the firefighting vigiles of Orlaun, she'd been able to use a wand to cast this spell on others. The wand was returned to the guild, leaving her with only a self-cast version. Thomena had originally used a wand for Rylak's Bubble, but she had only needed it to cast more efficiently, since she'd already known the spell.

Thamin nodded his appreciation. "Useful. Thank you."

The two of them resumed walking into the town center. They couldn't see any threats, but they did find a lot of bodies. A few dead lizardmen lay in the streets. Veldale did have a small garrison of men to defend the village, but it was not enough. The majority of corpses were human.

The scene began to overwhelm Thomena. She'd seen death before when Old Market burned. A new friend, Pommery, had died, despite her efforts to save as many as she could. These streets looked much worse. People lay where they had died. In some cases, whole families lay near each other. A few body parts were strewn about, and some corpses were burning. The stench in the air made her sick.

Thomena ran for the edge of the village. She barely had the time to disappear the bubble around her head before throwing herself to her hands and knees. The nausea caused her to empty her stomach. She retched for a couple minutes, unable to help herself or rid her mind of the images. Even when her body stopped rebelling, she knelt and stared into the field. It looked peaceful enough, and it distracted her mind. But the view wasn't free of all distractions; the school still smoldered at the edge of her vision. A school her father built...now gone with the rest of the hamlet. What about the children? Thomena knew the answer in her heart. Hopefully, some had escaped. She could also hear Thamin calling out several times for survivors, but no one answered.

It took several long minutes to muster the courage to look back at her father. Her eyes were blurred with tears. Somehow, Thamin held back his own tears. She saw him looking grim as ever, a steel set to his jaw, as he studied tracks in the ground. It seemed they were too late to help any survivors. Thamin's ranger abilities kicked in, trying to find clues in the environment to piece together that attack. Thomena restored another bubble around her head to fight off the smoke then walked over to his side. She could see Thamin was sweating. Thanks to her ice shield, the heat of the flames didn't bother her.

As they searched, Thomena used her magic to spray water over some of the flames, allowing them to peek into a few buildings that might still hide someone. They found no survivors. Thamin's search led to the outskirts of town. He checked for tracks to figure where someone had gone in or out of the village.

At long last, he stopped and just stared across a field. "Some escaped. A few families ran with their little ones while the garrison and some other men, including the old men I played games with, bought time with their lives."

Thomena watched his facial expression. His face remained stoic, perhaps grim, but only the heat in his words gave evidence of the emotions under his façade. She realized that her father's expressions often masked his deeper feelings. The tone of his voice when he spoke was the only indication of the deep hurt he felt within. Thomena couldn't hide her emotions near as well. Many tears had already streaked her cheeks and her stomach couldn't settle.

Thomena said, "I can't believe all this death and whatever hate lay behind it. How can such cruelty exist? Will there ever be justice done for this act?"

Thamin put up a hand, motioning for Thomena to stop and face him. His stern gaze kept her eyes locked on his.

"This. This is the answer I couldn't utter to you last night."

Thomena only managed to break eye contact for a moment, glancing back at the burning village. As soon as she turned to face him, she was once again trapped by his stare. "What? A burning village?"

Thamin took a deep breath. "Maybe I sent you away out of fear, for my lack of fatherly abilities, or the danger I involve myself in. However, this is also part of the reason why I couldn't raise you here. This is the second time this village—and this school—were burned to the ground. I didn't just build two schoolhouses; I built the same school twice to replace the remnants of the former one."

Thomena's jaw dropped in shock, but Thamin didn't slow down his explanation. She could tell he was having trouble staying calm. Palpable anger lurked just under the surface.

"People here are pioneers, living on the edge of the freedoms and opportunities Kaigal offers, but living at greater risk due to the dangerous races living in the hills and the jungle."

He looked down at the ground. "I didn't want to raise you in a place so dangerous as this. Out here, schools burn down, hamlets catch fire, and trolls play with their food."

Thomena's eyebrows rose. She chanced another glance at their surroundings. "Trolls?"

Thamin gestured at the massacre around them. "There were trolls here, alongside the lizardmen. It's not unknown." He paused momentarily. "Maybe I should have gone with you to Orlaun, but at the time, I was needed for Kaigal's safety. I didn't honestly see the long-term effects of our separation. You were somewhere safe, following your mother's footsteps, and I worked hard to keep evil away from our home. This has always been *our* home, if only from my perspective. I endangered friends and myself on many occasions trying to drive evil from these lands. I didn't stop to reflect how you would view that distance between us."

Thamin looked ready to say more, but he stopped. The veteran warrior stared across a trampled field. Thomena reexamined his reasons. He tried to protect her in the only way he knew how. She finally felt that she had more of an explanation, even if she couldn't truly understand it.

She tenderly put one hand on his shoulder but stayed a step behind so as to offer him a bit of privacy. "You sent me to a good school. I appreciate that. As for yourself, you were part of the army? You couldn't just leave?"

"I probably could but I didn't. I was with the best team of people you could ever be blessed to join. We stopped armies from moving against these people. We delved dungeons to excise the nests of fermenting evil. We discovered relics from the Godswars and delivered them to safe places for study, where they wouldn't be misused."

He reached out for her hand. She accepted it. Thamin closed his eyes. "Days like this...it feels like what we did never really mattered. There's always more evil arising in the world. The Wolves who survived have followed their own hearts to different places. I'm sorry I couldn't make this world better, and instead I've been away from you for too long."

When he opened his eyes again, Thomena saw the moisture welling up in them. His tears were a rare sight. He patted her hand and let it go.

"I'll make you this promise." A swallow interrupted his message, but there was a fresh look of steel to his jawline. "You are my most important thing from here to the next world. When we report back to Bael Cochaw, I'll resign my post."

Thomena couldn't help but be surprised. "What next? Where to?"

He shrugged. "You're the one on a journey of study. I can think of a few libraries across Diara that might have knowledge not common in Orlaun. I can suggest some destinations for you to consider. It's *your* journey, but I'll tag along and help."

A wave of relief coursed through Thomena. It was a desire come true. She could explore magic, and the world's mysteries, and rescue her father from this wild, deadly land. Amidst the haunting sights and odors of the village, it didn't seem appropriate to give herself over to any joy. She acknowledged his plan quite simply, stating, "That sounds good."

He stuck a pointer finger in the air. "There is one last thing to be done. I can't turn my back on it."

"What's that?"

Thamin turned her to face the burning hamlet. He gestured to the massacre. "The tracks of the lizards lead back toward the jungle. They've sated themselves on the killing and are returning home." He turned his head south, pointing into a field that had been heavily disturbed by tracks. "But they had half a dozen trolls with them. Lizardmen may be bad enough, but trolls possess more appetite, a willingness to torture their food, and a love of violence. These trolls turned south, heading deeper into human lands."

Any relief Thomena had felt reversed back to stress. "Aren't trolls..." She had to pause and remember her conversation with Mabry. She also had to remind herself that Diara measured by feet and yards, not meters. "...twice your height?"

Thamin took one last look back at the village. The smoke still climbed high into the sky. He made a motion with his arm. Thomena recognized it as a gesture of Yurtash to anything recently departed. The message translated to, "May your spirit fly free."

Thamin turned his body toward the southern tracks and gave a delayed nod to Thomena's observation. "Aye. Almost twice my height, tough skin, long reach. Hasn't stopped me from killing them before. You just asked if justice will be done for this act. Out here, justice is *my* job."

The Trollsbane began tracking his prey.

***

They located the trolls during the late afternoon hours. The trolls had settled down in a dell, next to a wooded pond. Thamin had educated his daughter about trolls as they tracked. Trolls preferred to move during the night, especially this deep into human lands. Their night vision was superior. It appeared as if this group had decided on a rest in this spot while awaiting nightfall. It was Thamin's raptor-like vision, one of his natura spell abilities, that allowed him to spot the trolls before the pair had stumbled into the group's awareness.

Father and daughter then spent the next thirty minutes crawling through the tall grass, angling toward another clump of woods that was within a decent bowshot of the trolls. Thomena felt itchy and tried not to get disturbed by the bugs and spiky grasses tormenting her. She'd never crawled around in the wild like this before. She couldn't match Thamin's stealth or ease of movement, but the presence of several intimidating trolls in the vicinity gave her proper incentive. It didn't take long for burrs and dried leaves to sprinkle her attire. They were soon sitting behind a fallen log, looking down on the camp.

"I can see the fear in your eyes," Thamin said, speaking low enough so as not to let his voice carry to the other camp. "It is my highest goal to keep you as safe as possible during this fight. I can handle a few trolls at once, and I can cut down their numbers before they can even run within reach of us. I know you must have ways to defend yourself, and you have that lightning wand at your belt. Tell me about your abilities. I need to know every spell that you can use to offer us an advantage."

Thomena had only been tested in battle once, but that was through the eyes of a water elemental. She hadn't really been in much peril until an unlucky set of events hurdled her into danger. By that time, she managed to out-talk her foe, not fight him.

She began listing her abilities. Many of her spells were basic ones that offered minor influence over water and air. She had a few which she assumed would be more helpful. "I can freeze a section of ground, making it slippery. For defense, I can cast a semi-circular ice wall around me, with large ice spikes pointing outward. The wall is only waist-high to me, but the spikes project upward as well as out."

She paused to get her father's reaction. He replied, "That might be too low to slow a troll, but if he slid across ice into it, that will do more. Please, continue. I'd like to get a complete plan."

"For personal defense, especially against a big threat, I might harden my skin rather than use the ice shield. It's an earth-based spell that will toughen me like I'm wearing armor. At the same time, I can summon a thick layer of air to cushion any hits coming at my body. I can throw sharp icicle spears into opponents or use my lightning wand to augment my electrical attacks. The latter would hit harder and be more efficient to my mental reserves, thanks to the wand. I can also bolster my own strength. It's impressive against a human, but I've nay comparison to a troll."

Thamin shook his head. "It would be good to have it on you, but you can't risk getting close to a troll, even with a strength spell. If a troll is trying to bash you, the most important thing is to get out of the way." The ranger cocked his head. "Do you have any fire spells?"

Chewing her lip, she began to fidget. "I do. I don't like to use it."

"Why is that?"

Thomena, still keeping her head and voice down due to the trolls in the distance, pointed out at the grasslands. "I don't wish to start a fire. The spell allows me to direct a concentrated stream of fire, but once it ignites something, it is out of my control."

Thamin nodded and put a comforting hand over her own. "Do you know why trolls have such a tough reputation, aside from their size?" Thomena shook her head, so Thamin continued. "Their blood vessels are quick to seal leaks if you cut them. Trolls don't bleed to death. They can withstand a stab or cut to a major organ and keep fighting."

The ranger drew his two swords and laid them on the ground. "However, there is a balance in all things. A troll's anatomy reacts badly to fire. Maybe it's some oils inside their body, but flames eat them alive. In fact, the only time I see a troll bleed is when it's on fire. It is as if their tissue is repelled by the heat, and wounds open back up."

He began chanting a natura spell over his weapons. Thomena saw orange and red glyphs appear along the length of Longclaw and the swordbreaker. Tendrils of smoke curled around the steel edges.

Still whispering, she asked, "Are those some type of fire runes?"

Thamin nodded as he returned his blades to his scabbards. He set down his yew bow and began to enchant it the same way. Orange and red glyphs appeared over the markings already etched into the wood. "Your lightning will be effective, but fire is the top weapon against a troll."

She saw him glance down at the lounging trolls. Thomena followed his gaze, her own thoughts in a scramble. *The Codex* pushed for Bravery and Valor, but these odds seemed too great. She would be frightened enough to face one ten-foot creature that didn't bleed. Thomena and her father would be facing six.

Maybe it was the fact she was chewing her lip again, or that her clenched hands were still trembling, but Thamin reached out and put a calming hand over hers. "What are you thinking?"

Honesty. She always gave an honest answer. "I'm thinking this is too much for us to face. Maybe we should get ahead of them and warn someone, or grab reinforcements from the castle?"

He looked her up and down. His reassuring hands still held hers in his grasp. "That could be a fine strategy. Except it would also chance getting other people killed. I can't be certain that I can return with help and track down these trolls again before they find more victims." He took a deep, steadying breath. "I'm not afraid of six trolls at once, especially if I can catch them by surprise. I only worry for you. If you prefer, I can wait until you've snuck back to those trees back there, and I'll find you when I'm done. I expect from the news I've received that you're a gifted wizard. I think this is a challenge you're capable of meeting. However, battles are never predictable, and if you have doubts, I'd rather you seek safety."

Thomena shot a look at the trees he mentioned. It sounded safe. Yet, she couldn't just abandon her father after finally meeting up with him again. If he felt he could face down this foe, then so could she. *The Codex* promoted Bravery, Justice, Courage; therefore, she would do her best to live up to those expectations.

In answer to her father's concern, she began casting spells to bolster her for the battle. Thomena cast the earth-based spells that hardened her body and lent her unnatural strength. She tried not to worry over the fact that her best spells, which utilized wind and water, were the least likely to help her in this situation. Her hand passed over the wand at her belt. At least the wand would allow her to efficiently throw several lightning bolts without overtaxing her mental energy.

"What is your plan?" she asked.

Thamin raised his bow slightly. Thomena got a second good look at the temporary runes his magic had just branded into it. Although she didn't understand natura magic, she realized they were the same fire-based ones he had on his swords.

"I'll be able to drop one from here with this. I'm going to have you stay behind me maybe twenty yards. I should hopefully be able to stop two with my bow before they reach me. After that, they're attention will be on me. I'll be able to slow down their movement. That's when you'll attack, hitting their backs with lightning or fire when they aren't looking. But stay low and hide as you do so. I want their attention on me. And don't overly worry about any stray fire. Especially since you have water abilities to help quench problems. Fire is part of the circle of death and regrowth even in nature."

Thomena pointed at the open area. "When they charge across that grass at us, I can use my lightning. Maybe then we'll have only three instead of four."

Thamin shook his head. "Your lightning will draw them straight to you. How well can you dodge three trolls when the grass and bushes around you are clutching at everything? My abilities will allow for the foliage around me to hinder my attackers while leaving me alone, but it won't discern friend from foe. The area affected will mostly be in front of me and won't move once I initiate it."

145

She gave thought to where she would be positioned, several long steps behind her father. "Likewise, I may freeze the ground near me. Enemies will be prone to slip and fall. Will that get in your way?"

"Thank you for the warning, but I should be fine. Set up so that you have an ice field in front of your spike wall."

Thamin looked at her face, judging her emotions. "You always used to have an appropriate phrase from your Codex," he inquired, "Do you have some wisdom to share before the battle?"

Thomena closed her eyes for a minute, sorting through passage after passage to find one she liked. She opened her eyes and recited it. Though she wanted to proclaim its message to the world, she humbled her voice so as not to be overheard by their enemies down the hill.

"Think of the tenets of The Codex as a guiding beacon in a storm.
Light your own spirit to discover your path.
The darkness of the storm will breed lies and deceit in your mind.
Let the Truth of your light illuminate your course and burn away illusions.
The cold of the storm will turn your heart selfish and uncaring.
Let the warm Love of your light create a haven to shelter fellow travelers.
The ferocity of the storm will sap hope and cause you to cower.
Let the Courage of your light rally your heart and overcome your fears.
The bleakness of the storm will make you feel forsaken.
Let the Spirituality of your teachings bolster your hope and faith to endure.
The storm will break, and your light will shine eternal."

Thamin's eyes beheld her with fatherly pride. Only a few times were such emotions so visible on his stoic face.

"That's a good rally. Are you ready?"

Her voice suddenly dry, she nodded. He pointed toward a fallen trunk several paces away before speaking. "Then go hide in your spot. I'm about to kick a troll's nest."

Chapter 16 – The Trollsbane

Thomena had set up every protective spell to survive the upcoming confrontation. Her strength was reinforced, skin hardened, the air around her formed a cushion, and an ice slick made the grass ahead of her slippery. She held her lightning wand ready. Her other hand reflexively checked the pouch containing a replica of a jade gem. She'd already withdrawn a trickle of energy to replace her preparation spells. The item held more reserves of her willpower in case the resulting battle drained her mental stamina. She wanted to erect her spiked ice wall or let loose her wand energy early against the trolls when they charged, but she trusted her father's plan. If even one troll saw and rushed her, she might panic. Her heartbeat pounded in her consciousness, interrupted by every little crunch under her restless boots or brush of contact with nearby plants. She swiveled her satchel of extra items towards her back, out of the way. Thomena had sweat on her that wasn't from the temperature.

The sight of her father...kneeling with his bow upright, holding a statuesque appearance, radiating calm while facing a frightening enemy...it bolstered her confidence. If he could retain some peacefulness in the face of this danger, then she could attempt no less. Deep breath in, slowly release out. She forced calm upon herself as she focused on his every action, while both awaiting and dreading that first shot.

He sensed his moment. She watched the bow rise, eventually coming horizontal at arm's length over his head. He nocked an arrow. Thamin drew arrow and bowstring back as he lowered the bow to aim toward the distant target. Thomena glanced at the trolls' position. She doubted that she could hit one from here with a straight lightning bolt. She prayed under her breath.

Thamin's bow twanged a note as the arrow launched forth. Thomena's breath caught for a moment. There would be no turning back now. The fight of her life lay before her.

Foreign exclamations came from those woods. The voices sounded deep and craggy. Even as they vented their anger and surprise, more red-glowing arrows crossed the open space.

Big and brutish, the five remaining trolls busted out of the other group of trees with enough force to send fragments of branches flying. Their monstrous roars sent a chill of dread down Thomena's back. Their intimidation didn't seem to shake Thamin, as the ranger rapidly shot arrow after arrow into the air in smooth repetition. As such, it was also easy for the trolls to see the source of the attacks. Each monster desired to be the first one to sate his anger on the flesh of the insolent attacker.

Thamin proved he could fire with great accuracy under pressure. He didn't have long before the trolls would traverse the open space; yet, it was enough to land critical strikes on at least one other troll. The arrows, enchanted by the fire runes of Thamin's natura magic, spawned fire in the ribcage and throat of one charging monster. Its limbs became heavy a few steps before it fell face first into the grass. By that time, flames had engulfed the creature's torso and head.

Two other trolls, each hit by a fire arrow, batted angrily at the flames but they continued a healthy rush to the edge of Thamin and Thomena's sheltering trees. Their rage and anger-driven hunger raised their battle roars, causing terror to rush through Thomena.

The moment they hit the trees near Thamin, the trees hit back. The monstrous war cry broke apart in complete disharmony as the trolls defended against nature itself. Thorn bushes whipped around legs, leaving their thorns embedded, even as the strong monsters ripped them from their roots. Thick branches hammered away at their bodies, causing the trolls to retaliate. They wanted to continue pursuit of the nearby human, but they also had to pause and tear limbs from trees to quell the battering. Despite the ferocity of the forest's assault, the strength and endurance of four trolls would have eventually won out.

But amidst the throes of branches and vines, a figure moved unimpeded. Orange-glowing blades whirled and flashed through the tangle, causing light and shadows to dance in the trolls' vision. They howled as they felt cuts more lethal than the briars wrapped around their legs.

One had his back to Thomena, and the rest had certainly been distracted by their situation. She knew it was time to act. Any fear she might have felt before was banished in the realization that her magic was needed to save her father. This would be a true test of her arcane studies.

Hands weaving through the air, she summoned cold air from the wind. A wall of ice and spikes formed, growing higher than her waist and forming a half-circle with her protected in the center. It would shield her front yet leave her room to retreat. Although she barely had time to muse, it was designed with normal-sized humanoids in mind...not giantkin.

The lightning wand had dangled from a leather cord around her wrist and thumb in order for her to cast the first spell. Her hand snapped in a practiced movement, flipping the foot-long wand into her grip. Although her father had explained the weakness trolls suffered with fire, Thomena talked herself out of using fire in the woods right away. She convinced herself that a brief flash of light from the wand would do less to reveal her position than an arc of fire lingering in the air for the space of a long breath.

Thomena felt a moment of apprehension, since she had never used this spell on a living creature, such as the frenzied one thrashing and shattering a tangle of branches. On the other hand, its size offered up a big target.

Her hand twitched in a practiced movement as she said, "Kee-lass!"

A flash of blue light lit up the forest. Her bolt struck true, causing the monster to spasm for a moment while its arms flailed outward. A pained wail from the creature caused one of its companions to stop and stare.

The moment passed too quickly. The troll turned to find its attacker, smoke curling skyward from its oily back. A second troll, within sight but beyond the first, paused to rip free of the suicidal shrubs wrapped around its leg. The first troll would see her soon. Its eyes squinted and pondered the existence of the ice wall. Thomena didn't dare delay her attack. If her father dared to handle so many trolls at once, she had to drop at least one.

"Kee-lass!"

The lethal, bright flash bridged the gap between them again. Thomena's aim faltered on the second bolt. Nevertheless, her lightning tagged it across one arm. The troll spotted her and yelled a challenging roar. The second troll also saw the blast, turning its attention towards Thomena. Her eyes rounded as she saw both enemies face her.

In that moment, she also noticed the impressive length and sharpness of their claws and fangs. Dread nearly shook her.

The second troll's charge failed before it ever truly began. The bright orange glow of a burning blade stabbed through its leg from the other side. Fire erupted along the limb. Thomena couldn't really see her father well. He moved among the trees like a blur, his enchanted blades drawing and misdirecting the eyes as they spun patterns. The monster turned a violent swing to catch the backstabber, but in doing so the weakened leg buckled. It fell, but all of the beast's attention refocused on Thamin's assault. It tried to stand again despite some trees' roots snaring it.

Thomena didn't have the luxury of time to observe her father's fight. The troll she'd wounded reached down and hoisted a large rock. Judging its size, Thomena doubted she could lift it even with her strength spell. Branches lashed at the creature, but it managed to heave the boulder in her direction.

She yelped as she ducked behind her ice wall. The wall cracked as the boulder deflected off to the side. The background noise of shattered icicles, from the forward-facing spikes, could be heard rolling across the ice-slicked field extending from the wall. Crushed ice showered Thomena.

When next she rose, her mind and muscles were prepared to fire the wand again. Thomena didn't want to offer herself as a target any more than was necessary. Coming up in a crouch, she peeked above the wall's edge with the wand pointed. She had to make a small adjustment to her aim. The troll held another boulder with one hand, but its other arm was tearing a branch off an animated tree. The limb wrenched to splinters in such a terrifying display, the girl knew she didn't want any trolls getting within arm's reach of her.

"Kee-lass!"

Her blast hit the troll square in the chest. Light and shadows played across its facial features in a way that was even more horrifying than before. Despite the hit, the monster threw the second boulder at her position.

Thomena crouched low again as the hunk of stone bounced over the wall, shattering more ice spikes and merlons before it continued rolling behind her.

She peeked over the wall, expecting to see the beast on the ground. It wasn't. Smoke poured from its body as it quickly patted out small flames. Thomena saw open scars in its skin, but none bled. She was hoping the wand would ignite it or drop it by now. How much damage could trolls endure?

The thing roared a challenge. The troll then rushed straight at Thomena, snapping a few vines and branches as it moved. Its momentum delivered it from Thamin's animated flora but left it barreling toward her slick ice field. Between its size and long legs, it closed the distance fast.

Eyes wide, Thomena scrambled backward, even as she straightened up. She retreated as fast as she could go, heedless of what might await behind her. Non-animated plants scratched at her arms and whipped across her gaiters. Something solid blocked one leg, toppling her into a backward roll.

Thomena lost her grip on the wand. Even the leather loop slipped past her clutching fingers as her world spun. Once her body settled, she scrambled to raise up on hands and knees.

A high-pitched yell from the troll helped orient her to its approach. Her eyes locked on the source, watching the large creature slide and roll across her ice. Its body impaled itself on a few remaining ice spikes as momentum carried it through the wall, crushed ice exploding out past Thomena's position.

A second hellish troll screech erupted many meters away. It wasn't hard to spot the owner of the sound through the trees. The distant troll had been lit from head to toe, like a bonfire. It faltered in its death throes as the one closer to Thomena tried scrambling upright. She hadn't succeeded in killing it yet, and time would be running out for Thomena.

Lucky for her, she spotted her wand next to her. Propped up on her right arm, she retrieved it with her left. Although she wasn't left-handed, her instructor had the foresight to have her practice movements with both hands in case of moments like this. Thomena raised her left arm and pointed her wand at the thing.

Unfortunately, she was now within the troll's reach. Its green, repugnant arm latched on to her arm, even though the troll was perched on its knees. Thomena resisted its pull with her spell-augmented strength. Her protective spells did little to slow down its crushing grip. An unprotected person would have already had their arm torn off, yet Thomena didn't feel like her spells were assisting her at all.

Thomena's scream filled the air. It had her. She was going to die. She had fleeting thoughts of Julia and her grandfather.

The monster picked up her body one-handed, leaving her dangling from the injured arm. It yanked her up and down twice before cocking its hand back. She gasped for more air. Her right hand ineffectively slapped at her entrapment. The troll pitched her with all its strength, aiming downward to insure she would land nearby.

Her body slammed into the ground several meters away, rolling until she collided with a tree. The impact blasted the air from her lungs despite Thomena's wind and earth spells absorbing the worst of the impact. She gasped several breaths quickly. Her ribs were sore but felt intact. Her arm had suffered the worst damage. Her left elbow had been wrenched into uselessness. Whether or not she had a broken bone, pain inundated her forearm and numbness hid her hand from her senses.

Thomena rolled onto her back, propped up by tree roots as she looked back at the approaching troll. The pain and fear almost paralyzed her, but it also gave a burst of adrenaline that fueled a clarity of mind. Her mistake had been relying too much on her favorite spells. Her father had told her to use fire, but he hadn't fathomed the emotions that weighed on her mind. She had seen the damage fire caused to the city of Orlaun. She'd watched a new friend die from it when she was only thirteen. Thomena had the ability to rescue him, but her efforts came too late. Even though her master trusted her with fire, and she practiced it enough to wield it well, the element's destructive nature sabotaged her willingness to use it.

Even if her lightning wand had somehow stayed in her hand, it had been entirely too ineffective. She needed fire.

The troll approached. This time, it didn't rush. It uttered an odd, repulsive, gurgling sound: laughter. Its laughter sounded like a person gargling fluid in their mouth. The sound unnerved Thomena. The troll easily shouldered a tree aside and ripped away a branch as it stood before her. It bared sharp teeth in a lopsided grin, unbothered by the wounds inflicted by her spells. Its large claws could easily launch out and kill her, yet it delayed its attack while savoring her apparent helplessness.

She remembered her father saying, "...trolls like to play with their food."

Thomena raised one hand as if pleading for it to stop, but she had a purpose in mind. First, she had to muster the concentration for her spell. It wouldn't be easy due to the pain and damage to one arm, as well as the soreness in her ribs. Her heart was also beating fast as she barely held her panic in check.

One last spell before I die. Last chance.

However, she'd had spent her last few years preparing for this. Her classmates had helped teach her to cast spells from the back of a moving, bouncing wagon. She'd had to work spells when a horse had thrown her into a fiery building filled with smoke. In the years since her adventures with the vigiles, she'd taken the effort to cast spells in a number of challenging ways: from her offhand, weights wrapped on her arms, blindfolded, under verbal insults, on the run, or even hanging upside down. Many of these attempts eventually became games of entertainment for her fellow students. For Thomena, she wanted to be able to cast spells under any interference.

Shoving all her distractions away, her mouth and healthy arm worked in conjunction to build the spell. The dull-witted troll failed to realize her intent. It reached for her slowly, out of curiosity. It only learned its mistake when Thomena's hand glowed with flames. Fire sprayed from her hand, bathing the monster's chest and neck, igniting its body oils.

The troll tried to cover up. It raised its muscular arms to shield its face, but the fires only spread across those appendages as well. It shrieked and batted at the flames. The troll twisted and squirmed, bouncing off trees.

Thomena struggled to maintain her concentration. The fire-spray heavily taxed the mental reserves of most young spellcasters. Her hand circled to spread the fire over as much skin as possible before time ran out. She could see the remarkable effects. The troll's skin actually shriveled away from the fire. The troll's earlier spell injuries began to bleed without any ability on its part for the wounds to scab and heal. Flames proved to be the bane of the towering creature. It collapsed into its own funeral pyre.

A brief flash of emotions played with her mind. Among them was relief at survival. That reprieve managed to dim the debilitating pain in her arm. She grappled with the realization of killing her first creature, one that had towered over her. Some part of her faith whispered that it was necessary, and that Justice had been served and Bravery upheld.

But what about her father and the rest of the trolls?

She could still hear the rustling of foliage and the roar of at least one living troll. It would have been better if she could just lay there and catch her breath. Her body needed to recover, and her emotions jumbled disjointedly. Instead, she focused her will and compelled her muscles into action. Thomena used her good hand to pull herself upright, using her legs to slide her back up a tree. Her left arm simply dangled at her side. She sucked in a forceful breath despite her sore ribs, knowing she had to get back into the fight.

A rock, spinning through the air, entered her field of view too late for her to react. It impacted the tree, stripping it of some bark. The deflection wasn't enough to spare her. Its spin still caused it to roll across her chest, driving her recently acquired breath out of her body. Thomena fell backward in a daze, spitting out blood.

She couldn't be sure if any ribs were cracked or broken. Her protective spells had never encountered such brute force. Fear returned as the dominant emotion. Thomena tried to seize another lungful of air as desperation emboldened her to return to her feet. Behind the cover of the tree, she pulled herself up once again as she heard the roaring approach of a new attacker.

I'm going to die! The thought screamed in her head. *I feel like I have nothing left in me.*

Thomena risked a glance around the tree. A troll, the last troll, strode toward her holding a small tree trunk as a club. Torn foliage still clung to it. Still-burning scars crisscrossed its body, likely caused by her father's swords. Fury twisted its purplish lips and pulled the monster's thick eyebrows into a glower. It gave no indication of wanting to waste time playing with this morsel. It stomped directly towards her and raised the club. Thomena, standing on shaky legs, gasped for a new breath as she raised a hand for her spell.

Then the tip of a bright orange sword burst from its chest. Fire erupted from the new wound, leaving the troll screaming in protest. The blade withdrew, only to be replaced by the tip of a different blade puncturing near the creature's grossly distended abdomen. The troll stiffened upright from the blows. The club fell from its grip as it slapped its hands over the new fiery holes.

Thomena couldn't see her father, but she did see the troll backlit by a play of light. The orange trails of fire swept high to low, side to side, several times in fast succession behind its back. Flames quickly rolled over its shoulders and engulfed its head.

The monster sagged to its knees. Another horizontal strike flashed a glowing trail, leaving it headless. The corpse fell over. Behind it, back by the thrashing trees, Thomena could see the funeral pyres of the other trolls. Their burning stench filled her nose. As difficult a task as it was for her to kill one troll unassisted, his tally for the day was five.

When Thomena's eye fixed on the figure that had been behind the troll, it wasn't her father. A wolf, large by the standards of any wolf, stared at her through brown eyes. The girl took a step back, fear crowding out other emotions again, but then she paused as she realized the truth of what stood before her. The wolf's claws extended abnormally long. They glowed with orange flame and looked like singular, foot-long sword points on each forefoot, not wolf claws. Long, brown fur covered the wolf's head and shoulders like a mane, and a braid of it near the top of the head was held in place by Thamin's elvish hair clasp. When Thomena locked eyes with him again, she felt like she could sense human expression in its eyebrows and form.

She held no doubts, only confusion, as she whispered, "Father?"

Once the word passed her shocked lips, his form morphed back into the human shape she'd known.

Chapter 17 – Champions of Yurtash

Ztakish stood upright from a recently erected throne, the movement so fast and intimidating that it silenced the speaker. The goblin had been singing a discordant war song about how his people planned to cook the humans. Behind the goblin, a room filled with various races and war captains went silent and still, awaiting the words from this war-priest they'd come to follow.

"You want to descend on the humans in a giant horde and sweep them in one mighty move?" His voice demanded attention, even as his tone expressed sarcasm of the goblin's plan. "Even I would like that to be possible. My own people have known me for a phrase: 'Respect through mercy is only earned after the foe has been beaten by your superior strength.' I've spoken those words many times to my legions."

The iztheran took a few confidant strides toward the middle of the room. He scowled, though it was lost on the fact that battle scars around his mouth already gave him a constant angry expression. Ztakish's stripes, bright red and gold lines running to his brow on an otherwise mottled green-and-brown scale color, accentuated the displeasure in his eyes. He flexed the ridge scales running down the middle of his back, an aggressive posture. Around the room, orcs, goblins, three trolls, lizardmen (who could not control the inner heat of their reptilian bodies like iztherans), and a host of newly enlightened iztheran (who formerly endured other races referring to them as "lizardmen"), gave space to his presence. Even the jovial goblin became meek and retreated to his kin.

"Some of your former warlords favored the same tactics. Our joined tribes outnumber many human settlements combined. We like to think that we can storm their fields and shatter their walls by the strength of numbers and ferocity."

His tongue flicked outward, smelling traces of fear among some of those gathered. Fear for him? Or nervousness of the coming war? It didn't matter to him. He only wanted their obedience and cooperation. The more assistance he could procure from the jungle humanoids, the better likelihood of preserving the lives of his own resurrected race. His eyes passed over the gathering. His clawed hand slowly swept across the emissaries and warlords that packed the tall, wooden chamber. The structure was only two weeks post-completion, and already it held more bodies than its design intended. Every eye riveted to his movements and words.

"I see the designs and emblems of many gods among you. I remember a time when our gods stood as allies, and we marched to battle in their favor. During that time, one could feel their god's presence as a close companion. I championed Yurtash prior to this 'Covenant,' of which I've heard tales told to me with resentment, fueled with scorn. I know not what bindings Yurtash and your gods endure from this ancient treaty, but I believe I have been called here and now as part of a plan. I am Yurtash's champion now as I was then. I must fulfil a calling."

He allowed a couple breaths for his words to sink into his audience. Even the trolls in the back of the room allowed him more patience than he would normally credit their race.

Ztakish flexed his arms. His scales hugged against well-honed muscles. "Strength and numbers have always been in our favor, but where has it led us? Relying on brute force and head-on attacks may win you a few battles, but our ranks would diminish before theirs." Seeing the confusion on some of their faces reminded the iztheran that they did not have as good a grasp of the most common languages as he did. He simplified his message. "If we lose soldiers faster than they do, we doom ourselves to a fall. We need the humans and elves to stumble blindly into us. We need to draw them out from their walls and defenses before we hit them. As of now, they can only guess at our numbers."

Ztakish walked around as he spoke. He timed his next message while standing among an orc tribe. Amongst their numbers, a half-orc stood prominently to the fore of the rest. "We have spies among them. Let them think the jungle forces are merely restless and mostly unorganized. Let us give them a target that is really a trap. Wait for me to draw them closer to us, and then we surprise them. We can catch their best warriors on an open field, rather than them hiding behind stone walls."

His words won over much of the crowd. A few gave half-hearted arguments about hungry bellies. After all, some of these humanoids had waged fights amongst each other for hunting grounds and food rights. Their concerns were assuaged as the iztheran hosts served up a generous dinner. A few stolen ale casks were introduced and the contents washed away the concerns from their lips.

Soon Ztakish found himself in a private conversation with the half-orc scout who would be key to his plan of deception. The shadowed alcove in which they shared a drink secluded them well enough for them to plot while undisturbed.

"Brogratch, is it?" Ztakish inquired, speaking in his own language, but using a miracle to convey the message. The half-orc would hear it in his own words, though he had been learning the iztheran language. "You are prepared to play your role in this plan? Your tribe boasted well of your abilities."

The half-orc, Brogratch, puffed up his chest and nodded. "I've scouted for the humans for years. I've led them to many enemies, enemies of my own tribe. They trust me."

The iztheran tried to offer a sly smile, but his facial scars made almost all his emotions seem like a scowl. "Benefitting your own tribe in the process, nay doubt. This is nay different."

Brogratch leaned closer, not wanting to be overheard by anyone. "What if the humans nay fall for it this time?"

Ztakish replied, "That is all up to you. I'll have to trust your judgment. Is there anything you need from me?"

The half-orc shook his head, leaned back, and gulped down a mouthful of grog. He didn't remove his stare from Ztakish. "I've heard stories about you. Some are hard to believe."

"Which ones?"

Brogratch pointed at the spiritual leader. "They say you turn into a big animal when you fight. *Monstrous* animal."

Ztakish, not wanting to disappoint the scout or downplay his abilities, bared his teeth. This time, the scowl was intentional. "By Yurtash's will, my body can transform into a large alligator whenever I call upon the need. I have sated my hunger for conquest on the meat of my enemies."

The half-orc ventured, "By Yurtash's will? Does he grant this shapeshifting ability to others?"

The iztheran's interested peaked. Did the scout know of something he was reluctant to share, or was he a possible convert to Ztakish's religion? Ztakish glanced at the few adornments the half-orc wore. He didn't see any holy symbols, but that wasn't a surprise. Since the half-orc walked among humans as an agent of his tribe, it could stand to reason that his religion might need to be kept hidden. Perhaps he still sought enlightenment?

"Sometimes, he grants his ability randomly. Even the arrogant races in their towering cities have seen members born with the primal urges of shapeshifting. It is rare. But the sure path to it is fealty to Yurtash. All his high priests can adopt a spirit form and morph into its shape."

The half-orc nodded then took a drink. He seemed to be digesting the information.

The iztheran decided to pursue the question. "Do you follow the calling of a deity? Would you seek more knowledge of Yurtash's way?"

Brogratch held a hand up. His answer started off hurried, as if unwilling to offend the powerful leader. "I pay homage to many gods, for different reasons. I ask because the humans have a shapeshifter of their own; a champion has guided and fought alongside their armies for many years. My tribe curses his name."

Ztakish became less worried about losing a convert and more curious about this potential enemy. "Tell me more, starting with his name."

"Thamin, but they call him the Trollsbane. He has led parties of adventures in the times of my father and cleared out lairs of dangerous creatures in the eastern hills. He has become a legend in fighting his way out of traps and dangerous battles. He is Kaigal's lead scout. He serves at Bael Cochaw, a large fortress more than a day to the east of the city."

Ztakish listened with rapt attention, but he hadn't heard everything he hoped for when the half-orc paused for a drink. "You say he shapeshifts? Have you seen this happen?"

Brogratch shook his head as he gulped the remains of his drink, a few rogue drops spilling over his tusks. "I have never witnessed it, but the stories are well-known among humans. He turns into a large wolf in some battles. His howl carries across the field to rally his men, or he stays silent and topples creatures as big as trolls single-handedly. He plunges into battle until his enemy is defeated and his weapons, or claws, are soaked in blood."

Ztakish pondered for a few moments. "And he worships Yurtash?"

The half-orc looked unsure. "They say his shape is a gift of Yurtash, and that he follows the god. I'm not sure. I don't know of him teaching Yurtash's ways."

The iztheran mulled this information over. He wasn't really speaking to Brogratch when he uttered, "Another champion?"

Before the half-orc could comment, Ztakish's eyes snapped back to him. "How much land has he conquered in our divine name? How much has he broadened human influence?"

The half-orc cocked his head at the unexpected question. "Trollsbane has not been a conqueror. Kaigal hasn't expanded their territory in generations."

It was Ztakish's turn to look inquisitive. The iztheran's eyes widened at the half-orc's news. "Tell me more."

Brogratch cleared his throat. "Kaigal has had its fill of enemies, going back as far as my family's tales. We've followed conquerors against its walls more than once. As long as Trollsbane has been around, he's been a stout defender of her borders. He has thrown back every attacker, often fighting against my own ancestors or other Diaran city-states. Even when he ventured with allies into the hills, he would kill large threats in their lairs, take their treasures, and return to Kaigal."

Ztakish considered those facts. "Would you consider him a guardian of the peace? A defender only?"

"Aye, I would."

When the diplomacy had been concluded with the other tribes and the moons began their climb to the sky's pinnacle, Ztakish thought long and hard on the half-orc's words. He had asked many detailed questions, but the half-orc's first thoughts remained consistent. Although Brogratch had rarely dealt with the human personally, Ztakish learned much about him. Ztakish sorted his thoughts in his most holy of religious chambers, inside the hulk of the downed Divine Chariot.

"It seems there are *two* champions of Yurtash on this campaign field. Is my deity conflicted by the two natures? On one hand, he has me as a conqueror and champion of old. Is it indeed time to reignite conflict?

"Or is it time to let old motivations die and cede them to the young defender? Did the Covenant truly sedate Yurtash's ambitions, and would he abide by it?"

Ztakish scoffed. "Maybe it is a contest between us to determine the divine course. If so, I know my path. My nature is not that of peace."

***

As father and daughter walked back through the prairie, side-by-side, Thamin saw Thomena reach over and rub at her left arm. Following the battle, his skills seemed to further amaze her when he reached out and used natura magic to heal her injuries. She told him that the numbness had gone away, but it still felt sore. She could flex her fingers and hold

160

onto her wand again. Thamin's healing skills were meager, (another natura gift from Yurtash), but they succeeded in relieving her of the worst of her injuries. Thomena also reported sore ribs but nothing broken. They'd shared only a few, brief words after the encounter. Aside from checking on her health, and her asking about his, they'd spoken only a few necessary words.

Now, they walked together to report the tragedy back to Kaigal. Out of the corner of Thamin's vision, he noted Thomena glancing at him several times. He could tell she had several questions on her mind. It seemed like her bravery could face a troll but faltered against her father. He waited at least a mile of traveling for her to speak her mind. He didn't mind giving her the chance. He still wasn't sure how to open the conversation after the tirade last night. *A tirade I deserved,* he thought.

After that first mile, he decided to break the silence. Thamin spoke as he walked. Mostly, he faced forward, but his watchful eyes kept roaming the horizon for more threats.

"When I was very young, I started discovering tricks and abilities that I later realized were natura," he started. "Jaena would have been able to teach you her arcane magic when you came of age." A sigh slowed him down, but he pushed the explanation forward with minimal delay. "But natura doesn't work that way. It's an internal magic that is somehow unlocked randomly in the user, usually while living a primal lifestyle or an attachment with nature. It advanced to the point that I could even adopt an animal shape. My kinship spirit turned out to be that of a wolf. I call upon Form of the Wolf, and my physical body becomes more than just myself or that of a wolf. If I'm fighting, it doesn't hold for long. If I'm only traveling, it can get me from settlement to settlement in as little time as riding a horse. There is a stronger version, druids named it 'Predator's Call,' but I haven't achieved that yet. I'm sorry my form scared you."

He looked at her out of the corner of his eyes. Despite all the rigors of the trip, Thomena started chuckling. Maybe the absurdity of the situation was more than her knowledge could handle. "It did vex me. It still does. I came to Diara wanting to rediscover you and my homeland. I don't think I knew what to expect. Just when I think I've learned more about you, I find something else surprising. And now…a wolf form?"

"A gift from Yurtash, I guess. In my youth, I learned about gods worthy of worship: Yestreal, Boyal, Dawn, and I even read from *The Codex*. When I started developing my natura abilities, Yurtash became my focus. His devotion is on a primal, natural level."

Thomena's brow furrowed. She chewed her lip before asking, "But many monstrous humanoids worship Yurtash as well."

If she offended him, he didn't show it. Instead, he nodded at her words.

"There are many creatures out there who don't enjoy, nor pursue, the civilized life we enjoy. Even the elves have branches of their culture that stick close to nature and the wilds, and they have worshippers of Yurtash as well. A number of monstrous humanoids revere Yurtash, and it's unfortunate that they carry racial hatreds as well as fears of stone-wall city cultures. They might even share the same god, but some gods are simply about a way of living and not focused so narrowly on good or evil. Besides, even good gods can have bad apples serving them."

Thamin paused for a moment. "My god came about because of my lifestyle, but my good morals are what *I* choose to promote in this world. I use his tools to do so."

Thomena nodded. "Thank you. That is a lot to think about."

"And it isn't even the biggest question on your mind." Thamin added, surprising her.

Her head darted up to read his face, but his last few steps quickened his pace. All she could see was the side of his hood. He knew she realized the truth of his comment. Though sometimes it felt as if they were from two different worlds, that was his own fault.

He interpreted her discomfort, and his own role in it. Thamin slowed and looked at her over his shoulder. He wished she could see herself from his view at that moment. Even though Thomena suffered from bruises and scrapes, and her outfit marred by events, her spirit appeared to be unbroken.

"Let's stop and catch our breath for a moment," he suggested.

Thamin watched both his daughter and the horizon. She stretched, relaxing muscles that were likely tensing up from the battle. When they'd left Bael Cochaw, he'd noticed that her outfit looked new and locally tailored. The leather gaiters covering her lower legs handled their abuse well, but they were already stained a tinge of green from striding through the prairie grasses. Her wool skirt and gray tunic had dirt stains, intermixed with some blood around a few tears. She'd suffered some lacerations from when the troll threw her. Pieces of dry leaves clung to the fabric. Some of her equipment straps had gotten twisted around during the fight. Her subdued-blue cape had another large rip in it. As the wind ruffled it, Thamin could see the pink and blue bruise around her left elbow. He would have to mend that with more healing spells when he recovered his energy.

The wear in her clothes didn't mean as much to Thamin as the physical details after his girl weathered her first big fight. He could tell that Thomena still labored through rib pain to take a deep breath. She did her best to keep her injured arm still. Although since Thamin had healed the bone and muscles, a little movement would keep it from getting too stiff. If Thomena felt any more strain from the encounter, she didn't show it. She wasn't smiling much...but after seeing what happened at the village, why would she? Nevertheless, she kept her head high, her back straight, and she endured the necessary march without complaint. The tears upon her face had long dried, and she shed no more following the troll fight. Even when she realized that her father was watching her, she met his gaze with an even stare. Her eyes seemed closer to a bright silver, compared to their normal gray. Thomena likely inherited her father's inner fire. Of that, there could be little doubt.

She probably hadn't even realized that Thamin had his own share of injuries following the fight. His bruises weren't visible, but he'd gotten thrown by the trolls a couple times. Nevertheless, he spent all his healing energy on her needs.

"What? Why are you looking at me like that?" she asked, confused about the attention.

"I'm not looking at you," Thamin replied. "I'm looking at the *new* you. My young girl is gone. There's a capable, strong, grown woman in her place."

Thomena blushed and averted her eyes. "I'm the same me. I'm only sixteen."

"Age is just a number. In many ways, other traits such as maturity, confidence, and responsibility define you better than your times around the sun."

Thamin shifted his weight and looked at the ground. He didn't know how to say it, but he needed to give her an apology.

He looked up again but couldn't quite meet her gaze. His eyes drifted northward, looking for, but not seeing, any smoke that might still be rising from Veldale. "I've been a bad father."

When he said nothing immediately afterward, Thomena swallowed a lump in her throat before offering an admission. "When I came here, I harbored some resentment over you sending me away and having to grow up without you or my mother. Questions lurked in my mind in a place I didn't want to acknowledge. Nevertheless, I wanted an explanation. I still don't quite understand."

Thamin nodded. "We can't control all our emotions, and you weren't wrong to question it. I just wished I had a better reason to offer. Looking at these monster-bordered lands, and the chaos that they can still cause...I feel that I also failed my task as a warrior."

"But you're a legend among these people."

He sighed. "I may have done some legendary things in their eyes. They ignore that I had a barracks full of extraordinary helpers once. However, even now, it seems emptier for not accomplishing my task. I haven't built you a safe, peaceful world out here."

Thamin tried to imagine the outlook of this land from her perspective. The violence of his world was almost incomprehensible to a child raised on books of knowledge, in the sanctuary of a major city like Orlaun.

She asked, "Is this how wild the settlements really are? How can one grow up in such savagery?"

Without looking straight at her, Thamin pointed a finger in her direction. "Exactly why I sent you away." As Thomena closed her eyes and thought on that, Thamin continued. "Things can be peaceful around a village for maybe eight-to-twelve years, but then some community tragedy always pops up. Rogue monster, a humanoid incursion, a bad spell gone wrong, disease...some things were appropriate for my people to deal with and some we could only relieve some suffering. I couldn't turn by back on people in need. Too often, justice needed a swordarm."

Thomena raised her head and nodded. "I'm glad that we stopped those trolls. I didn't think we had a chance, but we served Justice and saved the next victims without them ever knowing they were in danger. I can relate to the satisfaction of making a difference for someone. My soul was fulfilled when I helped the vigiles."

Thamin nodded again. This time, he felt he could look her in the eye. "I'm sorry I couldn't make the world a better place. I'd lost your mother; I didn't want to risk you also. You would not have been safe near me, and I always saw this as a home waiting for your return. I did a lot of good, but the world is just too big for me to tame."

Thomena straightened up her stance, lifted her chin, and did her best to hide any signs of pain. "I'm big enough to explore the world on my own now. I know I'm young, and the world is full of surprises. But...I'm as ready as ever to go explore it. Maybe there is something that I could do someday to help and protect people in such remote places, but only once I learn more of the arcane arts."

Thamin grinned. He reached his arms out wide, inviting a hug. She proved eager to the idea. Thomena launched into his arms. Her embrace helped him realize what his choice had denied him for so many years. Father and daughter shared a close embrace, one that Thamin had to relax slightly after a sharp intake of her breath reminded him of her sore ribs.

Once he released her, he wiped away a rare tear. He couldn't keep a swell of emotion from showing on his face. He even choked up when he spoke. "Seeing how well you fared against the troll, I believe you are ready to explore. You've been trained to handle the world, maybe better than I could have done. I'd be honored to take the journey with you."

Thomena smiled, the expression sharing the buoyance of a rainbow after a storm. "Then you are serious about what you said? You'll resign and travel with me?"

He nodded. "There will always be danger here, but I'm not the only champion Kaigal can call on. Since I only have one child in this world, I'd say she needs me more. It's time that I enjoyed some of the peace that I fought so hard to champion."

Chapter 18 – Soot Stains and a Bubble Bath

"Uffa! Your veapon will be looked at once Oye get to dese otter orders. De general gets his first, unless you vant to bodder him yourself!"

Julia flinched as Gunnard yelled at the soldier. She was glad that she hadn't yet started her swing. Mentally bracing herself for more shouting, she resumed pounding on the metal. The shop would have been a hot place, even without the forge running. They thought they had caught up on the previous smith's backlog of orders, but a new swell of requisitions hit faster than they could work. Requests were arriving from everyone in Bael Cochaw, and all of them begged to be served first.

The work distracted her from her thoughts, but Thomena's welfare settled uneasily in the back of her mind. The rumors from the countryside were worrisome and she could feel the tension building among the people.

Gunnard threw his hands up in frustration, his impressive muscles knocking wide his long, braided locks. "Dat's enough for me. Lia! You handle dese soldiers, Oy'll vork the metal."

Julia set aside her task, though the veteran smith scooped it up immediately and set to work. The girl wiped at her brow, not that it helped to stall the sweat running down her face.

"Yust make sure…" Gunnard started to say, but Julia interrupted him.

"I know. Take the names, take the piece, twine the request and price around the item."

She didn't mind being asked to man the counter during such a busy time. Gunnard was the veteran smith, after all, and Julia's expertise focused on tinkering with small gadgets. As busy as the requests hit the shop, Gunnard needed to utilize his skills to keep up with demand.

The next soldier needed a new blade. Another merchant, anxiety leaking through every sentence, asked for an old knife to be sharpened. While people stood around, all the talk focused on sporadic attacks on villages and raids on caravans. As rumors mixed with facts, everyone suddenly needed a new weapon or sought repairs on an old one.

The worries of her friend being out there, facing danger somewhere, frayed her nerves. Julia barked at another soldier who was trying to cut in front of the merchant. "You there, back off. There's a line."

"But he's a craftsman, I'm a soldier..."

"We'll give your request priority as needed *after* you've patiently waited in line."

Julia filled requests, placed new weapons alongside others tagged for work, and helped Gunnard whenever he called out "Lia!" As a side effect, she also built up her skill in rebuffing rude people.

The surge of business promised good coin, but the danger in the realm overshadowed any other good news. The populace knew that a struggle was coming; the old-timers could feel it in their bones. Julia barely had time to worry about her friend, alone in that wilderness with a negligent father.

Another crafter, a fletcher, grabbed her attention. "I need three hundred arrowheads for the fort's archers. If I can get as many as five hundred, I can get spare ones on the wall towers."

Julia posted the request without giving a hint at how overwhelming that sounded, taking a moment to grab a tool for Gunnard before another warrior approached. She didn't even register that it was Mabry until he asked if she felt well.

"Oh, hi," she said. "I guess so. I'm sorry for not noticing you. I loved that evening together, but I'm becoming so busy lately."

The tinker absently swiped her brown hair back over her left ear, brushing the scarred tip of her ear as she did so. On busy days like today, a string tied much of her hair out of the way. Her workload overweighed the self-consciousness or her disfigurement—until she happened to touch her ear with that handsome, persistent young soldier standing before her. She turned her head to the left, hiding it a little, as she spoke, and she couldn't help but notice that his muscular arms were bare again. His one flaw, the blunted nose from some previous injury, only served to even them out as far as deformities were concerned.

"I'm sorry to bother you, as I can see you're both very busy." Mabry glanced at Gunnard, but the smith just snorted and kept focus on his project. "We were practicing using full armor, and during the sparring, one of my buckles snapped."

He propped his chestplate onto the counter. It was one of the few metal armor pieces worn by the lightly-armored Gold Lions. Julia glanced at the broken part. It wouldn't be hard to replace it.

She offered him a shy smile. The effort worked against the native scowl usually painted on her face. "We can't have you going into a fight without armor. I'll get it done."

Julia took his info and bartered a discounted price. It wouldn't really cost Mabry anything. A portion of his normal soldier allowance was used for the sole purpose of equipment maintenance.

Gunnard eyed the piece with a frown but said nothing.

Mabry went on his way, soon replaced by another request at the counter, then another customer. At one point, a patron making demands got too close to Julia's face. It wasn't even a fighter, just a farmer from outside the fort who wanted a scythe blade sharpened for his defense. He showed amazing arrogance, claiming that his livelihood fed the fort, and he needed protection for his home outside the walls.

Julia yelled back at him in a perfect imitation of Gunnard's accent. "Uffa! Your veapon vill be looked at once Oye get to dese otter orders. De general's army is first, unless you vant to bodder dem yourself."

Gunnard looked at her with raised eyebrows. A second later, he let out a boisterous laugh. "Dat's my Yoo-lia!"

The farmer left quite disappointed.

In the evening, Julia and Gunnard closed the shop window but kept diligently working on their endless line of requests. The work left their hands blackened and soot-trails of sweat down their faces and arms. Neither of them enjoyed a proper supper, only a few handfuls of some nuts.

At one point, Julia picked up Mabry's chestplate. Gunnard shook his head. "Dat's not as urgent as some of dese otters. It can vait."

"I can make a new buckle," she pleaded. "If we're attacked soon, I want him protected."

Gunnard offered a knowing smile. "Dis da same boy yoo complained about ven ve got here? Da one gave us that ice treat?"

Julia nodded.

"Oye think yoo've gotten soft on him. Is he...vat they called it here? Courting yoo?"

Her blush almost hid under the soot. "Aye. He is."

Gunnard chuckled and nodded. "Oye'll make the buckle; Oye can do it faster. Oye vant yoo to be able to spend time on your special proyect." He motioned his head to the side yard of their shop.

Julia looked that direction, seeing Gunnard's wagon. A burlap sheet covered an object projecting up from the middle of it. Julia's new weapon model was nearly complete.

She almost found dreamland when the voice came calling. Someone repeated her name. A part of her registered it, but the bulk of her consciousness resisted rousing itself from the near slumber. Both her mind and body needed a rest. Her eyes cracked open a bit, barely recognizing the dilapidated old barracks room. The ceiling still harbored a couple cobwebs, which survived her literal whirlwind of cleaning. In her mind, she almost fooled herself that she reposed in a luxury inn.

The voice called again. "Thomena, are you there?"

Julia. Her best friend must be worried about her. How would she react when she found out the truth of the latest adventure? Thomena didn't really feel up to having a visitor. At the same time, she knew that she needed her closest confidante.

Languid and cat-like, she stretched her slack muscles. Her movements sloshed the water around the metal bathtub. A yawn delayed her response.

"I'm in the back, enjoying a bath. Don't fret, you can come in."

The water had lost a bit of its heat and most of its bubbles. Restoring both wasn't a hard task for her magic. As she heard Julia's hesitant footsteps enter the barracks, Thomena expelled the energy to bring back the freshness of the soak. The water warmed and bubbles repopulated the surface. Despite the cover of bubbles, she still reached over and grabbed a towel, dragging it into the tub and draped it to cover her. It protected her modesty, even though both girls had shared guild baths in the past.

Julia's head peeked into the room, then her eyes darted around nervously. "So, your father isn't here?"

"He's giving his scout report to the commander." Thomena perceived that much of Julia's nervous glances were due to fears of Thomena's father. Julia had reason to be anxious around father figures...and everyone here seemed to step lightly around Thamin. Thomena pointed at a simple chair situated across from her. "Have a seat and relax."

Julia did so and quickly switched moods since the two of them were alone. The tinker leaned forward in her chair as her eagerness surfaced. "Did you get to see some other hamlets?"

Thomena nearly choked on the response. She barely managed to utter, "Aye."

"What an adventure! You have to tell me what it was like." Julia had already averted her eyes and was looking around the room. Her excitement caused her to talk fast, but she missed the pall that came over Thomena's face. "Hopefully, they don't dress as drab as most of the people here in the fort. I know, not like I ever dress up in anything fashionable anyway. Did they have any people our age or any social events? How 'freely' do they live their lifestyle so far away from a city? Did any of those towns have use for a tinker? Any blacksmiths?"

Thomena sniffled, and it caught Julia's attention. The tinker looked over to see her friend in tears. "Oh, what did I say? What happened?"

Thomena took a deep breath to steady her thoughts. She could only speak in a soft tone or risk her composure breaking down. "We did visit a village. The elders treated Father with a lot of respect, and they played a game that Thamin always seems to win. But then..." Thomena paused, stuttering as she restarted her chain of thoughts. "Th-there was...a f-fight. After we left. We came back too late."

As her hands wiped away her tears, she saw Julia take notice of her clothes piled nearby. The garments had been stained with speckles of blood and ripped in a couple places. Her friend's eyes went wide with the realization.

Julia pulled the chair closer, taking Thomena's hand in hers. "I'm sorry to go off on questions like I did. Take your time; tell me everything."

Thomena did go into all the details, even her explosive tirade against her father during their night in the woods. Tears ran down into the bath, and her voice shook during her accounting of events. Julia offered encouragement and sympathy. At the end of the recollection, Thomena leaned forward in the bath, hugging her knees to her chest, exposing her bruised and scarred back and ribs.

"Thomena! You need a healer!"

Thomena glanced over her shoulder, but she couldn't see all the damage. "Father used some magical healing on me. He planned to do more once he got back. It feels sore, but it's not serious anymore."

Feeling self-conscious, Thomena leaned back against the support of the tub wall. She kept her towel over her front. She'd lost quite a few bubbles during the retelling of her experience, so she started whispering arcane words.

Julia's jaw dropped as she witnessed a change to the bathwater. "Did you just use your magic to replenish the bubbles and reheat the bathwater?"

170

Thomena, feeling tired and suffering from a dry throat at this point, simply nodded.

"Okay, I need to learn magic if only to cast that spell you just used."

The comment stuck a pin in Thomena's foul mood, popping her emotions with laughter that she couldn't restrain. When she recovered enough to reply, she said, "Even if you have the aptitude for magic, I think it might take a few years of study and concentration to do that trick. I am so well-versed in water and air spells that I'm able to perform some variants without much planning."

Her friend's brow scrunched up. Julia began playing with her hair again as she spoke, "I think you lost me there."

Thomena reiterated, "I can take known spells and alter their effect a little bit, kind of spontaneously. I can only do so through a very thorough knowledge of this subject."

Although Julia's observation had helped lighten the conversation, it hadn't finished Thomena's discussion. The tinker went back to the painful topic. "I can't believe you handled a big troll. I've never seen one, but I think I would have panicked."

Thomena nodded, reciting a common saying for one who faced a grueling test. "Talk about shoving the ingot into the middle of the forge-fire."

Both girls lapsed into silence for a few breaths. Each seemed unsure of where to guide the conversation next.

Thomena finally broke the stillness. "I guess I got what I wanted. I still can't believe that I shouted at him like that. Once I started, I just couldn't stop throwing my pain and questions at him from all those years. Resentment I didn't even realize just kept coming out." She paused for a breath. "It will be different now. I hope. He's agreed to step away from all this and go somewhere with me. We can have some time together to focus on our bond."

Julia stiffened. "Wait, what are you talking about?"

"Father's been giving too much of himself to everyone else, so he agreed to retire from his obligations here. I don't know what we'll do next, but we will be as a father and a daughter again. Maybe we'll travel a bit. I hope we can make up for lost years."

"That may be just fine for you, but what about me? I've been more worried about you than for myself, but you're about to change that." Julia's voice had taken on a higher, somewhat anxious, tone. "You just led me out to a place where I can have a future. But did you notice there may be a war going on soon? You're taking away the city's

171

legend as villages are getting burned to the ground. The people are beginning to panic."

Surprised at her friend's outburst, Thomena quickly defended herself. She struggled to keep her voice calm as she said, "He's been risking his life for everyone but me. Building schools for everyone but me. Talking to everyone but me."

"Just...consider your timing on this and the circumstances. When you were out, there was a minstrel performing at the pub while Mabry and I shared some drinks."

Thomena glanced toward her friend at that news. Her curiosity about Julia and Mabry's apparent budding romance temporarily allayed the feelings of her personal situation.

"The minstrel sang two songs about The Trollsbane. Your father is the local hero. Kaigal and Bael Cochaw once had dozens of bigger-than-life heroes defending their borders, commanded by him. Most of them are gone, but he remains. They idolize him. Villages are now burning, and yet stories of him are the comfort that helps simple folk sleep at night."

Thomena's head dipped forward, her shoulders sank, and a heavy sigh escaped her mouth. Chewing her lip, she put the fingers of one hand up to her temple.

Julia allowed her time to think.

Thomena gathered her thoughts and spoke. "All I desire is time to spend with my father...my only living parent. Is that so selfish?"

Her tinker friend tilted her head. "I want you to be happy, I really do. You have to look at this situation and these people's safety. He's their defender. What does your *Codex* say? I'm sure there is a passage in there on the subject."

Thomena nodded. "If you mean about selfishness, the scripture is 'carved into stone' regarding the dangers of that course. Favoring personal desires over the needs of those suffering goes against Mercy, Honor, Compassion, Sacrifice, and Humility. Yet, *The Codex* encourages believers to never be completely selfless that they surrender their own needs. It is hard for Compassion to flourish when the Love from others does not water it."

Julia put a hand out. "Let's take this a different direction. Maybe there is a passage about people like your father."

Thomena's brow scrunched up, sorting through her devotions for an answer. After a minute, her posture perked up as a memory came to her. "The Watcher on the Wall."

Before Julia could say anything, Thomena clutched the towel to her chest and sat up straighter. She pointed back towards the barracks' main bunkroom.

"My *Codex* is resting on the desk next to my bunk. Could you wait there for me? I'll make myself decent."

Thomena knew that it wouldn't be hard for Julia to find her bunk since only two bunks in the large barracks showed signs of upkeep. Also, both had curtains partially surrounding them. Thomena's side definitely reflected more of a woman's touch in finery, colors, and comfort; as much as could be found in the territorial fort. Her father's side looked pragmatic and spartan by comparison. Thomena exited the bathroom minutes later, clad in fur slippers, knee-high hose laced around the knees, and a lengthy robe. She couldn't conceal her troubled expression.

Thomena sat on her bed, grabbed the tome from her desk and then patted the bunk by her side. "Have a seat, I'll find it in a moment. Father has been a stout defender of this land during my whole life. I think I ran across this composition and thought about him even back in Orlaun."

"Poetry?"

The mage shrugged. "Aye and nay. There is a section of *The Codex* composed of poetry, songs, and tales that show examples of the virtues. 'The Watcher on the Wall' is in here. I don't think it is poetry, however, as it doesn't have rhythmic pacing or rhymes. Ah, here it is." She read it to her friend.

The Watcher on the Wall

As the people feast, revel, or speak their evening prayers, there is one who stands above and watches. He does not watch that which he can not partake this night. His senses focus beyond the protective wall, alert for dangers from the wild. He stands so that they may sit or rest. He uses his eyes and ears so that their pleasurable distractions may render them blissfully ignorant of the outside world.

He keeps an oiled blade at his side instead of dinnerware. Metal or boiled leather cover his front instead of a dining napkin. A helmet serves him better than a floppy nightcap. His stomach may growl from hunger while those dependent on him eat. He shares no conversations with others, hearing only the sounds of the night animals and the distant laughter through the windows at his back. His shivers and hunger are a sacrifice that spares the same fate for the meek.

Each nightly vigilance is a test of Bravery and Honor, of Sacrifice and Courage. He can never predict what fateful time an enemy may appear. A dark hour may come swift and deadly, so he must remain vigilant in his service. A failure in his care strikes worse for those behind the wall, who have relaxed their guard to enjoy life's comforts.

Some nights a watcher can join the evening revelers. He can sometimes dull his wits with drink or distract himself with pleasures. On those nights, another watches in his stead. But although any watcher can enjoy nights of revels, not all revelers can become vigilant watchers.

Another night, another ascent, and his watch begins anew. His loved ones may suffer loneliness this night, and he will carry them in his heart. He may endure loneliness and hunger in cold silence. Yet, the wall must not be breached, and his perception must remain keen. Through his service, the rest of the world may rest. Thank you, watcher on the wall.

Thomena lowered the tome, feeling conflicted. Her father sounded just like the watcher. People needed him, but she needed him just as much. She wanted to live guided by *The Codex*, and her father seemed to be living a life influenced by its tenets. She couldn't fault him for many of his decisions, but that didn't settle her upset emotions. While her friend sat quietly by her side, Thomena sought to think up an answer to her dilemma. What should she do? How would it affect those around her? What Sacrifice was paid by the family members of the watcher on the wall?

Chapter 19 – End of Watch

Thamin stood with a multitude of officers, scouts, and elders from nearby villages. In the middle of them all, Commander Shan Bedran glared across the map on the war table with a grim expression. He announced to all in the room. "As of this moment, we are at war."

Several of the younger attendants tensed up. Thamin surveyed the markers on the map. A skull emblem sat on Veldale, but it wasn't the only one ruined. There had been raids and violent incidents everywhere north of Kaigal and Bael Cochaw.

"I've never seen this kind of cooperation between humanoid monsters." The commander finger-poked the map as he spoke. "Orcs and lizardmen, trolls and goblinkin. Whoever coordinates our enemy is still faceless, but there must be a bigger plan at work. This has moved beyond any simple unrest or isolated tribal event."

Thamin listened to the commander detail the gravity of the situation and couldn't help feeling guilty. He hadn't yet been able to tell his old friend that he would now be retiring from service. The timing appeared to be nothing less than horrible.

The commander continued speaking in the background. "Assemble the men. Pull up all reserves in the southern outposts. Prepare a letter asking for conscripts from Kaigal's Senate."

Thamin mentally winced, though he kept his expression stoic. Asking to force conscripts to serve was an extreme action and likely to be denied. Despite the raiding of several villages, Kaigal's controlling merchant factions might not be willing to fulfill a levy except with criminals or people struggling under debts to them...not proper warriors.

"I need a list of arms sent to the smith, Gunnard, both fulfilled and requested. I have a feeling we'll be needing more, but I'm not sure how much he's been able to supply in the last few days. We'll have to prepare a caravan to get more arms and supplies from the city. They can deliver the requests and restock."

As the instructions continued, the ranger wanted to melt into the wall behind him. His skills would be invaluable to his commander, his old friend, but he needed to hold firm on his promise to Thomena. She

175

was the most precious thing in the world to him, yet he'd already missed much of her childhood. He needed to get her away from this land before her life would be at risk. An unbidden memory surfaced in his mind. Once again, he recounted the fall of a portion of Kaigal's wall, taking the life of his defending wife with it, while he helplessly observed from the battlefield outside the city.

Thamin shook his head. His daughter needed him now. The two of them could go explore the realm together. He'd always wanted to do that with Jaena, but they missed their opportunities. It was long past time that Thamin took such a trip, and Thomena had reached an age to enjoy sharing the experience with him.

Commander Bedran's words drew Thamin's attention again. "All scouts are going back north, in groups if needed. We must locate the heart of the enemy. At the very least, we have to see these threats coming and respond in time to save the villages."

The commander's eyes glanced across Thamin's. The army depended on their legend, but the legend knew he wouldn't be going.

Thamin got his opportunity to talk to his friend shortly afterward. Too many ears still lingered, awaiting their assignments, but Bedran was about to give his most experienced soldier an assignment. The aging officer motioned to Thamin and pointed at the map.

Thamin stepped in and interrupted him. "Commander. I know this timing is bad, but I have family to look after now. I am retiring from my service to Kaigal."

You could have heard a pin drop in the room during the sudden silence. Shocked, nervous glances darted between lower officers.

The commander stopped pointing and settled the palms of both hands on the tabletop. His weight sagged, giving the impression that those veteran arms were the only things still holding him up. After a breath had passed, he managed a slow nod. Bedran stood up with exaggerated effort and turned to face Thamin.

"You've done plenty for us over the years. Saved more lives than people know." Shan Bedran reached out and gave a firm squeeze to Thamin's shoulder. "I've asked enough of you, and Kaigal owes you an eternal debt. Go enjoy your time with that bright, young girl of yours, before you become as gray in the hair as me." His heavily-scarred face forced a smile.

Thamin tried to alleviate some of their worries. "There are good soldiers here. I've helped train some of them, and they show good promise. It's time for them to have a shot at becoming a legend."

Thamin met the eyes of everyone in the room on his way to the door. He nodded in deference to each, waved to a few. He hoped a brief show of confidence would lend support despite the feeling of a cornerstone being yanked from the foundation.

Once Thamin left the war room, he felt a mental weight slide from his shoulders. He had done his service. The former ranger and scout could now enjoy living life for his family more directly, rather than a general feeling of making a better future. He looked forward to traveling with Thomena and seeing the world. Thamin walked with a youthful spring in in his step down some stairs as he made his way toward the ruined barracks bearing the worn, red banner.

End of watch for the last Blood-Wolf.

***

Knowing that he now shared the barracks, Thamin stopped to softly knock on the door before entering. The fact that he sought permission to enter the home he'd used for years felt out of place. Given the trials of their journey, he wouldn't be surprised if she were sleeping.

"Thomena? It's me."

The muffled reply came from beyond. "Come in, I'm decent."

Thamin entered to find Thomena standing next to her bed, in the presence of another youth her age. He took a quick appraisal of the situation. The stranger in his barracks had short, brown hair, brown eyes, an ear damaged from an old cut (which he politely did not linger on), and she wore simple work clothes stained with soot. For a girl her age, her arms had respectable muscles. Thamin noticed that Thomena looked a bit red-eyed. Had she been crying? A wadded handkerchief almost evaded his discovery, crumpled in one hand.

He decided to focus first on the stranger. "A pleasure to meet you! Julia, is it?"

The teenager stared at him with eyes of dread. He assumed that tales of him had already influenced her reaction. He used kind words and a calm demeanor to help ease her tension. "Aye. Julia the tinker, smith's apprentice."

"And you journeyed all the way from Orlaun as Thomena's traveling partner, did you not?"

The girl glanced at Thomena, as if delivering a private plea for help. Julia turned back and noticed Thamin walking towards her.

She stammered her reply. "A grand adventure, the farthest from home I've ever gone. Thomena missed you a lot. When I found out she

177

was crossing most of the known realm to find you, I jumped at the chance."

Thamin noticed Thomena's head tilt up at Julia's words. The scout realized Julia's subtle game. The girl was trying to get him to appreciate or acknowledge his daughter's strong will.

"I joined her dangerous journey and things went well for me," Julia said. "I managed to find a new trade once I got here. Thomena is my champion." He saw his daughter blush.

Thamin acknowledged her words with a deep nod. "She is my not-so-little champion also. Thomena told me a bit about you and the journey. I'm guessing the garrison has kept you busy?"

"That is an understatement." Julia put her hands on her hips. "It's a little scary, wondering what I've gotten myself into. We've been hearing of dreadful events. I hope this isn't normal, and that everything will get quiet again."

Thamin shook his head. "I can't lie. It tears at my heart to see the threat currently biting at our people. Commander Bedran has able help, however, and he is taking action to safeguard everyone."

Julia opened her mouth, but tossed another look at Thomena. His daughter stood straight and strong, but she also gave a nod to the other girl. Some secret message?

"I'll be outside," Julia said, as she excused herself.

Thamin watched Thomena approach him. She stared at his gaze with her red-rimmed eyes. He gave her the chance to say the first words. Instead, Thomena glanced at the closest two bunks and indicated them. Father and daughter sat down and faced each other.

Thomena spoke. "How did the meeting go? They must have been shocked at the news."

He didn't mind that she seemed to be digging sideways for information. The ranger could tell when someone wasn't ready or willing to put their teeth into the meat of a discussion.

"I think Commander Bedran may have added a few gray hairs." Thamin's gaze never wavered. "You'd think I was a stout, dependable cane that supported his journey for years. I told him that I've trained a lot of good, young soldiers here, and that's true. He has helpers ready to take my place."

"But how bad is the situation?" she blurted with such eagerness that she gave away her biggest worry. "A village or two doesn't get raided like that every year, correct? Are the people here in danger?"

Thamin weighed the circumstances in his mind. He wanted to give her the truest answer, but the situation denied any simplicity. He had to rely on his gut instincts.

"Most of the time, the threats and the crimes are small. A village raid might only involve a hit-and-run strike against food stores in the night. Sometimes, a small band of humanoids would threaten residents of a ranch, departing with some furs or other valuables, but leaving behind only minor injuries. A few times each year, a caravan might get attacked, but Diara's city-states guard those well." He made a show of putting his hands close together, upright, as if holding a thick mug between them. Once Thomena focused on his hands, he spread them apart as if he was trying to throw a hug around the broadest oak trunk. "Every few years, someone riles up a host of trouble. This is one of those years. The humanoids of the swamp, as well as those of the eastern hills, outnumber Kaigal and all the citizens in its fealty. All the armies at our command would be hard pressed to stop a charismatic leader who unites those forces."

He winced before adding, "We would rarely get help from the other city-states. Each county in Diara wants to climb over the misfortune of the others and become the capital of a new empire. If any county offers help, the concessions they ask could cripple the commerce of the neighbor in need."

Thomena's lips pouted as she observed, "You didn't exactly answer my question about the danger to these people."

"Nay, I feel like I painted you a perfect picture." Thamin rolled his shoulders, dropping his hands together. He sighed. "This is as bad as it gets, and the whole army is anxiously waiting to spring any direction at a moment's notice. Blood will spill. Aye, the people here are in danger."

Thomena's shoulders already drooped, but now they managed to sink even lower. Her eyes looked aside, staring at a bunk. The bunk in question once possessed abandoned equipment and belongings when she had cleaned out the room. She absently chewed her lip.

"What are you really asking of me?" Thamin reached out, gently touching her chin and easing it forward so that her eyes once again faced him. Sometimes, Thomena's eyes shined silver, but right now, they were a dull, moody gray, rimmed with moisture. "I've kept the peace for these people, shed my sweat and blood for them, for more years than you've been alive. It's tough to turn my back on this predicament. However, you are now the star by which I chart my course. My guiding light. What do you need?"

Thomena slowly pulled away from his hand, sitting back farther on the bunk. She didn't avoid his gaze or display any avoidance of him. In fact, she nodded, though over what, exactly, he didn't know. The girl swallowed her nervousness, even as she clenched her hands together on her lap.

"When I was at Old Market," she began, her words drawing out slowly. "I was willing and eager to do anything I could to fight the fire with the vigiles. I could do little except offer them protective wards. The college supplied me with scrolls to control water golems, which I knew would be a great help. Due to the high cost, I wasn't allowed to use them unless ordered by the captain."

She closed her eyes for a moment. Thamin had the sense she was reliving some tough memories.

"They needed my aid, yet I stood helpless while awaiting orders. I knew lives were at stake. My friends stood in danger." She sniffled. "My heart guided me to a course of action."

"Which was...?" he prompted when her delay stretched too long.

Thomena met his eyes unflinchingly. "I knew that I honestly couldn't live with myself if I didn't help do something. I risked getting yelled at and owing an overwhelming five gold coins, but I saved several of them. I'm glad I did what I did, and they forgave me for it." She sighed. "But I didn't make my decision fast enough. I lost a friend that day."

She paused, watching for his reaction or waiting for him to speak, but he didn't. He sat across from her in a relaxed posture, his eyes focused on her every word. His simple response consisted of a slow, gentle nod, encouraging her to continue.

Thomena folded her arms over her lap, just so that her hands could keep from shaking. "I really desired to have you to myself for a time. I wanted us to reaffirm our family bond. But now I feel selfish for it." At that remark, he opened his lips to speak, but one of her hands shot up. "Let me say this. I have a friend here, starting a new life. She's at risk, and I can't walk away from that. I can't take away the people's hero while threats creep over the horizon. Can you really turn your back on them without guilt?"

"Nay. My heart cares for them, and it cares for you. But if my loyalties are split, they must now lie with my family first. I feel the need to protect them, but not if it risks you. I thought Jaena safe behind walls when the enemy came, but I lost her anyway."

"Well," Thomena said, "I have decided to stay and help these people. I'll do so in any way that I can. I won't deprive them of their protector."

"Things will get dangerous. Terrifying things happen in war."

She looked down, hands fidgeting. She glanced up and said, "Bravery is a virtue; one that is meaningless if left untested. I want to stay here and help out."

Thamin leaned forward, gently scooping both his hands around hers and gently cupping them together. "You're already brave, I can tell. Do you realize that some tenets of *The Codex* are self-rewarding? Compassion can warm your heart and earn friends. Justice helps rid yourself of evil. Knowledge arms your wits. But there are others that are truly hard to embrace because they demand from you. Do you know the toughest one that I fear?"

"Humility is my toughest challenge."

Thamin shook his head. "But bending to pride never seems to punish a person; not immediately."

Thomena inquired, "Which tenet scares you?"

"Sacrifice." He didn't bother to hide the deep pain in his eyes when he spoke. "Sacrifice is the hardest to conquer. Its cost is immediate and can take a heavy toll on the heart. You're making a sacrifice now on behalf of others."

Thomena rose to her feet. Taking a few steps, she arrived at her traveling gear, reagent pouches, and the belt with her mace. "What is the next stop?"

Letting loose a chuckle, Thamin stood and moved toward his own gear. "If we are to be helpful, we must go separate ways for now." Seeing her expression, he quickly added, "It wouldn't be my first choice. I'd rather be at your side since dangers are clawing out of the wilderness."

Thamin snatched his unstrung bow and weapon belt. "Shan's plan would have used me as a scout when he already has every scout running in all directions. I need to go convince him of a new plan."

"Will you share it with me?" she asked.

"We need allies but forced conscripts won't be enough. I intend to reach out to others who reside in the path of danger. I need to visit the ranger lodges and put out a call for help. Also, the elves of Syllatru were already attacked. I can call on them for aid."

Thomena tried to grab her gear in a hurry but ended up dropping a bag in her haste. "I can go with you."

Thamin shook his head. "You can't keep up with me when I'm running on four legs. I can outrun danger and get the message across in time for others to help."

She picked up her mess. "What do you want me to do?"

He paused to consider the request. "Shan has a few mages advising him. You can join them and see how they are preparing for war. I also know he'll be sending to Kaigal for supplies, including materials the blacksmith needs. Your friend, Julia..."

He suddenly remembered Julia had gone to wait outside. He wondered if she were still there, or even eavesdropping on the conversation. Either way, Thomena could fill her in soon enough.

"That means it's likely the smith's apprentice may be going along to Kaigal to ensure proper delivery. You can assist her."

Thomena replied. "I'll safeguard my friend, if I am able."

She looked resolute as she volunteered, holding strength in her stance and a firmness in her tone. Thamin didn't know the particulars of why she feared pride, but as a father, he was very proud of the woman she'd become.

He stepped to his daughter and wrapped her in a hug. Thamin whispered, "And if a troll happens to interfere, you are capable of dealing with it."

Chapter 20 – Macey Durant

The huge wolf bolted through the countryside, cutting across wild spaces more often than roads. Prey animals would scatter in fear, some only realizing the danger after it had already passed them. Thamin's lupine form ran through obstacles and terrain that would slow down a horse. Neither bristle bushes, nor dense grass slowed him in his quest, nor did he tire easily from the long run.

He only paused at the outer edges of Syllatru to establish his role as a friend to the elf sentries. Thamin wouldn't be so bold as to try running through the scout lines without identifying himself. A dignitary wouldn't want to scare them into raising an alarm.

With their permission, he pressed onward. Within hours, he had resumed human form and met with ambassadors from the city. Thamin handed them dispatches signed by Commander Bedran, and he discussed the attacks of the monstrous humanoids. Of course, the elves had already received word of the massacre of their kin in the old ruins at the edge of the jungle. Although the elf representatives stopped short of openly committing to anything, Thamin left the meeting feeling positive about the encounter. They knew his reputation. He'd also helped defend their borders in the past, so the ranger had already proven his trustworthiness to the elf city-state.

That was only the first stop in a list of locations he had to reach. Back into wolf form, he bolted over hills and through more unclaimed territory. The single-mindedness of his run carried him in a straight line, jumping hills and swimming creeks. More than once, he found evidence of monstrous patrols coming from the jungle. He couldn't afford to follow every track or inspect every campfire, not if he was to reach out to allies in time.

His wolf form panted and his human form felt the cling of sweat, but he made appearance after appearance to others who could help, or at least needed to be wary of the threat. Mostly, he visited the various hunting lodges found across the frontier. He pleaded to his fellow rangers. Some took up the call and prepared to journey to Bael Cochaw, others saddled horses and helped him spread word of the danger. His name and words carried weight among the woodsmen.

When the Trollsbane brought dire news, people listened.

***

The city-state of Kaigal had received news about the unrest and attacks upon its borders, but one wouldn't observe much of a difference as the merchants, entertainers, sailors, craftsmen, peasants, and laborers pursued their daily lives. Even a patrol of guards passed Thomena while joking and carrying on conversations without any gloom of war apparent in their faces. Maybe she misread them. It could be that the conversation and laughter kept them distracted from their fears.

Thomena felt burdened. Physically, she carried some bags and new purchases of clothes, potions, and equipment from the local merchants; mentally, the stress of her worries proved to be a constant distraction. She needed a rest, so she entered Heroes' Terrace well ahead of her planned rendezvous with Julia. Even though other people moved about, mostly children playing in the hedgerows, the overall peace of the plaza proved calming to her. She found a vacant bench and dropped both her purchases and her tired legs onto the seat.

She thought of her conversation during the morning with her tinker friend. Julia admitted more fears about coming out to this land. Thomena offered to help her get back to Orlaun, but Julia didn't take long to weigh her options. Gunnard's hospitality and support of the young tinker provided a place where she could finally practice her trade and be treated as an equal. Now, people even depended on her services. Julia planned on staying.

They separated after making plans to rendezvous back at Heroes' Terrace. Julia continued to supervise the resupply of materials requisitioned for the smith by Bael Cochaw. Some soldiers had accompanied them, including Mabry. The young man had his own agenda of orders to carry out while visiting the town.

This left Thomena free to pursue her own needs. The leather gaiters she'd bought the first time she was in Kaigal proved their worth in the grasslands outside of town. They'd saved her bootlaces and lower body from the burrs and grasping bushes. Her skirt and upper outer layers showed punishment from the brush and the trolls, so she bought some new sets of clothes with practicality in mind. The mage also emptied too much of her purse on a couple of sura potions. Like her spirit gem, the sura potions could help restore a worn spellcaster's flagging spirit so they could cast more spells. Despite the free use of her gem and its efficiency at holding spare spirit-energy for her, she feared that she might need the expensive potions in a drawn-out conflict. Thomena bought two healing potions from the merchant at the same time—the first ones she'd ever owned. She'd tasted them before, after a burn to her leg when assisting Orlaun's vigiles, but she'd never thought to need some until now.

Thomena would have enjoyed more rest if she didn't spend some of her time in the plaza energizing her lightning wand. She hadn't recharged it since the troll battle. The act sapped from her mental reserves, as if she were spending the time actively casting spells. Since she was safely in the city and staying at an inn for the night, she decided that the expenditure of her energy wouldn't put her at any risk today. Catching her breath after recharging her wand, her attention drifted to the statues around the gardens.

She could see seven statues, standing or kneeling at random intervals up and down the terraced plaza. Hoisting her bags, she decided to tour the artwork and learn more. The gardens of the plaza also gave space to decorative plant growths, smaller sculptures, and interchanging patterns forming mosaics down the walkways. Thomena decided that even if the people were forced to abandon their city, the culture of these people merited defense all by itself, lest it be lost and despoiled.

Each hero statue she encountered bore a plaque with their name and a summary of their actions. The few words displayed for posterity never went into deep details. Often, they only expressed a few appropriate words, quotes, or phrases which merely hinted at the person's importance. Thomena could only assume that growing up in Kaigal's area of influence allowed the local youths to learn about these heroes from historic events or even folklore. Figure after figure, she looked up from the plaque and tried to guess at the history.

The next one caused her to blush with embarrassment. Thomena looked up at the immodest female statue clad only in some kind of flowing fabric. The woman bore no clothing except a sheet or flag she held up at the corners, the wind seemingly blowing it up against her curves. The pose suggested that she held it up unabashedly, but the face resembled a young girl, with downturned lips marking her sorrow. Thomena averted her eyes from the display. She couldn't understand the unashamed nature of the statue compared to the other heroes. She noticed the name plaque displayed under her nose. Since she already stood that close, she thought she might as well read it.

"Macey Durant. The Last Bannermaiden. Forgive our hubris that led to your sacrifice."

Thomena reread it one more time, her lips moving with the words. "Bannermaiden?" she gasped, looking once more up at the statue. Her words whispered to the sad girl. "So that means...you're holding a flag. Covered only in the flag. What did that elder say?"

It took a moment for her to remember the words of Veldale's departed Elderman. *"After many years and countless events in which beautiful, young maidens met violent fates, the last bannermaiden fell. She didn't die...thank the gods...but her sad fate traveled the breadth of Diara and prompted change."*

Thomena understood part of the tale. Macey Durant was the last bannermaiden: the girl who rode with the army's banner in the center of a dangerous battlefield. Although female soldiers weren't unknown, this was an innocent girl close to Thomena's age. She fell in battle and prompted change that forbade further practice of the custom. The elder's speech had shushed the other men from sharing more of the story. Although the excerpt of the tale painted more to the puzzle, it still fell short of explaining why she'd been portrayed in such a manner.

In a fortunate case of timing, a historical resource happened to walk along the terrace gardens, looking for Julia. Having completed his own duties in Kaigal, Mabry Ingel headed toward her.

"Pleasant highsun to you," the soldier said, nodding. "Has Julia rejoined you, or is there a change in plans?"

Thomena set her bags down by the statue's pedestal. "She should be along soon. I'm glad you're here. I have questions I'm hoping you can answer."

Keeping a somewhat formal appearance, and dressed in his uniform, Mabry thumped his left fist against his heart. The motion imitated pounding a shield against his chest, which his company used as a salute. "How might I be of service, Thomena?"

"I was looking at all these statues in the plaza. Most of them are situated in heroic poses." Thomena's arm swept to indicate the area before pointing upward at the present subject. "Why is this girl...without clothes?"

Mabry looked up. "I thought they did a good job maintaining her modesty, given the circumstances..."

He trailed off at noticing Thomena's discontent glare. His cheeks flushed a bit as he backtracked to explain.

"All of these heroes are pictured as best as can be represented in their moment of glory. Most of these tales followed an impressive battle, so it's natural that they have weapons and armor." Mabry meekly waved a hand toward Macey's statue. "This was her...moment

186

of glory. At the same time, it was our moment of shame, not hers. I've heard elders say that it not only reflects her heroism, but our own guilt."

Thomena, noticing Mabry's discomfort, realized she needed to rein in her own emotions. He was here to help her, after all, and he wasn't a guilty party. She relaxed, softening her tone. "I've not heard any details about what happened. All I know is that the lords of this land once used young girls as bannermaidens at the heads of their armies, and that she was the last due to some tragedy. Please, tell me the full story."

Mabry nodded, but he didn't seem eager. "Macey Durant was a noble girl of Kaigal's lands, back when we were still ruled by nobles. She came from one of the smaller hamlets, I think, but that's not important. Apparently, she possessed both beauty and charm enough to win prominence among the court's social circles. From what historians tell us, she actively sought to be a candidate for bannermaiden when the army mobilized to deal with a threat at the borders. Back then, many noble lords encouraged fighting skills for their young men and tales of brave bannermaidens for their daughters. That isn't to say that women didn't fight on the front lines; however, bannermaidens came from young noble girls, who often weren't trained to fight."

Thomena perceived it was difficult for Mabry to tell this story. Was he having trouble recalling his history? More likely, Thomena realized, he wasn't understating the guilt his countrymen felt. Telling the story to a young girl, who might as well have been an outsider, posed a challenge. The soldier didn't even meet her eyes as he talked. As such, both of them turned their eyes to look up at the statue and imagine the subject in her former glory. Thomena silently admitted to herself that the subject did look like a beautiful woman who must have had optimistic prospects.

The statue's pose contradicted itself. The subject held the banner up like a display of triumph, but the figure's back was slightly bowed, chin dipped to the chest, and the eyes seemed dull and empty as they stared down at the two viewers. Both accomplishment and loss were exemplified in one frozen moment of time.

Mabry said, "Unfortunately, the enemy wouldn't be human soldiers. Our gallant human knights always treated the bannermaidens with civility. However, in this encounter, orcs from the eastern hills were sweeping through the plain. Such monsters hold nay respect and don't give quarter to defenseless victims. Bannermaiden Durant was only one of a few on the lines that day, her position occupying an outer edge of the line. Historians disagree on the why-for's of it, but orc forces cut her troop apart from the rest and began a massacre."

The soldier paused to collect his breath. His words slowed as the pain of the story forced its way past his lips. "The army tried to reunite but instead watched helplessly as the shine of knightly armor in that mass disappeared in favor of the dark hides worn by the enemy. Human cries diminished amidst the roars of orc berserkers."

He stopped, glancing briefly at Thomena without meeting her gaze. "I'm sorry, I go too far in the retelling. This is not for..."

"Not for a girl's ears?" she interrupted. "Mabry, on my way to Bael Cochaw, I enlisted to protect a caravan. I rode at the front with the guards whenever we approached trouble. At Veldale, I fought intimidating enemies alongside my father. Do not hold back on this story. I want the full tale, and I am too captivated in it to settle for a diluted version."

He nodded, his eyes fixed on the bare feet of the statue. "To understand the next part, you must know how we treat our battle standards. The flags must always stand proud and visible. No color guard would allow it to touch the ground, if possible. If the bearer fell, a new soldier would raise it aloft.

"That day, the banner fell and did not rise back into sight. Orcs swarmed over the defeated regiment. Dismay rose among Kaigal's forces as they feared the death of the young girl. All the lords on the battlefield knew of her through her courtly influence. The battle didn't end for another two days as various forces and reinforcements clashed. When Kaigal spared men to search the battlefield and found her regiment, they found no sign of her body or the banner. The latter was nay surprise, as orcs tear apart our banners and wear pieces of the cloth as a trophy. The loss of Durant's body struck a blow nay matter from what tier of society one lived.

"The battle ended the war, and orc forces retreated back to the hills. Kaigal mourned its losses, and Bannermaiden Durant presented a focus of that loss. Songs were sung, memorials observed, and the practice of using bannermaidens was openly scrutinized.

"Suddenly, two months later, Macey Durant walked into one of Kaigal's eastern villages, just like she appears here." The soldier gestured to the statue. "She carried the banner, but otherwise limped along, battered and naked from her ordeal. She held up the standard, presenting it for all to see. Somehow, she had hidden the flag on the battlefield and retrieved it after her escape. At least, that is what historians believe, as the orcs would have torn it apart."

For the first time in the tale, Thomena scrunched up her brow in confusion and interrupted his story. "What historians believe? Didn't anyone ask her and record her words?"

"There were nay words to record." Mabry sighed. "She never spoke of what happened. Bannermaiden Durant came out of the wilderness mute, for nay reason but her own. The clerics healed her bruises but found nothing physically wrong with her ability to speak. Silently, she presented the banner to the nobles. Every regiment would die to protect its colors—that's a matter of honor. She survived the massacre of the young men of her company, upheld their honor with the returned banner, but kept her pain hidden. Who could possibly possess the sight to confirm what she suffered in those two months of absence at the hands of the orcs? Her fate is one of the reasons Kaigal overthrew its nobles in favor of a different kind of rule.

"I'm sorry, I'm getting ahead of myself. We're told that she passed within the year, due to a self-inflicted withering disease. I guess that's what they call it when a person refuses to drink, eat, or otherwise take care of their needs. Can you imagine a popular, beautiful, young girl allowing herself to waste away like that? And now that you know the tale, how do you feel about this statue's presentation? Would you have her depicted in her armor, on horseback, holding the flag high for war?"

Thomena stared directly into the statue's vacant eyes. *Am I becoming too judgmental?* She asked herself. *Nay matter how things appear, I need to ask and learn more before I jump to conclusions. Assumptions mislead from Truth.*

Her Honesty provided an answer for Mabry. "Nay. Portraying her in any other way would seem like a lie."

The soldier nodded. "Her nakedness is for our shame, not hers. The bannermaiden custom ended. Our city-state eventually revolted and changed rule due to several reasons, but perhaps this one brought the most passion to the movement."

A moment of silence came over them. Thomena realized that Veldale's elderman had lied to her. He had claimed that the bannermaiden hadn't died, which seemed a half-truth given that she eventually succumbed to the incident. She assumed that the old man was simply trying to protect a stranger's ears. There might have even been some denial on his part that separated the event from the long-term result.

189

Thomena brought her hand up, using a portion of her half-cape to dab at her eyes. She only just realized the wetness at the corners. "Thank you for recounting such a sad tale for me."

The soldier nodded. "I'd be happy to tell you about any of the others. Almost all of them include some loss or tragedy, but the rest of them have better endings. Pick which are your most important, however, as I suspect Julia will be here before I go through all the other seven."

"Other seven?" Thomena pivoted her head up and down the terraced plaza. "I only count a total of seven."

After comparing notes with Mabry, he quickly deduced which one she had missed. He led her to a grove of tall trees. Although planted as neighbors, they'd grown outward to extend the reach of their branches. As they approached, Thomena could make out a silhouette within the ring. The statue didn't stand out like the others, mostly due to moss and lichen from the trees spreading to the statue's cloak.

That isn't really him, is it? she thought. *Nay, the figure is holding a two-handed sword.*

Thomena convinced herself that it wasn't her father. She assumed that the green fungi on the figure's cloak deceived her into seeing familiarity when there was none. Once she arrived at the front of the towering figure, she looked up into a familiar face.

She barely mumbled, "Nay...truly?"

Thamin's face stared outward in anger, a pile of severed troll heads and a broken bow at his feet. Rays of sunlight filtered through holes in the cloak. He wielded a large, two-handed sword, sundered near the tip. Thomena had never seen such a sword despite clearing out the leftover weapons from the barracks. The plaque beneath him declared: "Thamin, the Trollsbane. Our Watcher on the Wall."

Mabry, shuffling his feet behind her, said, "I told you what I knew about this one. This is from the battle four years ago. He led the wolves' charge that broke through the monsters' line and saved a good part of his company. He later broke the sieges at Bael Cochaw and Kaigal."

"Don't worry," Thomena said, standing in her father's shadow. "I can get these stories from the source."

Chapter 21 – Roster of the Wolves

Ztakish looked over the plains, imagining the cities of the humans as he'd once witnessed them from another age. The foliage of his home territory was behind him, along with the promise of safety. Venturing even these few hundred meters into the open posed a risk of discovery. As far as he could tell, and from what his spies reliably obtained, the human defenders didn't know the identity of their true enemy. He didn't think the humans could even tell the subtle physical differences between the iztheran descendants and their more primitive lizardmen cousins. Unfortunately, the humans did discover that the lizardmen had become more organized. Even so, the frequency of attacks from other monstrous humanoids had left them confused and jumping at the slightest hint of trouble. The iztheran had hoped to catch his enemies with a sudden surprise in numbers, yet the ensuing confusion from multiple, restless humanoids worked into his plans just as easily. The situation could cause the humans to reach out too far from their walls if given the proper motivation. All that the plan needed was the proper lure and a place to spring the trap.

As Ztakish studied the land, he noticed his adjacent observer likewise study him. Brogratch the half-orc, the turncoat spy who assisted the armies of Kaigal only to serve his tribe's own needs, was likely still trying to ascertain Ztakish's full ambition and intentions. Regardless of the half-orc's opinion, he likely found it irresistibly tempting to strike a blow against the mostly human city-state. Anything that weakened humankind's influence would grant more control back to Brogratch's tribe, one way or another.

Ztakish had learned that the half-orc scout, observant as he was, also had trouble picking out the small differences between iztherans and other lizardmen. Brogratch could only admit that the male colors, namely the red and gold stripes up Ztakish's neck, brow, and the back spine ridges to the short tail, seemed to stand out more than those of the lesser race.

Ztakish had greater concerns on his mind. "We need to draw them here. This would be a good field of battle," the religious warlord spoke.

Ztakish pointed down the valley. "There is a fortified tower and a ferry crossing, just down this river. Am I right?"

Brogratch nodded. "The Vaeklus river. The tower and crossing are barely two miles away. Much farther downstream, the river flows into a portion of the city."

The Iztheran's gold irises widened. "That's even better. A direct line of threat to Kaigal! The humans would be forced to intercept our approach, especially if they think we're not large but pose a grave threat to the river supply."

The half-orc glanced around, appraising the land features around him. Ztakish hoped Brogratch could visualize it like he could. The nearby jungle and trees could grant a lot of cover for movement. The river wouldn't slow down large creatures like trolls from flanking the enemy…in fact, it might embolden the monsters against the diminished threat of wizards' fire spells.

"Do you have a plan in mind?" Brogratch asked.

Ztakish nodded. "Even a portion of our force would still be considered enough of a threat to raze the tower. We let the humans underestimate our numbers, allowing for the trees to hide our reinforcements. We make them think that we're threatening to topple the tower and disrupt the ferry, and that we have plans to poison the river. They know we have a large presence, but I doubt they know the extent of our power. Make a camp here then let them come. The more they commit, the better for us."

Ztakish faced Brogratch directly. "Tell me the truth. Have you ever seen such numbers thrown against the humans in all of your life?"

The half-orc shook his head. "Although Kaigal has stood up to some tough invasions, many of those were human. We've never seen such numbers united between the tribes of the jungle." Brogratch cracked a smile through his stained tusks. "They won't expect such a huge alliance."

The iztheran nodded, looking back toward the southern plains. He considered his plans and the course of his past. He believed that his god had reawakened him to resume his prior service. He'd had some divine dreams lately, but the messages were never clear. Yurtash currently moved two champions on the playing field, though the imagery contradicted itself. Ztakish knew he had a choice, however, and that Yurtash left his historic path open to him. It was time for war.

"It's time to make a map and gather some false evidence," Ztakish told Brogratch. "We can get one of my druids to make a poison sample.

I'll set up a camp at the edge of these trees. This won't be the first time that I've baited an enemy."

***

Thomena's jaw hung open from shock. She recovered quickly despite the sting of the refusal. "But why? All this talk about spending more time with me...I even decided to stay here and support this fight! How can you deny me at this time?"

Her voice rang out louder than she intended, given the emptiness of the former Blood-Wolves' barracks. Her father stood before her, his crossed arms announcing his inflexibility on the issue.

Thamin's voice replied just as sternly. "I'm sure there is lots of help needed here at the fort while the army moves. You can support in that way; you're too young to seek out a battle."

"You were younger than me." She pointed an accusing finger, dropping it a moment later out of respect. "You said you were barely into your teens when you started adventuring."

"My first adventures involved helping out caravans that were attacked without warning. Adventure found me when I wasn't looking for it." Thamin gestured in a northernly direction. "That's a lot different than actually joining a marching army headed for a fight."

"What about the troll fight? You dragged me into that one when you could have avoided it."

Thamin's stern expression cracked ever so slightly. He glanced down, breaking eye contact. "Maybe that was an unnecessary risk," he admitted, "but I had more control over that situation than you think. That was a skirmish, and I wanted to see how you could handle yourself."

Thamin paused. Thomena was tempted to jump in and say more, though she had a feeling he was searching for the right words. Her intuition proved true.

He said, "You're both brave and capable. I am impressed by the person you're growing up to be. However, large battles have a tendency to discard plans within minutes. I've seen..."

His eyes changed from intimidating to haunted. The quick turnaround left Thomena a little scared. Everyone, including her, had seen his strength of character. Was the shadow that suddenly caused him to flinch brought on by a simple memory?

"I've seen my friends taken down beside me." He stared into her eyes, allowing her to see a reflection of loss and guilt. "Good people,

193

experienced people, fell in battle because we can't anticipate all the surprises we'll face. I heard a phrase once, saying death wears many faces. I've already seen too many such faces in my dreams, and some of them belonged to good friends. People can spout bravery and loyalty, but all too few can cling to those concepts in the terror of war. Our company did much to keep the peace, but there is always another fight awaiting its turn. I can't risk losing you."

Silence stretched on for a few heartbeats. Thomena doubted that he could find the words to express something that he clearly didn't intend to share with her. She found some words of her own.

"You said you watched Mom die from afar, and she was behind the city's walls. Am I really safer here than out there?"

"I worry about leaving you out of my sight, knowing what is going to happen," he admitted. "You are still safer behind these walls than you are riding with an army column."

Despite giving him permission to help the people, Thomena couldn't resist saying, "Wouldn't you be safer here, too? Someone needs to man these walls. Your talents might be better used to stop any siege weapons that come rolling toward me...and Julia."

"I would be better at making sure that an army never gets close to these walls." Thamin altered his tactics. "Thomena, you are the most precious thing left in the world to me. I want you to be brave in the face of danger, but I also want you to see the reality in this situation. Just because we won't turn our backs on these people doesn't mean that the only way to serve is on the front line. They will need help here at the fort or even at Kaigal."

During his speech she crossed her arms and paced away from him. At his latest pause, Thomena interrupted before he could say more. "*You* fight on the frontlines. You've been risking yourself like that all my life when I didn't realize how much trouble you faced. You could have died." Her left hand flung outward, indicating the room full of empty bunks. "I could have lost you, and you never really stopped to concern yourself with that. You might have become an empty bunk! How was I supposed to react after such news reached me?"

"First of all, they didn't all die." Thamin turned to the bunks and started walking among the rows. "These people were well-trained and reliable. We threw ourselves at danger time and again and pulled ourselves out of some rather dire situations. They were all very talented in what they could do. We covered for each other."

The veteran ranger pointed at some of the beds. "Terill and Sildaar argued all the time, but when they teamed up in a fight, you did not

194

want to be one of their targets. Willowbee, a druid, paired up with me on a few outings. When we sat down, we always faced each other. It wasn't because we were looking at each other. We were actually keeping guard by watching over the other's shoulder for any approaching danger. Ombras and Bificus were one of a few couples we had in the company. They actually explored deeper into the hills before I did and gave me my first tour out there.

"Like I mentioned, they weren't our only couple. One of our druids, Dugan, married one of our martial artists, Josie." Thamin looked up at one of the walls, seeing a memory outside the window. "Jara, one of our healers, did the ceremony up on that watchtower."

Thomena remained angry, but she realized Thamin was losing himself in the memories. She respectfully stayed silent, fearing that she wouldn't hear these stories at any other time. Thamin continued speaking, pointing to bunks as he walked beside them.

"Josie wasn't our only martial artist. Dotanis had the habit of playing 'dead' on the battlefield then rising up and hitting an enemy from behind. We had strong front-line warriors who stood tall amidst any onslaught: Legionnaire, Hodine, Ceneleny, and Wraithwolf. They were immovable. Ryche and Woopnyo were everywhere that we needed them. Memo was a good officer. If you had an arcane dilemma, you could count on answers from Emersum, Majentas, or Moyeera. We had Northwind, a supportive teammate as well as an artist. Wendol's rogue antics landed us into some interesting situations, but he blind-sided enemies so well that we kept his tankard topped in the evenings. In fact, one of the other rogues, Arcusan, cooked up some nice surprises. One of our minstrels, Liette, often bluffed our way out of trouble in such a way that we'd laugh over her antics afterward. We had other rangers: Findor and Wargto. Two half-orcs ran with us, Croflah and Mara'tir. Then there were Kamyena, Muldari, Zetaorionus, Odessya...all healers...who kept us standing and fighting nay matter how hard our enemies tried to kill us." His voice took on a more somber tone as he stared at one bunk. "Except in cases like Arleeya's. Died of a heart condition when the rest of us weren't around to help. We're lucky we even found the body."

During the pause, Thomena forgot her silence as a question came to mind. "Some of those sound more like nicknames rather than actual names."

Thamin nodded. "Once you get to know enough adventurers, some are like that. All you have is a nickname or some assumed name to hide their background. I mentioned one of our half-orcs, Croflah? C-R-O-F-L-A-H. Try spelling her name backwards."

Thomena's lips moved silently as she reversed the name. Once she worked it out, her eyes widened and her shoulders shrugged. "Truly?"

"True story, most people missed it. Here's another strange one. Look at the name carved on the head of this bunk."

She followed where her father pointed. She looked at the name. CTHEN.

"How do you pronounce that?"

"That's just it," he said, a grin interrupting his formerly grim expression. "We all saw his name, but it must have been weeks that went by with everyone just calling him 'you' before someone got the courage to ask. It's pronounced '*See*-then.'"

A bewildered Thomena thought to speak again, but her father raised his palm up, begging silence. She could be very patient, and so she waited while he gathered his thoughts.

"It feels good just saying and hearing their names out loud, at least one more time. These people formed the best team ever seen on this continent. I couldn't ask for better fighters, problem-solvers, trouble-shooters, and arcane masters. Jaena would have been there, too, but she was raising you. The Wolves emptied dungeons, knocked aside invasions, found old secrets hiding in the darkest places, defeated traps meant to destroy us. Their names aren't supposed to mean anything to you, but I'll never forget them to my dying day. What *is* important to you, is that despite how tough we were as a team, sometimes we paid a price. People still died."

He focused a hard stare right at Thomena. The intensity of it almost made her step back.

"Now, you are asking me," he said, "to take a sixteen-year-old girl, who has barely been outside civilized walls and only recently graduated beyond her apprentice status, to jump into a war. I will not do that. I can't, in all good conscience, bring you into that danger."

There was a finality to his words and gaze that indicated she shouldn't push the issue. The veteran warrior rose and began gathering his armaments. There was little left for him to collect in the way of gear and supplies. His belt and pack ever remained ready to travel at a moment's notice.

Thomena fumed silently as she tried to think of something else to say. She couldn't envision any method that might turn his resolve. She couldn't believe that he would be leaving her behind after she agreed with his decision to help these people. The situation reminded her of the test she had taken when young, which offered challenging philosophical questions that pitted the tenets of her religion against each other. The virtues of Honor, Humility, and Faith would likely have her staying out of harm's way, as her father commanded. Other virtues, such as Bravery, Justice, and Sacrifice would favor Thomena putting herself in the path of danger.

She admitted to herself that even her most important tenet, Honesty, would result in an unfavorable self-reflection. After all, her father brought up a serious point. What did she expect to do that could make a difference in war?

Thamin stood before her. He looked ready for war. His yew bow rested over his shoulder, sticking up like the full quiver of arrows on his back. The history of the leather armor he wore testified its usefulness in the form of scratches and patched holes. The swordbreaker, (which he claimed didn't really break swords), sat ready at his right side. On the opposite hip hung Longclaw, formerly the weapon of another of his departed friends. Thomena knew without looking that his pack likely contained neatly wrapped leskam for nourishment.

Although his face remained stoic as ever, Thamin reached his arms out wide as an invitation. Thomena couldn't stay mad enough at him to refuse a hug. After all, years of her life had passed by wondering when she'd get to hug this man again. *What will I do if he dies?* She stepped into his embrace and didn't hold back.

"If something does happen to me," he spoke, as if he read her mind, "think well of me. I know I'm not a good parent, but you turned out more wonderful than I deserved."

In minutes, he was gone.

***

Thomena allowed plenty of time to pass. She wanted to make sure Thamin had left Bael Cochaw before she ventured outside. She needed to put a plan into motion without his suspicion. She planned to go to war. It sounded dangerous, but she'd made up her mind to help. The situation reminded her of when she tried to help at Old Market in Orlaun. Her thoughts were similar to the choice she'd made back then. *In all Honesty, I couldn't live my life without guilt if I didn't help as much as possible.*

Much of her time delay had been well-spent preparing for the journey. Despite having made up her mind about her plans, she knew less about stocking up for such a venture. What did one pack when preparing for war? If warriors didn't carry their equipment into battle, where did they put it? How would you reclaim it if your side lost and ran? She knew she'd be preparing for a trip that would take days and could involve running and dodging.

At her adopted bed, she laid out her devices to sort their importance. Her one-shoulder satchel carried most of her arcane implements and her spellbooks. Some crisscrossing leather straps held her potions. The mage placed the sura potions on one side and the healing potions on the other. Thomena didn't want to get them mixed up in battle.

She laid down her lightning wand, decorated by blue symbols and pierced by a leather loop that could allow it to dangle from her wrist. Thomena felt the pulsing of her own soul energy when she dropped her spirit gem onto the sheets. The device almost overflowed with her stored spirit.

Thomena tilted her head to the side as she considered the importance of two of her items. One was a timing glass, which could be "stuck" to any surface and measure the duration of some of her spells. The second item, which looked like a magnifying glass, allowed her a simple translation of any commonly used language. Thomena doubted that either item would come in handy for the impending scenario, so she placed them off to the side.

Turning back to more useful devices, she rummaged through the set of scrolls that her friend Auney had provided before leaving Orlaun. Some would be useable in combat. Of course, trying to grab and read a scroll in the middle of a fight would be a tricky proposition. Nevertheless, Thomena rolled them up using colored varieties of twine. The color of the twine allowed her to know which scroll was which even when rolled up. She returned them to a scrollcase and set it down.

She knew she couldn't afford to leave the mace behind. Thamin had created a leather loop that matched her belt. A simple leather string could be tied over the head of the weapon, holding it in place. Her father showed her a way to tie the string, which allowed for Thomena to pull it loose quickly. Although the weapon's weight tugged her belt lopsided, she could still wield it easily as long as she used a strength spell when close to any battle.

Although she felt that she'd already sorted her essential gear, she still had a lot of decisions to make. Thankfully, she knew that the rest of the army would still take a day or two to depart, allowing her any last-minute foraging such as rations. But would she find a horse available? How many sets of clothes should she carry? Most of her personal grooming items fit in their own bag, but did she really need all of them? Should she take along one of the Wolves' spare tents in case of rain, despite the weight?

Thomena recently realized that Thamin wore a magical belt of pouches. She'd found out that secret as he packed his gear away. The pouches could hold a ridiculous number of small items, despite the apparent external size, but couldn't accommodate stretching their openings to accommodate large items. This meant that the veteran ranger could carry just about every small accessory known to civilized society without worrying about weight. Thomena didn't have the same luxury. She wanted to carry a bit of everything, but all those tiny things added up.

Sighing as she folded her hands across her body and stared at the equipment piles, Thomena knew she would have to set out and discover if she could even get permission to tag alongside the army. Beyond that, she would find out if she would have the luxury of storing extra gear on a horse or wagon. Even further beyond that, she'd have to avoid running into her father for as long as possible. He had enough to worry about.

Thomena decided that it was time to seek help from another source. She equipped herself with only enough basics to defend herself in a fight yet left the whole pack and her traveling supplies. Her mace, wand, straps of potions, and her healing satchel adorned a simple outfit. She wanted to appear ready but carrying a heavy pack a couple days ahead of the march might look foolish.

She exited the barracks and passed under the inner gate with barely a glance to the guards on duty. Her first choice could have been Commander Shan Bedran. He would be in charge, and she'd already met him. However, she'd already decided that if his long relationship to her father caused him to deny her, then she wouldn't have a good backup plan. Thomena had another option she could try first. She'd already impressed Lieutenant Kreshaw, commander of the Blue Boars, when she shattered the arm of the training dummy. He could likely get her invited to the army, and if he denied her, then she could go over his head to the commander.

Thomena wasn't even signed up in the army. It was with some distaste that she realized she would be banking her worth partly on her father's legend.

She spotted the lieutenant in question as soon as she got to the Boars' training area. Before getting too close, she cleared her throat and tried to swallow her trepidation. Thomena tried walking as confidant as possible. Her hands clenched in determination. The acts revealed some coolness of sweat in her palms and clothes. She recalled those inspiring words from *The Codex*: "Always strive to better yourself."

Thomena almost forgot about the low stone wall cordoning off the barracks from the street. She recalled the officer telling her before that if she wasn't part of the army, she was supposed to stop at the wall until summoned. Her pace broke as she hesitated. Stop at the wall, as she properly should, and show him that she could follow protocol? Or should she just walk up to him again since he had told her that he wouldn't deny the daughter of the Trollsbane from going anywhere? She spotted the gray-haired officer a short distance away, looking through papers in the shadow of the overhanging barracks' roof. The latest soldier to bother him had just left, giving Thomena a moment to catch him with few likely in hearing range. She decided to take his earlier words as permission. Stepping through the gateway, she judged that by not allowing the wall to stop her, he would be less likely to stop her as well.

She stopped at his side, assuming a pose of attention, just like she'd seen troops do in the past. "Lieutenant Kreshaw, if I recall correctly. I'm here to serve in Kaigal's defense." She saw his eyebrows raise in disbelief. "I'm led to believe that you would have use for magical support prior to fighting the enemy."

His eyes scanned her up and down as he stroked his long, grey beard. "Once again, I seem to be hosting you within my holdings. Lady Trollsbane, was it?" He made an obvious glance at the wall behind her.

Thomena didn't like that name, but she tried to hide her reaction. "Thomena GrayEyes, if you wouldn't mind. Hopefully, this is the place to be if one wants to serve the army, even if only for a short while. My father already headed into the grasslands, but his role is too stealthy for me. I can serve the Boars for as long as needed until the threat passes. These papers can prove my worth." She handed him some folded letters. "I once cast enchantments on the firefighting vigiles of Orlaun, prior to them running into burning buildings."

The officer accepted her papers. The documents included commendations for assisting Orlaun's vigiles, as well as approbations from her masters at the Brotherhood of the Circles mage guild. "So, you seek a limited-time contract with the army? Such as that of a mercenary?"

She nodded, forcing herself not to appear too eager...or nervous. "Aye. Although I possess more loyalty than any common mercenary.

After all, I was born in Kaigal, my mother died there, and my father yet serves its people."

"How old are you?"

"Sixteen...sir."

Kreshaw kept a neutral expression. "Well, you wouldn't be the only sixteen-year-old in this army. Residents of this continent learn to wield a weapon at a young age." His eyes dove back into the letters.

"Impressive letters." He handed them back to her. "Praetorians and your guild's masters speak highly of you. I'd like to see how you assisted the vigiles. Let's see you cast some spells."

Thomena's expression brightened. As the officer called over a few of his men, she saw something nearby that even prompted a mischievous smile. A rare look for the humble girl. As they lined up before her, she said, "If you want to truly judge my capabilities, allow me to cast protection over your men while on the move."

She pointed her hand. Kreshaw and the rest of his men followed her motion, noting a horse and cart parked beside the low wall. Within minutes, Thomena cast her protection spells on the men while hanging on to a moving wagon. At first all of them were dubious, but as the wagon raced outside the outer walls, and Thomena kept her balance while weaving her magic, it began to amuse the men. Most of her spells were limited to the same ones she'd used with the vigiles. Rylak's Bubble filtered the air around their heads, which would help block out smoke or poisonous air. Her skills had advanced enough to cast ice shields on others, helping protect them from fire. One addition to her spells included an air cushion. The spell would wrap a target in a layer of hardened air, which could help turn aside arrows or soften melee blows.

Kreshaw ordered the driver to slow down, then addressed her. "Here comes an enemy," he shouted, pointing at a tree stump sitting next to the path. "Hit it hard!"

Thomena drew her wand from her belt. Pointing it, she shouted the activation phrase. "Kee-lass! Kee-lass!"

The first lightning bolt missed, but she knew how to correct for the second one. Lightning blackened a portion of the stump as they rode past.

"How about something bigger?" The officer indicated the wrecked remains of a siege machine half-buried in vines.

Thomena allowed her wand to dangle by its leather thong at her wrist. She didn't like to use fire, but it was her best choice for impressing him. Thomena began to realize that she needed to get past her reluctance on using the element. She contorted her outstretched hand as she hurriedly spoke an arcane phrase.

When they passed the machine, Thomena launched a focused spray of flames at the wreckage. She kept up the stream for two seconds until the target was out of range. Fire and smoke rose as they left it behind.

The soldiers were entertained, but Thomena grew worried. "I need to put out that fire!" she exclaimed.

They didn't listen. Kreshaw and his men talked all at once, impressed and enjoying the fun. However, Thomena's thoughts drifted to the mage who'd caused so many dangerous fires back in Orlaun.

"I have to put that out!" she yelled.

Not wasting any more time, since the wagon was leaving the burning wreckage behind, she jumped over the back gate. The sudden act silenced the men as they gawked. Her muscles had already been augmented by her strength skill, allowing her to leap backward faster than the wagon rolled forward. She knew enough to land in a roll. The impact lessened to almost nothing due to the spells that hardened her skin and cushioned her with an air blanket. By the time the wagon had turned around, the disheveled girl cast a new spell. A spray of water doused the contraption.

When Thomena pivoted from the drowned fire, the wagon had turned around and rolled back to pick her up. Kreshaw nodded at her, grinning. She knew she'd convinced him. Now she could join the war effort and help her father.

She had no way of knowing that he intended to keep her in the back of the army.

Chapter 22 - Tokens

Julia worked up a fierce glow trying to keep up with Gunnard's work. For all their toil, the smith made sure to provide her with needed moments of rest and sustenance. She had a feeling that he was worried about her collapsing from exhaustion. Most smiths didn't seem to expect much from a female helper. With all the effort and skill Julia put into her job, she knew she had impressed him. In fact, their latest run back to Kaigal allowed him to officially add her to the roster as his apprentice. Julia now held a membership to one of Kaigal's crafters' guilds. She tried not to consider the fact that part of the act was to ensure her welfare and guild support in case something happened to Gunnard. Julia's membership would allow her to retain access to craft requisitions and job placement...even if the latter ended up like Gunnard's own assignment to a frontline castle.

She also knew she had impressed him due to his words to her during their last, brief rest.

"Lia? Oye just vant ye to know," he started to say, looking her in the eyes. "Oye'm glad you talked me into taking you out here, even dough you did it by picking my lock. Uffa! You know I vorship Dalios, and he's viewed as a muscular man. In Norvess, ve have strong vomen who can pull plow like a yak. Most ladies here aren't tough. Ve don't use vords like 'dainty' or 'delicate,' but that is vat I see in dese girls in Kaigal. But ye're as strong, tough, and enduring as any Norvess voman." He reached forward and gave her a hard clap on one shoulder as if congratulating her. "A Norvess compliment says, 'as strong as de ridge beam.' You know vat a ridge beam is?"

Julia shook her head.

Gunnard pointed to the angled top of a nearby roof. "De ridge beam runs along de top center of a longhouse roof. If you turned the house over, it vould be de keel at de bottom of de ship. For a longhouse, de ridge beam is de backbone holding it up." He held out both hands, palms wide, to indicate all of her and smiled. "You are as strong as de ridge beam."

Julia smiled, taking a moment to flex her arms. "You think these could hold up a longhouse?"

Gunnard laughed. "Vell, it isn't alvays just strengtt. It's endurance, toughness. You vork hard, and I daresay dese Diaran boys can't measure up to you."

Julia couldn't help but think of that compliment as they continued their work. If anything, she didn't want to let that man down. The two of them continued to mold the raw materials from Kaigal into stacks of shaped metal.

A messenger in a soldier's uniform brought a scroll to Gunnard. The smith's eyes rose as he looked over the message. He turned to address the soldier, but the man had already moved a few doors down, handing an identical scroll to another crafter.

He turned a serious eye towards Julia and waved her to a nearby chair. "The army vill be marching, and it needs its sutelers to follow."

"Sutelers?"

"Dat's a Norvess term. I mean deir crafters and provisioners. Vhen a big enough army moves, dey need some support people. Since I'm a smitt, dey'll need my expertise."

A chill ran through Julia's spine. "Wait…what…does that mean we have to go with the army? To war? I didn't know that a merchant life would lead to that."

Gunnard nodded. He gave her a few breaths to adjust to the news before speaking. "Boys in Norvess are expected to use a veapon to defend their homes at fourteen. At sixteen, dey are expected to join raids and patrols. You're old enough."

At her continued worry, he added, "Besides, sutelers generally stay in the back and are guarded like treasure. If an enemy did get close to us, ve could try out your machine."

Her eyes lit up. "We'd need the wagon to carry it!"

"Uffa! Ve're taking the vagon. I need supplies and tools to do my vork with the army. Ve better get it mounted right now."

A female voice called to them as its owner approached. "You two have been so busy lately. It's good to see you getting a moment of rest."

"Thomena!" Julia stood up and surprised her friend with a fierce hug. "You're not going to believe this, but I'm being conscripted for a war."

Thomena couldn't hide the surprise from her face, but once Gunnard stood aside and left them some room she said, "That makes two of us. I've been assigned to a wizard group by the head of the Blue Boars."

Julia didn't immediately respond, Thomena prompted her. "And you? How are you getting involved in this?"

"I'm being dragged along as a sut-e-ler." Julia stumbled to pronounce the word right.

"A sutler? You mean a provisioner attached to the army?"

"Suteler, in de language of de gods' favorite people," Gunnard insisted.

Julia barely glanced at Gunnard's interruption, more focused on her best friend's knowledge. "You *knew* of such a thing and didn't tell me?"

Thomena gave an apologetic shrug. "*Knowing* about a thing and *seeing* it in practice are two different things. I couldn't have foreseen this when we came over from Orlaun."

Julia crossed her arms but dropped her accusatory glare. "Well, at least we'll both be together on the same battlefield."

"And don't forget me," the blond smith added, crossing his own muscular arms. "Now, ve'd better get dat machine loaded on de cart."

The tinker turned back to her friend. "Do you have your strength spell on?"

"As it happens, I do. You need something lifted?"

***

Gunnard's promptness proved accurate, since the army marched from Bael Cochaw a day later. As their wagon had sat ready in a street between other sutelers, they'd heard the horns and shouts when the first ranks exited the gates. It took a long wait before the traffic cleared and Gunnard could urge his team forward. Even on the plains when Julia stood tall on the wagon seat, she couldn't see the front of the line. The dust kicked up by hundreds of soldiers, maybe a thousand, caused a dirt fog, which obscured their path.

She was grateful for having some cloth to guard her head from the dust shower. She'd bought a few men's handkerchiefs, large enough to cover her hair and her scarred ear. Julia lifted her hand over her eyes to help her see forward.

Although Thomena said she'd be with some wizards that were assigned near the Blue Boars, Julia couldn't see that company's banners. Her friend might not be that far away since the wizards wouldn't likely be at the front. Julia saw several members of the Gold Lion's forces. Mabry's company helped guard the supply train, including Gunnard's wagon. She occasionally saw Green Horse members riding back and forth off to the sides of the plains. The majority of soldiers marching near the supply train were, however, conscripted militia and spare guards from Kaigal.

And only one Red Wolf member somewhere out there, Julia thought with a smirk, before silently amending her count. *Or two, if Thomena inherited a membership.*

It wasn't long into the march before a familiar Gold Lion found his way to her wagon. "Julia, is that you?"

She turned her covered head and saw Mabry riding a horse alongside the wagon. She glanced up and down the animal before asking, "They gave you a horse for the battle?"

He shook his head. "Nay, just for guarding the wagons while everyone is on the move. It allows me to ride up and down the line and pass along orders. Once a fight starts, I'll be relying on my feet."

The tinker scooted as close to the soldier as the wagon bench allowed. There was something she had to admit, and it embarrassed her that other ears might hear it. "You stay safe and don't do anything rash if there's a battle. I've become accustomed to your visits and company and couldn't bear the thought of anything happening to you."

"I'll stay safe as I can, but I can't promise anything. I'm glad to hear that you enjoy my company. Once this is over, I hope to spend more time with you...if that's agreeable?"

Julia only blushed and nodded.

"I have to do my best to make sure that nay enemies get past me and threaten you."

Mabry fished into a pocket, drawing forth a pair of pristinely white gloves. The soft fiber indicated that they weren't used for hard work.

"These gloves are part of our formal uniform. On social occasions, at the fort or in Kaigal, we're required to wear them if we ask a woman for a dance." He extended his arm, offering them to her. "Take this as my vow of protection. I offer you this token to carry, so you might continue to think of me. I don't mind you holding them. If there is another dance, you're the only partner I'll consider."

Julia barely hesitated. She grabbed the handful of white in her hands, even as her cheeks flushed red. "This is...thank you. I'll keep them safe."

She held his eyes in hers for a moment. "Allow me to return the favor."

Julia had to think for a moment to figure out what she could offer. Suddenly inspired, she reached up and loosed the handkerchief covering her head. The wind blew her hair and left her ears exposed.

"I'm sorry it's not a fine, lacy lady's version. But accept this token from me and wear it as my champion."

Mabry accepted it and brought it close to his face. Julia knew it carried the scent of her hair wash. "I've never been anyone's champion. I'll do my best."

After exchanging a few more words, Mabry admitted that he needed to continue riding along the line of wagons. They bid their goodbyes and he started loosening the reins for the horse to speed up. A sudden thought came to Julia's mind, causing her to frown. She had to free one of her secrets before he rode away.

"Wait! Mabry Ingel!"

He pulled up short and resumed his pace alongside the wagon. "Aye?"

"I wanted to tell you something—a persistent thought that nags at me for release." She half-turned to Gunnard, who had been stoically guiding the wagon. "And you can continue to listen while doing your best to pretend otherwise."

The smith looked up, commenting out loud to no one in particular, "Vas dhat de vind howling again?"

It brought a short-lived grin to Julia's face. The emotion faded as she returned her attention to the soldier and adopted a serious expression. "You, and everyone else, get all curious about my ear. I'm ready to tell you about that now."

Julia closed her eyes a moment, clenched her hands together, and did her best to steel her nerves. "My family did well enough making precise mechanical items: clocks, locks, small gadgets. But for some reason, we ran into monetary problems, and my parents argued about it. I didn't catch all the words, but it sounded like my father did some drinking and gambling to excess. Their arguments became common during the last month before...the *event*."

The tinker sighed. Mabry was gentlemanly enough not to interrupt with any questions. He could see the difficulty in her explanation by her tight brow and hand wringing.

"I tried to help. I tried to work harder, redirecting my father toward our pending projects. I think he had been out drinking again. He didn't seem his old self. Finally, he grabbed a knife and slashed at me. Mother got in the way, so he slashed and stabbed at both of us."

Julia turned in the bench so that Mabry could get another look at the horizontal scar, which ended at the upper tip of her left ear. "He took off part of my ear, but I didn't even notice it until later. Worse yet,

Mother didn't survive. When guards were called out about a madman in the streets, they ended Father's life also."

She turned back to face him. "It's old news that I don't need to think about anymore. But I'll always carry this disfigurement and folks recoil when they see it. I'm glad the mage guild let me do odd jobs, which paid for a room. Beyond that, I am especially happy that Gunnard here gave me a good job and that I found a nice man that can see past my scar."

"Dhat vind sure is noisy today."

Gunnard's comment broke the gloomy mood. Julia gazed at Mabry. "And now you know."

In response, he held out his hand for hers. Julia reached out to accept the touch. Once clasped, he leaned over and risked his horse stumbling into the wagon. But it didn't, and he gave her hand a gentle kiss.

***

Thomena marched just behind a large wagon, which utilized a tall cover to shade those within it. She thought she might be on the wagon or given a horse, but both hopes turned out wrong. The wagon housed the senior magic-users assisting Bael Cochaw's forces. There were six of them inside, sitting and reclining on makeshift furniture as they plotted strategy for the battle. Thomena would have loved to be part of that conversation, but they lacked room for anyone else. A handful of other young magic-users suffered the same fate as Thomena, marching in the wagon dust while struggling with all their gear.

She knew she had overpacked. Few people who were walking had any spare clothes or provisions, although some of her fellow mages likewise struggled with carrying large bags. She had to admit she could have somehow shucked aside a few more items. After all, if they had to run for safety, Thomena would have to drop her entire pack and abandon it to outrun anything.

It didn't take long, however, for her to see an opportunity. Some of her stuff came in separate packs with their own straps. She noticed hooks and other protrusions for tying a load spaced all around the mage wagon. Thomena surprised the other walking magic-users when she suddenly picked up speed and ran alongside the lumbering wagon. She hooked her main pack and most of her gear to the side of it, falling back into the march with just a small satchel.

Within minutes, every other walking spellcaster had followed her example. Once that was out of the way, they made introductions and a light conversation flowed between them. Although their discussion swayed between personal stories, battle tactics, and arcane secrets, Thomena couldn't hide the truth of the conversation from her own heart.

She silently admitted to herself that the chat served to distract her thoughts from the reality of her situation. Her pilgrimage as a journeyman mage had been to learn from the world and set things right with her father. She shouldn't be marching into a battle, uninvited, against hordes of monsters. Thomena had criticized her father for risking his life and ignoring his family. Her current course seemed to parallel his choices.

Even serving alongside the vigiles of Orlaun, she never felt like she put certain virtues to the test. Thomena brought a renegade guildmate to Justice but didn't honestly feel like she had tested the tenet. A battlefield would bring forth the judgments of Honor, Bravery, and Sacrifice, and that ethical courtroom loomed over her current path. Thomena's faithfulness to Honesty had already forced her to face uncomfortable situations.

The future didn't settle for appearing uncomfortable; it clearly went straight to deadly.

***

Thamin crouched in a dell with a number of army scouts, lodge rangers, and elf allies from Syllatru. This group composed the advance scouting team. They all knew that Kaigal's forces were already marching to this area. Thamin understood how well an accurate assessment of the land and their enemy could leverage the battle for Kaigal's army.

The dell seemed an odd spot for a strategy meeting. Although sheltered from any eyes able to see them from the nearby jungle, it was a muddy spot with lots of tall grasses. The forces around Thamin used that to their advantage, smearing mud onto their exposed body parts and tying up lengths of grass. They spoke few words since most listened to a druid using his connection with nature to scout the area through a bird's eyes.

"I saw a camp just outside the fringes of the jungle," the druid informed them, his eyes fluttering nearly closed as his vision followed the bird. "It's occupied by orcs. Several battle standards and totems ringed the camp. I dared not guide the bird too close to those totems."

Thamin asked, "Any thoughts on numbers? Is it more than one tribe?"

The druid nodded. "I see more than one chief's yurt. Plenty of differing banners. Perhaps a couple hundred orcs? I spotted some moving in an out of the jungle."

"What of the approach? What does the land look like?" asked a Syllatru elf.

The druid motioned with his hands as his eyes continued to focus farther down the valley. "To get to the camp, we'll be entering some lowlands between two hill regions. The hills are steep and jagged enough to make it hard for most to climb them. The gap between hills is wide enough for the army to pass but would prove difficult to allow much flanking. The central part of the valley is open grassland, with some bush spots. The Vaeklus river flows out of the jungle along the west side, our left as we approach, between those hills and the open prairie. Our right side is bordered by a finger of woods stretching out from the jungle. It is a couple hundred yards wide in places, thinning out at the edge of the eastern ridge. Beyond the camp, the jungle is thick as it borders the river."

At this pause, Thamin asked, "There are nay enemies in those woods? It would seem a natural flanking spot. Also, no possible catapults on those hills?"

It took several breaths before the druid answered. "The orcs seem to have sentries only near their camp. I don't see enemies in the woods, but the animals in there are sheltering. They sense danger. The hills are clear. It would be next to impossible to build siege engines on those hills and use them well."

That last bit of news relieved Thamin. The ranger recalled a battle in which the Blood-Wolves suffered many casualties while pinned down by catapults on high ground. At least that didn't seem to be a worry here, but the eastern woods could hide flanking enemies.

Thamin mirrored the others in tying grass shoots to parts of his outfit and smearing dabs of mud on his face. As the others pried the druid for details, Thamin took a moment to consider the larger picture. At face value, it seemed like they would be catching a portion of the monsters' combined strength. Kaigal had more than a thousand fighters on the move, not counting the support personnel. If this was indeed a small band of orcs, they might be displaying their hand too soon. Thamin also considered that this might be a diversion. If the orcs were the only ones here, what about the goblinkin and the lizardmen? Even worse, were more trolls out and about somewhere?

Thamin wanted very much to scout the orc camp himself, but their orders were to use indirect means such as the druid's control over animals. The tactic posed less risk of alerting the enemy prematurely. Relying on such secondhand information, the ranger couldn't rule out surprises such as tunnels or hidden traps in the grass. The only concern he was allowed to alleviate was one they had shared when first eyeing the valley: the woods on the right flank.

The conversation had drifted to uncertainties, but it hadn't changed their tactics. Thamin called for their attention. "Make any last preparations now. Once we get up out of the dell, we're in for a long night of nay rest. We better hope they don't have any surprises lurking in those woods. That's *our* job now. We have all night to creep forward and get into hiding. Patience is the key. If someone sets off their sentries, we'll be undermanned and running for our lives."

Camouflaged faces nodded back at him. Within moments, a silent force moved out of the dell and began a long crawl across the tall grasses. Most of them began a slow skulk toward the distant finger of woods. The sun had already hung low to the jungle cover when they started forward, and dusk and nightfall rolled past as they took their time. Eventually, Thamin switched his approach by shapeshifting into his wolf form. He padded forward silently, just another animal in the wild. Several other lodge members and elves shared similar abilities, likewise advancing toward the enemy in animal forms.

Kaigal's forces knew that the orcs and their allies had an advantage seeing through darkness. However, even that bonus didn't give them enough advantage when dealing with distant forms on the horizon. The closer the scouts approached, the more dangerous it would get. Thamin and the others bore the brunt of the risk as they moved closer to the orc camp without any nearby support if the enemy spotted them.

Chapter 23 – Vantage Points

While Thamin still padded through the grasslands in wolf form, Thomena wandered through the parked army only about three miles from his position. She glanced up at the first stars of the night. She could see the constellation Theocris, the warrior, standing next to Adeline, the healer. These days, her once-favorite constellations only reminded her of Bealak's folly. Orlaun was still rebuilding from his acts of arson.

The sound of a whetstone sharpening a blade guided her to Gunnard's wagon. Not many fires lit the encampment, likely due to their proximity to the enemy camp. Some officers used arcane lights, such as Thomena did, dimmed so that they didn't send too much light into the sky. She approached the smith's wagon and saw him busy honing sword edges. The round whetstone sat on a supportive frame, small enough to be portable using the wagon. She couldn't see her friend.

"Fair eve, Gunnard," Thomena said. "Are you and Julia still working through the evening? Is she around?"

Gunnard lifted the new blade from the whetstone. "Velcome Tomena! Ya, dey have me finishing up some new items. Oye won't be using de hammer tonight...too noisy for de soldiers' sleep." He pointed over the wagon. "Lia is sleeping on de odder side, under de tent."

The tinker's voice sounded like it originated under the wagon. "Just because my eyes are shut that doesn't mean I'm getting any sleep. Please join me, Thomena."

Chuckling, Gunnard said, "I planned on sleeping in de bench tonight. You young ladies can share de space in de tent."

"Gods watch over you. I'll get my rest. Make sure you get some rest for yourself." Thomena curtseyed.

She walked around the wagon. The "tent" of Gunnard's consisted of panels of thick fabric attached to the side rim of the wagon as high as Thomena's shoulders, which sloped downward from the wagon to some meter-high poles propping up the low end. She was about to ask how to enter, but Julia started flipping free the wooden toggles holding the inside flap.

"Inside, quickly," Julia hissed and with good reason. As Thomena ducked into the opening, she saw that her friend only wore a long shift and socks.

From the inside, Thomena realized that a second curtain of woven fabric dropped straight down from the wagon, blocking both eyesight and winds underneath the transport. Thomena's spell brought the only light inside the tent, causing Julia to squint her eyes. The tinker fumbled to close the opening as Thomena adjusted to the space. Despite the low headroom, the tent looked cozy enough. Julia's bed, borrowed from Gunnard, consisted of wool blankets stuffed with something soft. A tarp lay underneath, fighting against any moisture. Another thick, wool blanket covered her.

Oddly, Thomena saw a pair of immaculate white gloves next to the folded cloak Julia used as a pillow. As the mage set aside her pack and cloak, she asked, "What are those gloves for?"

Julia scampered back to her spot, stuffing the gloves under her pillow with all haste. "Oh. Just in case of a nightly chill."

Thomena tilted her head slightly. "You know, I wouldn't lie to you."

Julia frowned. Thomena's light revealed a reddening of the tinker's cheeks. Julia huffed before answering. "They're Mabry's. It's something of his to hold onto...and we aren't discussing this."

"Dat vind is starting to blow again," Gunnard said from the other side of the wagon, only barely muffled by the tent fabric.

Julia slapped a hand over her face, covering her shame.

Thomena couldn't prevent a broad smile. She didn't want to tease her friend, so she verbalized her support. "It's fine, Julia. I understand, and I'm happy for you. It is good to have something wonderful to cling to when the future looks a bit scary."

Julia turned the conversation. "What brings you here? Need a place to sleep?"

"Aye," she nodded. "None of the mages have a spare spot for me, and that's fine. I'd rather stay with you if I'm not imposing."

Julia indicated the spacious bedding. "There's plenty of room here. I'd be happy to have the company tonight. As Gunnard said, he plans to sleep on top of the wagon. The wheels are anchored in place, and the horses tied separately."

A voice, spoken thick with a Norvess accent, started singing a tune. "I rest witt my drink, under stars so entralled, viewing de candles of the sky's great meadhall. My fahdder's look down, my brodders

213

gatter 'round, and under dese stars I pass out on de ground…" The voice drifted into humming.

The two girls giggled as Thomena found a corner to place her pack and outer garments.

Unfortunately, most of the mirth disappeared after that, leeched away by worries of tomorrow. Mage and tinker spent a mostly sleepless, silent night burdened by anxiety. Thomena felt too alert with every sound that came to her ears from the army camp. She worried that her father and the advance scouts would run into trouble and if they would be running back during the night.

He's the Trollsbane, she reassured herself in the darkness once Gunnard's snores could be heard atop the wagon. *If I need to be worried tomorrow, I should start worrying for myself. The Codex says always strive to better yourself. Nay matter what challenge I face tomorrow, I need to survive it as a better person.*

***

The morning light illuminated the Vaeklus River Valley, revealing a scene in which weapons were brandished between two opposing forces. Kaigal's army marched out of the southern plains in tight formations, drumbeats accentuating their tandem steps. Colorful pennants snapped as they rode the morning air, but none so large and imposing as Kaigal's signature banner. Due to the revolution that overthrew their nobles and established the rule of more modest men, the centerpiece heraldry involved a golden merchant's scale. In the background, a blue triangular field stretched along the staff's side and the top edge, diagonally meeting a field of red forming three angles along the bottom and the far end. Heavily armored troops bore the banner proudly in the center of their line as it moved forward. A few lightly encumbered horsemen rode ahead, looking to get a feel for their destination.

Just outside the borders of the jungle, the orc camp likewise looked alive with sights and sounds. Warpaint covered their faces as some waved serrated swords and others raised macabre-looking standards of their own, mostly decorated with bones and profane symbols. The humanoids beat upon their own wardrums as they yelled threats across the valley grassland. None seemed deterred by the approach of the mostly human army.

Walking several waves back from the front of the army, Thomena nervously took in the whole scene. The ranks of veteran soldiers

214

surrounding her did little to provide any sense of comfort or protection from the inevitable clash. A couple hundred meters to the rear, Julia rode in the supporting wagon train. The mage glanced back, wishing for the safety of her friend this day. Looking forward again, she saw the stretch of trees on the right that their advance team reportedly infiltrated last night. As far as she knew, her father likely hid in those trees, waiting to counter any similar ambush plans the enemy had for those woods...

If something hadn't already gone wrong in the dark hours. *If* they'd managed to sneak up to monsters that saw better in the dark than them. Thomena had no way of knowing her father's whereabouts or welfare. In a twist of humor, he wouldn't suspect that she stood in the middle of the marching army. She guessed he was there due to strategy meetings between the magic-users. They talked about limiting area bursts toward the woods due to the risk of threatening friendly units. Since they knew their lead scout team—likely including Thamin—snuck forward last night, Thomena assumed that was his most likely position.

The finger of woods extended out so far that the right flank of the army moved alongside it as they continued to close within bowshot of the orc tribes. Members of the Gold Lions marched on both flanks of the army, with several skirmishers following the edge of the trees and the opposing river.

The sutelers and other wagons pulled to a stop at the far extent of those woods. Although situated way back from the potential fight, Thomena still worried that any opponents in the tree line could pose a threat.

A messenger from Commander Bedran intercepted the group of magic-users, summoning them to his side for orders. Thomena followed in step as they jogged to his position. He wasn't hard to find. Although the banner of Kaigal waved at the front and center of the army, a banner indicating the Bael Cochaw garrison accompanied the command group. Even if not for the run, Thomena's heartrate would have quickened just at the thought of the commander seeing her taking part in the battle. He didn't notice her right away. His attention focused on the other end of the field, using a looking glass. When the messenger announced their arrival, Shan Bedran's scarred face looked them over. His eyes locked onto her for a brief pause, but he kept a poker mask as he turned and addressed the head of the group. She couldn't read his expression.

"As discussed spellmaster, pair up your people. Spread up and down the line." The commander paused to point directly at Thomena.

"That one stays back from the front waves. Put her somewhere in the center, where I can see her."

As the head magic-user assigned pairs, Bedran motioned Thomena to approach. She stood tall before him, even snapping a salute that she'd seen the soldiers use. "Aye, sir!"

He smirked at her actions and returned the salute. In all, a softer visage than she expected. "And just how did you end up here? Does your father know?"

Thomena honored Truth. "I asked to serve. Nay, my father doesn't know, but I'm old enough by militia standards. I saw what happened at Veldale. I can't just turn my back on that happening to someone else."

Thomena thought she saw respect in those veteran eyes, but she couldn't be sure. The commander nodded. "Well enough, I suppose. The spellmaster will pair you up with someone. Don't get yourself killed. I don't want to deal with those repercussions."

Moments later, the spellmaster paired Thomena with a half-elf druid whose name seemed unpronounceable at best. Together, they started marching ahead of Commander Bedran's position. The girl tried to quell her own worries about what was to come. Her heart beat as if she'd been sprinting. Ahead of her, she could see two lines of heavily armored Blue Boars in the center and farther ahead of them were more infantry, Gold Lions and Kaigal conscripts bearing Kaigal's banner. Even farther ahead, a scouting line of light horsemen led the rest.

If the monsters didn't have any more reinforcements, Thomena shouldn't have to worry about any threats against her or Julia's spot in the back. Maybe the only test to her Courage this day would be the simple act of taking the field and observing a win from a distance.

***

Even as the bulk of the Kaigal army advanced up the valley, and the orc encampment continued to demonstrate their disdain through war drums and bawdy shouts, a host of eyes watched from concealed positions.

Ztakish grinned as much as his reptilian face could allow as his golden eyes watched the neat formations arrayed against him. He respected a strong show of force laced with confidence. One thing that he loved even more involved breaking such formations and the screams as they eventually ran.

He spoke to one of his underlings. "Keep them calm. This trap will be won only through patience."

His supporter, as fanatic as most of his iztheran followers, disappeared to carry out his words with zeal. It proved to be a tough job, but one that his army managed with increasing difficulty. Their allies enjoyed witnessing the festive defiance of those orcs selected to portray a fake army encampment. They were bait, but they treated the honor with fine spirit. The war drums and shouts invigorated the rest of the orcs in hiding, making them want to go forth and join the display. Ztakish and his officers had their hands full trying to keep the forces in the jungle from making themselves known. Yurtash's mystic general assumed that the humans suspected more humanoid enemies in the area, but it was best to delay the confirmation until the opportune moment of surprise.

To Ztakish, it didn't matter that the human-dominated lands had summoned so many protectors to the battle. He had the numbers and enough tricks to win the field. Once he smashed this army, Kaigal would have lost their best warriors. He hoped that the other champion of Yurtash would present himself on this battlefield. The iztheran assumed he would take part. Ztakish hoped he could spot the Trollsbane before making his own presence known.

From another vantage point on the field, Julia stood up straight on the seat of Gunnard's parked wagon. The sutelers and supply wagons formed a nearly oval formation in the back of the army. Conscripts and older volunteers ringed their perimeter in case anything unexpected happened.

Julia heard Gunnard scoff at her dangerous act, even as she balanced as high as she could for a vantage point. Across the visible mass of sun-sparkled armor, horse-churned clouds of dust, and wind-whipped cloaks, the tinker found it difficult to see distant details. She couldn't spot her best friend, nor could she see the soldier bearing her token.

The girl looked down at her employer. Gunnard said nothing, nor did he wander from the wagon. The smith had no part to play in the battle, except for the watchfulness of any need to retreat. However, she noted that he stood by one of the ropes holding down the wagon's tarp. Julia's surprise lay hidden under the tarp, but they weren't expected to use it.

Unless the monsters launched their own surprise.

The tinker's eyes slowly swiveled to the right. Tall trees stood off to that side, beyond squads of Gold Lion skirmishers and Kaigal conscripts. If any monsters lurked within those trees, the wagon train could be bombarded with arrows. The wagoneers were told not to worry...but they weren't told why.

The vantage from within the trees came from a different perspective. Two groups of monster tribes skulked along those very same trees. They had a closer view of the encroaching Kaigal army than the camp of orcs facing them. They had to restrain themselves from joining in with the camp orcs' chorus of shouts, not that they knew many of the words. The primitive lizardmen, those who lacked the intelligence and hardiness of their iztheran cousins, slinked along game trails along the flank of their enemy. Hordes of goblins matched their movements, aiming to surprise the human army from the side.

They had all been told to expect the possibility of human watchers and swordsmen in the woods, but they saw no evidence of enemies. They weren't met with resistance as they first set out. That was a good enough sign to them that their path would be unopposed.

Those closest to the field of battle paused as the first action took place. They watched orc archers from the false camp's barricades began loosing volleys...intentionally disorganized volleys. The first arrows dropped across the open grassland like a scattered drizzle. A few lucky ones managed to deflect off the armor of the lead soldiers. The light horsemen veered erratically as shafts zipped down. One horse gave a shrill scream.

The lizardmen in the woods took it as their signal to creep forward, approaching the edge of the open meadow. Many of them began to ready bows and spears.

The goblins moved further away from the jungle line, continuing down a course closer to the far side of the woods. As much as they wanted to join in and fight, they had been asked to cause a distraction against a softer target. They snorted as quietly as they could as they stretched, unmolested, down toward the tip of the woods.

Unknown to the jungle humanoids, there were others watching them. Even as the monsters looked westward to the battlefield or looked southward down the line of woods, they were watched from more angles than they realized.

The elves, rangers, druids, and scouts of Kaigal's advance lurked in camouflaged positions. Some hovered in the trees, others waited and watched from artificially grown thick foliage, in between lines of goblin ranks.

The eyes of the Trollsbane watched a line of lizardmen form under his tree. The brown-eyed, dark-haired champion had already gone through several preparations. From the moment he first heard their advance, he had drawn Longclaw and the swordbreaker from their scabbards. He infused the blades with fiery natura magic before slipping them home again. The scabbards were protected from the spells, and the enchantments should last long enough for most battles.

By the time the creatures moved within visual range, Thamin whispered, "Fellunus."

The natura spell, another gift of the god Yurtash, flowed through his body and fused spirits to his will. He adopted a feline elegance of speed and agility. For the next hour, he would gain increased grace of movement.

Thamin watched his enemies move into position, and they didn't see him in the branches above them. He noted the goblins going farther south as groups of lizardmen took up positions underneath his concealment. He hadn't survived so long as a lone scout without obtaining a lot of skill at camouflage. Watching the monsters move into position, he constantly evaluated his battle plan. The numbers moving about made engaging them seem like contemplating suicide, but he wasn't alone. Looking to the side, Thamin started flashing hand signals to an elf hiding there. Once done with their conversation, they both turned and flashed new signals to other allies in hiding.

Unbeknownst to the lizardmen and goblins moving into their ambush positions, others were already set to ambush them.

Chapter 24 – Opening Skirmish

Thamin listened as birds called to each other in the woods that stretched down the human army's right side. Few out in the grasslands heard the calls since their attention focused on the scattered shots exchanged between Kaigal's horse archers and orcs in the encampment. Inside the woods, the lines of lizardmen and the groups of advancing goblins paid the whistles little heed. A few looked around, but their minds were too focused on the impending fight. The creatures could see the front line of humans advancing within range, the army's eyes focused toward the jungle line in the north. The light horse cavalry rode erratically across the field, much closer as the mounted bowmen skirmished with the orcs. Despite temptation, the goals of their commanders had been made clear: they were to hit the lines of human foot soldiers from the flank. Lizardmen nocked arrows onto strings before raising them. Deeper lines of melee fighters, mostly berserkers, moved up from behind so that they could defend the archers if rushed.

Meanwhile, they ignored the bird calls in the canopy...until the canopy attacked.

Thamin lent his own voice to a bird call, signaling to the elf troops. He extended one arm toward the line of lizardmen underneath him. The enemies were poised to fire into the unsuspecting Lions. The ranger drew on one of his many natura tricks. "Movreal," he whispered.

The thick underbrush of the woods came to life around the legs of the lizardmen. Branches encircled their limbs, pulling in a few directions at once. Only a couple of them released their shots, but those arrows flew wild.

Thamin's bow rose, the first arrow drawn back to his cheek as he aimed at the most vocal lizardman. In the confusion, the archers didn't notice their group leader drop dead from an arrow buried in the back of his skull. More fell in the next few heartbeats, so the act didn't go unnoticed for long. They tried cutting themselves free of the bushes while looking for the source of the arrows. One thought to look up, but an arrow stopped the warning from escaping his lips.

A flurry of bird calls heralded other wilderness warriors initiating their attacks. Up and down the line, battle cries or surprised screams echoed from the eastern woods. The style of attacks varied as greatly as the diversity of the attackers.

The elves of Syllatru had responded to the Trollsbane's call to action with great enthusiasm and numbers. It was a testament to the elves' woodland abilities that so many managed to hide their numbers without discovery. Volleys of arrows cut down lizardmen and goblin archers as they stood poised to deliver their own shots. Elf swordsmen rushed out of blinds and tried dropping as many berserkers as possible before the warriors' rage had a proper chance to start. Fighting erupted right under Thamin's perch, but the ranger kept a steady stream of arrows launching at targets.

Other lodge rangers struck from hiding. Some opened fire with bows in the canopy as Thamin had done. A few charged from hiding to take down leaders or enemy spellcasters.

Bows and blades weren't the only opening factors of the battle. Spellcasters…mostly natura users such as druids, shamans, and mystics…twisted the forest to suit their needs. Bramble branches slashed with thorns, vines sprouted and tugged at body parts, and trees slapped with their limbs. Some spellcasters had the ability to charm nature's animals, using them like attack pets. Both sides utilized these tactics, but Kaigal's allies were the first to strike. As a result, Thamin witnessed the jungle-based humanoids taking the heavier count of casualties during the battle's opening. Although the initial surprise went well, Thamin had too many concerns in every direction to afford any lapse in concentration.

***

Thomena followed in the path of her druid mentor as the spellmaster summoned them to his position. A slight swell in the land gave him a better vantage point to see the orc camp. To her, it also seemed like a bad spot to stand while both sides were firing arrows. She didn't have long to consider her worries.

"Look at the camp. Do you see it?" the spellmaster asked.

The half-elf druid and Thomena turned their eyes toward the camp as Kaigal archers sent forth another volley. The arrows' course seemed accurate until the last dozen meters. Some invisible force redirected the volley before it could strike the orcs. Arrows inexplicably spun or tumbled away from the camp defenders. The majority fell in such a way that the wind might as well have blown them backward.

"Like a wind wall of some kind?" Thomena asked.

"Nirahha's face!" cursed the druid. "They have totems planted around their perimeter. Mystics are using wind as a ward."

Thomena's arcane talents had revolved around elemental studies. As such, she knew that mystics could use natura magic granted by nature to likewise use elemental-based effects. She currently used an air shell to help deflect any nonmagical projectiles that came too close. The orc mystics were using a similar power, housed in totemic constructs, to protect the orc camp.

The three magic users watched as Kaigal's mounted archers rode erratically to avoid incoming fire. Orc arrows managed to fly through unimpeded, dropping a couple humans from their saddles.

The spellmaster turned to them. "Thomena, I need you to run a message back to Commander Bedran." He pointed. "He'll be riding near Bael Cochaw's flag. Warn him about the totems protecting the camp from arrows."

As soon as he finished his message, she took off at a full run. Thomena forced herself to move with all urgency to warn Bedran. Knowing that lives were on the line, Thomena ran faster than she'd ever run before. The flag hadn't seemed too far away, yet she gasped from lack of air as she jumped obstacles and kept pushing her legs onward. By the time she staggered to a halt in front of the commander's horse, she doubled over. Thomena couldn't deliver the message until she caught her breath.

***

In the distance, Ztakish had witnessed the same ineffectiveness of the humans' attack. He laughed at the success of his magical trick. The iztheran watched Kaigal's forces waste effort and resources while his own forces had the upper hand. Ztakish also saw the three spell-casters in the distance as they witnessed the truth of the camp's defenses. After all, they stood on an elevated position, and his own gift of natura allowed him to focus on long-distance targets. He plainly saw the young female run to the rear to deliver a message. If he had a spell that could reach that far, he'd have struck her down. The longer the humans failed to see his tricks, the better off his people would fare. He still took satisfaction in the signs of the commander's frustration. The leader of the "civilized races" could be seen making angry, animated movements while pointing his orders out to his men. The iztheran dismissed any further interest in the faraway girl.

"...light horse to move out to the flanks for support. Center infantry needs to advance to that camp and tear out those totems. I don't want our spellcasters that close to that jungle, just in case of ambush," Commander Bedran shouted to his aides. "The Boars will need to form front and center."

Having delivered her message, Thomena remained bent over, skin pale as she fought from retching. Bedran's next words were for her, still shouting, yet more respectful. "Young lady, don't run yourself so hard. It may be a long day of battle. Take the time to catch your breath then return to the wizards."

After a few moments, a subordinate watching the front lines relayed his observation. "The banner is moving forward, sir."

Thomena rose and turned her head. The blue-and-red banner bearing the merchant's scale bobbed slightly as men advanced toward the enemy camp. Although it looked to be some distance away, she was still mindful of the range of bows and spells across a battlefield. She couldn't accurately throw lightning that far, but a volley of arrows from either her spot or the jungle could still pepper that area.

She was just about to run back to her position when another messenger ran to the commander from the east. An elf! Thomena didn't recognize the heraldry of the patch on his tunic since she wasn't familiar with Syllatru. She decided to pause just a bit more to hear the message.

"I've been waiting all morning for news from the woods. What word do you bring?" Commander Bedran asked.

The elf jerked his thumb over his shoulder, pointing back at the eastern trees. "Reporting from Thamin Trollsbane. As anticipated, the enemy sent forces into the woods to flank us. We've begun ambushing lizardmen and goblins. Initial strikes went well, but more reinforcements are arriving from the jungle. The line is holding."

Shan Bedran shook a fist, glancing at the distant orcs. "This camp *is* bait; there must be more enemies hiding back in the jungle growth. I'm glad I didn't move on this with a smaller force." The commander returned his attention to the elf. "If the line is pressed hard, let me know so I can reinforce. I'll hold onto my troops for now. I expect more trouble straight ahead."

Thomena only casually listened after her father's name was mentioned. Her head turned to focus on the line of woods to the army's right. Now, she had confirmation on her father's whereabouts.

Unfortunately, she couldn't see any of the action past the tree line. She only caught glimpses of colors and movements, coupled with occasional shouts and battle cries in that direction. Even that was hard to pick out since the battlefield roared with individual shouts, moving armor, terrified horses, and screams.

Honor tugged at her to resume her duty. Thomena faced back to where she last saw her druid mentor and started a light jog in that direction. She couldn't spot them at first, but she knew roughly where they should be. As she headed toward the front of the line, she found more reason to be nervous. Kaigal's forces followed their banner forward, which meant she would be running even closer to the northern jungle than before. *A jungle that the commander thinks is hiding more forces*, she thought.

***

Julia and the sutelers remained far behind the front line, but she managed to get a good observation spot. She watched lines of heavily armed and armored Blue Boars advance forward. They were the apex foot troops of Kaigal's forces. Most sported thick steel breastplates capable of turning aside nonmagical strikes. Even the more mobile ones wearing chainmail held large shields to protect their front. Arrows pestered them but gave little concern to the troops. Most were human, and they formed the center line. A good number of dwarves and a few elves added to their numbers, but often the lines were grouped by similar heights for the sake of a uniform shield line, leaving many of the races separated into their own groups.

Julia knew that every one of them possessed a weapon on their belt capable of injuring large monsters. Heavy axes, thick-hafted maces, long swords...often paired with back-up weapons. The front lines also held pikes, whether spiked, hooked, or axe-like, that extended over a foot above their helmets. They bore the burden of their weapons without complaint, not that one could see their faces through their visor slits. Most primitive races possessed more strength and endurance than the average human, but these men and women were outfitted to take down any threat. Their marching steps stomped the grasslands flat as they advanced.

Ahead of them, several of the lighter-armed Gold Lions continued to fire bows or launch spears at the enemy. Julia worried, for the army and for Mabry, as all missiles were deflected by the totems and their wind magic. Only sporadic injuries occurred in the orc camp.

Julia didn't think that her weapon would come into play from the great distance between herself and the front line. On the other hand, the magic of their enemies seemed to render it useless before even a shot could be fired.

Following shouted orders, the Gold Lions fell back. The mass of oncoming Boars looked like they would trap the other soldiers in front. Both units stepped into a practiced movement. Two or three Lions would line up in rows along their line, leaving gaps between them. The Boars likewise had half their number step behind the soldier next to them, also forming mini rows. As the lines met, the rows of Boars slid easily between the rows of Lions and reformed a wall of shields once past their allies. The Lions resumed their line a few paces behind the Boars, ready to act as a reserve and fill in any gaps inflicted by the enemy.

During the passing of the two units, the banner of Kaigal changed hands into possession of the Boars, marking the new front line. Its blue-and-red cloth danced in the wind, displaying a few new arrow holes since the skirmish started.

Chapter 25 – Arrows of Green Horse

An arrow whistled its dirge as it embedded itself deep into a lizardman's chest. Another followed, inflicting a grievous injury upon the next in line. The jungle humanoids began to fear the shrill music that preceded their companions' death gasps.

Too many remained, seeking out their attackers and returning fire. The short visibility within the trees fostered a chaotic mess of glimpses among the distracting sounds of battle. Due to sheer numbers, a lot of them managed to catch sight of the Syllatru elves in their camouflage attire. However, most failed to capitalize on it as elven bowstrings twanged their song.

Fewer of the lizardmen bothered to look up. Thamin used his natura abilities to step among the branches in the canopy. He fed arrows into his yew bow so fast that the bowstring never had a moment of rest. Those lizardmen who spotted the threat before he claimed their lives noted the cool composure in which the ranger prioritized targets and delivered judgment.

But for all his kills, Thamin knew he could only hold back a small portion of the flood of humanoids infiltrating from the north. His bow would starve for arrows before the creatures would think of running back to the jungle. He reluctantly stored his bow across his body with less than half-a-dozen arrows still housed in the quiver.

Better to leave a few for later in case I need the range, he told himself as he contemplated the fall to the ground.

Someone forced the decision upon him. The tree moved of its own accord; its branches bucked him out of the canopy. Even as he dropped, Thamin realized a lizardman natura-user must have targeted him. He fell into a barely controlled tumble. No sooner than he got to his feet, he had to use one arm to bat a spear aside.

The ranger twisted his fingers into a clawed palm, shoving the air forward while uttering, "Mitsarum."

A spirit spark, gifted by Yurtash, jumped across three feet of air, and jolted the lizardman spearman. Although a quick spell, it generally lacked lethal force. Thamin didn't give his opponent time to recover.

He yanked the spear from the disoriented attacker, spun it, and then jabbed it back into its owner.

By the time his latest victim fell to the ground, Thamin had both of his own weapons in his hands. He looked for the natura-user who had turned the tree on him. He spotted a lizardman holding a long staff, whose outfit consisted of a shawl of beads. A couple of elves had already handled the problem, judging by the number of arrows in his hide as he crumpled to the ground.

Amidst the war cries, death shrieks, and sounds of weapon impacts, Thamin heard a fellow ranger shouting about goblins running behind them. The Trollsbane called out orders, trying to get friendly units to block any route by which the goblins could run around their flank.

The moments passed by too quickly in the flow of combat. More lizardmen swarmed into the area. Although several rangers and a few elves fought nearby, there were no organized lines in the woods. Longclaw and swordbreaker danced patterns as Thamin deflected attacks and returned strikes of his own. None of the lizardmen could face his skill, but they made up for it in numbers. Thamin risked getting skewered if he stayed too long in any spot. The last Blood Wolf wouldn't allow himself to go down easy. Lizardmen fell at his feet, yet more took their place. Over their shoulders, Thamin saw the first contact between Blue Boars and orcs at the edge of the monsters' camp. The air carried the sounds of steel and armor clanging together, accentuated by battle roars.

***

Ztakish received the reports of fighting in the east wood, even as he could see figures thrashing just inside that tree line. The combat veteran showed little surprise or any other reaction. He had expected some kind of challenge from there.

"Time to unleash the front wave of legions. Also, send signal to our allies by the river. We'll hit them from the other direction," he stated to those advisors closest to him.

War drums sent out a message: the majority of the army was to move forward. Tribes of orcs and iztherans up and down the jungle line made themselves known to the humans as they rushed out from hiding. Many reinforced the orc camp, but their numbers stretched more than two hundred meters to either side of it. Soldiers from Kaigal who thought they were too far right or left of the battle suddenly found enemies rushing straight at them.

Ztakish then used one of his spellcasters to send a magic-borne message to the western edge of the battlefield. Moments later, a rumbling could be heard from that direction. Ztakish eagerly watched for the humans' reaction.

***

Thomena stood alongside her druid guide. She couldn't see much beyond the backs of the troops in front of her. Over their shoulders, she saw distant polearms and axes chopping downward. The chaos of noise in her ears had changed slightly. Most of it had been directly in front of her, but now it seemed to come from everywhere. She heard weapons crashing against metal or the thud of them sinking into something softer. Commands shouted up and down the line from unit officers, usually directing them around the flag or encouraging them to stand firm. Most other voices formed a cacophony of roars and screams that the girl simply tried to ignore.

The druid brought his hands up to cast a spell. "The key to surviving a battle like this is subtlety in the casting, young miss." The druid bent his head forward, lost in concentration.

Thomena could see no visible effect, but she understood what he meant. Years ago, she'd been rewarded for her service to the guild by accompanying Master Korrelothar on his flying machine, Dovewing. Much of the trip involved enjoying the view from the sky over Orlaun. However, she had used the occasion to ask him about his adventurer experiences. One of the things Korrelothar emphasized included how not to make oneself a target.

"Although a wizard on a battlefield can inflict great harm," he had stated, "a flashy spell marks them as a target for every spellcaster on the other side. Even bowmen prioritize enemy spellcasters over other choices. Therefore, if you know you'll be in a big battle, ward yourself, pick your moments carefully, and prepare to move quickly."

Thomena didn't think she had anything subtle about her offensive spells, but she still found a way to fulfill the army's needs. Using a pair of scrolls supplied by her guild roommate, Auney, Thomena had already placed air shells around the troops marching past her. Like the enemy totems, they would deflect any nonmagical arrows that flew too close. It would assist in softening melee blows, but it was less effective at that. She hoped she would save some lives this day...maybe even her own. She'd never imagined such violence on a large scale, as far as her eyes could see. Having a job kept her distracted from much of her fear.

A few of the soldiers had turned and gave incredulous looks at her while she cast spells to protect them. A couple young ones actually looked her up and down. But the horrors of battle loomed ahead, so very little was said except "thank you" and they were moved along.

Thomena's thoughts jerked back to her situation as the druid mumbled, "Something new is afoot."

The druid's head snapped up and looked to the left. As he did so, a frightened hare sped from that direction. It zig-zagged, frantic to find safety. Finding none in a field full of soldiers, it kept on fleeing in an erratic pattern to the southeast.

The druid seemed ready to say something else, but both spellcasters couldn't miss what happened next. A rumbling and splashing sound came from the Vaeklus River near its exit from the jungle. More than a dozen trolls—towering over every other combatant on the battlefield—ran into the fray. Many of them wore thick hides for protection, including bear pelts that barely covered their upper region. A few wielded tree trunks for clubs, but some carried handfuls of sizeable rocks. Their sudden appearance sent the Gold Lions on that flank running. A few horse archers lingered in the area, firing from a distance. Trolls responded by throwing rocks at the horses. The horsemen reluctantly gave ground.

Thomena's wide eyes didn't want to believe the sight. Her father— and his reputation—were busy fighting on the other side of the battlefield. Korrelothar's words ran through Thomena's mind as she saw a Kaigal mage envelope two of the trolls in a ball of fire. The remaining trolls promptly stoned that mage to death.

The trolls came forward at an angle, heading mostly southeast into the mass of Kaigal's army. Not ones for elaborate tactics, the trolls didn't coordinate their movements. They soon began to spread out, chasing individual targets.

The druid grabbed her arm. "Quickly! We don't want to be between them and the knights."

Thomena glanced back over her right shoulder. As the druid pointed out, the youth did, indeed, stand directly between both forces as the Green Horse spurred to attack.

Without considering the consequences, Thomena strode briskly alongside the older spellcaster. She forced herself to remember what Commander Bedran had said about pacing her endurance for the battle. It wasn't easy advice to heed in the threat of the moment.

The two magic-users ran only a short distance ahead before Thomena realized the significance of their act. Their forward progress had been blocked by the lines of Boars and Lions. These soldiers stood in reserve, waiting to plug any holes in the line caused by the enemy. The shifting front line was less than fifty meters away. Most of the orc arrows targeted this area. One came frighteningly close to Thomena before her air shell deflected it away. She flinched back, only to be stopped by the sound of heavy horse hooves pounding the ground just behind her.

It wasn't easy to hold onto Courage at this point.

Thomena watched the horsemen thunder into battle. She'd heard that the Green Horse knights of Kaigal were all that remained of Kaigal's abandoned nobility. Despite being referred to as knights, they no longer ruled any homesteads or provinces and could not hire retainers beyond the few needed to help take care of the horses and armor. It was now a paid position, appointed by officers to those who showed aptitude and passed strenuous tests. All were expected to help train the next generation of squires, and none were above the law if they misused their responsibilities. Some equipped their own family armor and weapons; others were granted available armaments from those who had fallen before. As long as they upheld their duty, Kaigal paid to maintain their equipment and supplies.

The downside of such duty included dealing with a pack of trolls.

As the trolls continued to advance, Thomena watched soldiers retreat from their path. The monsters of the jungle probably thought the trolls' rampaging demeanor was enough to disrupt Kaigal's line. Indeed, nay Lions or conscripts had any wish to go up against those creatures without overwhelming numbers. However, the retreat had been designed, and previously rehearsed, for Kaigal's tactics. As the footmen got out of the way and the troll pack spread apart, the Green Horse could line up for their charge without threatening allies.

The knights formed groups called arrows. A triangle of three lancers would take the lead. Another three horsemen would follow in a line, each one handling a heavy, two-handed weapon designed to cleave foes. Each knight easily guided their mounts using only their legs and verbal commands. Several arrows of riders branched off to line up with separate targets.

Thomena felt scared enough if she had to defend herself from a troll using magic, she found it hard to contemplate charging at one with only steel.

The first arrow group approached the lead troll. At first, it seemed like the lead rider would go straight at it. At a critical moment, the horseman whistled a signal and swerved right. The far-right knight of the triangle raised his lance and veered off to give room. The leader's lance still stabbed to the left and managed to scrape along the target. As the troll tried to adjust to the rider passing by, the ignored knight on the left delivered a more critical blow. His lance shattered as the point skewered the troll.

Roaring in pain, the troll failed to protect itself against the next wave of the arrow formation. The three riders forming the shaft of the arrow lined up and took swings as they passed. The first one nearly severed one of the troll's arms using a chop from his two-handed sword. A sudden shift from the troll almost backed into the second rider. The horseman still managed to slash through flesh with his axe, passing on the opposite side as the previous man. The last rider in the formation had a free, undefended shot as the troll swung at a man who had already passed it by. The last weapon, a two-handed, curved blade, opened up a deep wound in the troll's torso.

The formation left the injured enemy behind them. The right-hand lancer, his weapon unbloodied and undamaged, switched with the leader for position. He prepared to guide the next charge. The previous leader adopted the right-hand side, his lance still useable despite the brief contact. The left-side man with the broken lance discarded the remainder of it and drew a two-handed weapon as he kept his spot. The lances were good insurance due to their reach, but the knights always needed another weapon handy to deal with the large creatures. The other three riders fell in line and reformed the arrow's shaft. They sought a new target, leaving the badly wounded troll wailing in the grass. Though trolls had little chance of bleeding to death due to their anatomy, they could still be knocked out of a fight with enough damage.

Across the left side of the line, Green Horse formations thundered into the trolls. Their tactics saved the line from collapsing. However, not all attacks went as smoothly. Some were disrupted by thrown boulders or broken up by trolls who managed to toss a knight or two. Four trolls still managed to get knocked down by the knights in the first pass, only to be swarmed by Lions and Boars.

Thomena could not stop to watch the action. She had enough excitement happening in her vicinity.

Chapter 26 – Primal Tactics

In the eastern woods, the fighting moved so fluidly that there were few places with organized lines. The trees were too dense to allow for solid formations. Only the elves from Syllatru managed to keep and hold any semblance of organization. The elves had a mostly unified front across the woods, but they couldn't stop all the goblins rushing around their flank. The ranger organization was loose-knit and informal, so many of them fought as individuals. The lizardmen and goblins would rush in packs but lacked military coordination. Of all the combatants in the woods, only those fighting near the edge of the grasslands could keep track of the main forces, and most of them didn't care for anything past their own struggles.

Thamin managed to recruit a few of the other rangers to fight near his side. Some used melee weapons, most preferred missile weapons, and a couple of them used magic. In all, he felt like it was a balanced team, much like the Red Wolves company he once led. The group had just managed to put down one band of lizardmen, but they could hear more approaching.

Thamin organized a plan. "You, druid, turn this patch in front of us to mud. Once they try to crawl through, use the foliage to snare their movement." The spellcaster barely nodded before Thamin moved on to the next members. "Melee folks, hold a line from that birch clump to this stump. Taunt the enemy when you seem him but stay low. Archers" —the hero motioned to those carrying bows or crossbows— "five steps back from this line. Don't just aim at the closest threat. Pick off groups of enemies but leave singles to be hit by our front line. I want to stagger their numbers."

He glanced around. Aside from the druid, only two other spellcasters presented themselves. He directed his first words at a gnome who hung out at the hunting lodges. "Chunar, protect our side over by the birch trees. There's more cover for you if they get past us." The gnome nodded with a smile.

Thamin didn't recognize the other spellcaster: a young elf maiden. Her appearance shocked him at first. In the dark of the woods, her cerulean eyes were shaped into vertical slits, like cat eyes. "I don't know you. Aren't you with Syllatru?"

She gave a brief curtsey. "Just visiting, though they brought me along for my magic. I hail from the continent of Quoros. Allisee Lentara, at your service."

"Thamin Trollsbane, at yours," he offered a quick nod, mindful of distractions amidst the battle. "If I have you stand closer to that stump, can you help keep anything from hitting us from the side?"

"I shall." The elf spellcaster took her spot.

The enemy arrived only a minute later. A band of more than two dozen lizardmen crashed through the undergrowth, hissing and hollering at the sight of fresh meat. It seemed like an overwhelming number, and these defenders lacked military discipline.

"Hold to the plan!" Thamin yelled. "Archers thin their numbers."

Arrows and bolts flew between and over the melee rangers. Lizardmen started dropping. The rest hit the muddy section and slowed down. Stubbornly, they slogged forward, some climbing over their tribesmen. Thamin's arrows whistled alongside the others, ending the threat of a lizardman mystic in the middle of a spell. Several lizardmen worked their way around the sides. The druid, Chunar, and Allisee let loose spells on each flank. The archers obeyed Thamin's commands, hitting the largest concentrations of enemies, allowing a few solitary warriors to approach. When the first two lizardmen came within melee range, they were quickly outdueled by the few rangers on the front line. Lizardmen climbed out of the muck alone or with no more than one partner then easily fell to the defenders' numbers. Allisee held her side easily, sending arcs of lightning along the ground. Chunar fired spells from the clump of trees, dropping several.

Thamin's tactics worked well. Although not all these people had seen him in action, he gave commands, called out adjustments, and the lizardman numbers thinned considerably. His military career had been legendary due to how well he could size up a situation and utilize his available resources in the best manner possible. Despite their success, the numbers still went against them. The gnome spellcaster got hit by a ball of acid, dropping to the ground. Thamin's bow sought and killed the lizardman druid responsible for it.

He had to toss the bow back over his shoulder. Too many enemies were swarming around the mud pit. Longclaw and the swordbreaker cleared their scabbards with a red glow of enchanted elements. While the rest of the rangers strained to repel the enemy numbers, Thamin's whirling swords became a fiery tornado. The blades burned through the monsters. As soon as the Trollsbane cut through the line, he dashed sideways. His run carried him parallel to the fight, but he ran behind the line of attackers. His natural dexterity, augmented by a natura spell, kept him from getting mired in the soft earth. Thamin delivered backstabs and fiery slashes against several lizardmen before they even realized an enemy had slipped behind them. Even his minor strikes distracted enough to leave deadly openings for his allies.

Within seconds, he reached the opposite end of his defensive line. He thought the elf maiden, Allisee, might be in danger of being overrun. She surprised him. The elf's hands had become deadly claws, allowing her to rake apart two lizardmen who tried tackling her.

In the momentary silence of the repelled attack, Allisee met his eyes. She looked ashamed. Her claws darted behind her back, reappearing a moment later as normal hands once again. She asked, "You won't tell anyone, please?"

Thamin shrugged before responding, "You don't need to explain anything. You are my sister-in-battle today."

He looked around, taking in the situation. Only the gnome lay dead. Most of his allies suffered non-mortal cuts and bruises. Around them lay four times their number of dead lizardmen. Due to the war cries and drumbeats coming from the direction of the jungle, the situation would likely be a short reprieve.

"Patch your wounds, share any healing potions. If they come at you again, slow and separate them as you just did."

The elf cocked her head to the side. "What are you planning to do?"

Thamin offered a rueful grin. "Pull out my bag of tricks and slow them down."

He turned toward the sounds of approaching enemies. Allisee's claws had given him incentive to give in to his feral side. Yurtash's gift of allowing him to shapeshift into an animal marked him as a greenman, also known as a feral warrior. Thamin was not the only one with this ability, though Yurtash had gifted him above others. His troops watched in amazement as the man morphed into a large wolf.

He howled as he rushed through the underbrush, putting out a primal call. Others heard his call stirring their inner nature. There were many among wildlands folk, such as the rangers and elves, who shared the gift of greenmen. The feral warriors could adopt an animal spirit and allow it to shape them. Many druids, plentiful in the woods that morning, could call upon similar abilities. The primal nature of Thamin's howl enticed them to adopt their inner beast.

As Thamin rushed through the lizardmen's ranks, biting and clawing on the run, Allisee and his other allies heard growls and hisses echo through the woods. Rangers and elves, morphed into animal forms, bolstered the fighting. Some of the animal forms weren't even native to Diara, yet they were spirit shapes embraced by those capable of the change.

Thamin wasn't the only wolf rushing forward; bears, panthers, wrelcats, hawks, snakes, badgers, gorillas, elephants, gussters, and alligators joined the attack. Most looked larger than the normal variety. Their savage fangs and claws ripped into the enemy.

The enemy took a while to understand what was happening before responding to the threat. The few lizardmen and goblins that possessed similar abilities also morphed to attack.

As grunts, roars, and howls accompanied the other cacophony of battle, the numbers of lizardmen continued to press forward, pushing hard against Kaigal's forces. Nevertheless, those tactics bought them more time. Allisee and the others continued to play out Thamin's tactics, aided by the lizardmen's distraction of a wolf running and slashing sword-like claws through their reinforcements.

***

"Lia! Uffa! Ve have trouble coming."

Gunnard hadn't strayed far from the wagon since the fighting began. In the span of a breath, he turned, yanked a large hammer off the wagon's side, and turned to face outward again.

His warning proved redundant. Julia heard the anxiety in the shouted orders from their guards. The tinker, standing on the wagon's bench to get a better look at the battlefield, turned her head to identify the excitement. She felt like her stomach leapt circles as she saw the threat: bands of goblins broke out from the cover of the woods and charged toward the suteler wagons. The wagoneers and suppliers in the vicinity began screaming and running.

The supply train had not been left unguarded. Barely trained conscripts formed uneven lines, offering support to squads of Gold Lion skirmishers. The troops clearly hadn't expected anything to get around the elves in the woods. Both sides began to trade arrows, with some of the goblins aiming at the supply wagons.

Gunnard shouted again. "Lia! Down from dat vagon. Run wit da odders."

She needed to gulp down some air before responding. "Nay. This is why we brought our surprise."

"Bedder get it uncovered den, and fast."

Gunnard ran to the side of the wagon and started unleashing the tarp ties one-handed. He kept his eyes eastward as much as he could. Likewise, Julia ran around the sides of the wagon, pulling ropes loose.

She had been eager to try out her construction in combat but hadn't really foreseen the fear inherent with such an act. She didn't even have the mindset to worry over Mabry or Thomena at that moment.

***

"Another push and we'll have them groveling," Ztakish said. "Vines first, then the spores."

The iztheran leader was disappointed in the superior coordination of Kaigal's forces up to this point. He never doubted that his force would earn a victory this day. He felt confidant that he possessed more tricks and numbers than his opponents.

The latest tactic involved bulbs of a type of vine only found in natura magic. Along the jungle line, iztheran druids used magic to fling their bundles into Kaigal's forces. They mostly targeted the reinforcements just behind the main fighting. The bulbs landed with a crunch to their outer layer. Within moments, roots pushed out of the bulbs and sunk into the ground. Though some soldiers gave them a wide berth or outright stabbed them, the next growth caught everyone unprepared. Vines grew amazingly fast, whipping around and strangling anything they could wrap up. Even some of the Boars in their heavy armor found themselves caught in tug-of-war between two plants. Kaigal forces began fighting a new enemy, disrupting their reinforcement of the front line. They barely had time to change orders before spores blew across them from the jungle. Men who avoided strangulation by vine ended up choking on noxious elements in the air.

The orcs and iztheran warriors began to push the Kaigal troops out of the fake campsite. Even the few remaining trolls gained some reprieve as the Green Horse riders distanced themselves from the cloud of spores.

***

236

"Reform ranks! Third battalion to the center." An officer called from horseback as he rode near Thomena's position. "Step forward men, don't let them take the day."

Thomena stood close enough to the main fighting to feel apprehensive and vulnerable. She watched as wounded men staggered to the rear. The sight of so much blood and so many injuries turned her stomach. Were they losing? Earlier in the battle, she couldn't see past the wall of armored backsides of Kaigal's troops, but now gaps kept appearing and closing, allowing her to spot howling orc berserkers and armored reptilian humanoids.

Kaigal's battle flag waved less than one hundred meters in front of her. The line of Blue Boars remained thick around the flag, blocking her sight of their adversaries. A couple wounded men crawled out from the area, replaced by another group of soldiers.

When the vines landed around the area and started lashing out, the druid next to her moved quickly to neutralize one. Thomena drew her wand and aimed. She didn't need to use it, for the druid's spell shriveled up the vines into a rotted mass. Other nearby areas didn't have as much assistance. She saw plant life trying to throw men or strangle them. The sickening cloud of spores descended upon Kaigal's forces. Soldiers gagged, a few bent over and lost their breakfast.

Up ahead, she saw Kaigal's banner dip then fall out of view beyond the wall of warriors. She gasped, recalling how important the banner was to the army and its movements. After hearing frantic yelling and the rapid ring of metal blows, the banner rose again. Moments later, Thomena happened to be looking its way as the conflict around it jerked it from side to side.

"A moment," the druid said, holding a hand to an earring.

The spellmaster used earrings to somehow communicate with the other spellcasters. Unfortunately, there weren't enough baubles for everyone, so Thomena didn't have access to command directions aside from the druid.

Her mentor looked worried; pointedly looked at *her* and wore a frown. He said, "Commander Bedran has asked the spellmaster to move all mages forward and assist the line. They want us to counter the enemy's spells and offer retaliation."

"Closer?" Thomena whispered so low she practically mouthed it.

The druid looked behind them. "They didn't mention you specifically, but they have their own worries. If you wish to run back and assist command, I'm sure they won't mind."

Thomena turned to look for the Bael Cochaw banner. It sat a much farther distance back than she was to the front line. The area between them did not look safe. A few trolls were still chasing people while the Green Horse formations kicked up dirt clods, maneuvering at a gallop around the monsters.

She brushed the sweat of her palms onto her skirt. Thomena chewed her lip as she teetered from one foot to the other. Any retreat looked just as dangerous as the route forward.

But my father and Mabry are out here too, and Julia may be at risk if the army fails.

She looked to the druid, swallowing a hard lump in her throat. "I'll stay by your side."

Both of them ran forward. The druid offered advice as they advanced. "If you can, use cold magic on plants. Use air spells to disperse spores. Can you do that?"

Thomena brightened up for the first time since the battle started. She appreciated having a part in which she could start contributing. "I can do both!"

She and her mentor moved closer to the banner. Thomena actually set the direction, knowing the flag would be central to the battle. The druid had the task of casting spells while trying to match the youth's endurance. Once they got close enough for the spores to become irritating, they started casting together.

The druid mostly focused on the vines, while Thomena's air magic blew the spore cloud back toward the jungle. One of the strange bulbs dropped near them. Thomena reacted, pinning it to the ground with the quick spell use of a summoned icicle. She fired off a second projectile for good measure.

A blast of heat and a flash of light shoved her sideways. Rolling on the ground, she retained just enough sense of mind to realize the fire burst for what it was. A glance down her body revealed singes in her garments and the feeling of a sunburn on her arms. Her ice shield protected her...but what of the druid? An enemy spellcaster must have targeted them. Thomena rolled to her stomach and pushed herself up. On hands and knees, her gaze sought out the druid.

Only a funeral pyre remained of the man, surrounding a dark outline.

Thomena quickly turned her head, but she felt the same queasiness welling up from her stomach as she had experienced at Veldale. She gulped down breaths. Her mind repeated, *Nay, nay! Not again.*

Thomena had seen death by fire before, but despite that, or maybe because of the memories, her stomach didn't hold back. The battle raged around her as she retched in the trampled grass. Her awareness of everything else dimmed as she focused on the reaction of her body.

Once her stomach finished, her head found clarity again. Relief soon turned to frustration. Thomena's hands balled up in the grass as she got angry...at herself.

I need to handle my emotions. I need to control my actions better, she thought.

Thomena glanced toward the woods in the east, knowing her father likely stood at the heart of any defense there. She pleaded, *How would you have handled this?*

In the ruins of Veldale, he talked about fighting the endless evils threatening his home...their home...and he eventually got good at it. Which meant that once upon a time, even the Trollsbane was an inexperienced young person who never gave up the fight. At the time, he certainly couldn't foresee the success of his actions and the legend he would become.

"All he tried to do," she whispered to the ground, "was defend his home and the ones he loved. I don't know how much difference he thought he'd make, but I know I can make a difference here."

Thomena momentarily wondered why an enemy spellcaster hadn't finished her off. Maybe they lost track of her when she fell or simply moved on to different targets. Targets like the men around her. She glared at the cloud of spores in the area, hearing soldiers still hacking at wild vines.

"I can handle those things," she firmly reassured herself. "I *can* change this situation."

Thomena pushed her shoulders up from the ground. "Honor, please empower me to stand firm under threats." The girl rose to one knee, then higher. "Bravery, lift my convictions to keep my feet facing my enemies." The honorary vigile turned a stern face toward the threats in the north. "Sacrifice, allow me the serenity to be willing to lay down my life to protect others. Faith, repeat these solemn oaths like a mantra, worthy of addition to *The Codex*."

Thomena withdrew a sura potion from her belt. She poured the fluid down her throat, revitalizing her spirit for the arduous spellcasting that would be sure to follow.

"Honesty, keep me truthful to my skills, and allow me to be that name I shy from...

"...let me embrace the title of Storm-Mage."

Chapter 27 – Storm of Battle

Ztakish's vertical pupils scanned the battlefield, and his tongue flicked outward, tasting the air. The campaign veteran watched all the developments on the field and understood more than he let on to his underlings. Kaigal's forces should have been routed by now. That fact disappointed him, but he still anticipated victory. Ztakish possessed unbloodied troops waiting for his command, while the mostly human army had few reserves remaining. The trolls hadn't delivered the impact that he hoped, but a few still dominated the field in places where the horsemen couldn't easily charge. The only information he lacked came from the situation in the eastern woods. The more primitive lizardmen didn't do a good job communicating enemy strength. He could see, distantly, goblins fighting near the rear of Kaigal's forces, but it wasn't the scale of catastrophe he'd planned for his enemy.

He needed to call on his last, most trusted forces to hold the middle of the line. Ztakish's prize troops were, of course, the zealots and other fighters among his iztheran people. He turned to several armored forms waiting impatiently behind him.

"Reclaim our old glory! Go forward for the will of Yurtash and crush the worshippers of the weak gods."

At his call, they passed his orders down the line. The army began to surge forward. Even as they moved, his scout returned to his side. Ztakish addressed him. "Brogratch, what is happening in the woods?"

The half-orc, former scout for Kaigal's forces, snarled a reply. "Animals in the woods, fighting our forces with intelligence, as well as elves from Syllatru. They seem to have broken the lizardmen's onslaught. The goblins went too far past the elf forces for me to reach."

This news intrigued Ztakish. Could it be other greenmen among the "civilized" races? "Animals, you say? They could be fellow shapeshifters of Yurtash."

Brogratch shrugged. "It could be the influence of the Trollsbane."

The iztheran commander already guessed as much. He hoped he would get the opportunity to test this hero one-on-one. For now, he had an army to direct.

"Take the remaining orc tribes and turn your attention to those woods," Ztakish commanded. "My people will stretch out from river to woods and push them."

***

Bodies clashed all around Thomena as she nimbly danced between fights. She'd already attended to her defensive spells, especially since her ice shield had been lowered by the fireblast. The girl augmented her strength, allowing the mace as an option, but she hadn't drawn it yet.

Thomena stayed wary of enemy spellcasters. She ducked behind groups of soldiers whenever possible to cast her spells. She found another vine plant and spiked a couple icicles through it, hitting from beyond its reach. A moment later, she called upon her wind magic to repel more of the spores. As she moved forward, Thomena realized that a number of fresh Blue Boar troops advanced alongside her. They recognized the protection she offered, and her life might likewise depend on them.

At the sign of another fireblast hitting some Kaigal soldiers, she made the group of men stop and pulled out one of Auney's scrolls. Moments later, they advanced again with the protection of ice magic to shield them.

"We need to support the banner," she said to them as they pressed on. "But I also need to spot their spellcasters and stop them."

The armored men nodded, faces mostly hidden behind steel helms. They set to work clearing a path forward, with Thomena protected in the middle. Orc and iztheran warriors came within striking distance, although the humans still regarded the latter as lizardmen. Kaigal's elite handled the first few well enough. Thomena held her wand in one hand and her mace in the other. The enemy didn't come close enough to her to tempt the mace, yet she held back from firing her wand lest she make herself a target for spellcasters.

She soon had evidence of one in the vicinity. Thomena saw a magical bolt hit the armor of one of her guards, sending a jolt through his body.

"There!" A soldier shouted, pointing. "Red topknot, holding a staff."

In between moving people, Thomena saw the orc figure barely twenty paces away. She had seen half-orcs in Orlaun while trying not to stare at their features for too long. The full-blooded version proved to be even more ugly. Red irises, protruding tusks, scarred cheeks, pointed

241

ears...and the fact that this one cast a spell that had dropped the druid made him twice as fearsome.

Her focus narrowed to this task. Thomena aimed her wand, trying to position herself as bodies traded strikes between her and her target.

"Kee-lass!" she shouted.

Her lightning bolt missed, yet it was a fortunate miss. The beam of energy struck the orc's staff instead, blasting it in half. This momentarily dazed the creature as the connection severed. A spellcaster's staff served as an extension of its owner's will. It helped carry a portion of the user's spirit-energy like a vessel. Sundering the item caused the orc some disorientation, but Thomena knew the effect would only be temporary.

She knew it would retaliate, but the fighting around them had grown fierce. They weren't far from where several Blue Boars stubbornly defended Kaigal's flag from orc berserkers. Thomena broke into a run, ducking behind several armored allies to shield herself from the enemy and find a better viewpoint. The terrain proved to be difficult. Bodies lay everywhere—some dead, some crawling for help. Discarded weapons and broken shields littered the front line.

Fire washed over her and a few other men before she could so much as scream in surprise. Her opponent, lacking any respect for catching its allies in friendly fire, swept the area between them with its attack.

Thomena reflexively put up her hands, closed her eyes, and wondered if she could find the other healing draught on her bandolier despite damaged eyes and fingers. Just as quickly, she realized the fire did her no harm. Her protective wards not only saved her, but they also shielded the men she'd readied earlier. Some warriors from both sides still fell aside or staggered away.

Following the orc's spell, Thomena had a clear shot at her attacker. She aimed again. "Kee-lass! Kee-lass!" Bolt after bolt of lightning blasted forth.

The energy blasts threw him backward, limbs undergoing spasms. Thomena kept her wand ready, although her own hand trembled slightly from the exchange. Smoke rose from the orc's body. From what she could see, he would no longer be a threat.

That didn't free her from harm. Iztheran warriors, wearing armor plates over thick hides, began replacing the orcs. The fresh troops hammered at the line of weary Boars. One targeted her as it approached. It threw a spear that Thomena's air shield deflected. It then wrapped both of its hands around a spiked club. Her concentration focused more on getting out of its reach, rather than using her wand again. She was momentarily saved as an armored human wielding a halberd launched himself into the creature. The two of them braced against each other, pushing forward with their weapons.

Thomena could have used a spell, but she was mindful about what Commander Bedran said about conserving her energy. Instead, she decided to tip the fight in her favor using her augmented strength. With hardly a thought to her actions, she ran closer to the duel and cocked back her mace. Weak points were not plentiful on the jungle monster, but as it struggled toe-to-toe for leverage against the human, it relied on its stance. Thomena approached from the side and swung her weapon across, smashing the iztheran in the knee. The jungle creature fell, chased to the ground moments later by a heavy halberd's blade.

"Don't retreat with the banner." someone cried out.

It was followed by a shout from another human, "Hold fast! If the flag withdraws, so goes the entire line."

Kaigal's battle standard stood proudly only a few steps from her position. The fresh iztheran troops pushed toward it. Men piled against the press of the scaled attackers, trading blows in close quarters. Some of the humanoids got through, landing blows on the beleaguered flag-bearer's armor, before being cut down by other Boars. Thomena looked for a clear target, but the intense fighting made it tricky to aim spells.

"Troll!"

The dreaded shout caused Thomena to seek out the threat, her throat suddenly going dry. Easily twice her height, the misshapen monster used a tree trunk to clobber soldiers out of its path. It headed straight for the banner, with Thomena caught in its path.

I have to use fire, she thought.

Thomena quickly slipped her mace into its holder and dropped her wand, feeling it tap against her arm as it swung from its leather thong. Both hands were now free to cast, but her terror caused her to stutter at the start of the incantation. She had to pause and swallow past her hesitation as the troll smashed a human flat.

The cruel, dark eyes of the giant looked down on her as its next victim. Thomena found her courage and concentrated on the spell. The arcane syllables flowed from her mouth as her fingers weaved a pattern in the air.

A fan of flames roared forth from her hands. The heat bathed the upper half of the troll, forcing out a roar that carried across the battlefield. Thomena's magical reserves began ticking away as she kept her concentration on the arcane attack. Flames coated the troll and eagerly scoured its hard hide. It raised the tree trunk in both hands, prepared to aim blindly at her. Thomena could only slowly back up while she tried to pour everything she had into the spell.

An arm wrapped around her waist and yanked her backward. She lost the concentration needed for her incantation. A moment later, she heard a distinct WHUMP as the tree trunk slammed the ground she had just vacated. The timber cracked from the blow. Tumbled across the ground as she was, it took her a moment to regain her bearings. Thomena got up to a kneeling position. The troll writhed on the ground, flames still licking at its oily skin. Kaigal's soldiers didn't give it a chance to recover. Several moved in and finished it.

She prepared to stand but noticed a new threat. A ball of ice, more specifically an ice comet spell, arced through the air aiming at her and the bannerman. Thomena could not yet cast one, but she had studied it. On impact, the ball would explode and send icicle spikes lancing in every direction.

A full-body shield lay abandoned on the ground next to her. She grabbed the edge of it and heaved upward. Her augmented strength made the task easy. One of the arm straps was broken but still dangled. That was enough for her to pull it upright and hold it in position. She barely took two steps back to help cover the flag-bearer when the magic exploded.

Icicles pelted the shield with dents. In a few places, the magical ice managed to puncture small holes in the metal without passing all the way through it. Kaigal soldiers and iztheran warriors both wailed in pain from the attack.

Thomena looked westward for the source. Down the line from her, but definitely originating from Kaigal's forces, a green glob flew toward the origin of the ice comet. It exploded in the middle of the iztheran ranks, splashing acid on their troops. It reminded her that she wasn't alone. Other wizards continued to fight nearby and support the front line.

Battle cries and exclamations behind her forced her to look back toward the banner. Thomena turned just in time to see the bannerman stagger. The young soldier dropped to his knees, one hand trying to stem a wound. A pair of reptilian humanoids launched at him. One got his hands on Kaigal's standard and yanked it from the man's hand. Both sides raged in a flurry of weapon blows over possession of the symbol.

Honor and Justice pushed at Thomena's heart, urging her to protect the flag. Arcane syllables left her mouth as an icicle appeared in her hand. It darted away with magical momentum, burying itself to the base in the iztheran thief's armor. A second one followed as she charged into danger. With a quick motion, she used the leather thong to snap the wand back into her grasp.

"Kee-lass!"

She ignored the first warnings of spell fatigue: a headache signaled that she was overusing her magic. Wizards who continued to cast beyond the warnings of spell fatigue risked the failure of their spells, perhaps even a loss of consciousness.

Nevertheless, she focused on the wooden pole that heralded Kaigal's colors. Thomena managed to wrap her left hand around the flagstaff. One iztheran still had a hand on it. The monster's other hand held a wicked, primitive, copper knife. It jabbed the point straight into her breastbone.

Her air shell slowed the blow while the earth spell that hardened her skin managed to stop the blade from leaving more than a shallow mark.

Thomena placed the wand's tip against the creature and spoke the command word. Sparks launched the humanoid away from her. The strength of her arm yanked the pole from its grasp.

Swaying on her feet, suffering from the headache of impending spell fatigue, Thomena momentarily stood as the undisputed bearer of Kaigal's banner...in the middle of the front line of battle.

***

"Gunnard! I see him."

Julia had been standing atop the smith's wagon, ready to test out her experimental weapon. Now, she extended her hand to point at a crawling fighter wearing the livery of a Gold Lion. Although it was hard to see any details that would differentiate him from the next Lion, he did seem to have a red handkerchief tied to his belt.

"Dere's still gobbers out dere." Gunnard shouted.

Julia looked for goblin threats. A few groups of them still fought other Kaigal defenders out in the field, but in small clashes rather than any lines of battle. "None are near him right now, but he doesn't look like he can defend himself. I've got to help him."

"Vat? Lia!"

Julia knew she wouldn't be much help with her weapon from this range, especially since they hadn't given it a thorough test. The young tinker vaulted softly to the ground and started sprinting away from the cluster of suteler wagons. She even caught sound of Gunnard swearing that unknown "Uffa" word as she sprinted. Julia didn't even have any kind of weapon on her. If she reached into her apron pockets, she might randomly pull out a tiny razor, cutting knife, or a small hammer used for light tapping. She continued to run, heedless of any danger. Julia only wished to pull Mabry to safety.

As she approached him, Mabry picked his sword up from the grass and swiveled on his butt to face the danger. One of his legs did little to assist in the turn.

"Julia? What are you doing out here?"

His last words were muffled as Julia threw her arms around him in a protective embrace. The girl whispered, "I'm not going to let you carry my favor and then stand back when I can help." Julia sat back and looked over the soldier. "Can you move?"

He pointed to his lower right leg. "I got bashed on the side, behind the shinguard. Broke something, it can't hold my weight."

She briefly considered dragging him using his cloak, but she knew that would still be difficult. "Can you walk if you lean on me?"

Mabry's eyes flicked around, looking for danger or other ideas. "I guess I can try. We can't stay here."

The couple struggled with getting him upright and limping. To her credit, Julia possessed stronger muscles than most girls her age due to years of hard work. But she still had to contend with Mabry's armor. They began establishing a rhythm, even if their movements matched a pair of drunken sailors leaving a pub.

A shrill, inhuman war cry greeted them once the goblin rushed into range. Neither had noticed the creature until it was nearly upon them.

A deep voice met it. "For Dalios above, in de hall of my fadders!"

Gunnard intercepted the goblin with an upward swing of a large hammer, held two-handed in the smith's solid arms. Ambusher became the victim as the small goblin stopped with a sickening crunch before falling backward.

Never one to leave a job unfinished, Gunnard Uunfred of Norvess slammed the hammer down a second time while the goblin still twitched. He sang a few words as he did so. Julia wasn't even certain whether it was in the native Hespal or a different language, for his accent made it difficult.

A moment later, he ran up and grabbed Mabry on the other side to help the couple retreat faster. They arrived at the side of the smith's wagon and set the soldier down.

Mabry pointed to several goblins forming up. "I think you grabbed some attention!"

Gunnard took a firm grip on his hammer and stepped protectively ahead of the wagon. "Lia! Da veapon."

Julia moved toward the wagon prior to Mabry finishing his warning. She jumped up on the footholds and vaulted to the top. Once there, Julia seized control of the large crossbow mounted on top of it. Some observers might have even labeled it a ballista due to its size, but the main reason Julia had it mounted on the wagon was due to its weight, and not any real difference in the mechanics of the device. A block, nearly the length of the weapon, sat over where the crossbow bolt would rest.

Goblins rushed at their wagon, yelling war cries and making noises that could almost be interpreted as singing. The ugly creatures had mixes of green and brown skin, similar to orcs, but they were shorter and had ridiculously long, pointed ears. Their armor consisted of hides, and their weapons were black and serrated.

Julia put one hand on the trigger and her other hand on a hand-crank at the base of the stock. She lined up her shot down a pair of rings front and aft of the weapon. The first goblin would be on Gunnard in seconds. She pulled the trigger.

The crossbow gave a slight jolt as it launched a two-foot-long bolt. The missile zipped over Gunnard's shoulder but missed the target. Julia growled as she cranked the gears of her weapon, drawing the string back and dropping a second bolt into place.

There was no time for a second shot at the first goblin. It tried to skewer the smith using a pointed spear blade with teeth. The man from Norvess proved that all his countrymen learned some fighting skills. He dodged the jab and retaliated with a mighty swing. The goblin rolled backward in the tall grass before stopping at its final resting place.

Now that Julia had a better chance to get used to firing her weapon, she aimed at the next threat. Her second bolt flew free and claimed her mechanism's first battle casualty. The bolt pierced a goblin's hide armor and knocked it down. Cranking again, Julia swiveled to the next target. Another bolt dropped from the box and landed in the crossbow channel. The tinker fired again, sending another goblin stumbling from a hit to one hip. That victim crawled away.

Mabry could only watch, propped up against the wagon wheel. His crossbow had disappeared in the heat of battle; all he could do was hold up his sword in case any got close. The young soldier had a front-row seat as Gunnard pounded flat another goblin attacker. The smith sang songs to Dalios as he swung his hammer.

Julia didn't reserve any spot in her mind to consider that she had killed her first creatures. A third and fourth goblin dropped from mortal hits as she kept cranking bolts into place. The tinker concentrated on her invention and setting it to work to protect herself.

Most of the other sutelers had run to the other end of the caravan or were hiding with little more than meal knives in their possession. However, at least one cheered on the smith and the tinker.

Julia missed again but soon loaded and fired another shot. This time, she watched a bolt trailed by a small, red ribbon hit the next target. It had been her idea to tie a red ribbon at the base of the last bolt in each ammo box.

"I'm empty." Julia warned Gunnard and Mabry.

The young tinker unhooked the empty bolt box from the weapon and set the next one in place. She heard fighting but concentrated on re-arming her crossbow. As much as she took pride in steady hands for her skills, she couldn't stop from trembling slightly while working in the midst of a battle. A part of her mind thought of ways to improve dropping the box in the right place in a timely manner while most of her consciousness screamed at her to get it ready and save her friends. The box finally clicked into place, and she used the crank to bring the first bolt into the groove.

When Julia looked up, she realized her efforts had been in vain. Reinforcing conscripts had arrived and were already driving back the few remaining goblins. Gunnard still sang a war song as he swung his hammer in the air, purely for show. She finally had time to realize how hard she was breathing, and that her hands still shook slightly. She looked over the side of the wagon to check on Mabry.

He gazed up at her with rapt attention, a look of complete adoration in his staring eyes. The soldier spoke softly, "You're amazing, in case you didn't know that."

Propped against the wagon as he was, he reached up one hand to hers, and she reached down a trembling hand to him. Their fingertips brushed each other. Julia began to feel heat in her face...from the battle? Or was she blushing?

Mabry slowly smiled. His eyes flitted to the wagon momentarily as he asked, "When can I get one of those?"

Chapter 28 - Bannermaiden

In the eastern woods, a clash of natura magic caused the fighting to become more primal than anyone could have planned. The elves had advanced north and joined the scattered rangers while the orcs shifted their focus east of the false camp and replaced the remnants of the disorganized lizardmen. Both elves and orcs fielded numerous natura spellcasters. Druids, shamans, greenmen, and mystics intensified the magic conflict originally put in play by Thamin and the rangers. The loosely-organized rangers had never been trained as a war force; therefore, they had been almost as badly routed as the lizardmen they had fought. Those with the will to fight still clustered in Thamin's vicinity. Despite fighting in wolf form, he called out to them individually and kept their tactics focused. The other force that had partaken in the east woods fight, the goblins, were too spread out and decimated to form an organized fighting unit. Most clung to hiding holes, awaiting the chance to loot from the fallen.

Though the average combatant in the woods had no connection with magic, the natura users proved numerous enough to spread chaos. Summoned animals and enchanted plants joined in the desperate fighting. The magic users dueled to counter the other side's spells as normal fighters and berserkers tried to fight through the unnatural conditions.

Thamin needed to change his strategy. With the lizardmen, he could get away with racing through their backlines in wolf form, striking and running to spark confusion. The orcs fared better at protecting against such tactics. The Trollsbane's opportunities diminished. He managed to kill one mystic chieftain before the orcs tightened their defensive formations.

Thamin retreated toward his allies to continue directing the fight. He heard the panting in his own breath, felt the wetness of blood on his sides as well as his paws. He realized he needed a break to recoup some of his spent vigor.

Slicing the hamstring of the one orc separating him from his allies, he still managed to scare a younger ranger as he ran through the lines. In wolf form, they couldn't necessarily recognize him from a summoned threat. Thamin's paws slid to a stop near a file of elf fighters.

He didn't get the chance to say anything. Someone dispelled his animal form, likely thinking he was a summoned creature. The elves' eyes widened as they recognized Thamin in their midst. His bipedal form reflected the effects of battle inflicted upon him as a wolf. The ranger bore minor injuries where blades managed to skirt the edges of his armor. His swords dripped blood. A new scar ran down the side of his nose.

Thamin quickly delivered a proper greeting in Elvish, coupled with a bow. "Sunlight favor you."

An officer stepped forward. He stiffly nodded in return. Most residents of Kaigal wouldn't receive as cordial a greeting, but the elves had learned to respect the Trollsbane as an ally, even though they couldn't always trust Kaigal's county.

The elf continued the discussion in his native tongue. "What have your eyes witnessed?"

Thamin pointed over his shoulder. "The lizardmen in these woods have scattered. The last ones that I faced ran when confronted. However, the orcs are shifting to this point in large numbers. They've left the middle of the monster line in the care of..." He paused to consider a description, "...larger, smarter types of lizardmen."

The elf officer turned to an aide. "Use orc tactics." The officer returned his attention to Thamin. "I think our rumors are true. The iztheran civilization has returned from history fables. This is like a ghost from the past for our people."

Thamin took a moment to perform some natura magic. "Sentorum."

A healing spell reinvigorated his body. The cut at his nose lessened, and his other injuries began to close. Though he lacked the true healing power of a divine cleric, his restoration spells mended small injuries.

After realizing the state of his remaining wounds, he resigned himself to drinking a healing draught also. The remainder of his injuries disappeared. Turning to the elf officer, he asked. "Orc tactics?"

The elf shrugged. "Let some of their berserkers bust through, sealing the lines behind them. Then our archers and wizards kill them out of reach of any healing support. Are you planning to join us?"

"As the tree goddess is witness, I would be honored. However, I must also see if I can rally whatever is left of Kaigal's rangers and scouts. We'll press forward side-by-side."

Thomena stood in the worst possible spot on the battlefield that she could imagine, directly under Kaigal's banner, and *she* was the one holding it. The hurricane of battle encircled her. Men and iztherans savagely struck at each other while focusing on the flag.

She tried to move, but the press of bodies limited her paths. All she could do was take cover behind the armored fighters. Even when Thomena looked down, she witnessed some of the trodden remains of the former orc camp. She tried to ignore the many bodies of the fallen.

The soldiers jostled around again as spell-explosions ripped through their ranks as well as their enemies. Some of the heat passed harmlessly by Thomena, but allies and foes fell. Another gap widened in front and left her exposed to the rush of more creatures.

She allowed the wand to dangle by its leather cord as she submerged herself in a spell. At its climax, she waved her hand from right to left in an arc. A wave of water erupted from the ground. The wave covered a semi-circle in front of her, but quickly hardened into ice as it rose and spread forward. The outer tendrils of the wave hardened into icicle spears aimed outward; the entire construction solidified slightly higher than her waistline. The aptly named spell, "spike wave," became a deadly barricade. A pair of iztheran warriors impaled themselves before they could slow their charge. Other enemies tried to swarm around the sides, where more Boars awaited.

A sting of pain lanced through Thomena's head, dropping her to one knee. She gasped for air, aware that her spell almost failed due to her exhaustion. Spell fatigue nearly claimed her. If she would have passed out...the implications were too scary to consider.

She grabbed at the last sura potion on her bandolier, hearing arrows whistle over head or impact against her wall. Her wind wall deflected many, yet Thomena watched it from a barely cognizant, dream-like state as her concentration flagged. One gulp allowed the potion to restore much of her spirit energy. Revitalized, she dared look up and saw troops clashing nearby.

Thomena switched back to her wand. The arcane creation would help her use her energy more efficiently...at least until it ran out of stored power.

"Kee-lass!"

Magical bolts shot over the ice barricade, knocking down iztherans in succession. Her enemies roared but had trouble reaching her. She saw the spears flying at her, only to witness them tossed aside by her wind wall. Scaled warriors tried to circumvent the spikes, only to meet resistance from Kaigal's fighters. One iztheran managed to leap over from one side. Although landing in a tumbled heap, he struck out at Thomena's leg. The flagstaff shuddered and let loose a cracking noise.

After his first blow sundered the last two feet from the pole, he reversed direction and scored a hit on her leg. Pain blossomed up her limb.

Half-wild with pain, Thomena firmly grabbed the pole and jabbed downward as she dropped to one knee. Her augmented strength drove the jagged base of the staff through the warrior's torso. From one side, a Kaigal polearm also stabbed the victim.

Breathing heavily, Thomena re-assessed her situation. The iztheran was dying from its wounds. Her left leg hurt, but the hardened skin from her earth-based spell absorbed a good portion of the damage. Despite feeling pain, it didn't seem like any bones broke. Suddenly, a hand grabbed the banner and yanked it. Protective of her charge, she pulled back just as violently, and her assailant lifted her back to her feet.

She looked to the source of the assault only to realize he was an ally. A young Blue Boar tried to take up the banner when he thought Thomena had gone down from her wound. Since she managed to hang on, he surrendered the standard back to her grasp.

As she stared at the wonder in his eyes, her mind found a revelation. Thomena realized a Truth: that whether relying on armor or spells, weapons, or magic, she stood on as equal footing as any of these armored fighters of Kaigal. She could be killed, but her chances were no worse than any of them. Her Honor and Bravery filled her heart with a resolve that she would not back down.

This banner was now *her* charge to protect.

She shouted for the benefit of any of her allies that could hear. "Rally to this banner! Our fight is here!"

Thomena faced the enemy and promptly fired another energy bolt into the mass of oncoming creatures. Using her ice-spiked wall for cover, the revitalized mage sent a combination of spells and wand bolts into the enemy numbers while they tried to flank her.

The nearby soldier spoke, with only the slightest hesitation at using a title his country had banished for over a hundred years. "A bannermaiden! Protect the bannermaiden!"

Soldiers rallied to the call.

"I can't see the line. All I can see is that the banner has fallen too many times already." Commander Bedran railed at his officers. "The enemy has drawn more strength than we assumed. Our archers still can't get past the totems, goblins broke through to our supply wagons, and I've had nay word from the eastern woods."

The grizzled war veteran scowled as he looked northward. Kaigal's banner could be seen bobbing slightly inside the perimeter of the smashed orc camp, but he had no confidence that it would stay up.

"I need a runner," he called.

A young man, one of the Green Horses' squires, appeared. "Your command, sir?"

Bedran pointed to the eastern woods. "I need to know the situation in there. Find Thamin, the elves, or anyone in charge that can give me an update. Watch yourself and return if it's too dangerous."

Once the young man departed, the commander turned to the spellmaster. "We have to stay away from the jungle. We can't do anything with those cursed totems aiding the enemy. Communicate to your people that we will be pulling back."

The spellmaster began speaking through his magical earring link to all his subordinates.

Commander Bedran grabbed a junior officer. He jutted a finger southward. "Have the train of wagons get moving. Have them head toward the guard tower south of here. They move too slowly, and if this falls apart we may not be able to cover their escape."

The veteran turned his attention back to the distant banner. "And tell the banner to fall back."

***

Thamin had rounded up two score of volunteers into a decent fighting force. Most of them consisted of rangers or Gold Lions that had been skirmishing near the forest border. Others included conscripts, a handful of elf archers, and two Green Horse knights who'd been reduced to fighting on foot. The terrain at where the jungle overlapped with the woods proved difficult for solid formations of troops to maneuver. This didn't deter Thamin, who managed to find a way to strike and move his smaller force. Most of his unit weren't encumbered by heavy armor. Even for those who wore hefty protection, they picked up shields in each hand and acted as mobile barriers to protect the elf archers.

The orcs and elves focused on each other due to old rivalries, hardly spending much thought on Kaigal's fighters. The movement of Thamin's militia didn't create any sizeable gap from the elf army. On the other hand, the orcs and iztherans left a gap between their forces. After all, the orcs kept moving eastward to take the woods, but the iztheran warriors sought firm control of the area around the original fake orc camp.

Thamin saw an opportunity but was forced to make a decision. He knew he should inform Bedran of the situation, but he had no runners to spare. Likewise, he couldn't track down a wizard to borrow their long-distance messages or he might lose out on this opening. Instead, he gathered his smartest helpers and gave them quick instruction on a tactic.

Within minutes, a hit-and-run strike racked up a few casualties on the orcs' western flank. Thamin's force disappeared before any organized orc resistance responded, slamming into the eastern reach of the iztherans while inflicting a dozen casualties. In quick succession, Thamin's group bounced between the two enemy groups in the gap they'd left open. The woods stood at their east, the jungle stretched before them, and the grassland framed their back. With planned strikes they began dominating that tiny spot on the field.

Despite the distance between them, it was then that Thamin locked eyes with the creature that he'd once thought a statue. He recognized the mottled greenish brown skin, the red-and-gold striped highlights running up to its brow, and metal scales protecting its torso and upper arms. The foe wielded a dual-pointed spear, but Thamin's old axe hung at its side.

The creature—most likely the leader—stared back in recognition. It watched the longsword that had belonged to Thamin's former partner, as it danced circles and stabbed opponents in tandem with the defending swordbreaker. Thamin felt something instinctual tug at his feelings. He felt the need to face this enemy and duel him. However, the lines of fighting weren't very clear or distinct. Forces from both armies clashed between the two opponents. The iztheran leader moved in the direction of the Trollsbane, but was forced to divide his attention to the greater engagement. Kaigal's line refused to be broken, and that seemed to be his priority. Thamin saw him command a group of warriors in the direction of the banner. Thamin couldn't see the flag bearer.

Thamin likewise wanted to go after the leader, but he couldn't do it alone. He needed to keep his current force intact and as safe as can be, and that didn't include delving deep into iztheran troops without more support.

The orcs reacted to Thamin's quick strikes by sending out a unit of their own. A wave of warriors, skirmishers, and a shaman crashed into them. The enemy pushed with the intention of forcing Kaigal's troops back out into the open grassland.

The last Blood-Wolf reacted to the attack and called out orders and targets. They managed to take out the shaman, but not before losing some of their numbers.

In a close clash of arms, a recognizable half-orc came straight at him. Thamin knew him as Brogratch, a former Kaigal scout. The traitor didn't make the assault on his own; a few tribemates joined in on the attack.

Realizing the danger as it approached, Thamin pointed at one and uttered, "Mitsarum."

A bolt of natura struck one and caused it to stumble. The ranger spun in a different direction, swords spinning like a corkscrew. Longclaw and the swordbreaker, still enchanted by fire magic, trailed orange swirls as they spun. His maneuver batted aside another orc's weapon before Longclaw took a deep slice of the enemy. Brogratch slashed at him with a serrated blade. Thamin reversed direction. Longclaw danced back and forth with Brogratch's blade while Thamin stabbed outward to one side with the swordbreaker. The first wounded orc continued its momentum only to stumble into Thamin's blade, his front catching fire from the enchantment. Thamin quickly withdrew his sword from what had surely been a mortal blow. Brogratch's skill demanded his full attention.

Neither opponent spared any words as their weapons connected. Their only communication lay in the mutual glares and sneers traded at point-blank range as they crossed swords and pushed each other. Brogratch finally displayed his hate of the people who had stifled the growth of his tribe. Thamin knew the traitor in front of him had arranged this battle site, and he was prepared to deal justice. He recalled the words he told to Thomena.

Out here, justice is my job.

Thamin shifted his stance, but it allowed Brogratch to push forward so the half-orc continued to press his attack. One of the many teeth of the swordbreaker caught the serrations of his blade. The ranger yanked to one side. To Brogratch's surprise, his sword was hooked by the weapon. Thamin braced it against a tree and swung Longclaw with great force.

He'd once told Thomena that swordbreakers didn't actually break swords. Normally, that would be the truth; however, great individuals and magic could sometimes make exceptions.

Thamin's blow snapped the orc's nonmagical blade in two. Brogratch looked stupefied at his broken blade for a moment too long. Longclaw swept across and delivered a killing stroke to the traitor.

Chapter 29 – Battle Trophy

Thomena fought on, unaware that Commander Bedran had ordered a withdrawal. She didn't have the communication earrings that the other wizards were using. The runners hadn't yet reached her. The army also used musical instruments to convey orders, but Thomena didn't know the tunes and everyone around her was busy defending themselves.

"Kee-lass!"

Another Iztheran reeled from the lightning, falling atop the mound of bodies near her ice-spike wall.

More continued to try circling the barricade. An Iztheran and a Boar got locked up in a wrestling match near where she stood. Thomena ran only two steps to the side, then kicked the monster in the leg. Her augmented strength dealt damage as if she'd clubbed it with a hammer. It crumpled backward while the Boar finished it with a dagger. Another arrow whistled past her head, its course altered by her wind wall.

The mage wondered why more Kaigal arrows weren't raining down to help. Suddenly, she remembered the interference of the totems. Those constructs had turned aside Kaigal's arrows and could use tricks to bolster the Iztheran fighters.

"Seek out their totems!" she shouted for anyone near who could listen. "Shatter those totems and we'll get more support!"

Someone heard, and the voices echoed around her. "Rally to the bannermaiden! Destroy the totems!"

Thomena didn't realize that the news of a bannermaiden spread faster through the army than the calls to withdraw. Young, tired men across the battlefield found new strength when they heard the call. All of them had dreamt at one time or another about fighting around the battle maidens of old. Also, every one of them remembered the tragedy of Macey Durant. They swore that her fate would not be repeated. Calls of "bannermaiden" swept through Kaigal's forces.

Troops who were once wounded or shaken turned back toward the fight. They looked across the field, saw the spinning and dipping motions of Kaigal's battle flag, and hurried to join the bannermaiden.

Oblivious to the effect she spread through her allies, Thomena just kept trying to stay alive. More missile weapons tried to seek her out but turned aside. Iztheran warriors tried to break through the ice spikes fanning outward from her wall. Enemies continued to circle it, clashing with soldiers on either side. The young mage frosted the ground in front of her barricade, causing enemies to slip. She used the banner to shove away an enemy who had nearly climbed over the ice barricade. Within moments, she fired another lightning bolt from her wand at a new target.

Thomena's wand failed moments later. She had finally drained it of all energy, so it became a useless stick. Crestfallen, uttering a tired sigh, she tucked it back into her belt.

Sweat soaked her garments, while her head pulsed with pain. Spell fatigue once again bore down on her concentration. Her eyes got intermittently blurry and lost focus. She began to feel like she might collapse at any time, and the possibility of dropping in the middle of the battlefield scared her like nothing else. She remembered years ago, when the timber beam had pinned her leg to the floor in the middle of an inferno. She felt the same fear as she did back then. Thomena believed that if she passed out, she'd likely never wake up again.

The young girl swept her gaze to either side. She saw Kaigal's troops smashing apart the totems, but was it too late? Could she find another wizard to help her before she collapsed? Could she find a place with more protection? Her stubbornness to hold the banner began to feel like vanity. For Humility's sake, she had to consider passing it to someone else.

Then, her eyes caught sight of her father to the northeast. He fought alongside a group composed of mostly humans, yet they were on the *other side* of the Iztheran's line! His force stood just inside the boundary of the jungle, maybe just over a hundred meters away. Thamin was flanking the enemy, cutting down the line of Iztheran warriors from behind as he made his way westward.

"Bannermaiden, we have to pull back." A soldier of the Lions stood next to her, leaning toward her ear to be heard over the battle. "They are calling for the flag to withdraw."

Thomena spoke. She surprised herself when she felt her lip tremble, and her words had to struggle out of a dry throat. "But, my father and those men over there...we can't leave them."

The Lion looked uncomfortable, as if he didn't want to be the one making these decisions. "The commander ordered it."

In moments like this, the young girl typically tried to balance her options using the tenets of *The Codex*. Her thoughts couldn't focus past the fact that her father wasn't far away, and that she just couldn't turn from him. Knowing you could die was one thing, but making a decision that could allow another to die for your safety was unconscionable. Sacrifice was one of the scariest virtues to uphold.

"Protect me for a moment," she begged.

She jabbed the sharpened, broken end of the flagstaff into the ground. While the other troops formed nearby, still rallying to the cry of "bannermaiden," she allowed her weight to sag against the banner lest she fall over. Thomena slid her right hand into a pocket. Her fingertips brushed against the warmth of her spirit gem. She could feel her stored energy pulsing within the jade construct. Opening herself to it, she felt a rush of energy surge forth. The headache disappeared as her head cleared. It didn't take long to absorb the spirit energy and drain it dry. Although the energy wouldn't restore her to full potential, it bolstered a lot of her mental stamina.

She had no more sura or healing potions available. This was her last chance to make a difference.

Thomena pulled the staff out of the ground and waved it high. "Forward! Follow the banner! We'll rally with the Trollsbane!"

Kaigal's troops charged ahead, sweeping past on either side of her barricade while cheering or roaring battle cries. She noticed the variety of uniforms which had joined the call of the bannermaiden. Most were Boars, but Lions and conscripts had joined the front line also. Wounded and shaken troops had rejoined the battle at the calls of a maiden holding their flag. Even some dismounted Green Horse ran forward with their heavy swords. Both the presence of a bannermaiden and the Trollsbane empowered them.

Thomena lacked the strength to cast many spells, so she did her part to wave the banner and shout encouragement to the forces safeguarding her. Her hand drifted near the mace on her belt, ready to rely upon it if needed.

Totems were smashed, taking away benefits for the Iztheran warriors. From a hawk's eye view, the lizard-like race still outnumbered Kaigal's front line. However, momentum swung in favor of Kaigal. The humans and elves could inflict more ranged damage on the Iztheran troops, through both bows and spells, without the totems' interference.

Commander Bedran watched in awe from the back as his troops disobeyed his command and pushed forward. He heard the cries of bannermaiden and could only wonder at who held aloft their standard. Troops were trained to align with the flag, and with the flag advancing, so did his army. He called out to his spellmaster to find out who was responsible.

"It's the girl," came the reply a minute later. "The Trollsbane's daughter. She doesn't have an earring, so I can't communicate with her. I'm trying to get someone over there."

The commander groaned. The worst thing he'd wanted to do was place her in any more danger beyond being present in the first place. "How did she end up there?"

***

Desperation began to claw at Ztakish. He knew the strength of his plan lie in his army overwhelming Kaigal's defenders. Diaran armies seemed trained to fight long engagements using teamwork between different warrior roles. The monstrous humanoids of the jungle had no patience or willingness to engage in such prolonged toe-to-toe fighting. Tactics for them involved overbearing attacks raining through with their numbers alone, counting on a quick victory. They might still claim the day's fight, but Ztakish couldn't be sure of it. Even if they did, the cost had climbed too high. No matter how many warriors survived, they would be little threat to the walls of Kaigal, Bael Cochaw, or Syllatru.

The signs of his tactical failure opened like a book of truth before him. He felt the connections with the totems fail as they broke. Already, human and elven bowmen raked arrows into the jungle line. The Trollsbane led a charge of heroes toward him from the east. To the south, the main army determinedly gained ground despite all he could throw at them. His army had the most luck on the western edge, but the fighting by the river was all spent. Both sides had pulled apart from each other. The humans followed orders to pull back and reform. The orcs and Iztherans pulled back to lick their wounds, countermanding Ztakish's commands. His goblins, all battle fodder anyway, failed in their task to inflict serious damage on the wagons at the rear of the enemy lines. Though his trolls had inflicted great harm upon the enemy, all seemed to be dead on the field or driven away.

Ztakish knew he should retreat and save his remaining kinsman, but he was determined to find some small victory or tactical trophy to claim. He would have easily settled for winning a duel against Kaigal's champion. The Iztheran considered personally moving forward and dueling him, but an honest duel would be impossible in these conditions.

As his gold eyes focused on the movements of his chosen rival, he noticed a distraction on the part of that hero. The Trollsbane's attention locked on something southwest of him, across the lines of battle.

Ztakish turned to see what drew his stare. He witnessed the young woman bearing Kaigal's battle standard as she led men toward the Trollsbane's position. She called out to him, and Ztakish's excellent hearing picked out the word "father." Since waking from his long repose, Ztakish had made a point of reacquainting himself with the changes of dialect in the common language. He listened only a few moments longer as the bannermaiden continued to bolster her troops and call to Kaigal's champion. He also heard the men around her cheer their "bannermaiden."

That would make a good battle trophy, and it would set up the duel he craved.

The Iztheran leader gave a quick conference to his closest advisors and divine casters. He directed them to target the soldiers around the banner, but not the bearer. Ztakish turned to take a final glance at his rival before acting. The Trollsbane's eyes were back on him, urging his strike force closer. Ztakish openly pointed at the young woman. He saw the panic blossom in the wide eyes of the Trollsbane.

Thamin had only just noticed that his daughter participated in the battle despite his wishes. Of course, the fact that she also held the army's banner in the most intense portion of the battlefield shocked him. All logical battle plans he could try to enact fell away as his priority focused on his only child.

The Iztheran spellcasters initiated their attack as ordered. Area effect spells concentrated in the vicinity of Kaigal's flag. While several attacks were deflected by the humans' own spellcasters, a barrage of fire and energy nevertheless pounded those troops. In the one quiet space in the middle of that maelstrom, Thomena also worked her magic to counteract the incoming spells. The ordeals of her efforts through the day reflected clearly in the strain on her face.

Ztakish used his divine magic to initiate his move. Calling upon natura and Yurtash's connection to spirits, he entered a ghostlike form. Becoming insubstantial, he swept with speed across the field, passing through the bodies of allies and foes alike.

Thamin saw the danger and abandoned his position to protect his daughter. He shifted into wolf form and dashed toward the flag, both dodging and colliding with legs as he ran. The lines of Iztheran warriors challenged his progress.

Ztakish reached Thomena's position in less than a minute. Distracted by the spell assault and the protection of the soldiers around her, the girl didn't see the spirit form coming until he phased back into physical form and grabbed her. Thomena, wide-eyed and trembling, barely gasped before he hit her with divine magic. Ztakish's spell, designed only to stun the target, knocked her into a stupor which blocked higher functioning thoughts. She might have resisted the spell if she hadn't exhausted herself. One of her hands stubbornly clutched the flagstaff, without any conscious thought of what she held. Ztakish didn't mind, since he wanted to claim both. Wrapping his arms around the girl and the staff, he shifted back into a spirit form.

It proved to be timely, as a large wolf's jaws clamped the air which formerly hosted the Iztheran's neck. Thamin ended his leap and whirled around to pursue.

Ztakish, however, had no plans to stand in the midst of Kaigal's army. His phantom outline flew with great speed back to the north, toward his jungle home. His spellcasters and fervent followers covered his escape. The Iztheran and his dazed captive moved unimpeded, but the monsters forced the wolf to fight for every step. Thamin had to shift back into human form to properly meet them blade-to-blade.

The jungle forces began a retreat into the dense foliage. Thamin fought savagely in a vain pursuit. Eventually, Kaigal's troops pulled back while the elves also withdrew and regrouped. The situation left Thamin no continued support. He couldn't fight an entire army alone and the spirit form left no trail to track.

***

"I'm sorry. I don't know how she ended up at the very front. She even moved forward when I'd already ordered the flag to fall back." Commander Shan Bedran spoke as his two squires helped him remove his suit of plate. "I dare not camp this army any closer to the jungle for fear of a counterattack. It's not even worth considering the thought of moving forward into the scales' territory."

Even as the commander spoke, the last bit of sunlight for the day still lit the top peak of his tent. The army had already pulled back a mile from the edge of the jungle. The wounded had been dragged with them and were being administered by the priests. Companies were still reforming and taking count of their remaining members.

While Thamin's tactical mind respected the move, his heart couldn't abide by it. He argued. "Time is precious, and this is as much a tragedy as what happened to the last bannermaiden. You have a chance to rescue this one before something happens to her."

The commander's retort came quickly, though his own guilt kept any anger in check. He emphasized with Thamin. Unfortunately, his trusted friend was blinding himself to logic.

"Your heart is overrunning your good sense. If it wasn't your daughter, would you normally advise me to take our forces into the jungle? At night? With a known army out there, still about as big as my own?"

Thamin scowled. "We may not have to go far. They're licking their wounds also."

The commander shook his head. "Nay. That's still not enough advantage and you know it."

He paused to take a drink of water that was offered to him by one of the squires. While savoring the refreshment, he thoroughly looked over his best fighter. "Speaking of licking their wounds, have you caught sight of yourself in a looking glass?"

Thamin's attire reflected the intensity by which the legend had thrown himself into the fight. Aside from the many rips ventilating his cloak, slashing weapons had left their trails across his leather armor and straps. His leather quiver, dented by some impact, housed a handful of broken arrows. Some enemy seemed to have gotten away with half of one sleeve. The most telltale sign of the battle's ferocity stained his hands, attire, and equipment a dark crimson color. Yet for all the damage to his appearance, few wounds remained as anything worse than half-healed scars.

Thamin merely shrugged before saying, "I'm not out of healing draughts yet."

Bedran snorted. "Maybe you can take more punishment, but the rest of us look like we're limping. We took their best shot and blunted their assault. This was supposed to have been a trap but we fought through it. However, we don't have the resources to attempt a campaign inside the scales' home. The Syllatru elves feel they have earned a costly victory and are heading back home. A jungle rescue attempt will end in failure."

The ranger knew the truth of those words, but his heart couldn't just give up. He'd already lost the love of his life; he wouldn't simply abandon his only child. *Not twice*, he told himself, realizing that she had felt that way.

The commander watched his longtime friend and advisor try to come to grips with the situation. He added more reasons. "I should also point out, that even if we corner their commander, he may kill her before she can be rescued. If you have a better plan, I'm all ears. The army, however, can't help with this type of mission."

As much as Thamin didn't wish to face the truth, the commander's words spoke logically. If he still had Blood Wolves to command, he would be taking a specially-assigned stealth group on such a mission. Unfortunately, he no longer had anyone he could trust to bring along. Even the other rangers and elves, skilled as some might be, were recovering from a long day of toil. They hadn't been able to rest the previous night while sneaking into position, and then they had to fight through a battle larger than anything for which the loose-knit rangers could be prepared.

Thamin had only himself, and whatever resources he could acquire from the camp at the late hour. He looked to his longtime friend. "Don't be too hard on yourself. I have my regrets also. I should have predicted that she'd disobey my wishes and take part in this venture." He began to turn for the tent's door flap before even asking, "If I may be excused?"

"If I can help in any other way, just ask," Bedran said, but the legend was already exiting the tent as the sun disappeared behind the landscape.

***

Julia and Mabry chatted near Gunnard's wagon as the night encroached. Mabry managed to get away from his unit after checking in and receiving a healing draught. Feeling much better on his feet, he took the first opportunity to make a supply run to the suteler wagons under pretense of getting the unit some provisions, which he already had procured. At some point during his resupply run, Mabry ended up in Julia's arms.

Lights around the camp, both natural and magical, gave off the perfect amount of romantic illumination. Despite enjoying the luxury of their time together, Julia noticed another familiar, hard-to-miss person making a late-evening supply run. It reminded her of a fear that was left unresolved. To Mabry's surprise, the tinker bolted out of his arms and chased a shadow moving among the suteler wagons.

"It's him!" came as her only explanation.

"Julia?" He called as he joined the chase.

Mabry, limping, nearly lost the brown-haired youth as she sped through a cluster of people, but the pursuit didn't have to go far. She suddenly pulled up short, leaving him to stumble to a stop as he recognized the person in front of them. He awkwardly held back, yet stayed near her side as she planted herself in front of Thamin Trollsbane.

Julia's impulsive plan faltered. Stopping him was one thing, learning to speak was another. She didn't know if he was aware of Thomena's involvement in the fight. How could she approach the subject of his missing daughter?

He looked her up and down, taking a moment to place her. "Julia if I recall? What are you doing here?"

The straightforward answer came easiest. "Gunnard is the blacksmith and had to come along with the suteler train. I'm his assistant."

His lowered brow and eyes gave her a hard look; a frown easily visible on his face. "Did Thomena hitch a ride to the battle using Gunnard?"

Julia couldn't tell whether the question implied that he knew his daughter took part in the battle, or simply accusing them of the possibility, but her first reaction caused her to blurt out the truth.

Julia said, "She managed to ask someone and get in on her own. She was with the wizards." Under his stern gaze, she hesitantly added more. "We...haven't seen her since the battle. I'm...worried."

Thamin's emotions were boiling, but he reminded himself at the innocence of the youth talking to him. He settled himself with a long sigh before continuing the conversation.

"She was holding the war banner in the middle of the front line when I saw her."

As he revealed this, both Julia's and Mabry's eyes widened. Julia brought up a hand to cover her mouth, fearing the worst.

Thamin continued. "The enemy leader used magic to capture her and the banner. They got away faster than I could follow."

Thamin's thoughts dwelled on the reptilian features of his foe. If he'd know the trouble Marl would unleash when he tried to take that necklace as a keepsake...but that was a senseless regret of the past. That creature was definitely something greater than a normal lizardman. It channeled Yurtash's power, so who could know its limits?

Returning more of his attention to the scene in font of him. Julia's breathing had increased through her covering hand. She looked at him in wide-eyed fright. He saw a Gold Lion soldier step up behind Julia and put a comforting arm around her shoulders.

Thamin shared his resolve with them. He felt that he should warn someone of his plan. "I intend to get her back. The army can't do anything, but maybe I can. I'm getting supplies and leaving."

"On your own?" Julia asked. "Maybe I can help..."

He forestalled her with an open palm. "I don't think company would assist me. I have to be alone, using all my gifts to pull this off." He paused to consider before adding. "And it may not work, but I trust only myself on this endeavor."

The young girl's eyes began to brim with tears. "Gods guide you. Bring her back if you can."

He nodded and brushed past her. Julia watched him go as Thamin moved toward an herbalist wagon to look at their potions. She felt Mabry nudge her back toward Gunnard's wagon, and she cooperated. The tinker couldn't realize it, but all her worries had turned her face pale even in the dim light. The soldier wanted to get her sitting down.

Julia took a last look at the legendary figure. Despite Thamin's words, she feared that her friend would be lost. "How can he go up against an army, in the jungle, all alone?"

Mabry also fumbled for hope. As he limped along, he offered what comfort he could find. "He's the Trollsbane. He ventures alone into places that groups of men dare not go. He has a better chance to succeed than any of the rest of us."

Chapter 30 – Jungle Interrogation

Thomena knew another interrogation would be forthcoming. Ztakish and his army, only composed of reptilian races now, had set up camp for the night. This was her third sunset as a prisoner, not that she remembered much of the first one. On the evening of the battle, she had been weary from her overuse of spells, and it didn't help that Ztakish and his spellcasters kept her docile through their own magic.

Like the previous night, however, she sat with her hands tied on a conjured chair. Kaigal's war banner, which she had been forced to carry through their jungle trek, was sarcastically planted in a place of honor beside her. She felt relief that they hadn't stolen the prize, but carrying it through the jungle hadn't been easy. At times it had been her walking stick, other times it snagged branches and slowed her pace.

The reptilian soldiers had put up shelter for the night: a mix of plundered tents from ransacked communities. Ztakish personally claimed an elvish pavilion with partitions creating side rooms. It required natura from his druids to bend aside the jungle in order to place it. A magic-siphoning totem sat on the other side of the tent. Despite the distance, it restricted Thomena from initiating any arcane magic. It didn't seem to affect natura spells.

Ztakish entered his tent with two others. As they had done before, the newcomers untied her hands and rubbed healing ointment on her wrists while Ztakish practically ignored her in favor of a meal and a drink. Her attendants, likely females but she couldn't be sure, offered her some kind of broth. She wrinkled her nose at it.

"I'm not trying to feed you your kin, if that's what worries you." Ztakish spoke with barely a glance.

From watching and hearing him speak, Thomena deduced that he used a magical translation spell. Sometimes he tried to speak Hespal, the common tongue. His command of the language wasn't bad, but he struggled too often with the proper words when he tried to speak it directly.

Thomena took the warm broth and downed it. She needed strength to carry the banner through this jungle...though she feared the outcome.

Ztakish set his finished meal aside. "I'm glad you decided to open a discourse with me. I prefer not to waste pleasantries on an angry glare."

The girl's head tilted at the translator spell's choice of words. Normally such spells spoke using only simple words. In his case, it implied that he used complex words from a higher educational background.

"I wasn't aware that lizardmen possessed such advanced language skills," she commented. Perhaps she could make the interrogation work both ways?

"And now the insults arrive. I am Iztheran, not some inferior breed of lizardmen. We once ruled this land prior to the Godswars."

Thomena said, "I did not mean to insult you, not that I care if I did." She could speak truthfully enough on both counts.

Her devotion to the tenet of Honesty kept her quiet in the face of his questions for the better part of their two-day journey. Perhaps her biggest liability was her aversion to telling lies. After hints by her host that her usefulness might be coming to an end, she decided to employ some conversation. She intended to turn the questions back on him whenever she could.

Ztakish stood and moved into the center of the pavilion to face her. His attendants removed the stolen mugs and kitchenware from his setting. One of Thomena's guards started to re-tie her hands, but Ztakish addressed them. Due to the spell, she understood his words as clearly as they did.

"Leave her untied for now. Go speak to the masses. Promote Yurtash's message; they need reassurance in their course."

Thomena reveled in the fact that she wasn't bound or gagged; unfortunately, the siphoning totem kept her from using her best talent. The constant drain of her spirit left her lightheaded. That didn't stop her from turning a question on him to try and seize some initiative, before he could voice his questions.

"How is it that you know so much of ages long gone? Yet, you lack knowledge of a common language and current events, despite your gift of complex words?"

"Your champion would possess the basics to infer the rest. He helped bring me into this time period, though unknowingly. I believe you addressed him as a father?"

Her breath caught in her throat. She found it hard to swallow under this creature's sudden, penetrating gaze.

He pushed his verbal advance. "What kind of father? A holy one? A bloodline?"

Thomena wouldn't truthfully answer, so she tried to redirect the topic. "What do you mean, this time period? How did he bring you here?"

Ztakish noticed a certain paleness come over the youth. He knew so little of humans, however, so he tried to confirm his perception. His forked tongue shot out and tasted her fear in the air. The action caused his prisoner to jump in her seat.

The Iztheran smiled in his small victory, but the scars on his mouth only conformed to a frightening display.

"I'm going to guess he is your birth father. I couldn't be sure until now. As a fellow champion of Yurtash, I didn't know if he preached to his own flock. If you want an answer to your question, you will answer mine first. Confirm your relationship!"

His shout caused a guard to peek past the entry curtain of the pavilion. The Iztheran leader angrily sent him away, insisting on privacy.

Thomena looked for a chance of escape during the brief diversion, but nothing seemed realistic. Even if she crushed the totem first, her spirit energy would need time to recover. An army that wouldn't hesitate to eat her surrounded the tent, deep in the jungle.

Ztakish swiveled back to face her. The Iztheran locked its arms across its chest. As if translating the back-and-forth, darting movements of her eyes, he said, "You will find nay escape. Also, if you do not answer my questions, you become useless to me. I may then resort to using you as a sacrifice to inspire my people."

Her heart sank. "He is my birth father."

The Iztheran leader nodded. *Then the human champion will come after me. Hopefully he will find an access through the openings left by my scouts. We need to settle on who is Yurtash's true champion.* Aloud, he said, "I know of the old days, because I fought in the Godswars."

Thomena's eyes widened. She couldn't believe such a claim to be true.

"I remember the time when the gods walked the land. My faith put me in charge of a Divine Chariot during the Godswars. I will not waste time regaling my victories to a prisoner, but suffice to say, the day came when Yurtash's enemies descended on me. I was...trapped, you might say. A prisoner standing still as time passed by." Ztakish looked down, clutching his fists. "I lived through time unharmed as my world, my people, fell to ruin. I could only observe, and my means was limited."

"How could something preserve you through so many years?" She seemed to be asking herself the question.

"Maybe I will show you." He sneered at her. Thomena didn't like what it implied. Ztakish continued. "The Trollsbane, and his old partner, discovered me."

Ztakish went over to his desk and pulled forth an axe. "Your father's weapon. He left it behind when they accidentally freed me."

Thomena eyed the blade while she shrunk to the back of her chair. Her captor laughed. "I don't intend to use it on you. Unless, you give me nay other choice. As I was saying, once freed, I began to lead my people out of the obscurity in which they've locked themselves. Yet, there is much about the modern world I don't know about. As a practitioner of arcane arts, you must be intelligent. Talking to you is my chance to learn more of the world."

He paused only briefly. "I believe it is my turn to ask a question. Tell me about your religion."

The young mage looked at him and tried to retrieve her Courage. She sat forward in her seat and straightened her back. Thomena didn't want to expose too much about her own beliefs. She knew this creature might twist them for its own use.

Noting her defiant pause, he said. "Are you so quick to choose the route of sacrifice? My people could use some entertainment."

Thomena realized that she had no choice. "I worship *The Codex*. To you, it would be a relatively new religion. It is a guide book on good philosophies, created by a number of beneficial gods working together."

"Why did such an act come about?"

She drew a breath. "Many people felt misguided in the age of recovery following the Godswars. Many turned away from worshipping their deities. *The Codex* was made as a guide for a good, moral life, without needing to place trust in one specific god. Its principles and virtues guide individuals to promote Bravery, Honesty, Justice, Mercy, and Love, among other tenets."

"Honesty?" he repeated, causing Thomena to wince. Ztakish paced the tent while talking out loud. "I see now why you hesitate to speak, and why I haven't detected any misdirection from you. You must uphold this 'Honesty' very highly; thus, you've been unwilling to say much."

Thomena slowly nodded, before lowering her eyes to the floor.

Ztakish strode forward, grabbing her chin and forcing her to look up at him. It was the first time he'd touched her since her abduction. She tried to resist, but the Iztheran proved to be too strong.

"Then let me answer, truthfully, the next question you should ask. You are here only as bait. I champion the will of Yurtash, but I feel frustrated to be unable to speak to him directly as I did in the days when gods walked the land. Your father, whether he intends it or not, also embodies Yurtash's will in this world. Yurtash is wild, instinctual, primal...a perfect fit for my people, not yours. The Trollsbane has acted to preserve the peace, but I would see the return of war, if only to bring my people back to power. Yurtash's will hangs in the balance. We champions must fight to the death to see whose vision of our god guides the future of this world."

***

During the late hour, as the jungle canopy descended into shadows, the Iztheran people settled into their camp. Many already slept, but a large number of zealots enjoyed a primitive party not far from Ztakish's pavilion. Priests and priestesses led the assembly to invigorate the spirit of their army, assuaging them after their recent non-victory. A powerful tempo beat on leather drums. Voices called out praises to Yurtash.

Even out on the outskirts of the camp, where pickets watched for danger, Iztheran warriors bobbed to the beat. One scout enjoyed the sound so much, his attention strayed too long on the camp. He didn't even register the sound of the fletchings riding the wind until the arrow sank into his brain. He died before dropping to the ground.

Another sentry allowed his eyes to rest for too long. He opened them just as an arrow zipped out of the darkness. In moments, he no longer shared the worries of the living.

None of them really expected an attack this deep into their own territory. The other primitives who once competed with them for space had just shared a battle with them as allies. Even though the battle felt like a loss, they all felt like everyone would return home and lick their wounds. The calls of the priests kept them in good spirits.

Those sentries couldn't know that their leader sought to attract an attack. Their lines had been left thin and undermanned intentionally. An irresistible bait sat in their commander's tent. On top of everything else, a legend among hunters used all his talent to rescue the last of his family.

Thamin's rough appearance reflected his trials tracking an army through the jungle. Course stubble covered his cheeks. Stains of brown mud and green foliage covered his already camouflage-prone clothes, and only a third of it was intentional. He reeked so much of sweat that he was mindful enough to approach from the downwind direction, not that there was much of a wind in the thick tree cover. Grime caked the buttons on his boots.

His skill and deadliness didn't suffer any ill effect from his disarrayed garb. His talents, aided by some natura magic, made him a shadow in the dark. The bodies of three Iztheran scouts lie disguised under leaf cover by the time he entered the tent area. Other reptilian humanoids went abut their evening routines, unaware how closely death's shadow passed behind them. The ranger ducked into a hut-shaped hanging of hides to avoid a group that was approaching his route. The lone occupant of the shelter, too startled to react in time, died before the other group got past. By the time Thamin left the hut, the victim had been tucked into a covering of hides as if asleep.

The ranger continued to move through the camp's obstacles, using every bit of cover to his best advantage. He often slipped by enemies using simple tricks. Every now and then, a thrown nut or rock managed to get them looking outward or upward and away from his path. Too many of them preferred to focus their attention on the priests entertaining in the center of the camp, paying no notice to the shadowy figure passing through their midst.

Thamin saw the large elf pavilion tent and scrutinized it from different angles as he approached. He recalled the massacre on the elf camp and had suspected back then that several items had been stolen. Of course, the recent raids by numerous humanoids on civilized settlements had also gained more pillaged goods. As he studied the structure and pondered its importance, he realized that it was likely the commander's headquarters.

Unfortunately, it stood near the center of the camp, not far from the drums and chanting.

The situation vexed Thamin. His primary goal remained focused on his missing daughter. So far, he didn't have a good clue as to her condition and where they might be keeping her. His only solace stood on the fact that he'd found her boot imprints several times while tracking the army. There could be no way to confuse her dainty boot size with the often barefoot and claw-toed reptilians. He could tell that she'd been struggling with some kind of weight, something which intermittently dragged narrow trails through the ground and snagged at passing branches.

Thamin couldn't know if she would be found in the main tent, but he also hadn't seen any guarded tents elsewhere. He even witnessed a lack of security around the elf pavilion. The guards weren't far from the entry, but like the rest of the camp they were focused on the central festivities.

The ranger made a decision, knowing the serious nature of the stakes involved. He would have to infiltrate the main tent and find answers there. If he set off an alarm in that place, he risked discovery within bowshot of the entire camp populace.

Thamin needed a little extra insurance to guarantee that he could slip into the main tent without notice. His eyes settled on an unexpected sight. A small monkey had been trying to sneak a meal from some bags near Thamin. It had frozen in place when Thamin approached, standing so perfectly still that he only just noticed it.

Using his natura connection, Thamin whispered some unintelligible noises to the animal. In effect, he urged it to flee in the direction of Thamin's choosing. The monkey, finally frightened over the presence of a predator, panicked and ran towards the large celebration. It didn't realize that its path had been directed by the ranger's suggestion. The monkey ran scared and screeching past the tent guards and into the midst of the religious gathering. As the Iztherans followed the antics of the monkey, a shadow slipped into the pavilion.

***

"A duel with my father is that important to you?" Thomena struggled to understand the reasoning. "You say that you are both champions of Yurtash; shouldn't you be finding a peaceful way to settle the god's will?"

Ztakish walked a lazy circle around the youth. Although he spoke calmly, his proximity and nature caused her to tremble. "Such cooperation is certainly with precedent. Unfortunately, Yurtash bridges a spiritual connection within their followers' primal needs. The Trollsbane is human. Humans rule the nearby land. They lack nay comforts."

Coming around Thomena, he casually reached out and touched Kaigal's banner staff in reference. She wanted to do something about it,

273

Courage and Honor practically demanded it, but she knew that her chances of accomplishing anything were slim.

Ztakish let his hand slide off the staff as he continued. "My people wallow in the soggy ground, cowering in darkness. Yurtash commands me to better their lives. There can be nay compromise between Iztherans and humans…and certainly not with elves either. In the past, competing champions have had to fight to prove Yurtash's true will. In my spirit, I know this is the only court of law."

He spun to face her, the abrupt movement causing her whole body to flinch. Ztakish declared. "I have more questions for you."

Thomena tried to pull together the frayed strands of her courage. "I have nay more to say. You only desire violence." Her lips trembled as she spoke. "You are evil. I won't feed you any more information."

The Iztheran commander could sense the truth of her words. She had, after all, admitted to championing honesty. He stared into her eyes. She didn't flinch, even though he could see her rapid breathing.

"Allow me to witness the strength of your divine devotion. I can respect someone who is sturdy in their faith."

Thomena couldn't help but be surprised when the Iztheran marched over to the magic-draining totem and crushed it underfoot. She felt the immediate effects. Her spirit energy began to replenish as if the dam had been removed from a stream.

Ztakish turned to face her again. Step by step, he slowly advanced toward her. "It will take some time for your magic reserves to grow. Maybe, just maybe, you will soon regain the concentration for one critical spell, by which you might escape my camp." He reached behind her back. She tried not to flinch or tremble at his proximity, but it surprised her when she felt the rope at her wrists cut.

Thomena refused to answer him, but he spoke the truth. Even with the totem gone, she required time to rest in order to regain her strength. If she didn't cast her first spell efficiently, the drain on her energy could cause spell fatigue and make her pass out. She tried to cycle through her spell options. The youth couldn't picture herself making any spells work well enough to escape Ztakish, nor flee the camp. Nevertheless, if she died, she had the chance to go down while fighting. Thomena stood slowly, feeling less faint but trying not to overdue any actions. She got her hands in front of her and tossed the remainder of her bindings to the ground.

He pointed a clawed finger at her. "Is that a hint of bravery sneaking back into your visage? Has hope been rekindled? Look me directly in the eyes and show me it is true."

The Iztheran's hand dropped out of sight, but she locked a defiant gaze on him. Thomena summoned her inner strength from any source she could draw upon. She cycled through memories of warm moments, friends, *Codex* passages, compliments, and her recent reunion with her father. The girl stood straight, jutted her chin forward, and lowered her eyebrows in a stern admonishment. Her hands clenched at her sides. She was past feeling any more fear. Thomena knew that her next spell might end her, but she could possibly end him too.

"Now *that*," he emphasized, "is a beacon of hope."

His next movement flicked past her vision too fast to track. She felt a very light weight roll down the back of her head, settling upon her shoulders. Thomena tried to jump backward.

Except that she didn't jump, nor move in any way. Panic started to reclaim the girl as she fought to move a muscle, any muscle, and failed. Despite a great deal of mental struggle, her body stayed rigid like a statue. The mage realized that Ztakish held a piece of something in front of her eyes. Focusing on it, she saw a thin necklace, seemingly of elvish craft. He had thrown it over her head, freezing her in her defiant pose.

"And may that beacon of hope stand forevermore frozen, trapped as I once was. You are an inspiring vision of your faith. I would never waste you as a sacrifice. I just want one individual to have their faith tested as mine was. I pray, that you may watch the centuries pass before your eyes like I once did, watching your race fall into ruin."

Thomena panicked, but not a trace of it showed on her face. She could see and hear, but her muscles wouldn't respond to her commands. She no longer even drew breath, yet she did not choke. She recalled Ztakish talking about being trapped in his body for centuries, and a sinking feeling settled into her gut.

Ztakish's eyes swiveled away from her, looking over her shoulder at the sound of movement behind her. "I wouldn't do anything hasty with your daughter so close to my whim and disposal. You and I need to settle something, champion against champion."

Chapter 31 – Champions' Duel

"It is not my intent to harm her, but she *can* be harmed if I will it."
Ztakish warned the figure behind Thomena. "I wanted you to find me,
Trollsbane, for a duel of honor."

The girl couldn't turn her head. Her father...here? Then again, who
else would track an enemy army through their home terrain for her
sake? The voice originating behind her confirmed her suspicions.

"Thomena? Look at me." A brief pause. "What did you do to her?"

The Iztheran leader extended a hand, palm up, toward her. He
stepped back a respectful distance while replying. "See for yourself.
She is unharmed, but trapped in a magical stasis field."

As Ztakish yielded space for Thamin to approach, his worried
expression came into Thomena's frozen viewpoint. Mud and streaks of
paint covered Thamin's face; part of his ploy to blend into the jungle.
Even with the disguise, he looked tired. His lower eyelids sagged from
lack of sleep. Thomena tried as hard as she could, but she couldn't utter
so much as a sigh or even wiggle her jaw. Thamin's stare shot to her
neck.

"I see you recognize her new necklace. I never had a chance to
express my gratefulness at its removal by your partner."

Thamin's hand crept toward the item in question. The movement
was not lost on either of the other two who were present.

In a sudden movement, Ztakish twirled a double-bladed staff into a
combat pose. "I wish to talk, then engage you in a duel of honor. If you
try to free her first, I will kill her before turning upon you."

Thamin's motion stopped. The ranger's eyes looked over the
predicament. Thomena could see, better than Ztakish's angle, how
Thamin's attention darted from focus to focus. The ranger seemed to be
taking in every detail: the necklace, her position, exits of the tent, extra
weapons, his distance from Ztakish. His strategic mind seemed to be
calculating every possibility and tactic.

The human legend threw one last, reassuring glance at his daughter
before turning his attention to their host. "You know my title, but I
have learned of you also. You must be Ztakish."

Ztakish offered a slight, respectful bow, without taking his attention from the dangerous human, nor allowing his guard to relax.

Thamin moved away from Thomena, but stayed within her line of sight. Yurtash's two champions shared a glare while standing closer to Ztakish's portable table. Thamin continued talking. "Why all this effort? Why the duel?"

Ztakish replied, but stayed light on his feet as both men slowly circled each other inside the tent. "I am a warrior of the Godswars, and that remains to be my worldly view. The necklace was put upon me by elves, and I only escaped by the dumb luck of your partner." The two opponents continued to circle warily, each looking for an advantage. "My role in Yurtash's future include conquest and expansion. I was bred and raised for such..."

Thomena tuned out their conversation as she tried to find a deeper focus within herself. Thomena still couldn't summon the strength or willpower to break her imprisonment. She tried to think up a spell which could help. Unfortunately, she only knew of one spell she could attempt while paralyzed and unable to speak: a spell she'd never managed to cast successfully. The flow of magic trickled into her, but would take a while to power any worthwhile spell. Even if she succeeded in using that one now, it would throw lightning at every opponent in close range. Thamin would also be hit. Thomena felt helpless.

"It seems I have nay choice but to agree to your duel. Make yourself ready."

Thamin's words yanked Thomena from her thoughts. *They were actually going to duel? Father was going to fight a powerful enemy in the middle of his army?*

As she watched, Thamin began setting down his swords just like he did prior to the troll fight. He knelt near her. Across the tent, Ztakish spoke words of natura magic. The Iztheran ran his arms along his staff as he did so, and the blades began to drip green droplets which hissed when they hit the ground. Thamin ran his hands along his own weapons: Longclaw on the right, and the swordbreaker on the left. The red glow of the firebrands enveloped both blades.

He whispered to her while acting like he was still in the process of enchanting his equipment. "If there is a way for me to knock the necklace free, escape if you can. He would come directly after you if I do it, so I can only try for such an opening if I've slowed him down. Worry not for me," he continued, speaking as if to his armor. "You have a wide jungle and an army to worry about, just run if you can."

He paused slightly. "I'm sorry that I separated us for so long. I'm honored to see the woman you're becoming. Jaena would be so proud of her baby girl."

Thamin stood. He straightened his shoulders and tightened the leather laces on one gauntlet. His face turned to speak more directly to her, though he dared not take his eyes off his opponent. "My highest values in life have always been my friends and family. My whole life I fought for them. Now most of my friends are either dead or parted ways. You are the greatest sun left to shine upon my life. If I must die so that you may live, it is a death worth enduring."

Thomena would cry if she could, but the arcane necklace denied that also. She didn't honestly believe she could run if given the chance. The youth would defend her father if she could.

At one edge of her vision, Ztakish spun his enchanted weapon. "Are you ready?" Despite the question, it was clear from his tone that he would only accept one answer.

Thamin's swords left a red afterglow as he spun them into a guard stance. "Let's not keep Yurtash waiting."

***

Thamin and Ztakish lunged simultaneously, their weapons sliding against one another while spinning in defensive circles. Thamin's two swords alternated roles. Longclaw attacked while swordbreaker parried, only to be followed by an attack from swordbreaker as Longclaw swept aside a spear thrust. For his part, Ztakish might as well have been attacking with two weapons of his own. Both ends of his staff ended in foot-long stabbing blades. He thrust and spun the weapon with speed and efficiency. The Iztheran jabs stabbed fast as lightening, yet Thamin kept parrying or spinning out of the way. Ztakish never left himself open, retracting his weapon in time to knock Thamin's attacks aside.

Thomena couldn't always keep track of the action, even when they maneuvered in front of her. Thamin's two blades trailed a red illumination, Ztakish's staff blades left green afterglows in the air, and both weapons sparked when metal met metal. Even the Iztheran's wooden staff seemed to be enchanted against magical blows, since Longclaw held magical strength even without Thamin's fire enchantment. Thamin tried to shear the weapon early on during their fight, but it didn't sunder.

Both warriors used their terrain to full advantage. The pavilion tent didn't possess much furnishings, yet they were used to launch attacks or block attack angles. Ztakish used a footrest to launch a jumping attack, moments before Thamin's low swipe turned its legs to flaming kindling. The Iztheran's attack missed, allowing the ranger to slide behind the table used for the meal. Moments later, Thamin launched over the table in a high assault, as Ztakish slid underneath it. They continued the fight from opposite sides of where each once stood, until a blow from Longclaw collapsed the middle of the table.

The table remnants caught fire. Thomena would have widened her eyes, or felt her pulse quicken, but her own body felt distant to her.

With Ztakish on the wrong side of the wreckage, Thamin dashed to Thomena's side and tried to lift the necklace free. She saw the enemy raise his staff like a spear, but she couldn't warn her father. Thamin hadn't ignored the Iztheran, and thus struck aside the weapon.

Part of the blade managed to scrape along Thomena's head and slide through her hair. Acid dripped from the blade onto the girl. Yet, Ztakish's words proved true. Thomena remained unharmed and unblemished.

Father and daughter understood that Ztakish was living up to his promise, that he would make her a prime target if released. Realizing the threat, Thamin launched himself at the unarmed enemy. The staff teleported back to Ztakish's hands with a thought, batting aside a dual whirlwind of blades. In the rapid exchange, Thamin managed to slash the tip of the swordbreaker along Ztakish's arm. It drew first blood, but the effects seemed diminished compared to the skill behind the strike.

Father and daughter witnessed the hit, as well as the lack of a deeper cut. *He's thickened his skin, like my "harden skin" earth-based spell.* Thomena deduced. *Father will have to hit him a number of times to wear down that protection.*

Thamin kept maneuvering close to the lizardman, assuming that proximity would give him an advantage over the Iztheran's staff. Ztakish dispelled that notion as it used its alternate weapons. It snapped at Thamin with its snout full of sharp teeth. Both warriors even found time to trade punches and kicks, but Ztakish possessed sharp claws and Thamin didn't.

At times, Thomena could only hear the grunts and weapon parries behind her, not knowing how her father fared. During those times, her vision fixed on the ongoing damage to the tent. Flames and acid burned away sections of the shelter. Despite the fear of her own situation, she felt even worse for her father. She recalled him saying how he had been forced to watch her mother die, unable to save her. Jaena had been a powerful mage, but couldn't save herself.

"Mitsarum!" Thamin exclaimed.

Ztakish fell back into Thomena's line of vision. He twitched as the remnants of an electrical attack danced across his body. Thamin pursued his opponent with vigor, his twin blades trying to snake past the spinning staff from both sides.

Ztakish mimicked Thamin's mastery of natura, as he also shouted, "Mitsarum!"

An electrical bolt hit the ranger. Instead of causing convulsions to Thamin's body, his cloak sucked in the sparks of the spell. Thamin continued his attacks without pause.

A realization came to the mage. *His cloak protects him from lightning-type damage! I can try to use my spell.*

Thomena tried to focus on the spell she knew as "Still Lightning." She'd been practicing it in the barracks' yard, blackening the grass, but she still lacked any proficient use of it. It was the only spell she could hope to cast without speaking or moving.

The two duelists fought without any knowledge of the girl's continued tries, and failures, to ignite her spell. The combatants' garb showed rips and stains as blood ran from wounds. Ztakish hated to admit it, but Thamin proved to be more gifted in delivering hits and dodging attacks. However, the Iztheran possessed more magic tricks, including the one that hardened his skin. The ranger had speed, but Ztakish had more strength. As such, both warriors had difficulty gaining any real advantage over their foe for long.

Thamin finally trapped one of Ztakish's blade ends in a hole on his swordbreaker. The ranger leveraged himself to try breaking the staff. Not to be beaten in such a way, Ztakish increased the amount of acid leaking from the enchanted blade. The sword began to sizzle. Thamin cleaved down with Longclaw, sundering the Iztheran's weapon near the trapped blade's connection point. He even tried to reverse momentum right afterward and catch Ztakish with a backswing. The Iztheran managed to dodge backward, with only three-fourths of his original weapon in his hand.

Thamin fared no better; the blade of his swordbreaker melted apart at midpoint, leaving him with only smoking metal goo on his hilt.

Ztakish glared at his broken staff, now nothing more than a short spear. His eyes swiveled back to the Trollsbane. He challenged, "Why not give in to our primal nature? I've seen you assume the form of the wolf, but have you truly heeded the predator's call?"

Thamin knew of the predator's call to which Ztakish inferred. The transformation involved a more primal connection with Yurtash than

Thamin would dare go. He attempted it in the past, but the wild nature of the call seemed too intoxicating, thus he had always resisted and settled for merely the form of his spirit animal.

Ztakish didn't give him much time to consider it. The Iztheran's snout elongated even further, his jaws grew wider, he bent forward yet managed to rise in height, and his tail thickened and lengthened. Just as Thamin had done during the army battle, the transformation helped urge the others around it. Thamin, a fellow greenman and thus feral warrior such as Ztakish, felt the wolf change coming and didn't resist. He embraced his wild nature.

Inside a pavilion tent being eaten by flames, the large wolf faced off against an alligator. However, while Thamin stayed in the form of the wolf, Ztakish gave himself over to the more savage version: the predator's call. His alligator form continued to grow to giant proportions. His body stretched longer than any normal alligator, lengthening to just over 25 feet from snout to tail tip. His legs bulked out as thick as tree trunks. They circled as they transformed, tearing through more portions of the tent.

The face off didn't last long. Ztakish growled at Thamin, then did something unexpected. His thick tail whipped around and slammed into Thomena. Her statue-like body launched through an opening of the tent, toward the revelry of the camp celebration.

Thamin immediately turned and pursued. The sounds of the ceremony fell apart in disarray as the Iztherans stopped to witness the intrusion. Thomena's stiff body bounced and rolled until resting against a sitting log. Although Thamin couldn't know for sure, his daughter felt no pain, only continued fear at her helplessness. The foremost iztherans moved away as the wolf charged into their midst; however, an army of them still surrounded the bonfire.

They all turned and stared again as their living god, Ztakish, casually ripped his way out of the command tent. Only a few had seen his prior transformation at the elves' camp, yet all had heard stories about it. Cheers rose up at the sight of him. Many prostrated themselves as the giant reptile advanced toward the smaller wolf. A chant rose among the army, elevating to pitch proportions as they prepared to witness their chosen one's wrath.

Ztakish called out something in his native language. A pair of Iztheran priests seized Thomena's form and propped it upright in the soft soil, giving her a front row vantage. They did this despite Thamin, in wolf form, baring his fangs and looking ready to attack. Yet even

Kaigal's legend had to keep an eye on his approaching enemy, as well as remember the threat if he tried to free her before ending the duel.

But under the current circumstances, what would happen even if he defeated their champion? It looked like such an outcome would be a short-lived victory.

Ztakish dashed faster than expected, launching his strong jaws at Thamin. The wolf dodged, managing a swipe of his claws against Ztakish's toughened flesh. One wolf claw still retained the sharpness and flames of Longclaw. He only had time to inflict a small wound before springing away from the larger beast's bite. Thamin used his better agility and speed to keep flanking the giant alligator. He knew better than to take those jaws head-on. Wounds accumulated on Ztakish's legs and sides, but the Iztheran managed to land a hard tail slap that sent Kaigal's champion sprawling.

The Iztheran almost had him at that point. The jaws clamped down as Thamin still rolled to his feet and tried to jump clear. Reptilian teeth drew blood from the wolf's haunches.

The chanting crowd gave them some room, but not as much as Thamin would have wanted. Even with natura magic bolstering his already gifted agility, he had a hard time slipping around those terrible jaws. Iztherans continued to cheer their idol as the wolf tried to keep from being cornered.

Thamin attempted a frontal attack. Ztakish tried adjusting to the change in tactics and snapped at his target. The attack proved to be a feint, as Thamin paused just out of range when the jaws slammed shut. As soon as those jaws closed, he leaped upon the alligator's snout. Thamin wrapped his legs around the nose, hooking his claws around the bottom jaw. The claws sank in even as the he bit into the reptile. Ztakish had trouble trying to open his mouth with his opponent hanging on. Alligator muscles can crunch down hard when closing, but are much weaker trying to open back up. Blood ran from his snout as fangs and claws tore into him.

Thomena watched helplessly as Ztakish began to perform a barrel roll. The giant alligator rolled one way, then the next, hammering the wolf's smaller body into the ground. As the alligator rolled back closer to Thomena, he managed to slam Thamin into a bonfire. They were so close that drops of blood splashed Thomena. Try as she might, she couldn't get her spell to work. She felt very tense inside. The frustration built up as she failed time and again.

The latest impact finally threw Thamin loose. His fur gave off smoke. He tried to recover but Ztakish's reflexes struck like lightning.

Those powerful jaws clamped down as hard as any vice. Thamin couldn't escape without ripping free of the sharp teeth anchored in his hide. The pressure exerted through the alligator jaws made death a certainty.

Ztakish reared his head up high, shaking Thamin like a trophy for the sake of his followers. Iztherans cheered their god's champion, feeling vindicated in their goals. Inside, Ztakish believed that his view of Yurtash's will was now justified. Even though the first major battle had turned against them, the renewed fervor of his people would ensure a long-term victory.

Thomena saw her father's gaze pass across her as he suffered in Ztakish's grip. She let out a silent plea. *Please Codex, help me hear my mother's voice. She was a good wizard. Help me understand how I am failing? What can I do to save my father?*

A wordless answer came to her as she began to feel some unknown serenity relaxing her body. Her mind calmed. In doing so, she realized a common cause to her failure. Even when she had first practiced the spell, knowing she couldn't move, she tensed up as she braced her muscles for the incantation. Maybe the point was just the opposite. Since she wasn't supposed to be able to move, maybe she was supposed to relax? Although her muscles felt no different, Thomena sought a relaxed state in order to cast the spell.

A passage from *The Codex* flashed through her mind. *Parents fill children with wisdom, but most children do not become adults until they face the truth of those lessons.* Had Jaena's spirit guided her from the dead?

Lightning arced outward from the mage's still form, covering twice the distance as her height. The blue sparks scorched the hardened skin of the giant alligator. The pain of the spell interrupted Ztakish's moment of ascension in the presence of his people and his deity.

Thomena felt a severe drain to her scant magical reserves. She witnessed the alligator jump, but its jaws still latched onto her father. Lightning dispersed prior to affecting Thamin's body, due to the protection from his cloak. This was her chance...but a thunderclap headache blossomed in warning. Thomena lacked the endurance to cast any large spell. Nevertheless, she launched a second assault immediately following the first success. Electrical bolts seared all the flesh on one side of Ztakish.

Tremors caused Ztakish to heave his victim from his maw. The self-appointed champion of Yurtash had trouble comprehending the sudden distraction. Who dared interrupt his victory? Though moving on unsteady legs, he turned to face the direction of the onslaught.

The statue of Kaigal's most recent bannermaiden still stood frozen, slightly tilted, with her boots sunk halfway into the mud. His people scrambled to get away from her form. Blackened roots at her feet smoldered. Her energy managed to ensnare two of his priests, who both now trembled in death throes at her feet.

Reacting purely from instinct and pain, Ztakish lurched forward and snapped his strong jaws on the youth. The necklace hardened her form, making her near-invulnerable, but Ztakish continued to bite down.

Thomena hovered on the verge of spell fatigue once again. It was entirely likely that her next spell would rob her of consciousness. She couldn't see anything beyond the confines of Ztakish's maw. She didn't even feel pain from his attack, but that brought no relief. The young girl gathered Courage and resolved to try one more spell, even if it dropped her out of consciousness. She managed to release the lightning again.

Hot energy fried the length of Ztakish's throat into its deepest recesses.

Thamin staggered to his feet, momentarily overlooked by all. His balance swayed from both loss of blood and cracked bones. Air wheezed past the red drips exiting his mouth. His blurry vision focused on the other beast's frenzied attack on his daughter. He witnessed the bright energies lighting up the outline of Ztakish's teeth as thunder caused the other Iztherans to cower.

Thamin knew the choice he had to make if there was any hope of saving them. As a greenman and one of Yurtash's gifted, he needed to embrace the deeper calling: the predator's call. Once he adopted that connection, he didn't know if his wild side would overrule his intellect. Ztakish seemed unconcerned about returning to his humanoid form, so Thamin needed to accept the risk.

A deep howl rolled across the camp.

Any Iztheran soldiers, who hadn't already started giving room when Thomena's lightning radiated out, began frantically backpedaling as a monstrous new version of the wolf charged in from the side. Standing over ten feet tall at the shoulder, its bulk slammed into the alligator. Sword-like teeth which rivaled Ztakish's clamped down upon the alligator's neck.

Ztakish released Thomena, spitting her form through the air in the process. The girl's vision went blurry due to the lack of spell reserves. Now, she became dizzy also.

Cries rang out among the lizard-like people as they watched their champion suffer pain. The crowd backed away for safety, their composures a mix of prayers, disbelief, and shock. As the giant wolf bore their living idol to the ground, trapped belly-up, the Iztherans wailed for justice.

Thamin had the upper hand, and would not surrender it easily. His dark eyes reflected the bestial nature of the call, with little hint of the intellect of the man within the form. His teeth continued to sink into the neck. As his enemy hit the ground, his forepaws raked the tender underside of the other beast. The attacks stripped away any remaining natura protections along with the protective hide. Ztakish would have roared his fierce cry across the miles of jungle, but his throat collapsed upon itself. The wolf-beast tore away at its victim without a hint of remorse or mercy. As its vanquished foe shrank back into its true, Iztheran shape, the creature howled at the stars winking past the jungle canopy.

The wolf turned its hungry attention toward the disarrayed crowd.

Yet, something gave it pause. Its eyes spotted the dirt-and-blood spattered figure of a young maiden, discarded among dropped items near the tattered pavilion. Her figure lie rigidly on her side, jutting her chin, fists on her hips...an image of bravery and undiminished hope.

Oh, father. Thomena thought to herself as she saw the savagery of the feral beast. *Don't give in to the wild. Remember your nature.*

The wolf's eyes...remembered. The wild spark left its demeanor and left a moment of disorientation. In that moment, the true soul regained control.

The wolf shrank back to the form it had used when the Iztheran people first saw it leave the pavilion. It stood next to the body of their fallen idol. Though anger no longer clouded its eyes, they feared the portents of this struggle. After being lost for so long, they found themselves lost again. Some knelt, some even prostrated themselves, calling out to Yurtash.

The wolf did not give them time to react. Thamin mentally shoved aside his hurts and exhaustion so that he could run to his daughter's side. With great care, Thamin nipped the amulet and pulled it over Thomena's head. Freed at last, the girl's body relaxed to the ground. Despite suffering a roaring headache from the drain on her spirit energy, she staggered to her feet as hurriedly as could be expected.

"Let me put that away." Thomena winced, holding out her hand.

Thamin, remaining in wolf form, dropped the necklace into her palm. He couldn't communicate very well, nor in very complex terms, as a wolf. He hoped she could understand that he continued this form to generate enough fear to hold back the Iztheran army from swarming them.

Thomena, the educated daughter of two intelligent parents, already knew what action she needed to take. The interrogations suffered at the hands of Ztakish over the last two days had revealed much to her. She hoped she had time to get her plea on receptive ears. Thomena dashed over to Ztakish's corpse, which had returned to its normal humanoid size and shape, and removed an earring from his body. Thomena believed that item to be the magic source of how he had communicated to her. Without dwelling on the oddness or health concerns, she snapped the earring onto her own ear. It was a necessary action for her to make the best outcome from the situation.

The youth stood tall, stretching out her hands above her. "Proud citizens of the Olangi jungle, please hearken to my words and heed my message!"

From the way that every reptilian head focused on her, the earing appeared to be translating her words well. Her weight shifted between legs, which helped hide how much her weariness made her tremble. "You looked for guidance from Yurtash in this fight, and he has sent you his message. Ztakish brought back your language and culture, in order for you to flourish. Ztakish believed that his duel was to show an omen of Yurtash's will. But in his downfall to another Yurtash champion, your god demonstrates that your gifts were not given for war. The Godswars is an awful relic of the past, and it destroyed your culture. You must seek a peaceful coexistence with your neighbors."

She took a deep breath, trying to stay calm in the midst of so many hostile stares. They hadn't killed her yet, so Thomena took it as a good sign to continue. She resisted the urge to hold her pounding head in her hands. Now was not the time to reveal weakness.

"This continent is my home, though I have been away for many years. I read many things about this jungle before coming here. Humans and elves value many plants and fruits that grow here. Many medicinal herbs can be found in your lands. The various people of Diara would rather trade with you than fight you. *I* would rather have you as my friend than my enemy. Please consider this omen carefully."

Thomena thought she'd said all she had in mind to say. She turned back toward the remains of the pavilion tent and the sight of her father. He stood with fur bristling and teeth bared, protectively watching over the situation. Despite trickling wounds and the weariness of battle, the large wolf looked ready to kill anyone who threatened her.

One more message came to her mind. She turned back to face the Iztheran army even as they had begun to whisper among themselves. Her eyes were wet with honest emotion as she made her last plea. "You have children to raise. Be there to raise them. Don't throw away your life or limbs in battle and miss sharing the future with them."

Thomena spun around, ready to leave. As heartfelt as she tried to make her words, there was no guarantee that these people would just let her and her father slip away. The youth didn't go directly to her father, however, passing him by as he watched her from the corner of his animal eyes. She strode purposefully to the ruins of the pavilion tent. The whole time, she worried that too quick a stride or too slow a stride would lead to the Iztherans taking action. Some chanted prayers, some whispered to their neighbors. Thomena understood their words, due to the earring. Some were even debating the fact that the Trollsbane seemed to be Yurtash's true, chosen champion. A group of priests moved to honor Ztakish's body. Most of the tent hadn't succumbed to the acid or fire. Thomena wasted no time, focused on reclaiming one item. Thomena seized hold of Kaigal's fallen banner. The blue-and-red fabric of the flag remained mostly intact, other than the previous battle damage. She knew how the army viewed its importance. After dragging it this far into the jungle, gods willing, she planned to drag it back.

When she left the tent, Thamin still retained wolf form, and continued to stare down the murmuring Iztherans. Thamin dipped a shoulder as she moved alongside him. In a guttural voice he urged, "Ride."

She didn't plan to argue. They both looked weary, but his way of getting out would be better than her walking and dragging the banner. Thomena hopped onto his back, holding the flag high. Thamin turned to the south edge of camp. He moved slowly at first, uttering a low growl. When no one moved to intercept, he quickly picked up speed and bounded for the thick jungle before anyone could change their mind.

Running away through the foliage, covering ground more quickly than they could on human feet, they left the camp behind without further incident. The fear of a chase gave them the incentive to keep moving despite their exhaustion. By the time they did collapse, Thamin seemed to struggle to shed his wolf form. He explained it to her. "I've heard that when people accept the predator's call, it is hard to find their way back to humanity the first time. I wouldn't risk that for anyone but you."

Thamin used his limited healing spells to patch the worst of his injuries. He and Thomena curled up close for warmth under a blanket. The next morning dawned with no apparent pursuit. Thamin returned to his wolf form, not saying much. Thomena climbed onto his back again, hoisted the banner, and they continued back toward human lands.

Chapter 32 – One Indulgence

Thomena fell asleep twice more on Thamin's back as he carried her back to Kaigal's domain. He didn't mind her resting after her ordeal. She didn't miss anything but miles of jungle followed by miles of grasslands, both mostly uninhabited. Thamin went out of the way a bit to avoid the battlefield. Kaigal and Syllatru troops would have removed their dead, but the jungle humanoids usually left theirs to rot.

When Bael Cochaw finally came into sight, Thomena signaled that she was ready to walk.

"Nay," he replied.

"What do you mean, nay? I'm fit enough. This is embarrassing; letting them see me ride you back through the gates."

Thomena realized that the earring helped her understand Thamin's wolf language better, since some words only came out as growls or grunts. His message came across more completely than it would for someone without that magical aid.

Thamin spoke. "You gave the Iztheran people a symbol. Now, give one to your own people. They would have worried for you as they did for the last bannermaiden. Give them a victorious return."

She balked at the idea. "That sounds prideful. I'm trying to obey Humility for *The Codex*, and it is nay easy feat."

"A little pride can boost one's self-worth. Besides, this isn't your pride, it's theirs."

She glanced to the east, in the direction of the broken gate by the old barracks. "I just suddenly feel as if we should slip in the side entry. You can deliver this to Commander Bedran later, with my compliments."

A guttural sound came from the wolf's throat. She soon recognized it as mirth. Thamin argued. "You asked to go to war without my blessing or knowledge. Surely that was more courageous than riding through a safe gate? If you chase after Humility here, you lose out on both your Courage and your Honesty."

She ran out of time to argue. Soldiers were already stacking up on the north wall as alarm bells rang.

Thamin growled. "Back straight. Banner high."

His logic had beaten her at her own religion. Thomena smirked as she followed his instructions. The smirk soon faded to awe as she saw the numbers gathering at the gate. Gold Lions and Blue Boars stacked three deep on the walls to get a view of what approached on the plains. An "arrow" of six Green Horse that had been patrolling veered to intercept them. As soon as their commander recognized the missing bannermaiden and Kaigal's colors, he had his troops fall into a double-line behind her. Their lances couched skyward. They acted as an honor guard as the wolf approached the gate.

The chance to slip in silently had passed by her like the wind. Whether she wanted it or not, she rode in like the conquering hero. She knew she must be making an imposing sight: riding an oversized wolf, the home banner held high, and looking no worse for her capture other than her clothes requiring a good wash and a few spindles of stitching.

People began to welcome her approach. One voice called out, "Bannermaiden! The bannermaiden returns!" Others quickly echoed the title and the cheers.

She passed under a gate swarming with young soldiers, each crying out for her attention. Some others simply cried, thankful that the fate of Macey Durant hadn't been repeated. The shouting almost made her cover her ears. The noise brought out every citizen from every shop door. Inhabitants peered out of upper story windows. To Thomena's growing embarrassment, Thamin moved at a deliberately slow pace. Dhea Loral featured common enough magic and strangeness that people hardly spared a glance at the wolf mount, focusing instead on the miracle of their returned flag-bearer.

Commander Shan Bedran finally stepped into Thomena's path. The commander was a mountain of a man, whose steps thundered just as imposingly. However, he gave a deep nod to Thomena the moment she came near. He even seemed to spare a wink at the wolf. It only lasted a moment. The commander shifted his eyes to the girl whose stance with the banner had belayed his command to withdraw, only to end up winning the fight.

"Thomena Grayeyes, daughter of the Trollsbane!" His voice called out over the suddenly silenced crowd. "It relieves us all that you have returned to us safely, after carrying Kaigal's banner unto victory. I hope you can deliver us more good news from Olangi."

The youth continued to sit up straight and stately. The people were eager for good news, and her highest calling lay in Truth. Thomena's eyes swiveled to look at the crowd as she replied.

"The one who led the jungle invaders is dead. Hopefully, his ambitions died alongside him. I offered his people a vision of peace, and seeded a future of coexistence with my words. Only time will tell if my pleas fell upon receptive ears."

As proper as Thomena presented herself, she felt a strong need to conclude any ceremony and disappear to the privacy of the barracks. Thomena shifted her focus to the banner in her hands. The breeze caused it to wave, displaying the holes and rips inflicted by the ferocity of the battle.

"Good defenders, I have recovered your honorable colors and present them back to you...but I would ask one indulgence in return."

Commander Bedran couldn't hide his curiosity. "What terms do you seek? We owe you much, and would like to repay you, as well as apologize for any discomfort suffered, if we can."

"The flag is yours, but I would plead of you to allow me to keep the flagstaff. It returns a bit shorter than when it left."

The banner's support pole had been ten feet tall when departing the fort, but the battle-splintered bottom made it closer to six feet long upon it's return. Commander Bedran didn't care if she kept it. He knew a thing or two about wizards and their staves. However, he made it a point to delay his response. People murmured as he seemed to waste time considering the offer. He cocked his head to one side. He rubbed the stubble of his beard. The more he made a show of "thinking" about it, more and more people in the crowd started shouting out their support for the young maiden. Bedran played with the crowd a bit longer, sending voices into a frenzy before raising his hands to indicate quiet.

"Granted!" he shouted, and the crowd roared its support.

Thomena unfastened the cloth from the pole. A color guard of Blue Boars appeared, accepting the flag from her and folding it properly.

The commander shouted for the sake of the people. "Let us not indulge in any more ceremony. You need rest, and you shall have it. We'll have some clerics bring food, drink, and healing miracles out to the barracks. I will not suffer anyone else disturbing your respite."

All the attention and pomp left Thomena realizing how weary she felt. She whispered so that only Thamin could hear. "To a bed, please, with all haste this time."

He obliged.

∗∗∗

Thamin walked into the barracks a few days later, noting that his daughter was still at work adding runes and gems to her newly-claimed staff. Even the bottom end, where it broke, had been re-shaped and tapered with an endcap.

He commented on the changes. "It's taking shape like artwork. I'd hardly believe it was just a flagpole before. You've got it decorated nicely."

Thomena nodded. "I have a good idea on what I need to do to prepare it. I didn't realize how much I wanted this until it came to me. As I'd said before, a wizard's staff works best when it has a personal connection to them. We went through a battle together."

"How will it help you?"

"I can store specific spells in it, spending my energy when I infuse it, not when I cast it." Thomena paused briefly before adding to her explanation. "That helps when I'm casting a lot of spells in a short period, such as a battle. I can also attune it to some elemental energy, which will increase the power of my spells. I'm still trying to decide whether to base it off air or water."

She set down her staff on the wizard's desk and looked over her shoulder at him. "Did you really go through with it?"

Her father nodded. He wasn't even wearing his traditional scouting attire. He had pulled an official dress uniform from a sealed case. It displayed an outdated rank and a handful of medals. Longclaw sat in a decorative bandolier by his side, a simple dagger hung on his opposite hip due to the destruction of the swordbreaker.

"Aye, it is done. I am now officially retired from Kaigal's army. He even gave me a requirement on when to clear out of the barracks."

Her face scrunched up, "He did?"

"Thirty years."

She giggled and returned her attention to her work. The young wizard picked up her staff and examined the new runes. "I can't believe you would give this place up."

Thamin unbuckled his sword and set aside the uniform's overcoat. "You don't think I can find a place that is less drafty and prone to mice? I thought you were just beginning to make yourself at home here."

Giggling again, she responded. "I guess Orlaun spoiled me. I still miss certain comforts. Perhaps I will need to leave soon, regardless. Do you know what I found out from Mabry this morning?"

"Do tell."

She set the staff down and pivoted on her stool to face him. Her expression turned serious. "One of the fort's wizards used magic to take an illusionary image of me when we rode through the gates with the banner. There is already talk about adding a new statue to Heroes' Terrace."

Thamin, well-aware of how Thomena felt about her shortcomings in the tenet of Humility, tried unsuccessfully to dim his resulting laugh. Her sudden frown didn't dampen his humor in the slightest bit.

He consoled her. "Allow the people to have a memory of a hero. Sometimes," his hands swept out to indicate the mostly empty barracks, "all we have are memories of them by which to inspire the rest of us."

"I didn't do much."

Thamin expected such a response from his child, knowing how much she wouldn't want to take credit for anything. In his mind, however, he couldn't help but be honored with all her actions. She went on a voyage across miles of dangerous sea and land with only a non-combat partner until she found him. She took over the ghost-town of a barracks before he even knew she had arrived. The girl stood up against everyone's 'legend' and shouted at him to make known her true feelings. Thomena took down a troll by herself, and also turned the eye of every young soldier in the fort. She survived her first battle despite running forward with the flag when she was supposed to pull back. Thomena managed to make a difference with her spells even when she was supposed to be helpless. Thamin wouldn't soon forget her parting words to the Iztheran people, delivering a message of peace when there was every reason for hate.

Choosing his words carefully, he said, "You did enough that I'm having a hard time balancing out my Humility."

"What do you mean?"

"I'm finding myself full of pride at having such a wonderful daughter."

Her face flushed red. She turned away to hide it, chewing her lip as she did so. Her hands inspected her staff, but only to look busy. Her mind ran in circles of distraction.

"Another thing," Thamin spoke, but she didn't turn to face him. "Those parting words of yours to the Iztheran race...they likely did more for future peace than all my years of soldiering. I might be optimistic, but maybe they will actually come out in trade next time rather than a raid."

Thomena spoke while facing the desk. "I can't take all the glory. You had to beat their champion first."

A couple minutes of silence passed as both of them looked to their own interests. Thomena appreciated the use of the tools on this unknown wizard's desk. She had all that she needed in order to complete her staff within a couple days' time. Thamin had tougher decisions to make. He knew in his heart that it would be time to move on. It was hard sorting what to keep and what to leave.

"Thomena," he called to her, hoping to get more clarity of her plan, "this is your journey. Where were you thinking of going next?"

Her head swam in indecision. "I don't really know. It's expected of me to take a year or two of travel, then share what I've seen and take the test for mastery. For that, I generally need to visit the big cities, libraries, enjoy places rich with culture and fluffy beds."

He grinned over her last comment. "I can show you around Diara. I've visited a number of the other big city-states here. I can think of a few libraries and guildhalls that might offer you something."

Thomena nodded, but didn't answer straightaway. She puzzled over something for a moment before speaking again. "I also admit, you're right about trying to make the world a better place. I resented being away from you, but maybe now we can make a difference together. I'll feel better if I can make this journey for others as well as myself."

Thamin nodded. "I could show you some of the lodges of the rangers. There's usually lots of good people needing a hand. Who knows? Once we get you back to the continent of Quoros, we could also join organizations like the privateers of Kashmer. I've heard of some bad apples in their group, but it sounds like they mostly do good."

"This reminds me of something." She mused openly. "Didn't you start your adventuring career as a guide?"

He grinned, "Aye. And now I'm *your* guide. This is your journey, your adventure. But, I'll be happy to show you to some interesting places along the way."

***

"Wasn't it supposed to be, 'two girls seeking their fortunes in Dhea Loral?' And now you're moving on?"

Although Julia didn't mean to hurt her friend, Thomena still ducked her head a bit at the reproach. "I'm sorry."

"Oh, don't act like that!" Julia reached under Thomena's chin and raised her face so that they once again met eye-to-eye. The candles in

Gunnard's smithy barely illuminated either of them. "It amazes me that you can be powerful and influential, but the moment someone lectures you, your gray-eyes look like some sad puppy."

The young mage said. "I never expected to stay here. At the very least, I knew I'd be returning to Orlaun someday." She chewed her lip anxiously. "At least you did find something here. Am I wrong?"

Julia's expression looked quite pleased. "I found a job. I even have a chance to grow my tinker skills. I also found a good man...which had *not* been part of the plan. I'm glad that I came out here."

The tinker turned to her friend. "And what lies ahead for you?"

Thomena cocked her head to the side for a moment. Possibilities and expectations ran through her mind. "I won't know until I get out there and look. I've reunited with my father, and our future looks good. I know that I'll be touring Diara and expanding my knowledge of the world."

Julia chuckled. "That reminds me of one of your book passages. 'Always strive to better yourself.' Is that right?"

"Aye," Thomena said. "If I don't keep testing myself, I won't truly know my boundaries. Everyone needs to keep turning pages and opening up the next chapters in their lives." The young girl stared ahead, into the closest candle. "Who knows what my next chapter will bring?"

###THE END###

Roster of the Blood-Wolves

Achaikos
Adelle
Adgurn
Arcusan
Arleeya
Bificus
Blurose
Ceneleny
Cherith
Croflah
Cthen
Dem
Dotanis
Emersum
Findor
Garnola
Hodine
Jara
Jarr
Jasmyn
Josie
Kaimito
Kamyena

Legionaire
Liette
Majentas
Mara'tir
Memo
Moyeera
Muldari
Northwind
Ombras
Odessya
Ryche
Sildaar
Terill
Thamin
Thorne
Tristca
Vorpoll
Wargto
Willowbee
Woopnyo
Wraithwolf
Xneedra
Zetaorionus

Appendix A – The Calendar of Dhea Loral

The calendar of Dhea Loral's realm is four hundred days long. That reflects the time it takes for one year to pass for the planet of Epos Goth. The calendar is divided into five seasons, with two months in each season, as follows:

Planting season: Primus, then Florum
Summer season: Jherad, then Doyal
Harvest season: Othgar, then Novak
Waning season: Tiquierum, then Norgrad
Winter season: Vientula, then Icethule

Each month lasts forty days and each week is ten days. The civilized societies of the land do tend to observe two-day weekends; however, much work is still done on these days. The value of a weekend in Dhea Loral is seen more as a time for socializing and public events, but even on these days many merchants are still doing business. There is also a midweek day by which many government offices in the civilized lands take half the day off. The evening on these days feature balls, feasts, religious observations, or other relaxing endeavors. Many people do not observe such luxuries, as the struggle to work and survive has bred a strong work ethic into a number of cultures.

The New Season Day, which commemorates the start of the New Year, is held at the traditional end of winter. Usually it begins to snow in most of the lands by mid to late Norgrad, and by the first of Primus the snow is melting away.

The calendar is measured by an important date in Dhea Loral history. In a time when war swept the lands, several immortals and demigods took sides. Some tried to attain more power, while others defended the realm's inhabitants. Several gods lent their powers to affect the outcome as well. It was a dark time in the world when great civilizations fell and new governments arose. During the waning season of 1 BC, (Before Covenant), the fury of the demigods and the use and destruction of several artifacts led to the destruction of the last great empires. Many races struggled for survival in the winter season that followed. Even those living in the vast cave and underground systems of the world, while not affected by the surface winter, were left weak and foraging for meager provisions. The major powers, those gods who exerted the most influence in the world, stepped in and forced an end to the conflict. On the first of Primus, in the year now called 1 AC, (After Covenant), the gods and demigods signed a pact regarding the involvement of the deities in the future of the world. Although the gods were capable of controlling the world much more directly, restrictions were placed and honored by all. In this way, they voluntarily gave up several privileges, and bound to their oaths. Even the most chaotic of gods can never break the *Covenant*.

This began the modern-day incarnation of the churches and clerics. Clerics became the necessary mortal vessels through which the gods move the races, although the gods retain the necessary powers over nature and magic to make the world run smoothly and stay in balance.

Appendix B – Deities Commonly Worshipped in Dhea Loral

This is not a complete list of all the beings that hold governance over the world of Dhea Loral. It is a glance at some of the major powers that exert their influence over the land, people and natural events. The gods make possible all the little things that keep the world from falling into disharmony. They each have agendas that are carried out by worshippers in the world, for the gods themselves are forbidden to tread the realms as they once did.

Abriana – Goddess of Love and Healing. She is the most loving goddess and a supporter of all that is good and wholesome in the world. She helps instill feelings in mortals of brotherly love, marital commitment, and care of the land. Many of her followers are pacifists and healers. There are others who do take up the call of arms, but only to fight for what they love and protect. Even those that become paladins are restricted from using weapons or incurring fighting on the first day of each month, as these days are sacred to Abriana.

Boyal – God of Justice. It is said when the Goddess of Death collects the souls of agnostics, unbelievers, and those who turned traitor to their god she must bring them before Boyal for sentencing. Once that is done, she is only too happy to carry out the sentence or deliver the wayward soul to its fate. The clerics of this faith often find themselves on city councils, in courtrooms, or even libraries of official records. The concept of law, and how it applies to different people, is carefully studied. Many clerics go on pilgrimages to explore how the cultures of other lands express their laws.

The Codex – Book on the Philosophy of Good. Not a god by itself, it nevertheless has inspired a large following. This way of life is based on a literary work that champions a strong belief in the morals and principles that are known as "good". The original *Codex* was brought into existence with the help of several deities devoted to good causes, and it took a life of its own. People who devote themselves to this following are able to tap into clerical miracles just as if they were praying to a genuine god. There are many that serve to fulfill the moral requirements set forth in the book.

Daerkfyre – Dwarven god of Strength, Valor and Courage. Worshipped as one of the dwarven "battle gods", this deity favors strong warriors. Daerkfyre is often referred to with the extension "the Valorous". Often worshippers of this god are as strong and stubborn in the mind as they are with their muscles. Physical strength is a domain honored by dwarven miners and certain craftsmen. Warriors often pray to this god before battle. Weapons blessed by his clerics are exceptionally strong and durable.

Dalios – God of War, as well as the humans' God of Strength and Courage. This deity can be wildly unpredictable. At times he sets forth destruction and strife, though sometimes for the benefit of oppressed people. Regardless, this god is a major influence on events that shape the course of the world. His clerics are often eager to go into battle on either side of the lines, and sometimes they do meet across opposite sides of a battlefield. To these clerics, life is met by facing trouble in a straightforward type of manner. The clergy spends their often short lives seeking out glory amidst fighting for a cause. Dalios is believed to look over the world from a huge feasting hall, toasting those who struggle and fight for their beliefs.

Dawn – Goddess of Life and Rebirth. Closely related to Abriana, this goddess shares some of the same ideals. However, this deity views life as chaotic, with a bit of mystery. She creates and shapes new life, from babies to new species. Sometimes the new species can be deadly, but that is only to balance out and strengthen other forms of life. This goddess has a special abhorrence of the undead, and her clerics fight to rid the world of their existence. Due to her zeal for all kinds of life, many of her worshippers include people who feel more at home in nature than in civilized areas built upon stone.

DeLaris – Goddess of Death. Death can never be anything but frightening. She resides in one of the many Lower Worlds, but travels between them often and freely to carry out her tasks. Her most ardent followers in life may pass into the afterworld to become *Karet-Atriul*, otherwise known as Death Angels. These souls become harbingers and servants of her will, assisting the goddess with the many aspects of her position. She ferries the dead across the other worlds and homes of the gods. Those souls who were unfaithful, traitorous to a god, and untrue in their worship may find an eternity of torture or simply a boring, never-ending imprisonment. Some of her most powerful clerics can raise the dead back to life, but only to prove her power over death. Her clerics are not very strong with social ties, for they serve as a constant reminder to others of the dark fates that might befall them in the next world.

Foyul – God of Balance. Foyul works on the principal that too much influence by one side or force tends to imbalance the world. He walks a middle line between anarchy and order, good and evil. His followers come from all walks of life, all serving to sway the balance in their own way when needed. Foyul has few friends among the gods or men, as he tends to fight for all sides in order to not let any one force hold too much sway. His clerics may be evil or good, and may act for any number of good or bad intentions, striving to maintain the balance of the world.

Ganden – God of Honor, Duty, Service. This god has followers in many races. Those that feel fulfilled by a calling of decency to their fellow man and sacrifice for the sake of others fit into his followers. Those who break promises, or serve only themselves, fall out of favor to this deity. Ganden serves the other gods in the same way, carrying out honorable edicts and being of service to those that require aid. Often symbols of this god can be found with militias, honor guards, healers, and others who perform even menial services to others.

Juliustan – God of Storms and Cataclysms. Many races fear the name of this god, without a full understanding of his focus in the worlds. The god has two sides that are apparent to people. On one hand, he strives to balance the natural forces of the world. This can only be done by allowing some of the pressure of the forces of nature to vent their wrath on occasion. He may hold back one storm, while allowing another to rage unchecked. On his other side, he also seeks to ease the suffering of the world's people through such terrible events. This aspect is apparent in his clerics. His followers bring relief to those who have been displaced by storms or cataclysms, and assist in rebuilding. People do not fully understand and tend to fear his name.

Many blame him for catastrophes in the first place, and fear that it is somehow anger or wrath. His clerics believe that the world would suffer worse destruction than the Godswars if Juliustan relaxed his control.

Kelor – God of Luck. Although the other gods maintain that followers must have faith, this god prefers blind chance more openly. He champions games of chance, gambling, and random fate. This god tilts the tables in the direction he prefers, so one never knows how chance will turn up. This god rivals Dalios in unexpectedly bringing down great warriors. Many adventurers worship him, or at least pray for his blessing. Clerics of this god often throw themselves at adventure, or raise funds for the church in gambling houses. This god excels in finding small ways to thwart big plans.

Krakus – God of the Sea. The water is home to many creatures, and the oceans and seas have their own unique atmosphere. This god provides a home for some, and can bring down wrath on others with the power of water currents. Sailors pay homage to this god in return for passage over his domain. In time, Krakus can reshape the land with his currents, or smash cities in great waves, (and would do so more often, if not for the interventions of Juliustan). The influence of his domain resulted in several of his churches being built to float out on the water. His clerics have much influence over the element of water and some can walk over its surface.

Laedelious – Elven Goddess of Forests and Wildlands. Commonly referred to as the "Treemother", or "Lady of the Green", this goddess has worked through the elves to further the protection of nature. Due to her guidance, many elves build their cities within the trees and current topography, rather than cut down the woods. Many elves enjoy a certain harmony with the woodland creatures through their history with Laedelious. Though the race of man shapes the land around his needs, elves have learned to shape their civilizations and homes around the needs of nature. Although this goddess has many cleric followers, there are also a number of mystics that work in her name.

Mothrok – Goddess of Earth and Stone. Born of the element of earth, this goddess has a strong connection to earth and stone. She believes in the superiority of everlasting stone, and the plant life that flourishes from the ground. She sees animal life as a type of vermin that infests the planet on which Dhea Loral can be found. Given her perspective, one would think that she would have few followers. In actuality, Mothrok has many worshippers among the underground-dwelling races, and others that work with the land. Even goodly farmers spare prayers to her out of fear for their crops. As part of her control over the land, she has been known to bring forth the corpses buried within the ground and use them as undead abominations.

Nandorrin – God of Fire. Worshipped mostly by dwarven smiths, this god is also often seen as a smith. Whenever tales are heard of volcanoes running with lava, it is believed to be Nandorrin reforming part of the world. Many candle makers use his image or symbol on their work. Many wizards praise him for their destructive fire-based arcana. His clerics perform a lot of ceremonies around fire, and to an extent they can shape fire as well.

Noyugon – God of Knowledge and Learning. Often known as the "Lorekeeper", this god strives to preserve histories and knowledge, and is said to be a recorder of deeds for the gods themselves. He promotes academies and centers of learning. Needless to say, he does not have many followers outside of educated cultures.

Scriptum Verash – A Book on the Philosophies of Evil. Made by several dark gods, and by Foyul for the sake of balance, this tome is the exact opposite of *The Codex*. It details greed and lust, power and glory, and encourages the strong and cunning to take what they will. It is in every way a document of "evil", yet at the same time it also has a life of its own. These clerics practice in secret, with no room for honor or compassion. In the past they have lead armies filled with hate against enemies for no more reason than the cleric's own selfish needs.

Taekbol – God of Underworld. This dwarvish and gnomish god favors those who dwell under the ground, away from the light of the sun. This god also spreads gems and metals under the surface of the world, sometimes in competition with Mothrok's stone empire. Some human miners even claim worship to him.

Westrealei – Elven Goddess of Wind and Air. This goddess communicates with her followers by means of various flying creatures. Her own image is painted in the shape of a pegasus, whose head and neck is replaced by the upper half of a beautiful elven female. This elven deity is of the sky, and a force of nature. Elven arrows need to ride her winds to strike true to their targets. In this respect, a windy day is said to be a bad omen for going into battle, as the archers will have a harder time hitting their targets.

Yestreal – God of the Sun and Weather. This nature deity, worshipped by many who till the soil, exerts his influence on harvests and crops. Many times this puts him in direct competition with Mothrok for the success of farmers, but the two gods were once allied during the Godswars. The sunflower is often used as his symbol. His followers often come from agricultural regions, and are generally good at farming. Clerics of this god never condone weddings on rainy days, as they feel their god shuns the marriage. Elves also have numerous followers to this nature god.

Yurtash – God of Spirits. It is hard to define what spirits are to the common man, due to superstitions and drunken fireside chats. In short, spirits are creatures neither living nor dead that perform specific tasks in the world. They are the after images of once-living creatures. While the soul may depart to another world, a part of the spirit may remain in the world, trapped, only to be harnessed by magical means. Yurtash seems to store and nurture these lost energies of forgotten souls until they have a use in the world again. Mystics, greenmen and some arcane casters call upon the spirits in spells. Many of this god's clerics share the powers of mystics over these spirits.

About the Author

Douglas was born on Nov 28th, 1971. He lived many different places while growing up, courtesy of the assignments the US Army offered to his father. Too quiet and too shy for too long, there were always dreams of other worlds and places … and the desire to write about them. He's played may tabletop RPGs, as well as online MMOs, and many of his characters developed their personalities and quirks in these games before appearing in his novels. Douglas continues to write novels and think up short stories, while pondering the changing literary world of print vs. ebooks vs. audio. He makes several appearances at conventions around Minnesota.

Douglas lives with his wife and raises two children in Minnesota. He works in health care, serving people's needs in imaging. When most people see him, he is wearing scrubs.

Other books by this author

Please visit your favorite retailer to discover other books by Douglas Van Dyke Jr:
(Current as of Summer, 2025)

The Earthrin Stones Trilogy
Inheritance of a Sword and a Path
Trials of Faith
Muster of Heroes

The Pilgrims with Blades Series
A01 - Pressed into Service
A02 - Grandfather's Castle
A03 - Caravan Road

Storm-Mage Chronicles
Apprentice Storm Mage
Daughter of the Legend
Quest for Truth (Future Project)

Other Titles based in the Fantasy World of Dhea Loral
The Widow Brigade
The Wooden Maiden

Other Worlds
Boxer Earns His Wings
The Pale Gunner
Streets of Fire and Shadow (Anthology)
OtherWorldly Volumes 1 & 2 (Anthology)
Wonders and Dragons: A Midwest Fantasy Sampler 2025 (Anthology)
Laser Cannons & First Contact (Anthology)

Connect with Douglas Van Dyke Jr

I really appreciate your continued support of Thomena's story. Keep in touch with me to find news on future releases, behind-the-scenes on older books, writing/publishing tips and to catch my blog. Here are my social media outlets:

Visit my website and sign up for my mailing list: https://dhealoral.com
Follow me on **Facebook**: https://www.facebook.com/DheaLoral
Follow me on **Twitter**: https://twitter.com/ThaminDheaLoral
Favorite my **Smashwords** author page:
https://www.smashwords.com/profile/view/DheaLoral
Amazon Author page: https://www.amazon.com/Douglas-Van-Dyke-Jr/e/B00LZDDRME/
Goodreads Author page:
https://www.goodreads.com/author/show/761586.Douglas_Van_Dyke_Jr_

Give my books a review at your favorite retailer! Reviews are a big way to support indie-authors like me.

About the Cover Artist

Thea Magerand is a 40 year old independent fantasy illustrator living in a quiet rural corner of the French Alps. She likes bringing to life epic characters, dark creatures, horror monsters and fantasy worlds. When not creating covers she draws a lot of fantasy and mythology-oriented illustrations. A self-taught artist with a background in paleontology, she is also an avid videogamer, motorcyclist, a self-professed bookworm, and amateur knitter. You can find more of her works and contact her on her website: www.ikaruna.eu

About the Editor

Rebecca Jaycox did a great job and gave me a lot of guidance developing this book. You can follow her on Facebook as www.facebook.com/slayerofadverbs

Want to experience more of the world of Dhea Loral? Explore the dwarf homelands through the eyes of revolutionary Duli! *The Widow Brigade* opened on Amazon with twelve critiques praising the story, and each giving it a perfect 5 stars! This story features strong women, in a fantasy setting, rebelling against the traditions of a male-dominated society.

"I felt the plot was well developed, well paced, and the motivations of the characters really drew me in, caring about what happened as the plot progressed. I felt the main character was not your typical shiny hero, or dastardly anti-hero. She just felt real. I highly recommend this book..." - Tom H

"This book is very well written and as always with his stories, the battle scenes are intense, with details that pull you in and fully immerse yourself in the story. The characters are well developed and allow you to enjoy loving and hating them." – Lockhart

Discover the series which introduced fantasy readers to the realm of Dhea Loral. The *Earthrin Stones* trilogy gives the reader the largest backstory and plot driving the scenes of this world. Open your adventure with *Inheritance of a Sword and a Path*!

"Over a thousand years ago the Godswars ravaged the land of Dhea Loral, shattering continents, laying waste to cities, and driving species to extinction. The people of the land are once again starting to prosper and flourish, while the gods stay aloft and watch from afar the recovery. Yet, not all the old quarrels have been forgotten. For some gods, the time is right to once again meddle in the affairs of mortals. Though the gods have bound themselves by a Covenant that bars their direct entry into Dhea Loral, they are able to send mortal emissaries to carry out their schemes."

"*Inheritance of a Sword and a Path* is a treasure trove of fantasy, eye-popping adventures, lead characters imbued with morality, humility, strength and humor…This saga opener had me turning pages, reading way (way) past my bedtime, and definitely curious for the next installment. Pure fun!" — Lori Crever "30 Minutes with the Author"

Strangers thrown together, forced into service on a common quest, form a bond of camaraderie. Each seeks to find their focus in the world, amidst their private mysteries.

The half-orc savage, who takes pride in a company he no longer serves. The dusk-skinned archer, carrying a bow from her forgotten homeland. The dwarf who studies the past so he can create a future. The knight who pays fealty to no lord. The elf sorceress seeking knowledge, but what specific question is she trying to answer?

They will band together, seeking separate goals. How far will pilgrims travel to discover who they are?

-Pilgrims with Blades: Pressed into Service-

Facing a crisis and looking for any excuse to strike in force against the orcs occupying the hills to their south, the city-state Kashmer conscripts privateers and adventurers into war. A band of strangers must learn to support and adapt to each other as a daring plan separates them from the main force in hostile territory. Each possess their own mystery, but without cooperation and trust, they will be doomed to failure.

Pressed into Service is the introduction to the bold Pilgrims with Blades series.

Dhea Loral